WINDY CITY

WINDY CITY

A NOVEL OF POLITICS

SCOTT SIMON

RANDOM HOUSE
NEW YORK

Published in the United States by Random House,
an imprint of The Random House Publishing Group,
a division of Random House, Inc., New York.

RANDOM HOUSE and colophon are registered trademarks
of Random House, Inc.

Library of Congress Cataloging-in-Publication Data

Simon, Scott.
Windy city : a novel of politics / Scott Simon.
p. cm.
ISBN 978-1-4000-6557-8
1. City council members—Fiction.   2. Mayors—Death—
Fiction.   3. Chicago (Ill.)—Politics and government—
Fiction.   4. Political fiction.   I. Title.
PS3619.I5626W56 2008
813'.6—dc22
2007038424

Printed in the United States of America on acid-free paper

www.atrandom.com

9 8 7 6 5 4

Design by Liz Cosgrove

For my mother

"WINDY CITY." Chicago's exposed location between the Great Plains and the GREAT LAKES—and the wind swirling amidst the city's early SKYSCRAPERS—lend credence to the literal application of this famous nickname . . . but the power of the name lies in the metaphorical use of "windy" for "talkative" or "boastful." Chicago politicians early became famous for long-windedness, and the Midwestern metropolis's location as a host city for POLITICAL CONVENTIONS helped cement the association of Chicago with loquacious politicians, thus underlying the nickname with double meaning.

THE ENCYCLOPEDIA OF CHICAGO   2004

UNIVERSITY OF CHICAGO PRESS
CHICAGO AND LONDON

WINDY CITY

"*S*ome people will vote for you because they like the sound of your name. Some people won't vote for you because you've got a name that reminds them of a malodorous vegetable. You get some votes from people who think you're Italian. You lose some votes from people who think you're Sicilian. Your name reminds some people of the kid who sat behind them in the third grade. Pray that kid never smeared snot on their arm if you want their vote. Some people think you must be someone, they saw on TV. Some people saw you on TV, so you must be an ass. People you've never met feel intensely about you. Some people—they can't quite say why—don't like something in your face. Don't complain that it makes no sense. It's life. It's nature. It's the birds and the bees.

"You think I'm kidding? You think you're above all that? You want to tell me that when you look down at nine names on the ballot for Water Reclamation District trustee, you know who they are? You know where they went to school, what they do, and how they plan to get the fish turds out of your drinking water? You say to yourself, 'I like her name, it rhymes,' or 'He's Cuban, they're smart.' Then someday, a bomb knocks out a grate, a wind whips up the water, and suddenly those anonymous souls are the most wanted people in town.

"Bills, votes, raising money? Every grand or noble thing you've ever done can be undone by the damndest thing. You forget Lech Walesa's birthday. You tell a joke about a rabbi. You say, 'Jeez, blacks really are better at basketball,' and next thing, you've got pickets in your front windows, from the NAACP to the Kosciuszko Society to the North American Man-Boy Love Association.

"But somehow, it keeps the tanks off the streets. Trash gets picked up, snow gets plowed, the trains make all the stops. I admire anyone who has the nerve to put their name on a ballot. You're inviting fifty, fifty thousand, or one hundred and fifty million strangers to heave a tomato at you. Or worse—ignore you. It's appalling and amazing. It's *ridiculous and irreplaceable. Hardly any of us wind up being Lincoln, Churchill, or LaGuardia. Most of us aren't even Hoover or Carter. But so far, no one here has been Pol Pot or Stalin. Of course the game isn't fair. It favors the rich, the beautiful, and the shameless. But everyone gets a chance to try."*

SUNDARAN "SUNNY" ROOPINI
ALDERMAN, 48TH WARD

ALDERMEN OF THE CHICAGO CITY COUNCIL

1st Ward: Artemus Agras

2nd Ward: Evelyn Washington

3rd Ward: Dorothy Fisher

4th Ward: Wanda Jackson

5th Ward: Vera Barrow

6th Ward: Grace Brown

7th Ward: Miles Sparrow

8th Ward: John Reginald

9th Ward: Daryl Lloyd

10th Ward: J. P. Mulroy

11th Ward: Alfredo Sandoval

12th Ward: Linas Slavinskas

13th Ward: Brock Lucchesi

14th Ward: Collie Kerrigan

15th Ward: John Wu

16th Ward: Shirley Watson

17th Ward: Evelyn Lee

18th Ward: Kevin Corcoran

19th Ward: Mitya Volkov

20th Ward: Janet Watanabe

21st Ward: Tomislav Mitrovic

22nd Ward: Jesus Flores Suarez

23rd Ward: Felix Kowalski

24th Ward: Sanford Booker

25th Ward: Alonzo Guttierez

26th Ward: Rod Abboud

27th Ward: Donald Stubbs

28th Ward: Astrid Lindstrom

29th Ward: Gerald White

30th Ward: Wandy Rodriguez

31st Ward: Luis Zamora

32nd Ward: Emil Wagner

33rd Ward: Patrick Tierney

34th Ward: Regina Gregory

35th Ward: Carlo Viola

36th Ward: Keith Horn

37th Ward: Vernetta Hynes Griffin

38th Ward: Aidan Ruffino

39th Ward: Salvatore Del Raso

40th Ward: Cyril Murphy

41st Ward: Ivan Becker

42nd Ward: Sidney Wineman

43rd Ward: Kiera Malek

44th Ward: Harry Walker III

45th Ward: Adam Wojcik

46th Ward: Jane Siegel

47th Ward: Cassie Katsoulis

48th Ward: Sundaran Roopini

49th Ward: Anders Berggren

50th Ward: Jacobo Rapoport Sefran

THURSDAY NIGHT

The mayor was found shortly after eleven with his bronze, brooding face lying on the last two slices of a prosciutto and artichoke pizza, his head turned and his wide mouth gaping, as if gulping for a smashed brown bulb of garlic with life's last breath. Blood from his gums had already seeped into the tomatoes, prosciutto, and caramelized onions. His blue oxford-cloth shirt was unbuttoned. His red tie had been slipped out of its knot and trailed forlornly from his collar. His heavy gray slacks were laid across the back of the sofa where he was sitting for his last meal, illumed by the cold glare of the television set.

The security guards who had rushed in heard the ice in the mayor's bourbon crackling while it melted (it was that fresh) over the cloaked gallop of their thick shoes against the great carpet. Three men's magazines were fanned across the sofa, each with the kind of cover that, in Indiana, would call for the woman's bosom to be enrobed with a brown paper strip. But the guards' attention was drawn to the bold red letters they saw marching across the mayor's boxer shorts: BIG DADDY.

One of them reached gently for the mayor's arms to feel for a pulse. Another slowly passed a hand over his eyes, and softly called his name—it was how they were trained—while the third muttered some kind of code, colors, numbers, alphas and tangos, into a minuscule microphone in his hand.

Mrs. Bacon, the mayor's secretary, edged close to their burly gray shoulders to peer into the mayor's blank brown eyes and shakily point her hand at the slogan on his undershorts.

"I'm sure they were a gift," she said quietly.

It was the mayor's habit to have one extra-large pizza from Quattro's delivered to City Hall by ten each night, after he had returned from an evening's round of appearances. His standing order specified extra cheese and prosciutto. When the kitchen staff at Quattro's deduced the pizza was destined for City Hall, they spontaneously contributed extra glistening strips of onions and grilled peppers. His security guards joked that two officers were required to carry the pizza across the threshold of the mayor's office; it felt like carrying a manhole cover in your arms. So much extra cheese had been loaded onto the pizza that when anyone took a bite—an endeavor that involved opening one's mouth as if for a molar examination—they had to pull gooey strings away from their teeth to almost the length of their arms.

Most politicians groused that over an evening of cocktail receptions, fund-raising dinners, and precinct meetings, they never got a chance to eat. They needed to keep both hands free for handshakes and clapping shoulders. They couldn't chance that a sprig of parsley from a canapé might blemish their smile and photograph like a vagrant's missing tooth. They didn't want to be seen swallowing steak *tartare* on a round of toast, only to be asked, "Do you know how that cow was slaughtered?"

But the mayor's immense appetite was too well publicized for him to plead self-restraint. He risked political peril if he appeared to be indifferent to the specialties of any neighborhood. This guaranteed that on any given night, the mayor consumed cheese pierogi, chickpea samosas, pistachio-studded cannolis, and/or sugar-dusted Mexican crescent cookies in his nightly rounds. And consumed them *in toto*, for half portions were considered fraught with risk. "How can I tell the good citizens of Pilsen that I have to go easy on this magnificent tres leches cake," he remonstrated, "because I'm saving room for the ale cake in Canaryville? They might suspect that I truly like only two of the tres leches. I mean, when they've seen me make room for the packzi in Logan Square"—a cream-filled, pre-Lenten donut that was popular in the city's Polish bakeries—"how do I explain any diminution in my commitment to the pastry of Pilsen? *A man has to consider the consequences before he keeps his mouth shut.*"

So the Quattro's pizza would be waiting at the mayor's office as a reward for his duodenal daring. He would lift the top of the box with a great, yeasty smile.

"Goodness gracious, our citizens mean well," the mayor would explain as steam from the pizza seemed to plump his whitening eyebrows. "I can't disappoint them. How can a man of my positively *legendary cravings* ever convince anyone that I can't have just *one more bite?* If I turn my nose up at a shrimp and ginger wonton, I risk offending the entire Fifteenth Ward. I just might have to put new traffic lights up and down Canal Street. Bibimbop, halvah, or chitterlings, a man in my position can't refuse hospitality. It does *not* promote domestic tranquility. These days that's practically a matter *of national security.* It is positively *antediluvian* not to recognize that."

The mayor sprinkled *antediluvian* over his conversation like fresh cracked pepper; he believed it made everything tastier. He excoriated all political rivals as *antediluvian*, the state and federal governments—which had a depressing tendency to be run by elected Republicans—and any other daily source of irritation, including the city's newspapers, banks, and any restaurants that did not deliver beyond a twelve-block radius.

It was the mayor's custom to remove his pants and unbutton his shirt while he sat at the coffee table in front of the television in his office and punch out the numbers of local stations to follow himself on the ten o'clock news. Mrs. Bacon would overhear him cheering or swearing loudly and ingeniously as he ascended the dial:

Two: "*Dumb*-ass *hay*seed! A year ago, you were reading *pork belly* *prices* on a station in *Iowa* that didn't carry farther than a *lightbulb!* Now you're some kind of *ex*-pert on pub-*lick fi*-nance. The *nerve!* The stupefying *effrontery! As if she knows any more about pork bellies than she does about finance!*" Five: "I am not going to listen to any grown man who wears *makeup* for a living and isn't dressed in velvet tights! And I know it's not cause you're gay, 'cause you wouldn't be so *ugg*-lee if you were!" Seven: "Un-comp-*reeehending*, ass-*licking* in-*grates!*" Nine! Eleven! "*Antediluvian enemies of the people!*" Thirty-two! "Super-sillius *ass*-hole! *You* couldn't show a *slug* how to curl up and *sleep!*" Forty-four! "*Oh, my, but I shine! I might have my annual bourbon!*"

On Thursday night, Mrs. Bacon had entered when she realized that she had not heard the usual fusillade. With rising alarm, she rapped her hand on the thick polished door; on hearing no response, she turned the heavy brass handle and found the mayor slumped onto his last meal.

The three guards who rushed in at her cry reacted with profession-alism. But their voices quavered as they called out to him gently, and their hands fumbled slightly as they undid the buttons over his wrist. Their attachment to the mayor was personal. They didn't really know—didn't really care—if he was a competent and incorruptible civic leader. They knew he was good company, a man who worked hard, laughed at himself, and batted down the darts and knives of political combat with contagious zest. The applause and smiles that crowds cas-caded on the mayor fell on his guards, too. They shared his chores, his travels, his foes and friends, his frustrations, his feats, his humor, his phrasing. When traffic snarled, when an elevator was slow, when planes were delayed, the guards shook their heads and exclaimed, "Pos-itively *antediluvian!*"

All of the guards had prepared for the chance that one day they might have to repel an obstreperous protester from the mayor's path, wrestle away a weapon, or even throw themselves in front of an assas-sin's shot. The mayor was a compelling personality. Some reactions he aroused were ferocious and threatening. But that they should finally be summoned to his side to protect him from a prosciutto and artichoke pizza . . .

"I should have come in earlier," Mrs. Bacon said in a small, quiet voice as the boots of a paramedic team squished ruthlessly over the thick olive-colored carpet of the mayor's office. The head of that shift's security team, a large blond man whose shoulders strained against the sockets of his dull gray suit, had taken Mrs. Bacon gingerly into his long arms and softly patted her back.

"It would have made no difference," he assured her. "It happened so quickly."

"I could have cleared out . . . all *this*," she said, making a small, stabbing motion at the melting bourbon, the curling pizza, and the mayor's abandoned slacks on the sofa next to the sheaf of Indiana-offending magazines.

"It doesn't matter," the security chief reassured her.

"It's just so . . . *pathetic*," said Mrs. Bacon.

A paramedic crew had been assigned to an anteroom near the mayor's office a few years before. It was more a sign of the times than of the mayor's conspicuous magnitude in the city, or even the robust demands he made on his health. In five years of duty, the crew had transported just one case to the hospital (an old alderman, Stefano Tripoli of the 11th, snipped himself while zipping up in the men's room; thereafter he was known as Lefty), and one case to the morgue (a homeless man who had frozen to death while trying to sleep through a snowstorm against the Randolph Street wall of City Hall).

A woman paramedic held up the mayor's gray slacks by a belt loop. They looked like the skin of a small elephant.

"No wallet. No keys," she announced.

"He wasn't robbed," said Mrs. Bacon.

"We carried everything," the security chief explained.

The mayor's empty pockets were renowned. He believed it was a mark of distinction to walk through each day unencumbered by the tedious need to fish out bills or coins. "You jangle with each step," he once told his guards. "How can a man concentrate?"

One day, Linas Slavinskas of the 12th discovered an old city ordinance that said anyone found within the city limits with less than a dollar in his pockets could be arrested for vagrancy. Linas stood up from his seat near the end of the first row of the council floor, to wave the regulation and point to the mayor. "Arrest that man!" he commanded the sergeant-at-arms. "City ordinance 91-5!" The mayor stood up from his high-backed burgundy leather seat, laughing as he turned out his pockets and pulled them out from his trousers, like a zookeeper demonstrating the wingspread of a bat.

"That man is asking you to approve a budget that's larger than Mongolia," roared Linas. "And he doesn't have a dime in his pants! He knows as much about budgets as I know about mapping the genome of a fruit fly! Arrest him for his own protection! And ours!"

John Wu of the 15th Ward, who owned the Big Bad Buddha gift store on Cermak, Tommy Mitrovic of the 21st, who sold insurance, and Jesus Flores Suarez of the 22nd, who owned a travel agency ("Jesus Saves—On All Fares!") pulled out plump money clips from their seats in the center of the second row and began to ball up dollar bills and throw them to the mayor. Miles Sparrow of the 7th, who owned Pedro's Blues Room on Cottage Grove, Dorothy Fisher of the 3rd, who ran a luggage delivery service at Midway Airport, and Arty Agras of the 1st scuttled under the balled-up bills as they unfurled in flight, and lunged to intercept them.

"Turn *awaaay* from temptation, aldermen!" the mayor exhorted, his arms splayed to suggest a figure on a cross. "Reee-*ject* these antediluvian moneylenders!"

"Credit cards? Driver's license?" the paramedic continued.

"I doubt he had a driver's license," the security chief said. The guards smiled at the thought of the mayor fulminating behind the wheel of a car at the *antediluvian* buses and trucks slowing his progress along the Kennedy Expressway.

"Credit cards?" another guard said, as if the paramedic had asked if the mayor kept a bowling ball in his pocket. The mayor had well-publicized financial difficulties—a record of uncollected debts and questionable tax returns—that not even two terms' incumbency could altogether improve.

"We carried whatever he needed," said the guard with growing irritation. "Are you paramedics or Woodward and Bernstein?"

"We just have to account for these things," another paramedic rushed to explain. "We don't want the family to think anyone took his personal effects."

"There is no family," Mrs. Bacon said quietly. "Every now and then, we'd hear from a cousin somewhere. Georgia, Jamaica. We'd send them an autographed picture. There are no personal effects," she said, her last words catching, and she finally put her hands over her eyes and turned into a corner of the room, her elbows holding her up against the wall while she shuddered.

Four uniformed officers who had been summoned to the fifth floor walked alongside the ambulance trundle bearing the mayor, down a windowless hallway that buzzed with a weak light. The wheels on the cart squeaked beneath the mayor's weight, at a piercing pitch above the slow, grave footsteps. The paramedics sensed the police were observing a ritual; wordlessly, they consented to walk behind the blue uniforms. The chief of security took hold of the trundle railing just above the mayor's head, and steered the cart. When the police and paramedics had all tramped into a service elevator, he spoke in low tones to the officers, who had all turned around to stand at attention over the mayor's body.

"Nothing gets out yet. Please."

The officers muttered *yes, sir,* as the fourth and third floors blinked by. At the stroke of the second floor, they could feel the elevator begin to brake.

"No sirens," said the chief, turning to take the paramedics into his sight, too. "Okay? A nice, quiet, last ride." He paused until the three men and one woman officer had all nodded.

"Hell of a guy. We had some times together."

The chief blinked his eyes dry as the silver doors in front of the trundle began to roll open. One of the paramedics reached a rubber-gloved hand quickly down to the mayor's chin.

"I'm sorry," she said with detectable alarm, "but there's some kind of green discharge here."

The chief pulled back on the cart before it could be rolled through the open doors. The officers surrounding the trundle stiffened, and mechanically dropped their hands to steady the cart. Then the chief let out a breath and seemed to smile. Then, he really did smile—a laugh even snuck into his voice as the paramedic held the bewildering green secretion on the end of her thumb, finally returning his smile.

"Artichoke," the chief announced. "You take him from here."

Sunny Roopini heard his phone warble through his sleep, raised his head, but couldn't reach it without upsetting Sheldon. His head was tucked just below Sunny's shoulder, and Sunny could feel Sheldon's breaths tug across his ear; he decided to keep his arm in place below his head.

Sunny had been astonished when Sheldon had first crept onto his collarbone. For months he had simply sat on the foot of the bed, peering over the top of the blanket's folds, as if surveying the Somme from a trench. Sunny's daughters understood why their mother was no longer around. After all, they were teenagers of their times. They had seen spacecraft fall apart, infants starve, subways burst, and skyscrapers smashed. They had already heard so much about lung, skin, thyroid, testicular, uterine, prostate and pancreatic cancers, treacherous car suspensions, trans fats, lasers blinding airplanes, AIDS blighting continents, sporadic bone spurs, swine flu, Christmas tree electrocutions, cholesterol, high-speed car chases, category five hurricanes, and mad cow disease that they must have wondered how any human being grew to be as old as their father. Sunny had just turned forty-eight.

But how to explain to Sheldon—it had been the one challenge of being a widower about which no book or counselor had cautioned— that the shoulder on which he slept was now cold and gone? Sheldon's trust was unswerving, stirring, and slightly unnerving. For months, he struck what Sunny and his daughters came to call his British Museum pose at the end of the bed, splayed on his stomach, front paws extended straight as train rails, his gray face impassive, his blue cat's eyes looking out from his small head with vast certitude: *she'll be back, she always has, I'll just keep watch.*

Sunny would wait until his daughters had shut their door and tried to drown out the sound of a late-night newscast with the blare of music to splay out on his forearms and speak softly to Sheldon: *I'm sorry, old boy, but Mummy is not coming back* (under no circumstances did he want his daughters hear him refer to Elana as *Mummy* to their cat). *We love you, Sheldon. She'd be here if she could. She just can't. But Daddy* (he dropped his voice even lower—he would rather his daughters overhear him booking a high-priced call girl than refer to himself as *Daddy* to Sheldon), *Rula, and Rita will take care of you.*

Sheldon's blue-rimmed eyes barely broke their gaze as he blinked. He looked back at Sunny with utter, unchanged certitude: *She'll be here. Lose faith if you must. I never will.*

Then one night, Sheldon just came crawling across the covers and rammed his small gray head into Sunny's chin. Then he burrowed his nose into Sunny's armpit, not demonstrative so much as desperate. Sunny stayed in place, essentially pinned, hearing Sheldon's breathing finally begin to slow to something that his slight chest could contain, until the sky lightened and Sunny could hear the grind of buses begin along Broadway.

"How did you manage it, Pappaji?" his daughters asked when he shared the story that night—brandished it, really, recounting it several times with newly remembered details. "How did you ever convince Sheldon to come over?"

"Nothing," he told them finally, surprising even himself with his own reflection. "He just had to decide that it was his idea."

So Sunny slowly rotated his free arm over his chest and around to the night table just beyond Sheldon's head. A woman's voice—an unfamiliar voice—was there.

"Mr. Roopini," she said. "I'm Sergeant Maureen Gallaher." She waited while she heard fumbling and throat clearing on Sunny's end. "I'm with City Hall's security detail. I have instructions to bring you downtown to the mayor's office. If you have no other commitments, of course." She heard another fusillade of phone fumbling.

"That last line was a joke, right?" But Sunny kept his voice sociable.

"I guess so, sir."

"Later than usual for this sort of thing. It must be—" Sunny tried to twist himself to see the unblinking green numbers on his bedside alarm.

"A little after midnight, sir," said Sgt. Gallaher.

"Mrs. Bacon usually calls," said Sunny.

"It might be too late even for her."

"Is something wrong?" he asked.

"I wouldn't know, sir," said Sgt. Gallaher quickly, and then understood the point of the question. "No, sir. No alerts. Subways and skyscrapers are fine," she said finally. "All I hear on the radio is a warehouse fire in Lawndale and a shooting in Pilsen."

She heard Sunny hold his hand over the phone and clear his throat. She thought she recognized the phlegm midnight coughs of a cognac drinker. The racket of clearing his throat seemed to remind Sunny to speak more softly.

"My daughters. Teenage girls. I am always available to the mayor, but it's the middle of the night, and, you know, we're alone now."

Sgt. Gallaher seemed to remember. "It's a quiet night, sir," she said after a pause. "I'll see if the Twentieth District can send over a car to sit on the street for a while."

"Do I have time to shower?"

"Your choice, sir. I'm passing Fullerton now. I'll be on the Lawrence Avenue side of your building in six minutes."

"Not five?"

"I didn't figure to use the siren, sir."

Sunny jumped in quickly. "I was kidding, Sergeant," he assured her. "I was just intimidated by your precision."

"It'll be five now, sir," she said without perceptible reaction. "Whenever you're ready, we'll be on Lawrence."

———

Sheldon had opened his eyes and yawned, so Sunny left him in the folds of the pink sheets and flowered covers. He showered and chose his clothes carefully, quietly sliding back closet doors and snapping on lights. A pale violet shirt worn open at the collar, he decided, so that the mayor would not forget they were working after-hours; a light gray sport coat, to suggest seriousness; tan pants, brown suede shoes, a white linen pocket square onto which he dabbed some Vetiver after splashing two jots onto his cheeks. Sunny snapped on a small reading light to appraise the results in a mirror: he was dressed like the lawyers and brokers you could see on television sitting in the front six rows of professional basketball games, cell phones set to stun-only, but dealing out business cards. *Just one of the boys tonight, but don't forget who I am tomorrow.*

Rita was up. She shuffled in on bare feet, wearing a man's—or at least a boy's, he hoped—red candy-striped shirt.

"Something wrong?" She rubbed her eyes with the tips of her fingers, as her mother had when the girls would totter into their room to tug on their sheets and demand milk and songs.

"No. The mayor wants me downtown."

"To watch TV?"

"Nehru listened to the radio with Gandhi. Same idea. You'll be okay?"

Rita rubbed the back of her neck with the palm of her hand, black hair shaking in a waterfall over her shoulders (she was the younger of his daughters, in her second year of high school; he was startled to see such a gesture of mature fatigue).

"We'll call our dope dealer as soon as you close the door," she assured him. Sunny had turned his face down to examine his watch in the low light: it was nearly 12:30.

"You need money?" he asked.

"We give him your best cuff links and have unprotected sex." Sunny reeled back from her joke and smiled.

"We'd never refuse an extra twenty," she said.

Sunny slipped two out from a thick clip and put them in his daughter's hands.

"This won't go far with the dealer," he said. "But River Kwai delivers until one. Tip well, they know us. I've got my phone. There's some beer in the fridge, and I won't mind so long as you leave one. There should be a cop car outside on Lawrence . . ."

Sunny's daughters were the ones who usually stepped into his embraces these days. It spared him the adolescent anxiety of wondering if his arms would be welcome, but also made him feel pitied. As Rita brought herself close, Sunny placed his lips softly against her smooth cheek.

"Nice shirt," he told her.

"An old one of Mama's," she said. "Wasn't it yours?"

Sunny stepped back and beheld his daughter at the end of his arms.

"Oh, good Christ, I think so," he said. "So long ago. I wore it on a Valentine's Day we spent in Boston and never really got it back." He squeezed his daughter's shoulders. "Back before you get up. To try to sleep a little, too." Sunny reached back into a pocket to find his clip and left a last twenty on the bedroom bureau.

Sgt. Gallaher was a tall, bony, boyish woman in her mid-thirties, wearing a crisp white shirt, blue pantsuit, and black topcoat. Her squawking black brick of a radio hung on the front of her belt, and her service badge was pinned over a floral pink pocket square. She was standing by the dark blue cruiser when Sunny came out onto the street, and had to stoop down to pull open the back door for him. He saw wispy strands of long, raven hair stray from the bun she had tucked behind her head and tried to hold back with a drugstore clip. Sgt. Gallaher slid into the front seat of the cruiser, alongside a young uniformed officer—Officer Mayer was the name Sunny picked up—with a pale neck.

"Sergeant Gallaher, have we met?" asked Sunny. She turned around in her seat to smile.

"Good memory, sir. I used to work out of Foster Avenue. I came to your restaurant a few times."

"And now?"

"First District."

"You never go back home for dinner?"

"Long trip for chicken vindaloo, sir."

"You won't find better," he said, and Sgt. Gallaher laughed. She had wide shoulders under the blazer—Sunny guessed, from the way she sat, that her gun was holstered under her right arm—and broad blue eyes.

"Actually, I remember the polenta alla Sarda. My mother's side is Italian."

"We've added a little more Italian. Come any time, we'll take care of you. That used to mean: cops eat free. Now it means free toothpicks. Well, nothing prevents the owner from sending a couple of cannolis or mango barfis over to his friends."

"I'll come by some night, sir."

"You too, Officer Mayer," said Sunny, lightly clapping his shoulder.

As the patrolman pulled onto the Outer Drive, Sunny noted that they had left his ward and crossed into Jane Siegel's 46th. Puffs of smoke, burped from car exhausts and brilliant as small clouds in the frigid night, scurried across the highways. The people who lived in those glass houses along the lake never had to draw their shades. Who would see them—Peeping Toms flying into O'Hare? Lake Michigan ore boats miles beyond the beaches that frosted the eastern face of the city? So what you could see from the street after midnight looked like campfires dwindling down on a hillside: small yellow hall lights, slivers of bright bathroom lights from where someone left the door ajar, aquarium lights, kitchen lights, or a lone table lamp somebody left on to find the bathroom.

The people who lived there had to be up early to get to the gym by seven, a breakfast meeting by seven-thirty, or the trading pits by eight.

They watched the news and went to bed. Perhaps they stayed up late enough to hear the first few jokes of a late show monologue while they brushed their teeth—after all, they were concerned about issues.

But just a few blocks west, past Broadway, people lived in apartments that could not look above the towers to the blank blue waters of the lake. They had to look out on each other—close the curtains, shut the doors, worry about what people might see across the way. The people who boiled eggs and brewed coffee for breakfast meetings might be just getting up when the people who cleared dishes and served late-night specials were just getting home, aching for sleep. Sunny was convinced that the critical differences in his constituency weren't between blacks, whites, browns, and Asians, or Jews, Gentiles, and Muslims. It was between those people who get enough sleep and those who never can.

Sunny stretched back slightly in the back of the cruiser, careful not to catch his suede brogues below the seat.

"May I ask, sergeant—where are you from?"

"Beverly, sir," Sgt. Gallaher answered without turning back. She had escorted a fair number of politicians. None dozed or read in the back. They all seemed to feel that it was vital to leave the sergeant with an impression of their personal concern. They asked where she had grown up, gone to school, and whom she had met in her duties, until they heard something they could match from their own lives.

At the mention of Beverly, Sunny sat forward, putting his chin above the front seat.

"East or west of Western?"

Sgt. Gallaher held her reply for just a moment.

"I'm surprised you had to ask a Gallaher," was how she finally put her answer.

"The Nineteenth!" Sunny cried. "My friend Mit Volkov."

"But I live right across from Curie High now," the sergeant added.

"The Fourteenth!" cried Sunny. "My friend Collie Kerrigan."

The 14th Ward alderman was an outlandish little turnip of a man—even the gray suits that he wore seemed to acquire a stale greenish cast encasing Collie's pasty neck—who unfailingly approached Sunny in the minutes before the mayor rapped the council to order.

"Come on, Sunny," he'd say, flicking a hand up toward the gallery. "The folks came to see an Indian. Give 'em at least a little war whoop. A rain dance."

Collie was one of the south side votes that Sunny routinely needed to approve the Parks and Recreation budget. So he would whisper back, "This one's for you, Collie," and pat his open mouth three times. *Whoop, whoop, whoop.*

Sunny began to sense an amiable challenge from the sergeant, and readjusted the crisp white points of his pocket square.

"So: you went to Curie?"

"No. No *sir*."

When Sgt. Gallaher turned around, her blue eyes blinked with triumph.

"Mother McAuley," she announced quietly, and Sunny sat back, fairly slapping his knees.

"My gosh. From parochial school plaids to police blues. *Mother McAuley*," he repeated, as if he had heard the most unexpected answer to a crossword clue. "Did you have a problem with boys?"

"That's why my parents sent me there," said Sgt. Gallaher, determinedly looking straight ahead to the towers along the lake looming before them. "So I wouldn't. But when we played hospital, I was always the cop who brought in the gunshot victim," the sergeant added. "Never the nurse or doctor."

The car clipped past North Avenue, into Sidney Wineman's 42nd. Sunny spoke before any silence could fall.

"Is security interesting?"

"Yes. But I don't see the mayor much. My detail precedes him to appearances. I do get to work with international delegations. That's an education, really," said the sergeant. "I've learned that all Mounties don't wear red tunics. British security people don't wear Sherlock Holmes capes, and they do carry guns. No Chinese policeman I've ever met knows any more about kung fu than what he's seen in the movies. And there aren't any *she* Chinese police. Polish policemen all have relatives in Jefferson Park. Anyway, they get discounts on Milwaukee Avenue by saying they do. And, you don't win any points with a Pakistani cop by saying, 'I've always wanted to see the Taj Mahal.' Sometimes, it's a short course in international relations."

"A lot of people think aldermen don't have to worry about international relations," Sunny observed. "But I don't think a politician can afford such an impoverished imagination."

Sgt. Gallaher noted Sunny's choice of words. Most of the pols she took down to City Hall called themselves public servants or legislators, but almost never a *politician*. Politician was a word, like sodomist, that was perfectly accurate, but had connotations.

"When I first started in politics," said Sunny, "the best way to draw applause was to say, 'Thank you. And in conclusion, I just want to say, up with Walesa, free Nelson Mandela, and hands off of central America!' You don't get ovations like that for vowing to extend commercial zoning on the forty-three hundred block of Sheridan Road."

The mayor, in fact, had been Sunny's tutor on the utility of foreign policy in local politics. He remembered one of their late night meetings, with the mayor hunched over a bourbon glass like a sly cat protecting a nibble, taking his voice down to a greatly jowly growl.

"You think that all we have to worry about here is picking up trash, plowing the snow, and keeping Al Capone in his grave? My God, man. There are *a hundred languages* spoken here. Assyrian, Lakota, Urdu, and Yiddish. The Yoo-nited Nations doesn't have to worry about how to say '*beans*' in as many languages as any diner on Western Avenue. All of these folks with five-day beards and black head scarves who are going for each other's throats over in Snowdonia? They send their kids to the same school here and tell them, 'Now behave!' This nation kicks a little ass some place, and soon we got thousands of them living in basements on Halsted Street. Next day, you're in the back of their cab while they're on their phones, plotting a coup. We've got nuclear physicists from the Poon-jab and goatherds from Namibia. We've got brain surgeons from Ogbomoso—that's in Nigeria, if you were too embarrassed to ask—and rocket scientists from Petropavlovsk—that's in Kazakhstan, as I'm sure you knew—working as doormen. One day, after they find life on Mars, we'll have bug-eyed, green-ass Martian-Americans bussing tables on Clark Street. This great heaving mass of diversity is united by a single, momentous desire: They expect *you* to get the snow off their street."

Their car looped left along the older stone towers along the lake. The car wheels threaded into a high-pitched whimper against the smooth new pavement. The blast from the car heater started to make Sgt. Gallaher woozy, so she wordlessly inched down the window on her side until a chute of cold air cleared her head.

"But foreign policy has pitfalls," Sunny added. "One night I was in Andersonville for a zoning meeting. Someone said that a new preschool in a basement would be named after Pope John Paul. I saw my chance and said, 'Pope John Paul, who did so much to help so many throw off the chains of oppression.' Notice that I didn't say communism. Over on Lincoln Avenue, there are still storefronts where people burn a candle for communism. And anarchism, syndicalism, and probably fetishism. Call them nuts. But a politician never forgets: *Nuts vote.* All the Nobel laureates teaching at the University of Chicago don't have any more votes than people who believe they've had sex with space aliens. So I drop the pope's name, softly, like a ten-dollar bill in the collection plate. Suddenly, angry women get up all over the basement. 'The Pope is a pig!' they shout. 'The Pope oppresses women!' That was one night," said Sunny, shaking his head, "when I should have stuck to zoning."

Officer Mayer had threaded the cruiser into the complex of streets below the Loop. Fringes of snow, which had been blown in by a storm but concealed by the streets overhead from the day's sunlight, looked like grimy gray rails lining the roads. The policeman steered the car into a landing alongside three other cruisers in the Daley Center garage. A gray iron door rocked open from the wall, revealing another blue uniform on the other side.

"Thank you, Sergeant," said Sunny. "I enjoyed our conversation."

"Me too, sir. That detail will take you up to the mayor's office. We'll be down here when you're through. Whenever."

Maureen Gallaher sat back down alongside Officer Mayer, leaving the door on her side open to let in some of the numbing night air. She inhaled a bite of the frozen river, and ashy, misty warm exhaust from trash trucks whining nearby. Officer Mayer patted his pockets for a cig-arette lighter. City police cruisers were no longer so equipped. Radios and laptop computers had pointedly been mounted in their place.

"Nice guy, Alderman Roopini," she told the young officer. "But conversation? I don't think we got in ten words, do you?"

Three blue suits briskly showed Sunny into a service elevator and whisked him to the fifth floor. The officers seemed distinctly more sullen than Sgt. Gallaher—Sunny decided that this unexpected meet-ing must have necessitated an extra shift—and were silent on the short ride up. A gray suit took him through a gray-walled and wired equip-ment room, and another iron door swung open into the mayor's official waiting room.

Three sat in the mayor's outsized emerald-upholstered waiting chairs. Artemus Agras of the 1st Ward, whose brown potato shoes just touched the top of the thick maroon rug; Vera Barrow of the 5th, whose stockings brushed silkily as she rose in her pink sherbet suit to extend her hand to Sunny; and Linas Slavinskas of the 12th, who flicked a speck of something unseen from the smooth sleeve of his buttery chocolate-colored cashmere sport coat and stepped up to Sunny to take his hand into both of his own.

"Your lordship," said Linas. It was his nickname for Sunny, prompted by the clipped British school accent of Sunny's boyhood.

"Linas, I'm surprised they could find you at home."

"They don't look for me at home, milord."

"If I was your wife, Linas, I'd have them staple a tag in your ear to track you," said Vera Barrow. "Like they tag grizzly bears in mating season."

"That's not where she'd tag me, darling," said Linas.

Sunny brushed his lips against Alderman Barrow's smooth copper cheek.

"Resplendent as always," he told her. "Whatever the hour. What-ever the weather." He put his hand out to Arty Agras.

"We've been trying to figure out to what we owe this honor," said Arty. "It's a little late for this pajama party." Arty had pulled on his hairpiece with apparent haste, so that it rode up on the left side of his head, like a picnic blanket flipped over by a breeze.

Linas Slavinskas was chairman of the city Finance Committee, the council's most powerful. Artemus Agras was head of Budget and Government Operations, which theoretically employed the most city workers, and Vera Barrow was the mayor's floor leader and chairman of Police and Fire.

Sunny chaired the Parks and Recreation committee. The budget his committee set was not nearly as large as many other city agencies. But the money employed between four and nine thousand city workers, depending on the season: grass cutters, baseball coaches, bridge tenders, lifeguards, and trash pickers, in more than five hundred parks, sixteen lagoons, nine museums, ten bird and wildlife gardens, nine lakefront harbors, eight golf courses, two arboretums, and baseball diamonds, soccer fields, swimming pools, rec centers, fountains, band shells, and plazas.

Sunny was also vice mayor. The position was more a title than an actual office, a name to imprint near the bottom of brass plaques. Sunny understood, without awkwardness or apology, that his appointment was seen as a gesture to the position East Indian immigrants had won in the city. They spoke English, often quite lyrically, and had grown up, like the Irish immigrants of a century ago, with boisterous and combative politics ("So many parties!" Sunny once told a delegation of visiting Indian legislators. "Indian National Congress! Bharatiya Janata Party! National People's Party! Here in Chicago, we find that just one party can be as chaotic as you like.").

In politics, ethnicity was just one of the immutable facts of a man's biography. A politician learned to make use of it, as he might guiltlessly exploit his brains, looks, or wealth.

Arty Agras and Vera Barrow resumed their seats on one side of the room, sinking into the cushions against a bare cream wall (the mayor enjoyed watching security cameras shots of people on those cushions, squirming and flailing; they were disheveled and exhausted by the time they were brought into his office). Sunny took the one seat left, which was on the other side of a lamp table from Linas Slavinskas. Linas twisted his head slightly and caught Sunny's look as he comically turned his head and pretended to shield his eyes from the blazing dazzle of Arty's diamond stickpin. Linas was convinced it was a glittering fake.

"You see ads for these tchotchkes all the time," he once told Sunny behind his hand during a break in a zoning committee meeting.

"It's not as if he can't afford a real one, Linas," Sunny pointed out, but Linas snorted. His suspicion of the stickpin reflected his dubiety about Arty's political reputation. Arty took lunch (moussaka, a lettuce wedge, a kourambie cookie, and coffee) every day in the front booth of Thessalonica on LaSalle, a simple steel, ceramic, and cream-pie diner just across from City Hall. His conspicuous companions were men identified in newspapers as Jimmy Glad Bags, Sally Snake Eyes, and Larry Lizard Skin (inspiring Linas to call Arty *Squid for Brains*). Artemus Agras was somewhere between "allegedly" and "reportedly" organized crime's unofficial emissary in the city council. He was a full-time alderman whose annual financial statements reported everchanging investments in 1st Ward restaurant linen services, a car park company, and, in recent years, trash recycling businesses (inspiring Linas to also refer to him as *Eco Arty*).

Arty did not decry rumors about such ties. In fact, he jovially advanced them. He'd pull up to the urinal next to Patrick Tierney of the 33rd, who owned a rug cleaning service, and mutter, "Can I show you something in a concrete overshoe?" Or he'd hail tall, bald, Wandy Rodriguez of the 30th, a retired high school basketball coach, at budget committee meetings by saying, "I don't care how big you are, amigo. You can still fit into the trunk of a car." But Linas Slavinskas thought Arty's jokes betrayed him as a small, mild man with wise guy aspirations.

"Total con," he often told Sunny. "He's not a made man. He's a *putz*. At best, he knows a couple of cheap goombahs that could tie your shoelaces together. You know how the outfit works. They need lawyers, they hire the best Jews on LaSalle Street. They want a suit, they get the best Italian on Oak Street. So if the outfit wants a man in City Hall, do you really think they'd have to settle for a half-spiced plate of pastitsio like Arty Agras?"

Sunny picked up a copy of the city's Cultural Affairs newsletter from the low lamp table between him and Linas. There were stacks piled in Sunny's district office. Occasionally, the office ran short of tax forms, liquor license forms, taxi complaint forms, and zoning applications. But never Cultural Affairs newsletters. No matter how freely dispensed, there was always a pile or two to be disposed by the time the next was delivered.

Sunny couldn't remember the last time he had opened one that he hadn't used as a placemat for a sandwich. On those few occasions that he opened the newsletter as mental refreshment of last resort, Sunny was always astonished at the astounding display the city provided in public spaces and parks.

There were films, lectures, and mariachi bands, symphonies, puppet shows, gallery opening, and lectures about the linguistics of Augustine of Hippo. Sunny drew Linas's attention to a small box that read, *Creation of the Sacred Mandala*. "Something for you," he said, and ran a finger across the text as he read: "The public is invited to observe Tibetan Buddhist monks from the Drepung Gomang Monastery as they meticulously lay fine, colorful sand into beautiful patterns created as prayers for peace and healing."

"Oh, that's just what we've been missing," said Linas. "Sacred sand. Sure has done the job for Tibet."

"You're more sophisticated than you let on, Linas."

The newsletter said that when summer came, the Grant Park Orchestra would perform Mendelssohn's "Midsummer Night's Dream," Elgar's "Sea Symphony" and "Cockaigne," and selections from Mozart and Mahler.

"Look at that," said Linas, pointing his finger as if he had noticed a rooftop sniper.

"Estrogen Fest," Sunny read aloud. "Live music, theater, dance, visual art, poetry, and performance art."

"Estrogen Fest," exclaimed Linas. "*Estrogen Fest!* Parks should have softball games, hot dog and taco stands. High school bands playing "Stars and Stripes Forever." Maybe polka and Motown. But Estrogen Fest?"

"It's just a weekend next August, Linas."

"Estrogen Fest! That's what's wrong with this city now. Every goddamn loopy group has their own fest. What about Colostomy Patient Fest? What about Falling Down Drunk Fest? Don't they deserve recognition? When is Shoe Fetish Fest? I really want to try to make that one. *Estrogen Fest!*"

"Should be a great place to meet girls, Linas," Sunny said with a smile.

"I'm sure the kind of girls who go to Estrogen Fest think so, too," Linas replied.

Vera Barrow looked up from her newspaper and flung a smile from across the room, like the queen of Spain flinging a brooch from her throne.

"They just haven't met you yet, Linas."

Linas broke into the yellow-toothed grin that he knew made him look like the conniving wolf in a child's fairy tale and said only, "Natch."

Two more blue suits appeared in the waiting room and showed the aldermen down a bright, buzzing hallway into a conference room. They sat for another moment in silent, almost silly expectation around a shiny golden oak conference table.

"Oooh," moaned Linas. "Principal's office." He rubbed a palm ostentatiously over the glossy table. "You know they make these at a federal pen," he said. "I wonder if I can commission the warden to make me a dining set."

"Build your own when you get there, Linas," said Vera Barrow. "Service for twelve. One a year, twelve to twenty."

"Naw, babe," said Linas, "I'm a lover—" he began, but Collins Jenkins, the mayor's chief of staff, came suddenly into the room, his brown tweed coat flapping as if he'd been running after a bus, a creamy, hairy Nordic scarf—Linas was sure it had been knitted by nationalist Laplanders—looped around his neck.

"For chrissakes, Collins." It was Arty. "For the love of God, if he got us down here just to have you ream our . . ." Arty Agras tucked down his chin as he looked over at Alderman Barrow and let his observation stop short.

"Give us the two-minute scolding," said Linas Slavinskas. "And let us get back wherever."

Collins Jenkins took the seat at one end of the conference table. Stuart Cohn, the corporation counsel, an aging eagle with his smooth head and sharp face, stood behind him to take a snip of any question before Collins would risk doing so. Collins Jenkins had a peculiar gesture of lifting his reading glasses onto the top of his head. The precious little prop seemed to suggest that he could see things far above that were lost on others.

Collins flicked his tongue over his lips, clicked it against the back of his teeth, and thrummed his fingers three times before speaking.

"The mayor of Chicago is dead," he announced. Sunny heard a gasp from Vera Barrow—a sound as unexpected as a yodel from a woman of her incomparable composure. Linas dropped a gold lighter that had suddenly come into his fingers, and Artemus Agras let his mouth drop so far he needed his right hand to push it back.

"He died at his desk," said Collins. "Working late at night for the people of this city. Alone. It seems to be some kind of heart arrest. He's at Rush Medical Center now. I am awaiting the call from the doctors to confirm . . ." Collins voice caught ". . . whatever happened."

It was Linas Slavinskas who finally spoke, softly.

"Well, God rest his soul."

"You didn't give him much peace while he was here," snapped Collins.

"He gave it back pretty well himself," said Linas a little more sharply. But Collins Jenkins resettled the glasses on his head and went on.

"You aldermen chair the most vital committees. I wanted to inform you before I make a formal announcement. I want to have the medical report in hand. These days, there are always questions. I'm planning to call in the chihuahuas at six this morning."

The chihuahuas were the mayor's name for the City Hall press corps, and for reporters generally (he made no distinction between the gossip tout of a free weekly passed out in bars, and the religion editor of the *Christian Science Monitor*). Reporters were silly, smelly, noisome, and inconsequential entities that yapped and snapped against the ankles of the great and worthy. They had brains as small as walnuts, and soiled sofas and rugs. They cared only about eating, mating, and scratching themselves.

"If the mayor is on a slab over on West Harrison," Arty Agras admonished Collins, "some orderly has already told his girlfriend, and she's called chihuahuas. Or it's on somebody's computer bog somewheres."

Collins turned to face Sunny Roopini.

"You are vice mayor," he began softly. "You now become the acting interim mayor. I've checked with Stuart here." Collins actually raised the glasses off his forehead and gestured over his shoulder to the counsel. "As you know, your legal duty is to preside over the special session we'll hold tomorrow," and here he cast a glance down at his watch, then corrected himself. "Later today. To memorialize the mayor. At the regular meeting on Monday, you preside to elect a new mayor. Then of course there are regular elections next year. But although you hold office for just a few days, Sunny, your portrait will hang on the fifth floor here permanently, alongside the mayor and all of his predecessors. Harrison, Medill, Daley, Washington, Daley—and Roopini."

"Hell of a firm, your lordship." said Linas Slavinskas. Even Collins Jenkins permitted a small smile.

"The mayor was my friend," said Sunny. "For just a few days—it's an honor I don't deserve. I'll try to serve him well."

But before their smiles could fall, a door behind them was thrown open so roughly it whacked the back of a chair and banged like a shot. Blue uniforms trooped in, two, four, then six. Sgt. Gallaher strode in quickly, bending her head to the black brick of a squawking radio she had drawn from her belt.

"I'm sorry, you have to clear this area," she announced. Maureen Gallaher looked flushed and breathless, her blue eyes batting hugely. "This whole floor, in fact. Now. *Now*, please. The fifth floor of city hall is a crime scene."

A blue uniform was suddenly behind Sunny, taking each of his shoulders as he stood. Alderman Barrow had already reached her feet, and was stepping back to squirm out of the clasp of another uniform. "What the hell," she began. "What's this shit?" asked Arty Agras. Blue uniforms surged into the room and surrounded the aldermen, and the aldermen and Collins Jenkins turned so that their backs and shoulder blades suddenly bounced off each other as they shouted, "Hey! Hey? Hey?"

"Something's happened, right?" said Linas Slavinskas. "What the hell has happened?"

A shorter man in a more splendid blue uniform, with gold stripes and squared shoulders, stepped through the doorway. Sunny knew Matt Martinez, the police chief, just well enough to nod if they encountered one another at the same holiday parade.

"I'm sorry about the upset, aldermen," he said. "And Alderwoman Barrow." The title was alder*man* by statute, and Vera usually insisted on being so addressed; she could be withering with city functionaries who thought they flattered her by revising the phrase. But she did not correct the police chief.

"I'm afraid you'll have to leave right now," he said. "The entire floor is a crime scene."

"What have you got, Matt?" asked Linas, speaking gently. "This wasn't just a sixty-seven-year-old fat man who put too much cheddar on his cheese fries?"

"The mayor was poisoned," said the chief flatly. "That's what the doctors say. I am not at liberty to share any more information." Chief Martinez seemed to recharge his voice. "Clear this area. Clear this entire floor. Go to your offices on two. Or go home—there are cars downstairs. Get a drink, go to church, go to Lake Geneva. But get off this floor. The mayor of Chicago has been murdered in his office, and we don't know what the hell is going on."

Sgt. Gallaher had moved to Sunny's side and whispered that she and Officer Mayer would drive him home. As Sunny was stepping around a ragged line of chairs, he could hear Collins Jenkins remonstrate with the police chief.

"I have to stay, Matt. Decisions have to be made."

The chief only had to shake his head two or three times before Cohn stepped forward. When he spoke it was to the police chief, not Collins Jenkins.

"Chief Martinez, Mr. Roopini is the only one who has any legal authority right now."

Collins's head snapped around as if he had been slapped.

"Mr. Roopini has no experience. I say that with respect, Sunny," he added, but too late to keep Sunny from raising his left hand to Sgt. Gallaher and turning his feet pointedly to the center of the conference room.

"I've been in City Hall for nine years. I've been the mayor's chief assistant since he was a ward committeeman. Where were you then, Matt—getting flat feet on a beat in San Jo-Nowhere? I know every precinct commander by name. I can get the president of the United States, the queen of the Netherlands, the head of Scotland Yard, Bill Gates, or the cardinal of Chicago on *this phone*"—Collins brandished his own small silver mobile only an inch under the police chief's nose—"right now, right now, *right now*," he said, boiling and scowling. "Can *you*? Can Sunny?"

"That's not germane," Cohn told Collins Jenkins, more shakily. "Mr. Roopini is the acting interim mayor."

But Matt Martinez had already cast his vote with his broad, black, boat-heavy service shoes. He turned away from Collins Jenkins and fixed his red-rimmed eyes on Sunny.

"Mr. Roopini—"

"Sunny, please."

"Mr. *Roopini*," he repeated. "Let me have Sergeant—" and here he looked over at Maureen Gallaher's brass nameplate—"Gallaher take you to your office downstairs." Then he turned around to face Collins Jenkins.

"And Collins—I need your help. My officers need to run a few things by you."

"Question me? *Question me?*" Collins's face had switched into red as rapidly as a traffic light. He bopped between his right and left foot, sputtering and spitting, like some mad cartoon duck in tweeds.

"Question me! Question me! What the fuck, Matt. The mayor has been assassinated! Do you know what could be going on? Do you know what kind of world we have? What the fuck, Matt? What the fuck! This city needs direction now, Matt, not amateur hour."

But two blues had gotten a nod from their chief and had taken Collins's elbows gently into their huge gloved hands. They had already lifted him from his feet like a cranky toddler. Collins noticed suddenly that his heels were no longer in contact with the floor, and he looked down, confused and startled, as if the law of gravity had been suspended and a water glass had floated by.

"Just help us out, Collins," Matt Martinez said soothingly. "Thank you." The chief turned around to face Sunny again.

"And perhaps you should stay in your office, sir, so we know where to reach you. Please give me about fifteen minutes to see to things here."

Sunny felt his face flush and swell. He thought he should sit down; then he decided that he should be seen on his feet. He could see the back of Collins Jenkins's shoulders duck through the doorway between two blue arms.

"Do I need to take an oath?" he asked. There was a pause before the corporation counsel answered.

"Not technically," he said. "You were acting interim mayor from the moment the mayor drew his last breath."

"But maybe under the circumstances," said Alderman Barrow. "So there is no doubt."

Sunny stood up stiffly, reflexively raising his right hand.

"Should we have a Bible or something?" asked Linas Slavinskas.

"What is it that you swear on, Sunny?" Arty Agras asked solemnly. "The Kama Sutra? Whatever they call it . . ."

Sunny turned to Arty with a wide grin; the warmth of it surprised him.

"I'll take that pledge," Linas declared. Even Alderman Barrow couldn't restrain a smile.

"I swear on nothing, Arty," Sunny explained genially. "I don't know when I was last in a Hindu temple. I haven't been to a synagogue since we said goodbye to my wife. I've only been to a church for political meetings in the basement. You know how it is." Sunny turned back to Stuart Cohn. "Is there some kind of legal requirement?"

"No sir," said the counsel. It was the first time Sunny could recall Cohn addressing him with the honorific.

"Is there any book that means a lot to you, Sunny?" asked Vera Barrow. Titles reeled by in his mind as if they were spilling visibly from the top of a shelf. A Bible was packed with poetry, narrative sweep, and heroic depictions. The Bhagavad Gîtâ might be a nice touch that would be widely and approvingly reported. But Sunny wouldn't know where to find a copy of the huge Hindu holy book at this hour, and besides—there were too many rabbis and Hindus in the city to attest that Sunny was a stranger to them except during campaign season. *War and Peace? Ulysses?* Sunny had never really finished them. *Midnight's Children?* Sunny found the ending depressing. *Leaves of Grass?* Sandburg's *Chicago Poems?* Lincoln's Gettysburg Address?

Sunny finally asked, "Is there a subway map around here?"

Vera Barrow unclasped the gold snap on her soft black purse. She dug a delicate hand down, past crumpled tissues, scuffed emery boards, sugarless breath mints, mini-Cooper keys, crimped parking stubs, castaway combs, and smiling snapshots of 5th Ward children who were now in high school or the army.

"Exactly right," she said, waving the map, a spaghetti swirl of red, blue, green, orange, pink, and purple strands.

It was folded along the Green Line on the city's south side, between Cermak and Garfield Boulevard. Sunny took the slick map from her hand and unfurled it so that all folds flapped down over Vera's two hands. She held the map lightly, like a bowl of water that might spill. Sunny placed his left palm down, the tips of his fingers all the way north at Howard Street, the base of his palm south, along the Indiana line. He heard an ensemble of breaths in the room, and recognized his own. He picked up the shriek outside of a lonely late-night El car, spitting steel sparks into the cold as it leaned into the Lake Street turn, as he raised his right hand as he'd seen men in browning old photographs do.

"I, Sundaran Roopini . . ." he began.

"What do you want, Sunny?"

The mayor kept the thick walnut-clad television set in his office burning constantly, like a peat fire in a cottage in Galway. He told visitors that the low din camouflaged all conversation from a wide, indiscriminate inventory of sinister interests.

"What? Who?" Sunny finally asked one night. "Who would possibly bug this place?"

The mayor rolled his eyes and held a finger to his lips. "CIA," he finally mouthed softly. "KGB. Russians, Chinese, and Israelis. Oil companies, pharmaceutical firms, Cosa Nostra, al-Qaeda, and the House of Saud. The IRA, IRS, and FBI. Prosecutors, Martians, and Klingons."

Sunny was suspicious of the mayor's avowals, but admiring. His warning had the effect of making his visitors hem, haw, and stutter; the mayor's replies could be efficiently embroidered and oblique.

"What do you want, Sunny?" he repeated, raising his volume as he slid the control on the television screen up another three digits. The late-night news had ended, and a wild-eyed man onscreen bellowed the letters and names of each vitamin he had been able to excavate from carrot pulp. "A! B! B6! C! D! E!"

"To die in my bed at one hundred, beautiful women sobbing and massaging my toes," said Sunny, pausing between his delusions. "The girl who wouldn't go to the junior prom with me, shrieking that she was wrong. My daughters bereft and sniveling. Lance Armstrong wail-

ing that I was the only guy who could keep up with him on the hill climbs. Much general weeping and lamentation."

The mayor snorted cigar smoke from his nostrils like a dragon toy in Chinatown. "Besides," he finally grunted.

"I don't know," replied Sunny. "At least, I don't want to tell you. That's—intimate. Something you tell a spouse, a lover. Something you put in a prayer."

"I can do things for you those others can't." The mayor slapped his lap loudly with the palm of his hands. "Want isn't a weakness, Sunny," he announced. "We'd still be trailing our tails if one of our ancestors hadn't decided he was tired of getting sand up his ass and came out of the water to walk. Want is the wind that spins the world around," the mayor declared slowly and musically. "Nothing shameful about that."

Sunny sat back on the sofa, so that the mayor would have to twist his shoulder and waist around to look into his face. He thought he could hear the mayor's lungs groan like a bus starting up as he twisted around to meet Sunny's eyes.

"Telling someone what you want—it makes you vulnerable," Sunny said. "You divulge your dreams, and you show someone the best place to hurt you."

The mayor held Sunny's gaze for a moment, looking back at him with new interest. "I'll show you mine, you show me yours," he said finally. "I want to be mayor of Chicago. Forever. Not senator, not president of the United States, or Coca Cola. Not the king of Monaco, the Aga Khan, or even Steven Spielberg. I can't imagine—I don't fantasize—about anything else. No women, no money, no boys, no goats. This is what I want. I'll do anything to stay here. Anything. Do you know how much that is? I would lie, cheat, steal—murder, if I knew how to get away with it. I get away with plenty as it is.

"I am useful to my friends and strike fear in my enemies. I get my name on schools. I don't stop for red lights. The owner always sends over dessert. Everyone laughs at my jokes. People who wouldn't hire me with my night school degree now beg me to give jobs to their sons. People ponder the significance of me clearing my throat. People compete to make me smile, like I was a two-year-old. I bestow a wink or a* *wave, and they tell the story till they die. It's a nice life. I don't want to live any other way."*

The mayor sat back heavily, the plush cushion behind him sighing deeply.

"So, what do you want, Sunny?"

"Nothing that—elaborate," he said finally. "I'll run for re-election next year. If I win—"

"If, if, if—"the mayor grunted.

"It's my last term. Enough. I'll get serious about the restaurant. Out of office, I'll finally be able to get a liquor license. Maybe open a classy place in Lincoln Park. Finally make some money for my daughters."

"Nobody from the Forty-eighth can run for mayor, you know," the mayor observed as he stood up slowly and shook out his right leg. "It's a piece of jagged glass. Sikhs, Koreans, bearded Jews, Bible-thumpers, hillbillies, Pashtuns, Oaxacans, Menominee, Jamaicans, Nigerians— and I'm just getting started.

"Everybody brags on being the most aggrieved," the mayor explained as he settled uncertainly onto the edge of the sofa table. "The Chicanos think the Cambodians have had it easier. The Cubans think the Haitians get breaks they never did. The Chinese say you can't tell the Vietnamese from the Thais. The blacks say Koreans are pushing them out. The Koreans say blacks are pushing them around. Whites say they pulled themselves up by their bootstraps. Blacks remind them: at least you were born with boots. African-Americans get huffy because the Jamaicans, the Nigerians, and that's right, Sunny, the Hindus all get off the boats, the planes, the buses, with your cute little British accents, holding advanced degrees from provincial universities in your hands like fresh bouquets. A man who wins elections up in your neck of the city is like the astronaut who jumps twenty feet on the moon. Up there, he's Baryshnikov. But back on earth . . ."

The mayor stood, listing slightly to walk back behind his desk, settled into his chair, and leveled his cigar at Sunny like a nautical glass.

"But I'm not telling you anything you haven't figured out on your own, am I?"

"I always learn from you, Mr. Mayor."

There was another smoky snort. "I can't be flattered, Sunny. I have too high an opinion of myself." The mayor let the cigar cloud lift before he gave Sunny a long, appraising pause.

"Stan Hamel is seventy-five," he said.

"Seventy-six."

"I hear the congressman gets tired."

"I heard he played two hours of squash at the University Club this weekend," countered Sunny. "I always ask Stan, 'Why do you hang out in places like that? Those people wouldn't let your father in the dining room. We have beautiful park district courts.' "

"Well, Stan might be enjoying public recreation facilities again real soon," the mayor said quietly and paused. "Okay, I'll show you mine first. An inch or two, anyway."

"I'm sure you have it to spare," answered Sunny.

"Stan has a terminal disease," the mayor announced.

"I'm sorry."

"An interminable investigation."

"Then there really is no cure."

"Taking free chips and trips at the Forest County Pottawatomie Casino," the mayor explained.

"Stan has always been interested in the welfare of native peoples."

"Casino and Dog Track," the mayor stressed with amazement. "A man who makes speeches about the government paying too much for toilet seats in submarines and subsidies for soybean farmers has been betting money on dogs chasing their tails."

"At least not his money," Sunny pointed out.

"Somebody in the Wisconsin prosecutor's office turned somebody in the tribe," the mayor explained. "Stan's scalp fell onto the table. He wants to see his granddaughter graduate from Northwestern. They're willing to take his plea."

The mayor tapped a blunt gray ash into a green glass dish on his desk. "Women, boys, money, I understand," he said softly. "Even drugs. But dogs running around in circles . . ." The mayor shook his head gravely as he reached into a small black slipcase on his desk and rolled a cigar over to Sunny. It had a mossy green tint and felt smooth and squishy between Sunny's fingers.

"Jack Mirelowitz has been getting ready to succeed Stan in Congress since. . . ." Sunny finished the sentence as the mayor paused to let him draw in a puff.

"Since Cro-Magnon succeeded Neanderthal."

"The honorable state senator Miriam Gilpin feels she's due." As soon as the mayor had uttered the name he waved it away, as if erasing a chalkboard.

"There's that DePaul law professor who's on TV all the time. He wrote the new constitution for Na-u-ru." The mayor enjoyed drawing out the nation's name in his mouth so that it rhymed with kangaroo. "In the Pacific."

"Peter Mansfield. Yes, he sent me a copy—signed. It must have been a hundred pages. There are fewer people in Nauru than in the Eleventh Ward. He gave them a constitution that's longer than Don Quixote."

"A clause for each coconut," the mayor suggested. "The professor is vitally interested in public service, you know. Most academics, you give 'em a peck on the cheek and show them out. However, the professor has been wise in love."

"Fortunate, I'd say."

"Emphasize fortune," agreed the mayor.

"Dolores Carroll is not only a real beauty, but a civic asset," said Sunny.

"Asset-sss," the mayor emphasized. "The professor tells me he's interested in public service. I don't tell him, 'You may write constitutions, but you've got to fill potholes and work a precinct before you can take a turn in our game.' A man like that can make significant contributions to the democratic process."

"The Democratic party," proposed Sunny.

"Democracy is held together by an intricate system of checks and balances, Sunny," the mayor advised. "Personal checks and bank balances."

Sunny beheld his cigar at arm's length for a moment; it conspicuously lacked the manufacturer's band.

"These aren't legal, you know," he told the mayor, who looked at the fat, prominent ash on the end of his own cigar, and shook it to emphasize its solidity.

"An act of civil disobedience," the mayor declared. "To protest an inane, depraved, and antediluvian trade embargo." The mayor slashed his cigar like a cutlass through the bluish haze.

"There could be half a dozen others running up there, you know," he went on. "Nobody up in your slice of town suffers from lack of self-importance. Could be nine or ten candidates, between the lawyers in their town homes on Dearborn, the academics in their brownstones on Clark, the well-heeled along Astor, and all the libertarians, vegetarians, and antediluvians."

"Republicans?" guessed Sunny, and the mayor flashed an affirming grin.

"Sounds like there's no room for anyone else," said Sunny.

"Or in a field that packed—just the right someone else. A familiar name. International appeal." The mayor let his silence finish the sentence for Sunny in his mind.

"I've never thought about running for Congress," Sunny asserted flatly, and the mayor coughed out so much smoke with his laugh that Sunny had to flail through it with his hands.

"We've all thought about what it would be like to be president, win the last game of the World Series, drown to death, or sleep with twin blonds. Come on, Sunny. You can't be asleep for your own dreams."

Sunny indulged in a prolonged pause before replying, watching the smoke from his cigar snake up to the ceiling.

"The U.S. Congress," he said finally. "It's no way to live. Washington—a small company town. People think they're still in summer camp. They wear baggy khakis and squeaky rubber shoes. Name tags on their blazers instead of their underwear. Right down the road from New York—but no one can make a good bagel. They never learn. That's Washington."

"But you can come and go, you know," the mayor reminded him.

"That's the problem," Sunny replied. "Tuesday through Friday you're there, working and voting. Friday through Monday you've got to be here, telling people how much you hate being there, where you asked people to send you. You wind up stacking clean shirts in a bookcase in your office, next to mail and magazines you'll never open. Night after night, you eat General Tso's chicken from a bucket while you watch the news, drink a beer, and fall asleep on a couch. You wake up wearing yesterday's underwear and tasting moss on your teeth. Day after day, year after year, you beg for money more times a day than a bum on the street. What kind of bum does that make you? And for what? Just to hold on. To be one of four-hundred something that gets to vote on a thousand things you can't remember."

Sunny shook his head and shoulders theatrically. "No thanks," he said, flattening his hands above the edge of the mayor's desk.

The mayor wordlessly slipped a hand into a coat pocket and came out with a white handkerchief, neatly creased into thirds and fragrant with dabs of peppery cologne. He held it out to Sunny solemnly.

"But it sure would make your daughters proud," he said, pausing to affix the emphasis: "Congressman."

Sunny got out of his chair and walked over to the long window overlooking LaSalle Street. The mayor followed softly behind him.

"Did I say the magic words?" he asked. "I served a term myself, remember. Nice title, nice office. They got a dentist, a barber, and a restaurant right there in the building. You get to hire Harvard PhDs to pick up your dry cleaning. For the experience. You earn less than a high-priced call girl. But you get a future. Congressmen become ambassadors, commentators, lobbyists." Then the mayor twinkled in Sunny's direction. "Free hors d'oeuvres, every night of the week," he added, while winking over his cigar.

"I'm not hungry," said Sunny simply.

"Every now and then, any man can use a nice snack," the mayor reminded him.

Sunny stepped back from the window and moved to tap his next ash into the green glass in front of the mayor.

"You can't make anyone a congressman," he told him. "First District, yes. Second and Seventh, it helps. But not the Ninth."

"Indubitably correct. Which is what I will tell Professor Mansfield when I endorse him."

Sunny shifted slightly from one foot to the next, choosing to make the mayor go on.

"An endorsement like that elevates me," he said finally. "People say, 'The old warhorse has world vision.' Some of those folks along the lake know more about Micronesia than Montrose Avenue. So I can let the professor expound on Comoros and East Timor, while I tend to Morgan Park and Canaryville. He speaks seven languages, you know, including basic politics: you scratch my palm, I'll scratch your back."

"Is that in Nauru's constitution?" asked Sunny

The mayor put the stumpy end of his cigar into the green glass.

"I'll say, 'Peter, you have my unqualified endorsement. You are a stellar candidate who distinguishes our party. I'll be proud to raise your hand alongside mine. Just invite me to your lovely home some time when Angelina Jolie is there. Her causes, past and future, have my passionate approval. But you know what a disappointing mess democracy can be. You can't rely on my endorsement to deliver votes. In fact, you can't rely on it at all. Our citizens are independent-minded, especially in the Ninth. Isn't that what we revere about them? In fact, I'm not sure my endorsement doesn't risk harming you, in the teeniest way. Folks up there can resent it if they think some politician—even a popular and beloved one, if I may say—is trying to dictate to them . . . ' "

"Put a 'Perhaps I'm being modest' somewhere in there," Sunny suggested.

"A deft touch," the mayor agreed. "I'd have to say, 'Peter, get out there and campaign! Educate the public! Don't talk down to them! Let them know how vital it is to reduce the proliferation of nuclear weapons, relieve world debt, and reduce our wasteful habits of energy consumption. By increasing fuel taxes.' "

"Quite a platform next winter," said Sunny. "When people are breaking icicles off their shower curtains."

"Someone has to have the courage to tell voters the truth," the mayor declared with imperturbable sincerity.

"I'm told the professor also thinks Jerusalem should be the capital of Palestine."

"So do I," said the mayor. "In my part of town, Israel is the wicked landlord. But I never got my picture taken French-kissing Yasser Arafat."

"It was years ago. A conference of legal scholars. Arafat kissed them all."

"Sunny, in your district a man could probably explain away a picture of him fondling a twelve-year-old boy. He could say he was drunk. The boy looked sixteen. He could promise to get therapy. But playing smoochie with Yasser Arafat . . ." The mayor made a face as if he had bitten a sour pickle and moved quickly on.

"I will make strong, clear, urgent personal appeals to Norm Krumholtz at Title and Trust, Warren Williams at Prairie Construction, Gigi Winstead, and Devi Ardalan at Imagine Industries. I will inform them that Professor Mansfield has my heartfelt, unqualified, warm, and effusive endorsement, and I hope they'll support him generously. Even though I realize his campaign has staked out some bold and challenging positions."

"I'm sure they'll do as you bid."

"No dictating to people like that, Sunny. It's a free country, when you're rich. It's a great country when you're that rich."

"There are limits on campaign contributions," Sunny pointed out.

"There was a wall in Berlin," the mayor said unflinchingly. "There were levees in New Orleans. Nature finds a way."

Sunny walked softly back to the far end of the mayor's office and thumped his hands softly on the back of one of the unremarkable visitor's chairs from along the walls. As he spoke, Sunny drew himself back and inclined his chin, as if looking just over the earth's curve.

"But if I ran and won—that would help you, wouldn't it? You'd get your hands into the Carroll purse. But their busybody son-in-law would be chastened. He'd learn that getting elected is harder than writing constitutions. But the Carrolls would be in your debt. Or think they were."

"Senate seat coming up in four years," said the mayor.

"And we can play this game all over again, can't we?" said Sunny. "Unless they catch on."

The mayor grunted, unimpressed.

"The professor wants a career in politics. I intend to give it to him. Know how the Carrolls made their fortune?" he asked suddenly.

"Insurance."

"Selling dollar policies to poor black and Latin folks. People who were paid just pennies an hour for washing floors on their knees, and hauling shit out of sewers managed to pinch out a few pennies each month for the Carroll In-shoo-rance man, 'cause he said, 'You can leave your family with $100,000!' When the time came, most of those policies weren't worth more than a few pesos. But the Carrolls made out."

"Like bandits," Sunny suggested.

"Like billionaires," said the mayor.

"Behind every great fortune . . ." Sunny began. "So now their children give it all away."

"Just enough to start a foundation. They purify their treasure by letting a little of the interest dribble over orphans and endangered wetlands. Bono, Nelson Mandela, and the Dalai Lama show up at their parties. A smile from them sanctifies each cent. That's where we can lend our hands, too."

The mayor clasped his hands prayerfully and cocked his head to the side like a stained glass saint. Sunny took his time to reply, finally speaking in a cold, steely voice scorched of all jesting or veneration.

"My God you're shrewd," he said. "Dazzling, really. But you're like one of those greedy industrialists who pays a gang fifty million dollars to steal a Vermeer from a museum. You can't hang it anywhere. You can't show it to anyone. So you call in a few select souls late at night into your small, creepy chamber so they can marvel at how craven you are. What a fat, lonely, broke, smart, powerful, impotent, pitiable old fuck you are. I wonder how good you've been for anyone other than yourself."

The mayor had heard variations of Sunny's declamation. Being called a pitiable old fuck by an ally was no more unnerving to him than hearing a six-year-old scream "I hate you! I hate you!" at his father. It was how men who owed the mayor their jobs, reputations, and prosperity preserved a morsel of self-respect. The mayor had self-respect to spare. So his answer was gentle.

"I hope I haven't done bad by you, Sunny."

Sunny walked out from behind the chair. He absently slapped his thighs to wake up his circulation and placed a hand behind his neck.

"Stan Hamel." Sunny shook his head in sorrow. "I thought he was incorruptible."

"Don't be hard on Stan, Sunny," the mayor admonished. "Don't call anyone incorruptible. It's like saying that they don't get hungry, thirsty, or lonely. It's like saying that gravity doesn't apply."

The mayor had returned to mashing the channel changer. One animated man vacuumed sugar off a concrete floor. "Isn't that amazing!" Another ran a notched key over the glossy chassis of a bright red car; the audience gasped at the long scar, as if one more skyscraper had been struck from the sky. Sunny exercised the effrontery to walk over to a dark cabinet and began to unthread the cap off a bottle of the mayor's Remy Martin.

"Glasses over here," the mayor rumbled as he stooped down to pull back on one of his small drawers. On the next channel a woman poured hot fat from a hamburger into a clear cup to cheers and adulation. At the roar of clapping, the mayor squeezed up the volume.

"Let me see," said Sunny. "I should run for Congress. But you won't help me. In fact, you'll endorse someone else. In fact, you'll urge your wealthiest supporters to help someone else. But you expect me to win. And when I do, you expect me to be grateful."

"Sunny?"

He had the cognac positioned over two short glasses the mayor had plunked onto his green desk blotter and was just beginning to aim the first shot into the rounded bottom when Sunny felt the mayor's hand grasp his wrist and tighten, fiercely, suddenly, like a man who had lost balance and was trying to keep from falling down a staircase. When he spoke, the mayor's voice was hoarse, thick, and sounded slightly strangled.

"You're one of the few people who understand me."

"Who would want to kill the mayor?" Chief Martinez asked aloud, after all politicians had been safely removed from the premises. The mayor's office brimmed with brass-buttoned district commanders, blue-suited security cops, and investigators wearing gloomy gray suits. A growing parade of police technicians in blue windbreakers loudly stretched yellow crime scene tape across the length of the mayor's office, unsnapped equipment cases, and hailed patrolmen to hold this, hold that, and use their investigative acumen to discover where to get coffee at this hour.

"I mean, who would want to kill the mayor?" Chief Martinez repeated. After a mute moment, at least twenty hands shot up around the room.

"Let me rephrase that," the chief added in the general laughter. "I mean, which son of a bitch actually went ahead and did it?"

The mayor had been at once the most popular man in the city and the most despised. He was the most powerful and the most desperate for approval. No one else *knew* quite so many people. Between handshakes, winks, and waves cast out from podiums like blessings; between staffers, allies, adversaries, police, teachers, bus drivers, CEOs, parish priests, brokers, bakers, beauticians, street people, storefront reverends, and all forty players on the current roster of the Chicago White Sox (whom the mayor had made it his business to meet), Chief Martinez figured that at least fifty thousand people had the impression they knew the mayor personally.

The police had compiled an inventory of 1,476 people described, in the parlance of the times, as *persons of concern*. They had personally, if usually indirectly, threatened to kill the mayor of Chicago, either in a letter, a phone call, or increasingly, by e-mail. Of this accumulated number, 617 had said that they wanted to "kick your fat ass," "break your fucking neck," or apply some other force that, while technically short of homicide, was nevertheless regarded as threatening to the mayor's person.

Other correspondents obligingly listed the kind of details that experts found signals of forethought and sincerity: 349 said someone should shoot the mayor—"Shoot you in your big black head" was a common expression; 320 avowed that they would be gratified to see someone "blow up your fat black ass." A much smaller number, 89, said that the mayor should be slashed or stabbed, while 64 said that the mayor should be hanged.

(Of that number, 13 were so explicit as to specify "by his balls," rather than his neck. Department psychologists suggested that this desire was so precise as to merit its own category.)

Another minority of 9 said that they wanted to *fuck the mayor's brains out, fuck him up the ass,* or otherwise desired to hasten his demise with ferocious sex. When Chief Martinez once suggested that some of those correspondents might be more carnal than murderous, department psychologists pointedly asked the chief to recall his days on foot patrol: how many husbands' and wives' heads had he seen cracked by a beer bottle an hour after a couple had been in bed? Desire and murder, they reminded him, were compatible passions.

Then there were other, utterly distinct threats that were imagined with almost breathtaking intricacy. Twenty-eight (a number so unexpected that authorities wondered if it was the product of an organized campaign) said that they longed to pour honey over the mayor's private parts and sprinkle fire ants over the spill (which sounded excruciating; but arthropod experts at the Lincoln Park Zoo had evaluated the possibility and said that the bites would not prove fatal).

The overwhelming number of threats, 843, made mention of the mayor's race. Some 217 seemed to believe that the mayor was a closeted gay; 209 assumed that the mayor had to be some kind of furtive Jew, a covert convert, or in the thrall of Jews; and 107 blamed the mayor for not hiring them for a city job, for causing them to be fired from a city job, or for the fact that they couldn't seem to find or keep any kind of job as long as he was mayor. They implied that in his city only blacks, gays, or Jews got jobs.

Interestingly, most of the threatening messages did not express themselves in the conventional vocabulary of racial invective. They might threaten to kill the mayor for being black, a closeted gay, or secret Jew; but not for being a coon, a fag, or a kike. A generation of enlightened instruction had managed to adjust the language—if not much more than the language—of bigotry.

An amazing number signed their threatening letters with addresses or imparted some other bit of information (a place of work or worship, the name of a friend or neighborhood) that assisted police in finding them. Two plainclothes officers, a man and a woman (*a mommy and daddy,* as the teams became known) would ring their bells shortly after ten at night. (Psychologists had counseled that anyone who sent a menacing message to the mayor would almost certainly stoke their revulsion by watching the late-night news.) The mommy and daddy would introduce themselves as *Citizen Satisfaction Officers,* eager to hear complaints.

The mommies and daddies often noticed the same signature artifacts in the suspect's apartment: browning newspapers, forsaken coffee cups, a permanently unfurled sofa bed, discarded wrappers, and an uncombed cat snoozing on piles of soiled clothes. Daddy would play with the cat— this was considered unexpected and disarming—while Mommy kept up an unthreatening line of conversation as both officers scanned the apartment for signs of weapons, explosives, or some kind of plotting.

The mommy was encouraged to suggest to the suspect that she make tea (in fact mommies soon learned to carry their own teabags—

any the suspects had were usually musty and untrustworthy). While Mommy boiled water, rattled the suspect's two cheap pans, and unrolled the kitchen and bathroom drawers, Daddy turned off the television, hefted stacks of newspapers from the couch to the floor, and told the suspect in the most concerned and solicitous way that their letter, call, or e-mail had certainly *captured their attention* downtown.

The suspect was usually flattered. Then, they acted contrite. They blushed, stuttered, and professed to only half-remember whatever they had written. The mommies and daddies would return smiles benignly, and then Daddy would deliver a trim speech that the department's psychologists called *pre-emptive counseling*.

"We are watching you," he would say, affably but firmly. "Call a lawyer, call a priest, call your alderman, it doesn't matter. Threatening a public official is a crime. If we ever see you within a mile of the mayor, we will pick you up, put you in the back of a cruiser, and take you to the last place you will ever see. No phone calls, no court dates. We are the Chicago Police Department, okay? Not social workers," and here the mommy would put down her cup of tea, and the daddy would let his blue jacket slide back just far enough on his white shirt for the suspect to get a discreet glimpse of shiny black holster leather. "We don't give a damn if you grew up poor, if your father hit you, if your uncle diddled you, if your mama loved your dog more. We're the police. We get rid of problems. If anyone even notices that you're gone, the department will say, 'You know, sometimes people just disappear.' Your neighbors will say—you know this, too—'I'm not surprised. He was strange.' Call the FBI, call the ACLU, call Oprah. But really, who's going to believe you? Who's going to care?"

As a group, Chief Martinez noted that the 102 people who had received preemptive counseling from Citizen Satisfaction Officers seemed thereafter to be a very law-abiding group indeed.

The chief could remember when 1,476 case files would fill at least fifteen long brown file boxes. Now the contents were all purportedly encoded onto a single shimmering piece of plastic, which he balanced delicately between his fingers so he could inspect his unshaven 2:00 a.m. reflection.

"One thousand, four-hundred, and seventy-fucking six files," he said sharply to no one in particular, spinning the disc slowly on an index finger. "What the hell are we supposed to do with this Christmas ornament?"

Stuart Cohn hovered near the chief's elbow.

"Copy it for the FBI," he suggested. "They cross-check what they have. We can use their databases, their labs."

The chief signaled Walter Green, the commander who was his principal lieutenant, to step closer.

"Wake up what's-his-name," he told him. "The Mormon—"

"Christian Scientist," Green corrected him. They were speaking of the head of the local FBI office.

"He must live in the western suburbs." Green, a tall, slow-smiling, middle-aged black officer, was already pressing the keys on his phone as Chief Martinez turned back to Cohn.

"We need permission to enlist the feds?" he asked.

"We have cause already," said the counsel. "The perpetrators could already be in Indiana or Wisconsin."

"Draw up something anyway," said the chief. "*Now*. I don't want to have some guy holed up in a motel near Midway, only to be told we can't storm the place because we got his name off a federal watch list. Mr. Roopini should sign it?" Cohn nodded. "Can we get it in five minutes?"

"Two," said the lawyer, reaching into his coat pocket. "I only need a piece of paper." He already had a gold ballpoint pen that an old client had given him, unsheathed and poised. Chief Martinez nodded tightly and turned around to face the mayor's desk, now covered in some sort of ash-white downy spray laid down by the investigators.

"Jesus, this is unbelievable," he said softly. Commander Green had made his call, and approached the chief quietly.

"I know he was your friend," said Green.

"Well, I hope he had better than me. How many teams of mommies and daddies?" he asked.

"On all shifts?" said Commander Green. "Should be a dozen."

Cohn had returned to their circle with one simple sentence written in inch-high block letters on a plain white sheet of blue-marked City of Chicago stationery. He had drawn a line about three inches long on the right side of the page, and written in smaller letters below: *Sundaran Roopini, Interim Mayor.*

"Take it downstairs," the chief directed. "Roust everyone—chefs, servers, customers, bartenders, toilet cleaners—at that restaurant. And wake up the mommies and daddies."

4

"I'll have to ask you to stand back from that window," said Sgt. Gallaher.

Sunny stepped back from the cool glass of his single office window as he watched the first soft flakes of an overnight snow hover and fatten slightly in the moon glow of the streetlights. He turned dutifully around from the window to sit carefully on the rounded edge of a radiator cover. At this after-midnight hour, it felt cold under his slacks.

His aldermanic office amounted to two small, bright, boxy rooms on the fourth floor of City Hall behind a simple lettered sign saying SUNDARAN ROOPINI 48 in characters about as tall as a headline reporting the score of a high school basketball game. The flimsy plum-painted wooden door opened directly onto a reception desk that held small schoolroom flags: the stars and stripes of the United States, the state flag of Illinois, the city flag of Chicago, and the six-striped rainbow flag of the gay liberation movement.

The first office turned a corner to lead into a second small room that Sunny shared with his aldermanic secretary, Eldad Delaney: a gray steel desk for Eldad, a small round conference table for Sunny. On one wall, there were framed portraits of Yitzhak Rabin, Mahatma Gandhi, and Cesar Chavez (unsigned, owing to the deaths of the subjects some years before), and signed photographs from the mayor, the state's senators, and the Reverend Jesse Jackson.

Sunny had humbled himself to get the reverend to hold a pose beside him when the two were trapped in the same grim offstage passage at a 3rd Ward rally. The reverend held back for a moment. He seemed to recognize Sunny. But he had to rummage his mind. Did they meet in India? Davos? Devon Avenue? Was Sunny the commerce minister of Sri Lanka? The ambassador from Nepal? A cab driver? A cab driver who used to be the commerce minister of Sri Lanka? Sunny thought he saw an expression of imprecise distaste cross Reverend Jackson's face, as if it had suddenly struck him: *I could be posing with Heidi Klum.* But in a flash, the reverend gripped Sunny's hand with a great joshing guffaw, clapped his arms around his shoulders, and said "How you doing, buddy?" A ward functionary had time enough for a single, unsteady snap. Sunny sent a print over to the reverend's office for dedication; it was back later that day, efficiently if impersonally inscribed, "Keep Hope Alive! Jesse."

The adjoining wall had the spattered look of a patchwork quilt. There were cheaply framed citations of thanks to Sunny for sundry gestures of support from the Swedish American Museum, the Korean American Women's Association, the Japanese American Citizens League, and the Clubes de Oriundos. There were vanilla-colored certificates, listing slightly from vibrations of passing elevated trains, that attested to the gratitude of various holy assemblies for Sunny's appearance before them, from Saints Gertrude, Gregory, Henry, Ignatius, and Ita, to the Bong Boolsa Korean Buddhist Temple, the Bait-ul-Salam Masjid mosque, and Anshe Sholom (Orthodox), Anshe Emet (Conservative), Temple Sholom (Reform), and the Or Chadash Congregation for Lesbians and Gays (also Reform).

During rush hour, when three and four elevated trains passed through the Wells and Washington station, the scores of plastic frames on Sunny's wall rattled *tappa-tappa-tappa* against the plaster like a chorus of applauding beetles.

"Quite an explosion," was all Sgt. Gallaher said after Sunny had snapped on the overhead light.

"You can't put up one without putting up all," he told her.

"I don't think the mayor puts up any," said Sgt. Gallaher.

Sunny knew that the mayor displayed only a few refined canvases sent over on loan from the Art Institute. Sunny recalled one late night when the mayor had swept his arm past a Grant Wood prairie landscape, a Homer Winslow seascape, and a Hopper still life of a quiet night in a Chinatown restaurant.

"Americans are safest," he once told Sunny. "Some ties to Chicago, if possible. An undisputed master helps. No new pieces by any dissident Chinese, Burmese, Chechen, or Turk, or next you know, folks expect me to help get them out of the guuu-lag. Nothing too *interesting*. Nothing explicit. Nothing abstract—people will think they're nudes. And, *no nudes*. An occasional old communist painter is okay, as long as they're foreign. It makes me look cosmopolitan. Diego Rivera? Perfect—a dead foreign communist. I also believe he was an adulterer. Some people think that a portrait of Lincoln is safe. I think it just invites comparisons. I once saw Lincoln up on a wall in Bangui. The president-for-life there had a gold-plated swimming pool where he fed his opponents to hippopotami. He told me, 'Oh, Lincoln is my hero, Mr. Mayor. He knew what to do with rebels.' "

The mayor let a curl of cigar smoke enfold his small gray moustache as he smiled.

"The hippos?" asked Sunny.

"Naturally, I inquired," the mayor replied, drawing out a long, slow puff. "But the zoo here said that a diet of aldermen would be insalubrious. I know I find Linas Slavinskas and Felix Kowalski indigestible, too."

Stuart Cohn had stepped tentatively around the corner, holding out the sheet of paper.

"An ounce of prevention, sir," he explained, as Sunny was already moving Cohn's gold pen from left to right above his name, and Stuart Cohn was already turning back to the door. Sunny sat back against the wall, the radiator cover groaning.

"That's the first time I've seen my new, momentary title spelled out. A few hours ago, my signature on a credit card slip maybe could have bought a new refrigerator. Now, I think I just signed something that will get people out of bed and cost a lot of money."

Sgt. Gallaher raised a hank of her dark hair behind her head, and looked pointedly somber.

"You're going to declare war on Indiana?" she asked.

Sunny smiled as he stepped down and finally brought himself to sit at his round white table.

"They'd better watch their step."

There was a heavy old black phone, several models behind the most current, sitting on Sunny's table. Taped to the faceplate, old numbers of people he no longer needed to reach were fading into light blue scratches. He punched in the mobile number for his assistant; it rang off into voice mail. Sunny heard a recording of Eldad's maladroit imitation of the mayor's growly voice, intoning, "El-dad is not home right now. He is working for the betterment of the city of Chicago against all of the antediluvian forces that threaten her. You can leave your message after the beep."

"Eldad, I need you," Sunny said quietly into the phone. "I'm at the Hall. Call when you get this. Or just come down immediately, please. And Eldad," he added more gently. "You might want to change your phone message."

Sunny put down the handset and looked across to Sgt. Gallaher. She had kept her black topcoat on—Sunny thought that its long cut conferred a kind of elegant sweep to her tall stride—and when it fell open as she hiked her leg onto a chair, he pointed to the black brick of a radio on her belt.

"Chief Martinez said fifteen minutes, didn't he?"

"Half an hour ago," said the sergeant as she turned her wrist to look at her round steel watch. Sunny noticed that she was wearing nail polish, but it was clear; he wondered if that was a department regulation.

"Almost forty minutes ago," she amended.

"I wonder how long he'll be."

"I suppose you can tell him you'd like to see him now, Mr. Roopini," she suggested. "You are the interim, momentary, temporary, Acting Whatever, after all."

Sunny stood up from his table and stepped back to his single window, staying within a measured and respectful step of the unseen boundary that Sgt. Gallaher had set. He could see snow beginning to glaze slickly onto the cold stone ledge outside.

"Let's give him a few more minutes," said Sunny, and Sgt. Gallaher stood up and slipped off her long black coat, giving it a single, proficient shake to tuck it over the back of the chair.

In the mayor's office three floors above Sunny, a balding young toxicologist whom Rush Medical School had sent over informed Chief Martinez that the mayor had died of heart arrest, leading to a nonreactive coma with mixed hypokalaemic acidosis and central hypothermia, induced by a plasma nicotine concentration of 3.7.

Chief Martinez was speechless; then his vocabulary contracted to a single word.

"Nicotine?" he exclaimed. "Nicotine! Fucking nicotine? " Or two. "*Nicotine*! Nicotine! Fucking *nicotine*!"

"Cigarettes kill," remarked Stuart Cohn, as if reaching the conclusion of a Bible lesson.

"The mayor didn't smoke cigarettes," Chief Martinez pointed out. "A cigar now and then. Every day. But he talked too much to inhale."

"He couldn't absorb this amount of nicotine through smoking," the toxicologist informed them. "In fact—not to encourage anybody— flammable heat dissipates nicotine. At those levels, he had to ingest it directly."

"Ohmigod," said Walter Green. "You mean that the mayor *ate* cigarettes?"

After an astonished silence, the men let out their breaths, as if putting down chairs they had carried over their heads.

"But I saw him eat raw corn once," Chief Martinez recalled. "Coming back from a conference in McHenry County. He saw a farm stand, shucked two ears, and ate them raw, right in the backseat. Had corn silk dangling from his mouth for the rest of the ride."

"Those levels of nicotine seem to have been delivered by a distillate, probably sprinkled over the top of the mayor's pizza," said the toxicologist.

"Wouldn't he have tasted something funny?" Commander Green asked.

"Maybe some bitterness." The toxicologist tugged on the small end of his tie and nodded his head from side to side. "But among all those onions? That's why nicotine is used in some insecticides. It's bland. The insects don't get bait shy."

"The mayor was the least bait shy man I've ever known," Chief Martinez said with a mild smile.

The toxicologist had a small stack of X-rays and slick-surfaced facsimile pages that he struggled to keep orderly as he sat on a worn green velvet wing chair. But every few questions, something slid off; the young man would lurch onto his knees to retrieve it. It had the effect of making him look like the chief's constant supplicant.

He explained that there were two factories within a few hours drive that used nicotine in the manufacture of insecticides. But sufficient toxicity, he explained, was probably contained in two standard packages of nicotine patches—"No-Smokems, Smoke-No-Mo, whatever," he said. "They call it 'therapeutic nicotine.' "

"Some therapy," said Chief Martinez. "And what—they boil the stuff down? A lethal tea?"

"Trap the steam into drops. All you need is a burner and some tubing. Like a still," said the toxicologist. "Freshmen in high school—teenagers serving ten to twenty for armed robbery—figure it out."

Chief Martinez stood and rubbed the back of his neck. His elbow pumped back and forth as if he were trying to take off by flapping of a single arm.

"There must be half-a-dozen drug stores that sell those patches within two blocks of the restaurant," he said. "Hundreds in the city."

"And liquor stores," Walter Green suggested. "Gas stations sell them, too, right next to the salami sticks and puke-pine deodorizers."

The commander turned away and began to tattoo a sequence of numbers into his phone.

"But whatever the mayor ingested tonight wouldn't be enough," the toxicologist advised. "The nicotine would take two to three applications to kill—to affect—even insects, much less an average human being."

Chief Martinez and Commander Green exchanged embarrassed smiles as Green folded his phone back into his hand.

"Two to three. What about eight?" the commander asked. "On a man who weighed three hundred thirty pounds and who exercised by unrolling a burrito to check for extra cheese?"

"Applications?"

"Servingsss," he said, emphasizing the plural with his long, dark fingers. "Slicesss."

"Eight slices of deep dish pizza with extra . . . stuff?" The toxicologist's eyes widened, as if he'd just heard about an especially lopsided football score. "At one sitting?"

"Every man and woman on that detail is all over those pizzas," the police chief called out as he began to move slowly toward the door. "Get them tested."

"Of course," replied Walter Green, then paused, raised his eyebrows, and kept a large hand folded over the keys of his phone. "Immediately?"

The two men shared a frosty laugh as Stuart Cohn and the toxicologist looked on, squirming slightly in their seats and exchanging puzzled looks, uncertain if they were expected to join in.

"Tested, yes," said Chief Martinez. "Treated? I'll get back to you," he called over his shoulder, his words springing back from the hard walls in the empty hallway.

Sunny decided to splash water on his face. There was a men's room about twenty steps away in the warren of aldermanic offices, and Sgt. Gallaher nodded for two uniforms to open the door for Sunny and stand by.

After he'd had a pee to clear his head, he ran the tap and sloshed cold water onto his face with both hands as he looked into the mirror. When he was forty, Sunny had been happy with his face. He had ink-black curls of hair with discreet licks of gray, above a smooth almond complexion, and bright eyes, black and brown like a horse's tail. Most Indians would mark him as being from the south—Tamil, Tulu, or Kannadigas. Others in America sometimes wondered if he might be Egyptian, Brazilian, or Portuguese; or when they heard "Roopini," guessed, "Italian?"

At forty, Sunny's face had fit his name (Sunny had become his primary name at his father's instigation. A Tamil would not give his son a high-caste name, like Sunil. But he could urge his son, Sundaran, to go by the nickname Sunny, which conveyed the same implication). Sunny's face had shone with vitality, yet had a patina of silvery distinction.

But just eight years later, Sunny looked at his face and saw a distressed property. His eyes were rimmed with yellow, like the edges of an old map. They bubbled inexplicably, like leaky plumbing. His cheeks sagged like old lead paint dripping sadly down a wall. He noticed stray hairs growing from his ears and nose, like sprigs from cracks in a sidewalk. His hairline rolled up, like a cheap bathroom curtain, another millimeter every few months.

Sunny heard people around him assign each bulge and wrinkle to his tragedy. But he was sure that much of it was the passage of time, the pull of gravity, and the toll of politics.

The yellow tinge in his eyes could be bile from twenty years of slurping hot, sour coffee from unwashed urns in ward offices as he asked for votes or money. The jelly filling that upholstered his chin could be the bloat of twenty years of bagels, biscotti, and donuts put out at precinct meetings and police stations.

Sunny heard a rap of knuckles on the bathroom door and Sgt. Gallaher's voice, calling softly.

"Chief on his way down, sir."

Sunny scooped a last bowl of water into his hands and lowered his face into his palms. When he blinked water from his eyes, he noticed a uniform holding out a small stack of paper towels.

"You go to the academy for that?" he asked, and looked at the young man's nameplate. "Officer Harris?"

At first, the officer seemed taken aback, then grasped that Sunny was joking.

"Yes, sir. Firearms training and towel handling."

Sunny pressed the scratchy paper against his forehead and looked into the mirror. It was remarkable, he thought: what a man could try to hide in his own face.

On his way downstairs to tell Sunny such details of the mayor's death and suppositions and implications that seemed responsible to advance, Chief Martinez decided that he had to stop to strip a few pieces of flesh from the limbs of the chief of the security detail.

Francis Joseph Conklin shuddered with dry tears as he sat uncertainly on the edge of a folding chair that grated against the floor as he rocked from side to side, his stocky blond hands squeezing the sleeves of his putty-colored suit. A mommy and daddy team, Alex and Meg, had hugged him manfully, consoled him sincerely, and taken him into a room in the mayor's office suite that held office copiers. They sat him down, wordlessly patted him down, and took his service revolver from the holster under his left shoulder and a six-inch blade from a slipcase on the back of his belt.

"Just a formality, Frankie," Alex reassured him.

"I loved the son of a bitch."

"We know. *He* knew," Meg said soothingly. She was a tall, rangy woman who had won a couple of state archery titles, and officers looked the other way—or rather, looked *her* way—when she chose to wear sleeveless shirts on the job, baring the arms she used now to knead the security chief's clenched shoulders.

"He loved you," she added. "He trusted you."

"I fucked up," said the security chief.

"You couldn't have known," said Alex, and when a police tech stepped into the room crinkling some three-page report that she intended to copy, Alex waved her back. He stood so that Frank Conklin's right shoulder rested for reassurance against his hip. It was also a position from which Alex could smash the heel of his hand into Frankie's shoulder and grind Frankie down into the floor if he tried to leap up, run off, or grab for the gun he might assume Alex had holstered under his own left shoulder, but, according to plan, had actually removed. Between the security chief's coughs and sniffles, they could hear a low, dull drone from the copier.

Chief Martinez stepped into the small room. Alex stepped back and sat against a heavy white box of paper, but Meg kept her sturdy thumbs along the security chief's shoulder blades, rolling her fingers lightly.

"Did you tip him?" asked Chief Martinez. Frankie Conklin looked up in puzzlement.

"*Did you tip him?*" Chief Martinez repeated, and this time Frank softly mouthed, "Who?"

"The delivery man," explained the chief. "Whoever came over from Quattro's. In a while, I'm going to have to tell the world just how it was that the mayor of Chicago was killed by a pizza delivered piping hot and fresh into his own *fat fucking face*. What does Dear Amy say about tipping home delivery assassins? Is ten percent too little? Is twenty percent extravagant? Oh wait—Quattro's. *I'll bet they didn't send a bill at all!* I hope you gave the kid at least a ten-spot for making the trip!"

"I loved the mayor," the security chief was able to finally say through a clotted throat.

"*I didn't!*" Chief Martinez shouted for the first time, so loudly that Alex and Meg had to hold up their hands when a couple of blue uniforms sprang to the copy room door.

"So what?" he went on in a lower tone, his face boiling and purpling. "I don't think you grasp this, Frankie. These days, people expect to be protected from 747s smacking down skyscrapers, bombs on the Red Line, nerve gas on the Blue Line, anthrax under their postage stamps, and teenage girls putting bombs in their training bras. They expect us to stop a million tiny pins and needles from being snuck into crates of dates or toilet paper and then assembled, like a Christmas toy, into an atom bomb. *And they throw a fit when the security lines get a little long!* God knows—I wish I could say—how many things we've stopped. And what brings down the mayor? A shoulder-launched missile? A blinding laser? A crack shot by a crazed sharpshooter?"

Each example seemed to extract another inch from Frank Conklin's spine, until his head seemed to disappear below his shoulders.

"I would have taken a bullet for him," he said hoarsely. Chief Martinez bent down so that he could look levelly into the security chief's face; when he spoke, he sounded as if his wrath had made him weary.

"I wish you had, Frankie," he said. "He'd be alive. You'd be a hero. The department would be honored. Instead, your family is going to have to be smuggled out and resettled in someplace like . . ." The chief faltered while he rifled through his mind, as if trying to recall the name of a distant star. "*Nebraska,*" he said finally.

New tears bubbled in the security's chief's eyes; he batted them out furiously. The tears slid and seemed to trace red tracks into his cheeks.

"I wish I had a big fat cannonball hole in my chest," he said.

Chief Martinez was tempted to tell him, "It could still be arranged. . . ." But the chief knew that he already risked charges from the police officers' union.

The security chief sat back on his folding chair. Meg stiffened her thumbs along his shoulders when she looked down and saw him reach under the left side of his gray jacket. But Frank Conklin just slipped his heavy gold badge from where it was pinned in his chest pocket to hand it over to the police chief. Chief Martinez slid it into the breast pocket of his dress blues.

"I'll keep it here, Frankie," he told him, and rose to go down to the fourth floor of the hall.

6

Sunny's office window whitened as flakes of snow flattened and thickened against the glass, looking silver in the luster of the street lamp. An *a cappella* clop of new alligator shoes heralded an arrival from the hallway. Sgt. Gallaher took two long strides through the doorway, holding each side of the frame and standing at full height.

"Palace guards already, your lordship?"

"Please let Alderman Slavinskas in," Sunny called out. He could see the top puff of his sandy pompadour just above Sgt. Gallaher's shoulder. "But watch him carefully."

Linas stepped in as the sergeant stood back, theatrically smoothing creases from his cashmere sleeves. Sunny stayed seated while he offered introductions.

"Sgt. Maureen Gallaher, alderman." Maureen Gallaher did not extend her hand—regulations dictated that she keep both hands free in security situations—but smiled down at Linas.

"Alderman."

"I've seen you around the hall," said Linas. "You're in good hands, Sunny."

"Where's Vera?"

"Grieving," said Alderman Slavinskas. "Working the phones. Circling the wagons. Rallying the troops."

"Where are your troops and wagons?"

"Ready to roll," Linas said almost casually, as if acknowledging a thread from his sleeve. "So—what do you hear? I've got a pallie in the Ogden Avenue district. She says it was some kind of poison. On the pizza."

The aldermen looked over at Sgt. Gallaher, who lifted her eyebrows and chin slightly and inclined her head gently.

"I hadn't heard. Anyway, it's not for me to say."

"Oh good Christ, the pizza," said Sunny. "How many times—"

"But we never touched his," Linas reminded him. "His were always special." He turned to Sgt. Gallaher, fairly twinkling.

"Ever have a slice of the mayor's pizza, sergeant?" he asked.

"No sir, that was the body detail." Linas let that phrase pass.

"You strike me as more pasta sciuè *sciuè*. You know that dish?" he asked. Sgt. Gallaher shook her head.

"A tender penne, ripe red plum tomatoes, a good golden olive oil," Linas went on. "Just let a snowfall of fresh white moist mozzarella fall over the mound"—and here Linas tinkled his fingers, like a first-grade music teacher imitating flurries—"a gentle cover of basil leaves, then slivers of pecorino. Not heavy, not garlicky, just *e-squi-sito*. Downy and inviting as a fresh bed. You see the plate and say, '*Come sei bella.*' I'll bet you know that phrase. I know a place on south Oakley—"

"You must bring me there sometime," Sunny cut in.

Chief Martinez had entered the room softly. Sunny stood reflexively at the glint of brass. Chief Martinez nodded to Sgt. Gallaher and told her to take up a post just outside the door.

The police chief quietly explained that the doctors at Rush had determined that a distillate of nicotine had been trickled over the mayor's pizza. Officers could certify the integrity of the pizza—even the chief had to fight down a smile at that phrase—from the moment it left the restaurant, so their operating assumption was that it had been doused with a lethal dose at Quattro's.

"License, health certificate, building inspection?" asked Sunny.

"Current. Impeccable."

"Fines?"

"None. Never."

"Wish I could say that," Sunny told him, then asked, "You looking at everyone who worked there?" The police chief seemed to hold back.

"From head to toe," he said finally.

"The Faride brothers, Nabieh and Tannous, own it."

"For years."

"Someone will point this out," said Sunny. "They're from Syria."

"A long time ago," said Chief Martinez.

"A good, loyal American family," agreed Sunny. "And every time I'm in the restaurant it seems as if a new, distant cousin is passing through and working there."

"So what? They come to this country, work hard, and hire their relatives. My Uncle Julio's story, too," said the police chief, and at this Linas Slavinskas took a step away from the doorframe, dug his hands into his pockets, and swayed lightly on his heels.

"My Uncle Steponas's story, too, Matt," he said. "But I also had a great uncle Herkus, who blew up trains all over Klaipedos. If he were still around, you'd want to get your hands on him tonight."

"Is every employee on their books?" Sunny asked, and when Chief Martinez seemed to wrestle with a response once more, Sunny added, "I run a restaurant myself, Matt. Not everyone who asks may be as understanding."

"The brothers say they employ five people off the books. Part-time—if you call wiping floors fifty hours a week part-time. A couple Mexicans—or Salvadorans posing, if you ask me—a Polish kid, an Irish guy. Some guy who sleeps in a box on Clark Street. They were paid in cash. They only used their first names. I'm sure we'll never see them again."

"Those five," Sunny wondered. "Did any of them ever mumble to themselves? Hum the 'Internationale' or 'Come All ye Black and Tans'? Wear a Timothy McVeigh T-shirt?"

"Everyone says they worked hard and said nothing."

"I'm sure," Sunny observed. "Though someone who figured they're illegal could threaten to turn them in—unless they performed a small favor. Like sprinkle extra seasoning on somebody's pizza."

The police chief kept his arms locked onto his knees, sitting motionless for one long moment before replying.

"If we had started some kind of dragnet through the kitchens of this city, the courts, the mayor, businesses, banks, the press—you aldermen—would have been all over me."

"Like they will be now," said Linas Slavinskas, who chanced to place the palm of his hand softly just above the brass button that held down five enameled stars along the police chief's right shoulder. "This is Chicago, Matt. Nobody plays hopscotch."

"The mayor of San Francisco was shot by a city councilman," the chief sternly reminded them. Sunny chose to make his own tone almost chatty.

"Look, Matt," he continued, "I think that a six o'clock appearance is a sound idea. For both of us. The formal announcement about—what's happened. There'll be some questions only you can handle."

"Yes. Well, it's an ongoing investigation," said the police chief. "I can't say anything except that."

"I understand. Just flash some brass and reassure people that the Chicago Police Department will pursue the mayor's killers to the ends of the earth."

"We can't go north of Howard Street," the chief reminded him. "But I'll send Walter Green, my deputy."

Sunny sat forward, bringing the back of his knuckles lightly in a companionable graze against the police chief's folded knee.

"I'd like to speak again at about five."

"Of course, Mr. Roopini."

Sunny and Linas looked at each other silently for a quarter of a minute as they listened to the police chief commend Sgt. Gallaher and stride back toward the fourth floor elevators, his wet shoes squeaking like small birds. When they heard the distant ding, Linas raised his eyebrows, but kept his voice low.

"Mattie didn't just fall off the chile truck. Walt Green is a smoothie. He's also black."

Sunny looked up with a tight smile, and splayed his hands in front of him along the table. He did not invite Sgt. Gallaher back in.

"You want to show me your scorecard?" he asked softly. Linas sat back in his chair, turning up the soles of his shoes and lacing his smooth, well-kept hands across his stomach, enrobed by folds of black cashmere. Sunny could hear a slight, elegant sound, as the sweater under Linas' jacket slid against his coat, like the swish of velvet drapes.

"I make eighteen for me, first round."

"Vera?

"One more. But one round only. Daryl Lloyd will go once for her, then he'll feel the call and jump in himself."

Dr. Lloyd was the 9th Ward alderman, a dentist with offices and billboards strung across the city's far south side. *From Morgan Park to Calumet Heights, Dr. Daryl Lloyd has the smile that's right—for you!* Because Somalis, Sudanese, and Ethiopians had moved into his ward, Dr. Lloyd had taken to adorning himself in African robes. Grace Brown of the 6th, who had been a high school principal, recognized the designs as Ashanti, a Ghanaian tribe. She suggested to Daryl that whatever political magnetism he wished to establish by his wardrobe might be misplaced; it made as much sense—or as little—as someone wearing a Fraser of Lovat clan kilt to endear himself to Belgians. But her example clearly missed its mark. "An African robe is the cloak of royalty," Daryl Lloyd told her. "It is *not* some kind of skirt."

"Third round, Vera will be down to fifteen," Linas continued. "Arty will hold on to eight." Linas turned up his palms and hitched up his shoulders. "A jump ball could bounce anywhere."

"Which devil gets Rod Abboud?" asked Sunny. He was the 26th Ward alderman, and a West Town labor attorney with a hard, unfunny laugh that punctuated finance committee meetings like a tree saw in a cemetery.

"Undecided and open for business," replied Linas.

"I'm for her, you know," said Sunny. "I owe them. Simple as that. The mayor and Vera brought me to the prom."

"That's how I've got you scored," said Linas. "You owe me nothing. That's how we can be pallies."

"But since I'll be presiding, I won't vote. I've got to be neutral. Until she really needs it."

"She really needs six." Linas held up one full hand and one thumb, looking like some incongruously sly preschool teacher.

"Where have you got Cassie Katsoulis?" She was the 47th Ward alderman, a real estate broker who occupied the seat to Sunny's right at council meetings. The large red trawler of a bag she parked between them rattled with small internal seizures every few minutes from the vibrations of one or another of her mobile phones.

"You've got a lot of artsy downtown types moving into her ward. Gay couples adopting children," Sunny pointed out. "A segment of the electorate FDR never considered."

"*Homeowners*," stressed Linas. "They want to dump their kids at school without worrying about drugs, guns, Chechen rebels, and festering trash. *My people.*"

(Sunny remembered a similar insight from the mayor, who had once hung up on a call with a north side ward committeeman and scowled.

"What the hell happened to gays?" he asked. "They used to buy abandoned places and fix them up. Brass doorknobs, stained glass, skylights, hang the cost, 'cause they don't have kids. They didn't care if the public school down the street was Sesame Street or San Quentin; they just wanted a farmer's market in the playground every Saturday. Gays used to go to theater, guzzle pomegranate martinis, and gossip. You could talk to them about movies, music, and clothes. Listen to them now, will you?" the mayor asked as he clamped his hands over his ears. "Chattering like married couples at a backyard barbeque. 'Where do you get diapers? Can you believe what they charge for kids' shoes? Have you met the third-grade teacher? She looks a little slutty.' ")

"Luis Zamora?" The 31st Ward; a beer distributor.

"Luis is vitally concerned about improving the Department of Constructions and Permits. He's even kind enough to suggest a couple of people to help."

"Hiring laws," Sunny reminded Linas, who lifted his eyes toward the ceiling and flattened his hands beseechingly before a higher authority in the heavens, or on the fifth floor.

"As the man upstairs so often said: God helps those who help their friends."

The two men sat silently for half a moment, counting and calculating the implications of such wisdom.

"I play this absolutely down the middle while I'm in the chair," Sunny finally told Linas. "But if Vera gets to twenty-four—"

"You could name your price," Linas finished the sentence. "But there's no prize unless she wins."

Sunny hunched in closer over the round table, which prompted Linas to lean in, too.

"You could name your price right now, Linas. Have you thought about that?" he asked. "Lay back. Let her have it. Say it's to continue the mayor's legacy. You keep the finance committee. The press can extol your statesmanship. Then start running for next year. The real term."

"Is this an official tickle?"

"In no way," Sunny assured him. "I'm neutral until I vote. But I'm sure I can sell it."

Sunny thought that Linas paused longer than was necessary to convince him that he considered the offer fresh, sincere, and valuable. Then he shook his head almost mournfully.

"It's a little late for me to play statesman," he finally told Sunny. "Next year? Jesus will jump in, too. You figure Jesus, you've got to plan on Miguelito Torrez." A state senator from the west side. "Mexicans against Puerto Ricans, against African-Americans against Africans, against Koreans against Cambodians. Like the Irish against Italians against Poles."

"Divide and prosper," Sunny reminded him.

"Vera knows that, too. She's smart, your lordship. Tell her I said so. I lay back now, she knows how to pile every piece of the furniture against the door to stay there. Four years from now, eight years? I'll be too rich, fat, demented, or bored to be mayor. Or be in jail. I've got a running start now. I have to jump."

It was the response that Sunny expected; he didn't try to convince

Linas otherwise. In private, politicians almost never disputed each other. They might freely offer advice about romance or marriage, children or restaurants. Sunny had heard politicians argue about baseball, movies, or whether a man's shoe size correlated to the length of his penis. (Wandy Rodriguez, who wore a size fourteen, vehemently supported the proposition. Vernetta Hynes Griffin of the 37th, who had played piano for a roving gospel group, said that axiom was unsupported by her own observations.)

But politicians couldn't change their minds. They had raised money, won votes, and formed coalitions around fixed positions. Any revision was denounced as hypocrisy and taken as retreat. Changing your mind only made both your supporters and opponents agree: you couldn't be trusted. So Sunny went on.

"Christ, Linas, this is unbelievable," he said. They sat for another silent moment, looking at the walls of Sunny's small office, before Linas finally spoke.

"You know, we got along better than people knew," he said. "When he brought us up here, you, Arty, and Vera got lectures. I got winks. What was there to fight about? There's only one side of the aisle here. Everybody here is in favor of a woman's right to choose from the age of twelve, and nobody's right to own a gun. We all want to welcome poor immigrants to wash our dishes and diaper our kids. Or your folks, Sunny, to fix our computers and heart valves. Clashes on issues? Some of us think it's fine for gays to get married, we don't care. Just spare us the details and tell us where to send the espresso pot. Some others think the city ought to invite all gay couples to throw out the first pitch at Wrigley Field. That's as much as we get of ideological disagreements.

"You know what really spills blood here?" Linas asked. "Jobs. Favors. *Goodies*. Who gets to sprinkle candies into the hands of his friends. That's where the mayor and I fell out. But we were *use-full* to each other," said Linas, stressing the word as if it were the name of an ancient religious precept. "Do you think I ever lost a single vote in my part of town because of anything he said about me? Do you think anything I ever said pried any of his supporters away from him?

"A supporter can be like a lover, Sunny," Linas said slowly. "They might prefer to see you lose. It keeps you close. The mayor and I didn't have any claims on each other, and we never disappointed each other."

Linas sat back and laughed, as if to give Sunny the chance to laugh away what he had said, which Sunny did not. He pushed out a long breath and just repeated: "Christ, this is unbelievable."

"I've got to go home," Linas suddenly announced, standing and smiling.

"I thought you were performing constituent services tonight. Face to face."

"Got to be up early," he explained as he ran a finger down one of his smooth sleeves, as if about to lick frosting. "I've got a daughter who has a band recital tomorrow and wants me to hear her play 'The Wolverine March.' I've got to be at yoga by eight, or the young girls get all the good mats. Then back here. You've got a few eventful days in front of you too, your lordship. Call me—if. If anything."

Sunny shook hands and held Linas's grip for a moment.

"Is there anything?" he asked softly.

A range of possibilities was implied. But Linas already practically controlled scores of city jobs in his ward and committees. Major corporations already saw the sense of hiring his neighborhood law firm to advise them on property tax. And any promise Sunny might make for Vera to support Linas for state office was flagrantly worthless. Linas knew—he was even proud—that his sharp political charm would sour when uncorked outside the city limits. He held Sunny's hand only long enough to grin and throw the smooth thumb of his left hand over his shoulder toward the hallway being guarded by Sgt. Gallaher.

"Hey, Mr. Interim Mayor," he said. "Could you give me a police escort home?"

As Linas took leave of Sunny and sauntered past Sgt. Gallaher with one of his thick-lidded reptilian winks, the mommy and daddy team questioning Mrs. Bacon sent word to Chief Martinez that they had what promised to be the first break of the case.

Peter and Jessica were on duty in the 12th District on south Racine when called to City Hall. Mrs. Bacon had discovered the mayor; she was the only non-police person on duty at the time of his death. While she was immediately dismissed from all suspicion, Peter and Jessica muttered to uniformed officers who dusted the desk and lifted fibers that they wanted some ranking officer to quickly extract Mrs. Bacon's phone records, her emails, and her voice messages while they spoke with her in one of the bland beige conference rooms along the hallway of the mayor's office suite. She had been offered tea, water, coffee— "Hell, Mrs. B, if you wanted a little shot of something, I'm sure we can oblige"—and when she quaffed down a cup of water in half a dozen hurried gulps, Peter chivalrously snapped his fingers for another while Jessica took the first from her clenched fingers and motioned for it to be bagged, so it could be dusted for fingerprints, lip prints, traces of saliva, and droplets of DNA.

Mrs. Bacon quickly established that nothing had seemed out of place for a late Thursday night. The mayor had returned about 9:30 from an appearance at St. Kevin's Church on 105th, vowing—only comically, she stressed, it was a practiced monologue—to murder Father Walter for making him eat the half-baked *fiske farse* prepared by a parishioner.

"Fish balls, Doris!" he had thundered. "Fish balls! Have Father Walter lined up and shot. No blindfold. If it weren't for the succulent maroon-colored sauce served alongside, I doubt I could have finished. The sauce was faintly grainy. A tang of horseradish was discernible." He turned to his security guards. "Did you get the name?" They shook their heads, and the mayor grunted. "You're supposed to serve and protect. Call the church. Describe the sauce. Find the old Swedish lady who made it. Name a street for her. Bring Father Walter's head to me in a pastry box and a pint of that nice dark red sauce. And call Quattro's," he said, before standing up to take down his trousers and watch the late news. "*Fiske farse* my arse . . ."

Mrs. Bacon had cried again in re-creating those excruciating and sorrowful minutes in which she had found the body of the man she had served so long and loyally, slumped across the sofa. Jessica joined in with her own tears. Peter heard his own voice straining as he tried to get Mrs. Bacon to recall if the physical disposition of the mayor's furniture and artifacts was exactly as it seemed before she left him in care of his pizza; it did. When Peter read the paramedic's report revealing the slogan on the mayor's boxer shorts, he was glad for the respite of laughter.

"Mercy," laughed Mrs. Bacon, "but I had never seen those before!"

"And how often would you see the mayor's undershorts?" asked Jessica, with measured mischievousness, and when Mrs. Bacon answered, "Oh, all the time," the small room broke up with flabbergasted laughter. It was like hearing a grandmother repeat the punch line of a naughty joke she didn't quite understand.

"*I mean*," she added quickly, "it's like the theater. I'd be in his office while he changed before speeches, dinners. We'd go on talking while he dressed. He'd dictate letters, tell me to make phone calls. So I'd see his shorts. We all did."

"We?" asked Peter.

"The security detail. Assistants. It's nothing, really. I mean, you work for a man for thirty years, you know so much more about him than undershorts. You see people in their undershorts on billboards."

"Now Mrs. B, where would—" Peter had begun to speak before he had quite formulated the question—"or who, or how would those shorts get to him? It must have been a close friend . . ."

"I knew all of his friends," said Mrs. Bacon primly.

"So—I'm looking at the report now—so, when you said, 'I'm sure they were a gift. . . . ' "—

"I mean I hardly think the mayor got them for himself. He couldn't buy a stick of gum for himself. People used to kid him because he didn't have a dime in his pockets. But he couldn't go anywhere without being mobbed. That was the reason. Can you imagine having to buy socks and underwear with an audience? A few times a year, he'd call out to me, 'Doris, I need some socks,' or, 'Doris, I need some shoes.' I'd call someplace to send them over."

"Undershorts?" asked Peter.

"I'm sure."

"And you knew his sizes?" Peter looked down at the paramedic's report. "Like, they have the shoes at nine and a half D."

"They're written down somewhere," said Mrs. Bacon, and for the first time, Jessica recognized that they had been told one of those negligible lies, as easy to pass as a penny on the street, that training had taught her to detect. A woman who had been buying the mayor's underwear for thirty years would know his expanding size by heart.

Peter was about to observe that they didn't want to spend too much more time on the undershorts when he saw that Jessica had brought herself up onto the rim of her chair.

"So—let me get this straight, now, so we'll know how the office ran—if the mayor couldn't buy something like those shorts for himself, and you didn't pick them up for him, how would they get to him?"

"People send him things all the time," said Mrs. Bacon. "He's the most popular man in town," and for the first time, Jessica could see Peter take a furtive look at the lens of the small camera that the patrolmen had set up on a side table, looking for the small green light.

"Right," said Peter. "Cookies, cakes—am I right?"

Mrs. Bacon smiled.

"And you'd see those?"

"Never," she explained. "Everything gets opened in a warehouse by the Stevenson Expressway. They send the cards and letters over. But cookies, cakes, pies, hats—things people knit for him, you'd be amazed—they all have to be destroyed."

"I just wonder," asked Jessica, with the same slow, studied show of barely middling interest with which she might ask about the wallpaper in a motel lobby. "Why not send stuff to a homeless shelter? A senior citizens home?"

"You can't take the chance," Mrs. Bacon explained. "You have no idea what someone might put into a brownie, a pie, a tie, a bunch of flowers. Brownies could contain peanuts. Send those to an orphanage, some poor child has an allergy, and you've got a tragedy."

"Courtesy of the mayor's office," one of the uniformed officers volunteered. Peter thought his interjection was disruptive, but correcting him might alert Mrs. Bacon that the questions had grown more pressing. Peter was relieved when she just picked up her answer.

"Exactly," she agreed. "People send T-shirts with funny sayings, baseball hats, needlepoint pillows. But they all have to be incinerated. You can't take a chance. Everyone's scared of white powders."

"Anthrax," the officer inserted himself again, and this time, Jessica leaned forward so that the patrolman might see her curl a pink-topped finger almost teasingly into her long auburn waves, while Peter caught the officer's eyes and burned him with a scowl that, he hoped, could shatter the window on a shark tank.

"They went over a list with us," said Mrs. Bacon. "They warned us. Gosh, they scared us. They said the particles can perch on the lip of a coffee cup."

Peter rubbed an index finger across the rim of his own cup and wiped it absently on his sleeve.

"So if someone—an adoring constituent, say, or someone with a peculiar sense of humor—sent those over, you wouldn't see it, right? Over in the warehouse, someone there would see the shorts, Notre

Dame gym socks, and Greek Easter cookies, and send everything down the incinerator?"

"That's how it works," Mrs. Bacon confirmed.

Peter flicked his right eye to check the camera's green light once more.

"You and the mayor go back," he said finally.

"Since 1970," she said. "I walked into his campaign office on Ellis. He was so bold. So funny."

"No one else like him," Jessica said softly. "You were—?" She let the question hang.

"Just a grad student," Mrs. Bacon answered. "Modern European History. I never finished. The mayor was a state representative then, and I was already working in the district office on things that seemed more important than Hegel, Schopenhauer, and Descartes. Crime, jobs, and public housing. 'Doris,' the mayor used to say, 'stick with me and we'll *make* history.' "

"Mr. Bacon?"

"Another student. It—we—didn't last long. We were too young for each other, I guess. He went on to teach at Grinnell. We didn't really see each other until our daughter, Amy, got married a couple of years ago. It was—fine. The mayor was so charming with him. The mayor arranged for the reception in the Cultural Center. He put his arm around Amy in her long, lacy ivory dress—he's known her forever— as they danced in those big bay windows looking over the park. He said, 'My dear, the great Daniel Burnham had this night in mind when he put these magnificent environs at your feet.' You can't imagine," said Mrs. Bacon softly.

Peter leaned back quietly, to erase himself as much as he could from Mrs. Bacon's view. Her face was almost rosy. Her blue eyes brimmed, but in happy reminiscence. Her arms were folded around her chest, as if she were hugging a small girl from behind. Jessica gently touched the top of Mrs. Bacon's hand with two fingers. She leaned forward, as if she were trying to whisper in that child's ear.

"Mrs. B," she said gently. "Those undershorts are being put through every test known to man."

When the break came, it seemed to work its way up. Mrs. Bacon's feet fluttered, her knees began to buck, her hands and arms twitched, her shoulders shook, and then her jaw opened like a dropped drawer, just before tears began to spill from her eyes. She struggled, as if trying to get up, and then fell back before rasping, "They were a gift, alright? A little joke between us. What happened between us happened a long time ago. I wasn't always like . . . like *this*, you know!"

Peter and Jessica let Mrs. Bacon take their arms and led her over to a small brown couch in the back of the conference room. They gently laid her down; the small, scratchy cushions crinkled under her shivering bird's weight. One of the patrolmen rushed off and wrung out a towel with a trickle of cool water. Jessica laid it gently against Mrs. Bacon's forehead. They snapped off the lights in the room and left Mrs. Bacon to rest, with only Jessica sitting close by.

Peter sent word to Chief Martinez over in the mayor's office. The patrolmen had their recording cued up to just a couple of minutes before Mrs. Bacon's teary disclosure. Chief Martinez took off his service cap to get close to the small screen as it played, and Peter explained that while he and Jessica took no personal pleasure in Mrs. Bacon's breakdown, there was inescapable professional satisfaction. They had been charged with getting information from the person most above suspicion in the crime. They discovered, through pointed, intelligent questioning, a potential suspect with classic motivation. The long-spurned love. The daytime spouse who at long last realizes how many years she has devoted to a futile relationship. No one knew the victim better, his appetites, customs, precautions, and routines; no one knew better how and where to hurt him. Peter said they had already isolated calls to the restaurant on her phone logs.

"I wonder, Chief, if we should get a lab sample from her daughter?"

"You think she's involved?"

"I think maybe the mayor was involved. In her beginnings, if you follow."

Chief Martinez's laugh stuck in his throat and came out a snort.

"The mayor liked boys," he told Peter, and anyone else close enough to hear. A half-dozen others cut off their conversations and lifted their heads. Peter paused.

"I never knew."

"It was never any of your business," said the police chief, and when he was quite sure that the assertion had shaken Peter's certainties about the mayor's death, and sex and life generally, he looked over at a patrolman who was going over a gray evidence box of Mrs. Bacon's desk possessions.

"Daughter?"

"Amy. She's membership director of a sports club in Oakbrook." A western suburb.

"There's your answer," said the chief flatly. "If she were the mayor's love child, he would have put her in the City Treasurer's office." The chief tucked his thumbs in at his hips and turned back to the small video screen. "Again," he ordered quietly, and as it played through, Peter spoke into Chief Martinez's ear.

"We've let her rest just enough. She's just begun to get the stone off her chest. We'd like to go back right now." The darkened conference room was on a second small screen, but Chief Martinez could only make out the silhouette of Jessica's knee and shin, resting on a coffee table. He heard soft breaths from Mrs. Bacon emanating from one screen, and the gasps and tears from her replayed through the other.

"I think you got hold of a nice old lady whose been bursting to tell the biggest secret of her life," said the chief without moving his head. "Do what you have to," he told Peter. "But nothing more."

Sunny's phone trembled and began to dance in a line like a bug trying to scurry off the table before he could reach it. It was Eldad.

"Where are you?" asked Sunny. He could hear clatter, clinking, whirring, and the tremolo of "De Nina A Mujer" swallowed in a bustling, tiled room.

"Out."

"Eldad, I'm not your parent." In fact, it was a tone of voice Eldad had overheard Sunny use only with his daughters.

"El Comandante's," he answered quickly. A Mexican restaurant northwest of the Loop. "I just checked messages." he explained, "I'm not quite dressed for City Hall. I thought I should call . . ."

Sunny had been feeling a hole simmer in his stomach.

"Give me a few minutes," he told Eldad. "I could use a change of scenery."

"Of course," said Eldad, with reflexive politeness. "I'm with some friends—"

"I'll need your full attention."

"What's happened?" For the first time, Eldad's tone was unguarded. Sunny told him.

"Ohmigod," was all he said, and softly. Sunny could hear new whirring, a burst of laughter, and grease flaring from a grill.

"Not a word, please. We call in the press for six."

Eldad looked at the beer clock above the bar. The short red hand had settled onto the upper-thigh of the raven beauty shaking out her hair on the terrace; it was twenty to four. After a pause he said, "I'll have something waiting for you." Sunny could make out "Despues de Tanto Tiempo" and the sound of cutlery spilling into a gray bin before he clicked off.

Sgt. Gallaher had returned to Sunny's doorway.

"I'd like to run out," he told her. "To meet my assistant, Mr. Delaney. To get something to eat, I don't mind saying."

She spoke in a low voice into the radio on her shoulder.

"El Comandante's—did I hear right?" Sunny nodded. "Well, there should be enough cops there to protect you."

She kept about three paces ahead of Sunny as they walked to the internal staircase just off the council chamber that emptied onto City Hall's ground floor. Sunny had been in the hall late at night many times over the years, but had never taken those stairs at a time of such consummate silence; he thought he could hear a soft groan from the piling snow beginning to weigh on the iron slats of the fire stairs just outside the large window between the two floors.

They reached the bottom landing, the toes of their shoes sounding muffled and smooth on the worn bone granite. The lobby lights had been turned on, revealing blue uniforms on folding chairs squishing cigarettes into paper cups as they saw an authority descend from the floors above. Sunny made no mention of their violation of a city ordinance. Officer Mayer was recognizable from behind, blue shoulders and a pale neck. He had brought his cruiser around to the LaSalle Street entrance so that the department's emergency and investigation vehicles could thread into the underground delivery zone below. Wordlessly, he took up a position in front of Sunny, and Sgt. Gallaher fell back alongside.

"Do I get a nickname?" Sunny asked.

"Sir?"

"Don't the people you surround and protect usually get a nickname?" Sunny thought he could detect Sgt. Gallaher's cheeks pinken slightly as they came out of the brass security door Officer Mayer had shouldered open and felt tiny, glassy specks of snow in their eyes and nostrils.

"People seem to like them," she said.

"What was the mayor's?"

"O and O."

"I remember now," said Sunny as Officer Mayer wrenched open his cruiser's rear door. "One and Only."

The car had nosed down LaSalle and turned left onto Wacker Drive before Sgt. Gallaher spoke again.

"We talked about one for you. When you, Mr. Slavinskas, and the chief were in conference."

Sunny had let his mind slip into a kind of free fall for several blocks, counting streetlights through the tinted windows as they drove. Now, he sat forward.

"And?"

Sgt. Gallaher slowly squirmed to turn her broad blue shoulders around slightly to look back at Sunny.

"They said it wasn't worth it for just a few days."

Sunny was still smiling slightly as Sgt. Gallaher led their approach into El Comandante's. Bright confetti-colored placemats, *Bienvenidos* punched across the bottom, were taped onto pipes in the ceiling and fluttered in the wind Sgt. Gallaher had ushered in with her shoulder. There were uniformed cops standing hatless against the wall, perched against the tops of the brown vinyl booths to kill the last few moments of their meal breaks. Sunny heard a few officers—male officers—say, "Hey, Mo," but the sergeant was on duty; she returned greetings with just a tight, polite smile, and stood with her back to the window.

Eldad stood up from one of the booths. He wore a tight black T-shirt and black leather jeans, and had changed earrings for the evening. These were steel with a small violet stone, curled like the foil scraped off the neck of a wine bottle. He took Sunny's right hand in both of his before they each sat down, the slick seat of the booth squealing as they settled in. There were small brown bowls of a bright orange sauce and a pea green sauce between them, gleaming like traffic lights, next to a small plastic basket of beige tortilla chips.

"This is . . . unbelievable," Eldad said softly. "Do they know . . . ?"

"Nothing."

A waitress had appeared above them, and set down a small round red plastic-covered dish.

"Next round," she said to Eldad.

"I got you that stuff you like," said Eldad. "With green sauce."

With her other hand, the waitress produced an oval dish of chilaquiles, a crispy litter of yesterday's tortilla strips bubbling under a pale jade sauce. Sunny inhaled until the tart steam seemed to reach the back of his throat. Absently, he picked up a soft tortilla from the red dish and held it lightly against his chin before curling it into the sauce.

"This is unbelievable," Eldad repeated. "Do they know? Was it personal? Political?"

Sunny was famished. He shoved a forkful and a half of chilaquiles against the tortilla, then onto his fork, and began to swallow. He shook his head back and forth until he could speak.

"A den of conspirators or a lone assassin with a pizza? They don't know."

"Christ, I saw him just two days ago," said Eldad. "He was fine. He was strong. People loved him. What do you have to say at six?"

Eldad cast his eye to the beer clock over the bar. The long hand was now crossing luxuriously over the brunette's long foreleg: it was 4:40. Sunny took his voice down even more.

"Tell people what happened. Present a deputy police commander. Announce a memorial council session tomorrow, another on Monday to choose"—he hesitated over a personal pronoun—"the successor. Say that the police are investigating. The police department," he revised himself as he went, "which is mounting its largest investigation ever, which it damn well better be after we raised their salaries and had to hold the line with the garbage men."

"Shall I sketch out something for you?"

Like most aldermen, Sunny had to say something somewhere most nights of the week. But the demands on any alderman's oratorical powers were scarcely Churchillian. Aldermen didn't deliver state of the union speeches. They were usually introduced to equivocal applause, told a few gently self-mocking jokes, flattered their audience for their good citizenship, then lauded the mayor for his foresight and statesmanship.

"I don't think we need Ted Sorensen for this," Sunny said gently. "I'll just jot a few notes on the back of an envelope." But Eldad stayed serious.

"You should call some people."

"I don't want to wake up my daughters until just before."

"I meant some of our friends," said Eldad.

"That would be friendly."

"Make three calls," Eldad suggested, opening the red dish and reaching in to roll a tortilla between his fingers. "I'll make a couple, too."

"Peter Mansfield, too," said Sunny, and Eldad's eyes widened.

"He wasn't on my list."

"I want to keep him informed," Sunny said simply.

"Are we . . . reaching out?" asked Eldad carefully, and Sunny's smile might have come from a laxative ad on the subway—it presented no clue.

"Don't get talked into or out of anything. A situation like this? You can never tell how tiles get rearranged. Would you be surprised if anything ever broke about Crispus Foster?" The long-time, intricately profane county board president who infamously threw his amphibian arms across the doorways of conference and copying rooms to thwart the exit of any woman whom he wanted to fix with his gnarly smile. "Or if Ray Potash doesn't run again?" The peach-faced state treasurer from Collinsville was being treated for depression.

"Running statewide?" said Sunny with melodramatic derision. "In southern Illinois, they think Roopini is what you plant next to the squash."

"Name recognition helps," Eldad pointed out, and when the two of them had tucked away their chuckles and shoved aside their plates, Eldad leaned over.

"Linas must have taken a few inches out of his pants."

"He says he has eighteen, first ballot."

"Vera?"

"One more. But he says she can't keep more than fifteen."

Eldad smoothed out a napkin between them, with a hand that was already folded around a long black pen from the meat delivery firm run by Brock Lucchesi of the 13th. BROCK'S CHOPS, it read along the barrel. DOWNTOWN CUTS, STOCKYARD PRICES (although the stockyards had long ago moved to lower-taxed precincts in Omaha).

Eldad wrote down an *A*, and directly under it a small stroke to represent the indubitable vote of the alderman of the First Ward, Arty Agras, for himself. Further down the space of the napkin, Eldad scratched three strokes for a *V*, and five more below that, representing rock-solid south side votes for Vera Barrow from Evelyn Washington of the 2nd, Dorothy Fisher of the 3rd, Wanda Jackson of the 4th, Vera herself, and Grace Brown of the 6th ward.

"The African Queens," Eldad announced simply. Sunny smiled at the thought of their lemon, raspberry, and lime-colored suits and flower-petal hats sunning in the front row seats of the council chamber. Eldad began on another bunch of five by carefully pulling on an end of the napkin and applying three small strokes under the *V* for Miles Sparrow of the 7th, John Reginald of the 8th, and Dr. Daryl Lloyd of the 9th.

"But that's one round only," said Eldad, tapping the point of his pen over the last stroke.

"Still," said Sunny. "Eight? Almost a third there."

On the lower third of the napkin, Eldad drew an *L*, and four quick lines below it: for J. P. Mulroy of the 10th, Alfredo Sandoval of the 11th, Linas himself, and Brock Lucchesi.

"But if Brock thinks Linas will be stopped . . ." Eldad's voice trailed off.

"He'll park with Arty," Sunny agreed. "On his way to Jesus next year. He's running for a county seat and has the Chinese guys cutting his rump steaks already calling them *bifstek*."

Eldad put another mark down for Vera from Shirley Watson of the 16th, and one for Linas from Evelyn Lee of the 17th. But watching Eldad's casual stroke reminded Sunny how much a single mark could mask. Evelyn was Vera's best friend on the council. They shared jokes behind their hands. On the floor, they looked for each other's reactions. After long council sessions, they would often clip-clop down Randolph Street over to Macy's, chortling as they departed the chamber, "Quorum call in the shoe department!"

But Evelyn could not cast a first-round vote for Vera. For her, it would be as unthinkable as a politician saying that paroled pederasts deserve a fresh start.

Evelyn's 17th and Vera's 5th ward were separated by just a few blocks; indeed, their wards shared many of the same south side street names. But their constituents beheld their slices of the city in distinctly different ways. Most of Vera's supporters had been Chicagoans for generations. They had come up from the delta, fields, and marshes to fuel steel mills, auto plants, and packinghouses. They had improvised and polished the jazz, blues, and gospel the city now claimed as heritage. But any grasp that blacks had on the levers that actually turned the city felt fragile. The mayor's great, burly presence was the triumphal force that finally seemed to wring some of the rewards for which they had worked.

Most of Evelyn's constituents had arrived over the past generation from Korea, Cambodia, and Vietnam. They didn't understand why African Americans complained about being overlooked, because everywhere in Chicago that *they* looked—the mayor, the council, senators, the city's police, bus drivers, and basketball stars—they saw African Americans exercising power. Evelyn could support Vera once she became mayor, but not while she was a candidate, which Vera understood. Politicians rarely had to explain to each other why they voted as they did. They cast the votes they had to. It was all pressure and expectation. Most votes were as easy to predict as the flow of water down a bowl.

Eldad's pen hovered over the *L* for Kevin Corcoran's vote, but Sunny put out his hand before it could bear down on the napkin.

"That ward is changing. Kevin says he's burying as many Baptists as Catholics now." He ran his family's funeral home, Corcoran & Sons, on South Kedzie.

"The dead don't vote," Eldad reminded Sunny. "Any more." He went ahead and added a slash under the *L*.

Mitya Volkov of the 19th would be for Vera. The mayor had bestrewn city jobs, consultant contracts, festivals, and community centers up and down Western Avenue for Russian immigrants and indeed, so that point would not be lost, had renamed the street Anatoly Sharansky Way between 87th and 90th Streets, just in front of Mitt's ward office. Eldad kept his pen poised above the *V* but held back for Janet Watanabe of the 20th.

"She's touchy," he said. "She thinks the mayor and Vera have been trying to move Janaya Williams into her seat."

"Vera needs to tell her it's a terrible misunderstanding," which Sunny knew it was not.

"She'll want something more than understanding," Eldad pointed out. "A new police station on 66th."

"Then Vera needs to reach out to her. Before Linas promises to put Strategic Air Command headquarters in there."

Eldad finally put his pen point under *V*, then another stroke under *L* for Tommy Mitrovic of the 21st, who had a neighborhood insurance agency.

"Linas gives out Tommy's business cards," he said. "He's so far up his ass that Tommy burps Lithuanian zither music."

Eldad was just putting a stroke under Arty's *A* for Jose Flores Suarez when they heard a stutter step of high heels, an unexpected whoosh of silk, and a luxurious whiff of floral notes. The alderman of the 5th Ward stood just behind their booth, softly beaming the half-smile of an indulgent monarch.

"Doing homework at the table, boys?"

Eldad stood up in a scramble. "I was just leaving," he said, as the alderman put her smooth bronze head alongside his cheek and mouthed a kiss next to his earring.

"I just wanted to sit with my friend here for a few minutes," she said in a husky voice. She seemed to glide over the slick cushions when she sat, without causing them to squeal. The room seemed to catch a breath. The coral bloom across her lips looked fresh and neat. Her suit jacket looked unruffled and rosy. She sat against the brown vinyl booth as if she were about to play Chopin. A small forelock of her fine, downy dark hair falling across her right brow was the one visible smidgen of a hint that Vera had been awakened for an emergency in the middle of the night.

Sunny held up his hand before she could clear her throat.

"I think you should know," he told her, "that any napkin you use here is going to be framed behind the cash register."

Vera turned her head down.

"I hope you don't mind me tracking you," she said. "I think my police guard always knows where your police guard is."

She inclined her head over her shoulder where a hefty-shouldered man in a blue coat was standing next to Sgt. Gallaher along the red radiator in the restaurant window.

"It's a long, sad night," Vera Barrow said simply. Sunny muttered something in return.

"You've got a busy few days ahead."

"Not like you," said Sunny. "Or Linas, Arty, or from what I hear, Daryl Lloyd."

"I hope you won't think it's inappro—" she began, but Sunny held her off with a mild right hand.

"I'm with you, Vera. No other choice. The presiding officer casts his vote last—that's traditional. If Anders can get you to twenty-four . . ." Anders Berggren, a business consultant, was the 49th Ward alderman, who had grown a long gray ponytail down his neck to enhance his appeal among young constituents and business contacts. In fact, they were only reminded of the sort of men who talked to themselves on the subway. "I would have the honor to put you over. And Jaco might move to make it by acclamation." Jacobo Rapoport Sefran of the 50th, and an orthodox rabbi.

"All good things are possible," she said. The waitress had approached softly with a shiny dented pot. Vera nodded gratitude and held out a chipped beige mug. She sipped the coffee carefully, like a cat testing cream.

"Jesus, Sunny, this is unbelievable. I thought he had another ten years. I thought somebody, somewhere, might take a shot at him. But this . . ."

"Best way to a man's heart is through his stomach," Sunny said quietly. "I can't imagine it was personal. He had no personal life. No kids, no golf, no—" Sunny adjusted his phrasing for Vera—"sword-swallowing interns under the desk."

"Everyone has a personal life, Sunny," she said gently. "Sometimes, they just don't know it. What the mayor promised you about the Ninth," she announced in a brisker voice. "That's my promise, too. Anything he said, I say. Tell me what it was, and I'll agree."

"He promised me nothing," said Sunny. "It wasn't his way."

"He showed you a treasure map."

"I haven't starting digging."

Vera ran her sharp oval coral nail over the rim of her coffee mug.

"Your daughters like the idea?" she ventured. He nodded.

"They don't mind going to Washington?" she asked.

"They don't mind *me* going. Leaving them here."

Vera brushed aside his joke by placing a hand on Sunny's forearm.

"You'd go back and forth," she consoled him.

"Yes. Out of my mind." He sat back on the slick brown seat. Vera leaned forward over her mug to smile.

"Two pretty teenage girls. Traveling Dad. Two-bedroom apartment right off Broadway? You've got the makings of a comedy there." When she saw Sunny shudder, she added soothingly, "You can hire a house-keeper."

"I'd prefer a regiment of Gurkha soldiers," said Sunny. He cast a glance at the brunette on the beach blanket on the beer clock. The long black hand passed slowly over her ruby smile. It was just about five, and Sunny began to shake out his feet.

"I just might get more serious about the restaurant business," he told Vera.

"Not a good way to see more of your family."

"But the best way I have of providing for them," Sunny replied, and paused. "Honestly. I talked to Linas," he added, after a pause.

"That's what my guard said. That your guard said you were in conference."

Sunny looked over at Sgt. Gallaher and Vera's guard, both standing with their backs against the wall above the radiator, their heads turning toward the door each time a cook tapped the bell on the stainless steel counter where heavy brown plates of *huevos* and *chorizo* thudded and clinked.

"There's nothing you can offer," Sunny told her. "He says he has to run now because if you win now you're smart enough to figure out how to stay there for twenty years. He said he didn't mind me telling you."

Vera absorbed this without flinching or being flattered.

"Rod Abboud called," she said finally. "Linas called him. He's certainly open to suggestion."

"The lake is always east," said Sunny. "You could suggest vice mayor to him."

"When you run for Stan's seat?"

"When, if, if I don't. It doesn't matter. A new mayor gets to pick. That's traditional," and with this, Sunny leaned forward. "Don't give away a nice title for nothing."

Vera pulled back in her seat at Sunny's bluntness, as if the booth had accelerated through a traffic light.

"You know my policy, Sunny," she told him "A job should go to the person who is best qualified. "

"You're not putting his finger on the nuclear trigger. Just his name right under yours on the cornerstone of the next water treatment plant. It's a nonsense job, Vera. Rod qualifies."

Vera listened, a smile moving over her face like a parting of clouds.

"And you should get with Janet Watanabe," Sunny went on. "She wants a police station."

"I know. I can't," Vera said smoothly. She was chairman of the Police and Fire Committee. "We had to put one in the Nineteenth—all the gangs. And we already need an annex because the gang units need Russian and Ukrainian interpreters."

"What about one of those miniature ones?" Sunny suggested. "A couple of uniforms behind the desk. Move one in the next time a nail salon on Sixty-sixth shuts down."

"Cop-in-a-Box? Janet won't be fooled," said Vera. "She won't be satisfied."

"You don't have to satisfy her, Vera," said Sunny. "Just pleasure her a little."

"I pity your wife," said Vera, who suddenly thrust her hand out, as if she might spear the phrase before it could bite and bring it back. But Sunny took her hand and pressed his lips, softly and quickly, against her smooth knuckles.

"I'm so—"

"It's okay. Sometimes I slip too," he told her.

Vera sat back, blinking moisture, kitchen smoke, or a speck from her napkin out of her eyes.

"I think Dr. Lloyd would do fine with the Parks and Recreation Committee," Sunny said in a pointedly firmer voice.

"And what if he wants to be vice mayor?"

"Another south sider? Then he doesn't know politics. Don't worry about him." Of course there were white, Hispanic, and Asian south side aldermen, too, but Sunny and Vera understood that this was not what Sunny meant.

"Parks and Rec has a budget and jobs," he reminded her.

"Nine thousand in summer?" Vera asked. "And he knew them all, Adams to Zebrauskas. Kids' names, birthdays, and their favorite ice creams." Her voice suddenly toughened. "Why should I do that for Daryl?"

"It's a deal, not an endowment. You'll owe each other. But you'll be mayor, Vera. You can live with that."

Sunny turned his face up into the room and began to smile for their check. Vera dabbed her napkin against her mouth and tapped the band of a plain braided gold ring against her coffee mug, once, twice, and a third time before she asked a last question.

"Do you want to take a swing yourself?"

"That was never the deal, Vera," he said in a low voice. "You were always next."

"Only because he thought I'd grow old waiting."

"He made me vice mayor because he needed a north sider," said Sunny. "You couldn't have both the mayor and vice mayor be south siders."

Vera turned her face up slightly and snuck a look into Sunny's eyes.

"You can say 'black' in front of me, Sunny," she said, and Sunny felt his face grow hot.

"I read the fine print before I signed," he rushed on. "Being mayor never made it into my dreams. Besides, dreams scare me now. I try to stay out of them."

Sunny let an instant of silence seep across the table while pans banged and mugs clinked. Vera Barrow wound a paper napkin three times around a spoon, as if dressing a small doll, before speaking.

"Never been through an election like this one, Sunny," she said finally. "Just fifty people. No strangers. No ghost voters, payrollers, precinct captains, or hanging chads. It's like voting for Homecoming queen."

"In an insane asylum," Sunny observed, and after he had stripped another twenty from his clip and handed it to their waitress, he stood and offered a hand to lift Vera up from their booth.

"It's still politics, Vera."

She laughed more loudly than she expected to and patted a hand over her mouth.

"My God, Sunny," said Vera Barrow. "I feel like our parents have gone to bed and we're still up, playing house. But all we can do is imitate them. Do we really know what we're doing here?"

A mommy and daddy named Charles and Deborah from the Grand Crossing district drew the duty to take home Collins Jenkins, who was feeling angry, disrespected, and dismissed, to his one-bedroom, one-cat apartment on North State Parkway (though a co-worker at City Hall had convinced Collins that he kept such impossible hours, it was better for her to take possession of the oleaginous brown-and-orange patched cat, Richard J).

Deborah drove, choosing a route along local streets that would slow them in the snow and afford more time to engage Collins in conversation. Charles sat on the gray vinyl seat in the back of their black Buick alongside Collins, who recognized instantly that he was not being chauffeured so much as kept in mobile observation.

Deborah's part of the play was to be interested and nurturing: "This must be a terrible shock to you, Mr. Jenkins. You've lost your best friend. How bad do you feel?" Whereas the role of Charles, who was also an ordained Jehovah's Witness minister, was to be unimpressed and provocative: "The amount of *shit* you and the mayor must have had on each other! Mind if I ask—what did it for him? Boys? Shoes? Bicycle seats?"

But instead of crumpling and crying or losing his grip on some incriminating revelation of the kind powerful men sometimes made to impress the Lilliputian police, Collins Jenkins became truculent. He taunted them.

"Oh please. Milk-and-cookies from Mommy? The back of the hair-brush from Dad? Shouldn't you folks reverse that?" he sneered. "Isn't that what you're trained to do for us faggots? Dominate me, Debbie! Squat on my face!"

Charles and Deborah looked at each other wearily across the interior of the cruiser. They wished they had laid out a shorter route.

It had been easy to confirm that Mrs. Bacon had called Collins on his mobile phone at 10:37 p.m., within five minutes of finding the mayor slumped over in his office, and perhaps a minute since overhearing the paramedics mutter, "Nothing. *Nothing*," and hearing a shrill, unnervingly unwavering hum from one of their medical monitors. Collins was at home. He had fallen asleep on the same old gold tasseled brocade sofa he had inherited from his family for his first apartment after Antioch and hadn't had the time or taste for comfort to replace after twenty-six years. The left-hand arm of the sofa had developed a melon-sized smudge from where Collins had fallen asleep about a thousand nights previously, his phone injected into the chest pocket of his white button-down shirt.

It had taken Collins roughly twelve minutes to rinse his face, re-knot a slumping red-knit tie, send a brief, mournful message to Vera Barrow, and scramble into the brass elevator cage of his building to descend nine floors that clicked by with excruciating slowness; and just under a minute for him to flag down the American United Cab #510, which pulled a U-turn at North and delivered Collins to City Hall's central entrance on LaSalle at 11:02 pm, where he was admitted by a security team that had just begun their shift at the top of the hour. He was standing over the mayor by 11:06, wiping tears with the back of his hands.

Charles and Deborah saw Collins into his apartment. Warrants that had been signed by an insomniac circuit court judge whom the mayor, in his wisdom, had promoted for appointment with post-midnight complicities in mind, had already been executed to tap Collins's phone line (which they discovered had been disconnected thirty-one months before for non-payment), his mobile number, and his computer accounts. Walt Green had stressed to Charles and Deborah that they should try to encourage Collins to invite the officers to stay; it was paid companionship from a grateful city. Deborah plucked up some of the newspaper broadsheets that were tented and turning tan on the living room floor—some were so old they had baseball scores from the previous season—and Charles tried to entice Collins with the prospect of food.

"I make some really superior fluffy scrambled eggs," he volunteered, and after Deborah made a point of fairly shivering in appreciation of her partner's talents, Collins cut them off coldly.

"I would rather share a dead rat with a swarm of maggots than scrambled eggs with the two of you," he told them. After so complete and categorical rejection, there was not much more the two of them could do than sit in front of Collins's building until and if any of the taps turned up something that would give them license to storm through his door.

Collins used the bathroom, washed his hands, splashed his face, and stretched out on his sofa, his head high up on the armrest so that he could see the TV screen as he scrolled through a hundred channels. His set looked implausibly small in a time when screens filled walls.

(Once the mayor had dropped in on Collins's apartment after he had appeared at a fund-raising reception on an upper floor. The mayor brushed aside the litter of cups, take-out cartons, shirt cardboards, folding chairs, and unopened envelopes scrawled with phone numbers to regard Collins's television as if it were a working Colonial cotton loom.

"My God man, where do they still make these, North Korea? The news on this screen must still be in black and white! Leonid Brezhnev is still watching missiles roll through Red Square on Channel Two! I'll bet they're still singing "Love Grows Where Rosemary Goes" on this set!")

Collins found skipping through the channels now unnerving and reassuring. The world he saw onscreen was spinning on as previously recorded. A man vacuumed blue-steel nails off a kitchen floor. A silver-haired man, eyes rolled shut like rocks over a cave, beseeched the Lord for health and prosperity. A woman pulled unsightly hair from below her nose with what looked like refrigerator tape. Collins lingered for a moment on that; it must have been excruciating; she smiled on. Basket-ball and hockey plays—which Collins did not follow, his only interest in sports being to determine whatever Dominican athletes were star-ring for the White Sox, so that the mayor could send them encourag-ing notes—showed men leaping high toward hoops, and scudding across bright, white ice to flail after one another with curved sticks. Four men cast lines for trout in a brown Colorado river, chuckling, joshing, and chuckling. A Hollywood couple was divorcing because the wife had become involved with a witches' coven. Men in tight blue or red shorts ran after a ball and tripped one another in a language that Collins deduced to be Portuguese. Hugh Grant fluttered his eyes at wedding number three. A man roasted a chicken, which browned and sputtered behind a glass. Set it and forget it! Quick and easy cleanup! A man dried apple slices into leathery strips under plastic. Easy, nutri-tious, and fun for the entire family! Great for snacking, car trips, and camping!

Collins left the set on a low burn and crossed over into his kitchen, suddenly hungry. The light in his refrigerator had burned out a few weeks before, and Collins had to stick his head over tawny, crusted car-tons of two percent milk, stir-fried bitter melon, sag paneer, and white rice, turning chewy. He felt the foil top of a half-full box of chocolate-covered cherries sent to him by the Teamsters Local 714 Machinery, Scrap Iron, Metal and Steel, Chauffeurs, Warehousemen, Freight Han-dlers, Helpers, Alloy Fabricators, Pharmacists, Theatrical, Exposition, Convention and Trade Show Employees. He felt the tin lid of a barely touched jar of red chile peanut butter that had been buried in a gift bas-ket from State Senator Raul Rico of the 20th District. Collins closed the refrigerator door, as if it were a dark closet holding the clothes of a dead stranger.

Thoughts about the mayor kept breaking through. Collins swatted them away, like swinging a broom at bats in an attic. He remembered the night the mayor had been elected, defeating a nominal Republican who owned a string of high-ticket organic fruit and vegetable stores. (The party had persuaded him to squander his own money on a fore-doomed campaign on the promise that the next Republican president would make him an ambassador, and so he did—to Liechtenstein. The mayor was slighted. "Don't my vanquished adversaries deserve at least the solace of someplace warm? Grenada?")

On the gilded roster of a Hilton ballroom, the mayor had spread his arms as wide as the girders that held up the El trains and declared, "I open my arms in love and respect to *every living soul* in this city!" On that night it seemed as if six million souls could easily cling to his linebacker's girth, with room left over for Los Angeles.

Collins banished the memory by masturbating. He slipped his hands under the flap of his undershorts. Against all expectation, Collins found that he could make himself hard. He closed his eyes, and thought about Ralph Fiennes, Dirk Bogarde in *For King and Country*, and the hands of a blondish stockbroker who used to live on the top floor of his apartment building on Belden. He thought about a man with sea blue eyes who wore a scuffed brown jacket when he looked across at him for all of six blocks, a year or so ago on the LaSalle Street bus. He remembered the soft brown hair enveloping the ears of Chris Siewers, the tall boy who sat behind him in the fourth grade; brain cancer killed him when they were thirteen. He recalled the back of the legs of a Brazilian man he had met while changing planes in Dallas. Collins soothed and squeezed himself for about a quarter of an hour, but to no result, and no pleasure; his eyes hurt slightly from sustained squinting.

He stood up, stepped out of his pants, and crossed to his computer terminal. Sunny Roopini needed his help. The interim mayor was a reasonably well-spoken man, but he had never had to address an audience more noteworthy than the Andersonville Kiwanis Club. In a few hours, he would speak to the whole city; for a few moments, even the nation. His statement would have to reassure them that the city would continue to be guided by the mayor's genius.

Collins typed smoothly, without reverses or deletions; a sign of inspiration, he was sure. He suggested to Sunny that he begin:

The greatest leader in our city's history has been struck down by the foulest deed in our history, and I who cannot fill his shoes must occupy his desk . . .

(Sunny would stop reading after that first sentence. He did not want to begin by ranking the mayor's death above the Chicago Fire, the St. Valentine's Day Massacre, or indeed, as he reread the middle of the sentence, the Holocaust. And the phrase, "I who cannot fill his shoes," smacked too much of a grinning, obsequious Hindu caricature.)

Collins clicked to send Sunny the draft of his remarks and crossed to his apartment's one large French window, overlooking an alley between Dearborn and Clark. From nine floors above, he could see blue trash bags, nestled under the new snow like fresh-cut logs in a bundle under the small bugle lights behind the popcorn shop. The gray terrier with a lopsided left ear that bedded down in Esther Kim's beauty shop was on patrol in her back window, alerted by unaccustomed quiet as snow began to seal the slit under the door against the wind.

The charcoal sky behind the pipes and rails along the roofs turned smoky with suddenly discernible clouds. Collins heard the first gassy grinding of the LaSalle Street bus, nosing slowly over the snow past Goethe. He heard the low hum of a radio from a neighbor: a deep, quiet voice talking between bars of piano music. He remembered his mother holding the back of his head as he peered over the kitchen counter to see his small face in the gleam of a waffle iron. With a toe, he pushed hard against a bar to unbolt the large window. If it wouldn't work, he would go back to the sofa and watch the hens turn brown and drip fat into the easy-clean tray. But Collins's toe pushed down the latch and the heavy windows blew back slowly onto his chest. Collins could taste glints of snow in his teeth. He remembered his little brother sitting smack in the middle of Astor Street in his small red snowsuit, adamantly refusing to move until Collins took him over his shoulder; he felt his brother's sweet tiny breath against his ear. The Dan Ryan was clear; he could make out from voices he heard through the walls. The Stevenson has a small backup at Harlem. The cold air, filling with light, perfused his lungs and seemed to open his chest as he reached out as wide as the girders that held up the El trains.

It's nineteen degrees at O'Hare. There are short delays for wing de-icing. The pipes and rails on the roofs across the way began to burn along the top with a thin scarlet stripe. Use only as directed. Come to our web site. Twenty-one convenient locations all over Chicagoland. Collins could see his arms and hands suddenly alight, and felt the glow in his bones. His toes lifted him above the thin white ledge at his waist, and then above his knees. He blinked snow from his eyes as he reached out to grab the sun and tried to ride it through the air and down to the ground.

FRIDAY MORNING

"Mummyji?"

Eldad had begun to place his calls, taking care to use his mobile phone so that not so much as a scintilla of conversation with a sliver of political implication could be charged to the city's taxpayers. Sunny heard him murmuring reassurance from a corner of their office.

Sunny had called Peter Mansfield and then three other people of means who had supported his campaigns. Each conversation began, "Something has happened, and we wanted you to be the first to know. . . ."

It was 5:37 by the time he had punched through the call to London. He imagined the low, slate mid-morning sky strained with sun, the beaded curtains swishing and clacking in his mother's room in the large apartment of his brother's family on Lambeth Road.

"Mummyji," he repeated, "it's Sundaran."

It was not a time that he and his daughters would usually call. He heard gurgling water, a cabinet clicking shut, and guessed she was carrying the phone out of the bathroom.

"Are you alright?" Her voice electrified the phrase.

"I'm fine. But something terrible has happened. Not the girls," he added quickly. "Not Sheldon. Mummyji, the mayor has died."

She took a moment to turn over images and memories of her visit last year.

"That delightful man?" she finally asked. "Who kissed my hand? Who said—I found out later he was right—that curry is taken from the Tamil word, *kari*? He told me you were strong, that he would take care of you. He asked me if you had been an Eisenhower as a child."

"*Wisenheimer*, I think." Sunny chuckled softly. "A cheeky boy," he explained again.

"Goodness gracious. He was old?"

"Not particularly. Sixties."

"He took care of himself?"

"Not especially. It looks like—a terrible thing—that he was murdered."

"Oh bloody hell," said his mother. "Bloody Americans and their guns. I had not heard. They're playing Andrzej Panufnik on BBC now, and I doubt they'd break in for that."

"It wasn't a gun, Mummyji. Besides—we're just going to announce it. I do that, in fact. In fact, Mummyji, you might recall that I'm the vice mayor—"

"Of course, yes—"

"I've already been sworn to duty and all. I will be mayor for a few days. Until we elect someone else on Monday," said Sunny, rushing on, "I guess you can call me the mayor of Chicago."

Sunny heard the squeak of a drawer, the snap of a purse, a low, steady male voice being turned lower. Friday was already in progress in London, and it was his mother's day to take lunch with friends at a tapas bar on Kennington.

"That's wonderful, dear," she said. "You know, there are more than twenty Indians in the House of Lords now. Isn't that amazing?"

Sunny told his mother he hoped she would like the escabeche de gambas, explained that he was busy, and had to go. For a moment, he snapped the two ends of the phone together, like an alligator puppet, to gnaw on his index finger. Sgt. Gallaher shifted her weight in the seat behind Sunny's table.

"Mummyji. Your mother?" she guessed.

"Yes. In London with my brother, Vendan, and his family."

"Does he run a restaurant, too?"

"I hope not." Sunny smiled shyly at the sentence ahead. "He's a urologist."

Sgt. Gallaher let her head slip back onto the wall while she laughed. Sunny had not seen her excuse herself since being assigned responsibility for him more than five hours ago. But the color in her cheeks seemed fresh, even as more unbundled long black whisps of hair splayed over her shoulders.

"My mother stayed with us for a while last year," he explained. "After what happened. But . . ." The tail Sunny left on his words seemed to invite the sergeant to pick up the thought.

"I'm sure it was tough."

"It was *February*," said Sunny. "My mother must be the only person who now lives in England for the weather."

It was a quarter to six. Sunny had written some words out in large block letters on an index card, if not quite the back of an envelope. He looked at them every few moments, as if looking to catch something that had changed. Eldad talked away in his corner. They could hear shoes trudge by, worn by men and women on their way to bathrooms at the end of the hall. Sgt. Gallaher spoke up.

"Almost six, sir."

"In the real world," smiled Sunny. "In politics, six means six-fifteen. For something like this, you don't want people straggling in breathless. Let's let the snowflakes pile up a little longer."

"Six meant seven with the mayor," said Sgt. Gallaher.

Sunny held the index card out at the end of his arm; nothing on it had changed.

"There is something I have wanted to say since you got into our car last night, sir," Sgt. Gallaher said quietly. "There just wasn't the opportunity. Oh, what a silly goddamn word." She reddened and stammered but went on. "I remember your wife a little from the restaurant. Honestly, I remember her more than I remember *you*." She ducked her head slightly. "Beautiful, funny. Gracious. I'm—sorry. It must be—I can't imagine."

Sunny looked up from his toes and into the sergeant's face, but more into the bridge of her nose and the bloom of her mouth; he didn't want to get caught by her eyes.

"Thank you," he said, simply and finally.

"And—may I ask—the two guys?"

"They took a plea," said Sunny. "There must have been a dozen witnesses. But half had already slipped out onto Devon and couldn't be found. The time, the money—the chance that they might walk on some technicality . . . So they're in Stateville for the rest of their lives. Well, my life anyway. Just as well. I don't like the death penalty."

"I don't either," said Sgt. Gallaher in a stronger voice. "But I believe in it. I've seen evil."

"You're a cop." Sunny seized on the obvious.

"I'm a good Catholic girl," she replied, which was just as obvious to her. "Eye for an eye."

"That's not what the bishops say," Sunny reminded her.

"It's what the nuns taught us," and when Sgt. Gallaher saw the alderman sit back, smile, and slap a hand softly on a pocket of his soft gray sport coat, she decided to try another question that might not pierce so personally.

"Does Hinduism teach anything about the death penalty?"

Sunny paused as he took in the clock overhead.

"Only how to be as hypocritical as anyone else," he said. "There are Hindus who won't eat an egg because that kills a budding chicken. But they're happy to see a rapist hang because a rapist is guilty and an egg is innocent. And there are Hindus who guiltlessly slit the throat of a goat to make guthi mutton pulav—goat with coconut milk and ginger; not one of my favorites—because the goat isn't human. But they think that a killer who slits the throat of a child is."

Sunny shrugged and held up his hands, as if to show them both how gauzy any argument could be to enfold a belief.

"But jumping on hypocrisy is just a way to score high school debates. How do you expect anyone to get along without a little hypocrisy?"

Sunny stood up slowly, as if stepping out of a car after an overnight drive. Sgt. Gallaher bolted upright directly across the way, and found their faces at about the same height.

"I want those two to be tortured every day for eternity," he told her quietly. "That's why I don't like the death penalty."

It was six o'clock in the morning. In Sunny's office window, the sky was brightening around the streetlights. There was a hum of muted coughs and voices in the hallway. Eldad began to press the keys for his last call, and so Sunny stood against his window, turned to face the glass, and fumbled for his phone. He was grateful for the smothered racket of a snowplow, rumbling and rasping up LaSalle Street toward the Board of Trade.

Rula answered. She was left-handed and quicker on the turn to answer the phone between their beds. Sunny was reassured to hear her throat thick with what sounded like a few hours slumber.

"Darling. Is your sister there too? Good morning."

"Of course," she snapped. Sunny was glad not to hear his daughter have to splutter some deception.

"And Sheldon?" He received a languorous groan.

"He slept in your bloody bed, actually. What the bloody hell. Is the mayor just letting you bloody go?"

"You're going to have to learn more than one adjective. Even to get into reform school," he told her. It was a current joke between them. "Turn on the television," Sunny said, and Rula caught herself in midmutter.

"Bloo—why? What station?" Sunny heard the rustle of pillows and sheets as his daughter reached for the remote, and the sounds of unspecified protests from Rita's side of their room.

"Any," he said. "Not the one with animal rescue stories. We have an announcement coming up."

"You and the mayor?" He paused.

"The mayor is dead," Sunny said flatly. He heard his daughter gasp and bobble the phone in the heel of her hand—and felt rewarded. His daughters, like most youngsters of their age, could be as self-absorbed as quicksand. (When they had seen Hopper's *Nighthawks* at the Art Institute, Sunny thought he caught them peering deeply into the diner's lifelike window glass only to search for their own reflections.)

Sunny took Rula's gasp as a sign that he had not lost all of his old power to surprise them.

"What happened?"

"They don't know. It looks like poison. He was in his office."

"Oh bloody hell," said Rula. "Oh bloody goddamn." Sunny did not correct her language.

"You may remember that for the next few days, I serve as mayor."

"Of course. What do we do?"

"School like any other day. Well, it's hardly like any other day. This will be the talk of things. People may ask if I know what's going on. I don't. Go to the restaurant," he advised. "Wilmer and Oscar will have coffee. Matina will be along. She can make toast or dosas for you. I should be done here by 6:50." Sunny had the trait of a man who had to carefully observe cooking times. He did not say forty-five or sixty minutes when he meant fifty. "I can try to hurry and meet you both there."

"I have to leave before that," said Rula, as automatically, thought Sunny, as if he had pulled a bowstring. "You always forget. Mrs. Miller's class is 7:45. Rita doesn't have to be in until second period, but—"

Sunny could hear Rita make fierce, breathless protests, and her sister keep her away with swats from a pillow.

"I can get a ride," he said, catching a nod from Sgt. Gallaher.

"Well we can't stay. We have things to do too."

"Of course. I know. Leave when you need to." He heard the chorus of a carpet cleaning commercial from the television coming up behind his daughter, and blurted as artlessly as a sixth grader, "I love you."

"We know. Good luck. Take care."

Sunny despised the drip of self-pity he heard in his voice. "It's just a good thing to say today, okay? Tell Sheldon I love him, too."

"*Sheldon* loves you, Pappaji," he heard Rita shout across from her bed.

"And bloody hell," Rula added on, "if he does, so do we."

Eldad Delaney had finished his conversations in the corner and come back to Sunny's table. He tapped two fingers across his wrist, although he wore no watch, and then raised a full hand in front of his face.

"Five minutes," he said loudly enough for whomsoever was on with Sunny to hear him and feel hurried.

Sunny felt his pink shirt crease and stick to the small of his back. He slid his white card into the right-hand pocket of his gray sport coat. He took out his linen pocket square and drew it across his forehead, then took in a breath of last night's squirts of cologne before settling it back in, this time tucking the edges just slightly above the line of his pocket.

Sgt. Gallaher, rolling slightly as she strode, led him past open doors and upturned faces. Three blue uniforms fell in with their steps. The sergeant held up slightly before they could turn into the large walnut room just outside the council chambers that stirred with lights and men and women standing in small knots of mutters and whispers. Sunny stood behind a thicket of black-headed microphones. Bright lights gushed over his shoulders. A swarm of cameras began to chatter, pop, and whine. Blood, feathers, and bones shone in the large oil painting behind him. *Oh God*, Sunny remembered, *it's the Ft. Dearborn Massacre.* Sunny reached into his right-hand pocket, but kept his hand inside as he drew back a breath and began to speak.

"Good morning, ladies and gentlemen. I'm afraid that we begin the day with sad and shocking news. . . ."

11

Collins Jenkins fell to earth without a sound, or with a sound that only his neighbors on the backside of his building on North State Parkway heard and sleepily dismissed as some damn idiot slinging a couch or refrigerator into the alley. In fact, it was the crew of one of the city's blue sanitation trucks that saw Collins's right foot from a block away, and the brown buckskin that the velocity of his descent had shorn from that foot. They ran ahead and found Collins in sections, his wallet sticking from the right hip pocket of his black woolen slacks, which trailed from his torso, pressed chest down onto the top of a green Dumpster, as if he had been trying to scale it.

The first uniforms that arrived from the 18th District removed the wallet with their gloved fingers and squeezed out Collins's driver's license, credit cards, his Northwestern Hospital medical card, and an appointment card for next Monday with Tomas at Truefitt and Hill.

"No cash?" asked the ranking sergeant. The garbage men began to get busy behind their truck.

"Many people keep a little money in their wallets," the sergeant explained, as if trying to describe the behavior of puffins to a class of sixth graders. "For coffee, a bagel, a half-caff skinny latte. This guy's wallet doesn't have any."

"Maybe where he worked, they brought in bagels and coffee," one of the garbage crew suggested. The officers walked around to the back

of their truck, where their heads were bent down as if they had suddenly decided to scrape sludge from a bumper.

"Look, fellas. I don't begrudge any man—especially in your line of
work—who sees a chance to nick a few bills off a man who—I don't
want to be an insensitive prick here—wouldn't know it's missing," said
the sergeant. "But this is a crime scene. There are penalties for tamper-
ing with crime scenes. Anything in his pockets could contain clues—
fingerprints, traces of drugs, telltale stuff that only the lab guys know
about. Understand what I'm saying? Unless this guy had just won the
lottery, there couldn't be enough in his skinny-ass lizard wallet to
make twenty years in prison a smart move for you. So I'm going to
turn my back now. We've got work to do for the next minute or so. It
would really help us if, when I turn back, anything missing from the
pockets of the deceased—or his wrists and fingers; I didn't notice a
watch—was laid out right by the son of a bitch's head."

A minute later, four twenty-dollar bills, two singles, a stainless steel
Omega with a blue face, a gray star sapphire ring, and two blue Viagra
lay on top of the Dumpster, in memoriam.

The senior garbage man, who was one of the most effective precinct
captains in Sidney Wineman's 42nd Ward organization, overheard the
sergeant utter Collins's name into his patrol car radio and said, "Goddamn."

"You knew him?" asked the sergeant.

"Of course." It gave the garbage man some satisfaction to see a
policeman—who often complained, "We're paid like *garbage* men!"—
interested in his next words.

"He was connected."

The youngest man on the garbage crew put his hands up to his face.
"You don't mean—"

"Not *connected*. That's Godfather stuff. This guy was the mayor's
main man," he said with a note of swagger. But the sergeant turned to
the crew with a triumphal smile.

"And I guess you boys have had your heads stuck in the rubbish.
You mean you haven't heard what happened to the mayor? Every cop

has." He patted the black brick radio on his belt before adding, "You ought to get your heads out of the trash bins once in a while."

Commander Green took Sunny's arm after the last question of their press conference—"Mr. Roopini, what do you think the mayor would say to the people of Chicago now that he's dead?"—and whispered the news about Collins Jenkins.

"Good Christ," Sunny said to Walter Green. "Is there a note?"

"They're looking. Nothing in that high rent rat-hole where he lived. But these days, people send suicide text messages from their phones. We're checking."

"He was alone?"

"In all ways," said the commander. "We had a team outside, and a tap on his numbers. But . . ."

They had walked back to Sunny's small office, between the shoulders of three uniforms and Sgt. Gallaher. But Sunny kept his voice quiet as he leaned into Commander Green's left ear and asked softly, "Grief—or guilt?" The commander turned his large, dark hands down toward the floor—Sunny could finally read the lettering sculpted into his Coast Guard Academy ring—and held them steady for a moment at his belt.

"All we know for sure now, sir, is that he wasn't Peter Pan."

Sunny turned around to his window, where the LaSalle Street buses scorched black rails across the last fine layer of snowflakes, and the sun spilled sparkles into the fresh drifts that had blown up against light poles and garbage baskets.

"Good God, I remember something now," said Sunny. "He had a fat, patchy cat named Richard J."

"Nobody there said anything about a cat," said Walter Green.

"That big window swinging open . . . it's a small matter, with all that's going on. But it's something we can do something about."

"I'll have someone at the crime scene take a look, sir. The citizens of Chicago have a stake in finding Richard J."

"Crime scene," asked Sunny. "Isn't that rather a strict Catholic interpretation?"

Commander Green, who had had an even longer night of it than had Sunny, seemed to check each of his fingers before replying wearily.

"As the scene of this suicide may or may not be related to the crime of the mayor's death, sir," he said a little more sharply, "until we know what happened, the chief and I find you can get more things done if you call it a crime scene."

Green excused himself with exacting correctness.

Sunny suddenly remembered to reach for his phone. When he heard his own voice answer, he waited for the tone and said, in a nervous rush, he was sure, "Darlings, I'm sorry. I won't be able to be there. Something else—something terrible—has happened. Eldad is calling Matina to get me some clothes for the memorial session. If you get this in time—would you like to come, too? Please let me know. I love you."

Sunny had practiced politics long enough to hear voices in his head that would know how to knock his arguments back to him ("Don't tell me what I'm thinking, dammit! I don't even know myself!" Elana would sometimes reproach him after Sunny had said, "Now, I know what you're thinking. . . ."). Now, he could hear his daughters saying, "No thanks, we're busy. With you, something else is always happening. We'll see you later." Click. Ouch. Shit. Well, dammit, something was.

Sunny's best black suit with silver pinstripes had hung in a closet of the restaurant since Mr. Kim, the dry cleaner a block down on Broadway, had brought it by personally one afternoon several weeks after Elana's funeral. Sunny was still at the point where he was discovering things—a card in the kitchen drawer with her handwriting, a bar of soap that she had once rubbed along her arms—that he couldn't bear to see and couldn't bring himself to shed.

When the young police officer presented himself to bring back some clothes for Sunny, the pinstripe was the first suit Matina saw, wrapped in cellophane and swinging against white kitchen smocks, nylon windbreakers, and broom handles. Sunny shook it out in a conference room that had been appropriated for his use on the second floor of City Hall. Matina had also sent a plain white shirt, undershorts, black socks, and a silver tie, but it wasn't until he stood in those socks and tried to knot the tie in the gray reflection of a window that Sunny flexed his toes and looked down at his feet.

"No shoes," he announced to Sgt. Gallaher, who had entered the room with a new officer. They were just a few minutes from the start of the memorial session, and the Loop's many stores were not yet open. "Just the brown suede brogues I've had on all night."

"You can get away with brown suede, sir. I've seen it in magazines."

"Yes," said Sunny, who was now standing on his toes, as if testing the temperature of the surf. "Snake-hipped male models in Milano tooling along the Via Mascarpone. Or whatever the mayor called it." He smiled.

"They're not basketball shoes, sir," Sgt. Gallaher suggested gently. "They're respectful."

Sunny had slipped on his brogues and now rocked back on his heels as he looked down, watching silver pinstripes run into brown suede.

"Brown shoes with a black suit. I just look like such an *alderman*," he said.

Sgt. Gallaher waited a moment before bringing the other young officer to her side.

"This is Sergeant Ed McNulty, sir. He'll take charge of you now. I may—probably will—see you later. The chief has appointed me chief of your detail."

McNulty had round shoulders, sandy hair, a crushing grip, and the smile of a forest animal in children's storybooks.

"I'm out of First District, sir. Seen you a couple of times at Alderman Corcoran's picnics."

"Gallaher to McNulty?" asked Sunny. "All the hiring laws and diversity workshops, and this is what it comes to—Gallaher hands off to McNulty?"

"After all the laws and workshops, sir, Gallaher and McNulty *are* the diversity." The sergeant stood back on his heels and waggled the toes of black shoes that had been shined to glaring.

"I'm a twelve. Any use?"

"I'm nine and a half," said Sunny.

"Sorry, sir. You'd look like you're wearing Bozo's shoes, and I can't go barefoot on duty."

Sgt. Gallaher had stepped back from the circle of conversation and began to steer them toward the door to the hall that led into the council chamber. They could hear a hubbub of voices, struggling to be soft, bubble from the floor of the council chamber, and saw hot lights making the city seal glimmer above the mayor's rostrum. Sunny sensed that the young officers were holding back, waiting for him to take the first steps out into the council chamber.

"Did you ever hear Alderman Rodriguez's theory about shoe size?" Sunny whispered to Sgt. McNulty. The sergeant shook his head.

"I'll send him around to tell you."

Sunny stepped through the door, felt the hot lights blister his forehead, and walked to just in front of the mayor's mammoth burgundy chair on the podium. Someone had placed a single red rose across the seat.

Sunny saw schoolgirls in the balcony seats behind the glass, in blue and green plaid smocks, white tights, white boots and pink boots, and pastel snow jackets, with red Bulls' scarves looped around their necks. An enterprising teacher must have heard the news at six and rapidly deployed a field trip. Christa Landgraf, a blond woman with white cat's-eyes glasses from the Corporation Counsel's office, who customarily sat at the right hand of the mayor, inclined her head toward the gallery and began to write out a note for Sunny on the top of her long yellow pad.

Sunny had presided over the council scores of times, while the mayor excused himself to gossip, agitate, or flagrantly nap in his office. He would send word down through Tina Butler, the sergeant at arms, "Wake me when the children are done squabbling, Sarge." But Sunny had never called the city council to order. The mayor had always reserved for himself the special pleasure of bringing down the head of some glossy new mahogany gavel, fulsomely inscribed from a local Order of Hibernians, Knights of Pythias, or the Benevolent and Protective Order of Elks, and declare, "This council *will* come to *order*."

There was Arty Agras, looking weary but his hairpiece reinvigorated, slowly rolling back on the wheels of his chair in the first spot on the council floor, listening to Miles Sparrow of the 7th, with his Dizzy goatee, standing just over him to hurry through a hushed story; Daryl Lloyd of the 9th Ward, enrobed in mournful black and sorrowful violet, turned around and sitting on the edge of his smooth wooden desk to speak in whispers with Felix Kowalski of the 23rd, who occupied the dead center middle seat of the chamber in the unchanging black suit of his trade that was suddenly so apt for this morning.

Thirty-six aldermen were men, fourteen were women. The balance was scarcely equal, but the direction of history was clear. There had been just six women when Sunny was first elected.

Twenty-four, or almost half the council members, were not white. Sixteen were African American, and six were Hispanic, though Sunny had been admonished by Jaco Sefran not to assume any greater affinity between, say, Mexicans and Puerto Ricans than Frenchmen and Germans (or Jamaicans, Somalis, and African-Americans). Three and a half aldermen (the half being Carlo Viola of the 35th) were Mexican, two were Puerto Rican, and Jacobo was Cuban, a slight underrepresentation that was usually blamed—though not for much longer, thought Sunny—on meager voter turnout.

The count of Asians in the council was increasing. There was John Wu of the 15th, Evelyn Lee of the 17th, Janet Watanabe of the 20th, whose mother had been African-American, and Sunny. Evelyn Lee once suggested that they form an Asian Caucus. Sunny was tepid to the idea, but felt that he could not refuse to go along. He recommended that they call themselves the Pan-Asian People's Congress.

"It confers more authority," he explained. "We'll represent a realm of billions, from the steppes of Kazakhstan to the shores of Micronesia."

"Four of us?" asked Janet. She had already been a member of the council's Black Caucus, which had more or less disbanded when the mayor took office and summoned Daryl Lloyd up to the fifth floor and said, "I'm sitting on a couple of million votes here, Daryl. Do you still want to lecture *me* about what black people want?"

"We have to make it clear that Asians are an important minority," said Evelyn.

John Wu raised a steely eyebrow on his solid vault face and just asked, "Minority?"

Three aldermen were Jews, which had only recently come to be considered white. Three were immigrants: Mitya Volkov of the 19th, who was from Murmansk, Jacobo Sefran of the 50th, who was from Santiago de Cuba, and Sunny.

Three aldermen had been indicted and awaited trial.

Against all expectation, reputation, and lore, just six aldermen could be called Irish, and three of those, Aidan Ruffino of the 38th, Cyril Murphy of the 40th, and Keira Malek of the 43rd, were from families that married Italians, Slovaks, or Poles. They emphasized this mixed lineage as needed. There were two Poles, two Italians, two Swedes, a Croat, a Slovak, a Greek, one Serb, one German, one Russian, and a Lebanese.

Two aldermen were forthrightly, even boastfully gay. In recent years, gay political groups had mastered the nuts and bolts of politics more successfully than trade unions. Linas Slavinskas professed, "I used to tell young people who wanted to learn politics to join the Boilermakers, Iron Ship Builders, Blacksmiths, Forgers and Helpers Union. Now I say, 'Be gay.'"

In the whole Chicago City Council, there was just one authentic white Anglo-Saxon Protestant. The Reverend Harry Walker III, whose grandfather had been a founder of the Dearborn Bank, lived in a handsome old gray-stone family home, one of the few three-story buildings left on Stratford. (Harry had to spurn all entreaties from developers. He had run against them for twenty years, even as he had begun to feel like an elf living in a toadstool beneath the sixty-story residences rising around him).

But Harry was a hell-raising man of God who flung chicken's blood on the windows of Army recruitment centers. He ran a colonic irrigation clinic in the basement of his church. He was the gay father of three children, born to three mothers (an organic foods activist, a homeopath, and a Wacker Drive investment analyst) who had specifically enlisted his semen to seed a new generation of activists. With his sandy-white prophet's beard curling in fury around his chin, Harry's appearance recalled John Brown, not Cotton Mather.

Harry and Jacobo Sefran were the two clergymen on the council, though, as Jaco said, "What we really need is a priest around here, to hear confessions and keep his mouth shut."

(There had been a nun, Suzanne Suzinski, who represented the 30th before Wandy Rodriguez had been recruited to run against her.

Suzanne had irritated the mayor by always talking about "agape," and increasing property taxes.)

Nine aldermen were attorneys; in politics, that was unavoidable. But five aldermen were teachers, from Evelyn Washington of the 2nd, who taught first grade at the Cyrus Colter School, to Keira Malek of the 43rd, a professor at Northwestern Law. Five were full-time aldermen, who claimed to get by on their aldermanic salary alone (which, at $101,000 a year, satisfied some, but only whet other appetites). Daryl Lloyd was a dentist, Collie Kerrigan was a pharmacist, Janet Watanabe was a veterinarian, and Sunny was a restaurateur. One alderman was a dry cleaner, another a meat packer, one a beer distributor. There was a rug cleaner, a car dealer, a professional pianist, and someone who ran a string of senior citizen's centers.

"If we could all open up for business here," said Sunny, "there'd be no reason to leave City Hall for the rest of our lives."

In fact, there was no reason to leave thereafter: Two aldermen, Kevin Corcoran and Felix Kowalski, were funeral directors. Kevin said, with utter sincerity, "In Chicago, deceased Americans play a vital role in civic affairs."

Lewie Karp, in the clerk's chair just below Sunny's left elbow, called out: "Wojcik, Forty-five! Siegel, Forty-six! Katsoulis, Forty-seven!" Voices called back, more softly than usual. Lew reeled in his voice from the back row of the chamber because Sunny was out of his usual seat, and now standing in the rostrum.

"Roopini, Forty-eight."

Sunny bowed slightly before saying, "Present."

After Anders Berggren of the 49th and Jaco Sefran of the 50th had affirmed their presence, Lewie spoke with unusual formality.

"Fifty aldermen have answered present, sir."

Sunny was empty-handed. Tina Butler had offered him use of a gavel that had been inscribed to the mayor—"Our Champion"—by the Friends of Battered Women and Their Children of Rogers Park

shelter. But Sunny said that he would feel queasy about using it—
"Like a novice picking up Tiger's driver"—so he simply rapped his
folded hand on the desk just below the microphone and said in a measured voice, "The council will please come to order."

The chamber quieted. Christa Landgraf tapped the end of a pen on
the note she had written across the top of her pad.

"We welcome students from the St. Angela School on North Mas-
sasoit and Sister Mary Finnegan, who are seated in the gallery," Sunny
began slowly. "They join us on a sad day. And yet a day that I suspect
they will never forget—none of us will—as those who loved and admired the mayor in this chamber gather to pay him tribute."

(Sunny thought to himself, *I should have gotten my daughters
here,* and then another thought rolled in just behind: *And I should have
had the Stockton, Stewart, Pierce, Audubon, Clinton, and McCutcheon
schools send a few kids, too.*)

Vera Barrow looked up at Sunny from the fifth seat in the first row
and inclined her head just below his line of sight. Christa Landgraf
caught his eye with her cat's-eyes and mouthed a phrase, but Sunny
couldn't decipher it. He leaned forward just enough to finally see an
identifiably broad back and shoulders in a stately charcoal suit and said,
"We will now receive a benediction from the Reverend Jesse Jackson."

(Vera Barrow had the number of the slim mobile phone that the
reverend kept, turned to vibrate and tucked in the leg of his left sock,
and had reached him just as he had landed on an all-night flight from
Amsterdam. He was shocked, saddened, and instantly available.)

As the reverend's voice began to roll through the chamber, Sunny
leaned back to Christa Landgraf, who pointed to the minutes of their
last session. He straightened in place as he heard the reverend intone,
"his last, full measure of devotion. Amen."

The aldermen sat down, softly, the wheels on their chairs making
small, chattering mice sounds. Sunny stayed on his feet.

"Thank you, Reverend Jackson. We are grateful. No matter where
in the world your important work takes you, you take the time to still
be this great city's pastor. Thank you."

Sunny paused for a moment and looked over the chamber. The Reverend Jackson, ringed by four uniformed officers, was whisked away from the council floor.

"Do I hear a motion to suspend the reading of the minutes?"

"I so move." It was Vera.

"Without objection?" A stroke of silence went by. "It is so ordered."

Whether the residue of Hindu ceremonies or early British schooling, Sunny found the familiar civilities of parliamentary routine reassuring. Even sense-worn words seemed to assert order and a touch of majesty. He leaned into the small microphone and began in a low, subdued voice.

"It is the purpose of this meeting to pay tribute to the mayor of Chicago," he began. "He died last night in his office just above this chamber. We recognize the loss of the mayor's chief of staff, too, who also rendered many years of service. But with the council's consent, I am going to ask aldermen to speak about the mayor this morning. For millions, in and out of our city, he was a singular and irreplaceable part of our skyline. As a great man might say, 'The loss is positively antediluvian.' "

Laughter flickered over the chamber, and there was a squeaking of seats as aldermen sat back.

"I will also respectfully suggest that some of those aldermen who knew the mayor longest—the alderman of the Fifth Ward, Ms. Barrow; the alderman of the Second Ward, Mrs. Washington; and the alderman of the Forty-fourth Ward, Mr. Walker—speak for five or ten minutes each. I am sure that the rest of us will so closely identify with their eloquent memorials that we can express a small portion of our own grief in two or three minutes, which should take us to about one p.m."

Sunny tried to add up those numbers as he spoke: the math was hopeful to impossible.

"The chair recognizes the alderman of the 1st Ward," he directed, and Arty punctiliously buttoned the middle button of his gray jacket as he bowed to Vera on his left.

"I will certainly excess myself later," he said. "But first I yield to the distinguished alderman of the 5th Ward."

Vera bowed slightly in return and walked around to the front of her desk. In the shawl collar of her smart navy suit, she had pinned a rose of dark crimson. As Vera began in a low, sober tone, Eldad leaned down into Sunny's left ear.

"The president of the United States," he said. "On the phone in the conference room."

Sunny held still for a moment, thinking that Eldad had chosen a poor moment in which to spring a prank. Then he understood that he was serious. Sunny motioned for Donald Stubbs, the bull-chested courtroom bailiff who represented the 27th Ward, to leave his seat in the second row on the council floor to come up to the rostrum and preside. He walked out between the sergeant at arms and Sgt. McNulty, his brown suede shoes whimpering with each step. *I look like such an alderman.*

Sunny put his shoes below the conference table while the president, his voice twanging like wire fencing, reassured Sunny that help was already dispatched from the FBI, CIA, and DOJ, which Sunny had scrawled down beside a question mark. Claudia McCarthy, the faun-eyed assistant whom Sunny had noticed from the mayor's secretarial corps, had been sent down to the conference room, saw the scrawl and whispered to Sunny, "Justice. *Justice.*"

The president offered regrets that he could not be present at services for the mayor. He would be busy all weekend with meetings on nuclear proliferation. But the vice president (whose ideas on nuclear issues were apparently disposable), and the secretary of Health and Human Services (who had been the mayor of Houston and was visibly African-American), would represent his administration.

"You just call the White House, Mr. Interim Mayor, if your investigation needs something. I enjoyed the mayor, you know, differences be damned. We talked barbeque."

"He told us."

"The mayor sent a whole mess of things once, overnight. Pork ribs, beef ribs, wings, Memphis rub, St. Louis sauce. A Secret Service guy runs up to me, real serious, holding a card out like it was a list of kidnapper's demands. The mayor had written, 'Gnaw on these instead of the federal money we need to resurface the Kennedy Expressway.' "

"Must have worked. *Sir*," Sunny amended. He remembered that the funds had been restored.

"Smart gift sixty days before an election," the president agreed.

A call from the governor of Illinois was put through next. In the dry, flinty voice of a conductor on a commuter train, the governor took a couple of minutes to certify that he and Sunny had never met.

"St. Patrick's Day parade?" Sunny tenuously suggested.

"The mayor's show. Awkward for my party, unless you're Irish."

"Mexican Independence Day?"

"I go to the one in Des Plaines. Do you go to the Gay Pride parade?" asked the governor.

"Never miss it."

"I send a note," he explained. "Cordial but noncommittal."

The governor assured Sunny that the state police were at his disposal, but when he scratched "ISP" on a pad in front of Claudia, she held her nose and Eldad whispered, "Amateurs."

Claudia had a crawl of other names scrawled on her small secretarial pad. There were messages of concern from the Vatican secretary of state, his eminence the cardinal of Chicago, the mayors of New York, Boston, Milwaukee, and Iowa City, six U.S. senators, nine congressmen, Donald Trump, the owner of the Chicago White Sox, the Illinois secretary of state, the presidents of the University of Chicago and Notre Dame, Helmut Jahn, the Cook County sheriff, the owner of the Chicago Bears, a member of the U.S. Olympic Relay team, the Czech who conducted the Chicago Symphony, and the managing director of Skidmore Owings & Merrill.

"Just the ones we think we recognize," Eldad explained. "Hundreds more are coming in." He looked down at his own pad. "John and Catherine from Brighton Park. Rick and Leilani from Roscoe Village. Claire from West Englewood."

Of the names before him, Sunny had only so much as shaken hands with the mayor of New York. In fact, it was not much more than a nod,

at an Urban Issues Conference in Vancouver a few years before, where
Sunny had spent three days shuttling between symposia about Noise
Pollution, Light Pollution, Sprawl, and the Urban Heat Island Effect.
The mayor of New York had flown in to accept a plaque for opening
neighborhood farmer's markets. Sunny encountered him, surrounded
by a retinue of sharply creased assistants, by a bank of elevators and
pointed to a tan hemp briefcase in the arms of an aide.

"Are you keeping that, sir?" he asked. Every delegate had received
a case. Green letters along the side said, THE 21ST CENTURY CITY: GOV-
ERNANCE, SUSTAINABLE ENERGIES, A CIVIL SOCIETY. The mayor cast a
quick glance.

"Doubtful. My grandson wants something with a Mountie on it."

"Sundaran Roopini from the Chicago City Council, sir. I have two
daughters, but only one briefcase."

The mayor of New York nodded to his aide.

"Sold."

Sunny brought a beige conference room phone closer to him from
across the table. Each light seemed to be blinking. When one winked
off, he stabbed his finger down and tapped out the 212 number on
Claudia's pad.

"Sundaran Roopini at City Hall in Chicago," he said. "Returning
the mayor's call."

Eldad nodded approval.

When the mayor of New York came on the line, he remembered
that he and the mayor had bet competing pizzas, deep dish against thin
crust, on the outcome of various sports championship series.

"Jesus Fucking Christ," said the mayor of New York. "Knicks-Bulls,
Yanks-Sox. Every time we won, your mayor sent those fat, artery-
choking motherfuckers to us. Same place, right?"

"Probably."

"Now I know what the mayor's real agenda was," the mayor of
New York announced. "I just popped them open for my staff. Staff is
expendable. You'll see. Oh fuck me dead," said the mayor. "I didn't
mean that guy who just jumped onto the street. My deepest fucking
condolences on that, too."

"We appreciate that, sir."

Sunny, who had lived in three of the world's great cities and was generally adjudged to have a keen sense of humor, still found it difficult to tell when a New Yorker was joking.

"Are those Scientologists putting their fingers up your ass?" Sunny understood this much.

"The FBI is doing everything they can to help."

"If you can use anything from our people, you let my people know. The service?"

Sunny had to pause to remind himself of the day.

"Saturday, sir. Tomorrow."

"Our comptroller is going." Sunny remembered—an African-American businessman from Brooklyn. "He and the mayor were friends. I've got to be on a plane, or else. . . . Christ, mayors' conferences are going to be duller. I like Vera. Beautiful gal. But you knew the mayor. Once we had to sit through a whole morning seminar on composting programs. The chairman of the conference that year was from Austin or Madison—some place where composting is the pastime. The mayor looked over at me and whispered, 'I do believe I have heard all the *pig shit* about *pig shit* that I can bear. Why don't we run out on these pygmies and see if some place in this burg'—we were in Des Moines or Dayton; I can't keep them straight—'can manage a decent penne alla San Giovanni?' "

The one with the sage and walnuts, Sunny remembered.

"And he *found* some place, wouldn't you know? Fuck me dead. Wasn't half-bad."

"Well, that was fun," Sunny announced after the line from New York had clicked off. Claudia McCarthy held out a new sheet of paper with the U.S. Attorney's number. The sergeant at arms had returned to the room with a harder step, and Eldad Delaney received a whispered report in the doorway from Wandy Rodriguez, who had to stoop down to reach Eldad's ear.

"Alderman Stubbs might need some relief," said Eldad. "Alderman Lloyd is in full flight."

Wandy stayed down in his confidential crouch, even as Eldad began to sweep up pads of paper and prepared to move back onto the council floor.

"It's getting ugly," Wandy reported. "Daryl just said that the oil companies, Latin drug kingpins, Judas Iscariot, and the Chicago police killed the mayor."

"Can't keep a secret from Alderman Lloyd," said Sunny, but he was already rising and moving swiftly to the doorway. Sgt. McNulty had stepped into the hallway and held up his hands, should someone else be moving toward the chamber.

"And I may have left out a few," Wandy added, as Sunny wiped the palm of his hand across a hair that had fallen onto his forehead and prepared to step back under the bare, blaring light of the rostrum.

Donald Stubbs turned around to Sunny from the mayor's chair, unfurling his large, black-suited arms in despair. Sunny could hear Daryl Lloyd call for the police department to be indicted, "for what they did in conspiring to assist in the murder of our mayor." Jesus Flores Suarez had leapt to his feet in the middle of the council floor to pump his fist like a piston and shout, "Bullshit. *Bullshit!* Bullshit. *Bullshit!*" and more, while Luis Zamora of the 31st, sitting on the far side of the chamber, scrambled onto his desk, his knees slipping on the slanted surface.

"I'm sorry, Sunny," Donald whispered. "It was his turn. And you know—Daryl."

"Exactly right. I'll let you get ready for your remarks," said Sunny smoothly, and when Alderman Lloyd heard steps on the rostrum, he turned around from his microphone position in the first row and saw Sunny and a passel of uniforms.

"I see that word of my comments has run priests out of the inner temple," he declared. When Sunny heard Dorothy Fisher of the 3rd, John Reginald of the 8th, and Sanford Booker of the 24th bark with laughter—like Daryl, they had supported the mayor, but often felt excluded from his circle—he decided to draw out his response, as if wringing wet laundry.

"I regret that city business called me away. I usually try to follow Alderman Lloyd's appearances with the devotion of a Grateful Dead groupie. I think that Commander Green was explicit this morning. The investigation into the mayor's death is—" Sunny paused slightly for a choice of words, then made a politician's judgment to include all—"intense, wide-ranging, and unrelenting. It extends from those who have been closest to him," an unmistakable reference, he thought, to Collins Jenkins, and the mayor's own police detail, "to parties presently unknown who may be involved. In these times, no possibility—*no possibility*—can be ruled out. But it is important not to rush to judgment. It is not my desire to restrict any alderman's powers of imagination," he went on. "I simply want our mayor to have a proper remembrance today."

But as soon as Sunny had rounded into the last few words, Daryl Lloyd was on top of his microphone, holding the slender stand in a markedly tightening fist.

"What better memorial than the truth?" he sang out. Sunny could see Dorothy Fisher of the 3rd, John Reginald of the 8th, Gerry White of the 29th, and Rod Abboud all stand to applaud, and could even hear teenagers thumping gloved hands through the windows of the visitors' balcony.

"I appreciate what the alderman has done to put these issues before this chamber," Sunny said more loudly, and inclined his head toward the dozen television cameras blinking alongside the aldermen's seats. "And before the people of this city and beyond. But timeliness is a virtue, too. The members of this assembly will be unable to go about their important work until we have memorialized our late mayor. May I ask the alderman if he is near his conclusion? He must be as eager as I am to hear what our colleagues have to say."

For the first time, Sunny heard small squirts of applause for his own remarks, from Alfredo Sandoval, sitting just two desks down from Daryl Lloyd, John Wu in the second row, Mitya Volkov, and Wandy Rodriguez.

"I concur with the chair," Alderman Lloyd said after a pause. "These are emotional times," he said in a quieter key. "I apologize if the loss I feel today makes me uncharitable. I do not envy the chair his duties. I thank him for his courtesy. There are times, I'm sure, when he would like to be able to use a whip and a chair," and as the glad sound of gentle laughter began to roll from row to row in the chamber, Dr. Lloyd reached his right hand under one of the violet silk stripes that adorned his glossy Yoruba robe and pulled out a gun.

Sunny had heard that gun barrels gleamed. But this revolver had a grim, gray snub barrel, and a dull green grip, which Sgt. McNulty, who had instantly taken down Sunny from behind, as if he were folding a picnic chair, recognized as a Walther P99 with a green polymer frame, a red-painted striker tip, four internal safeties, and an ambidextrous magazine release in the trigger guard. He carried one himself.

There were gasps, then silence. Daryl laid the gun down, almost daintily, on the top of his desk (which Sunny couldn't see; McNulty had him pressed flat, from head to toe, against the spongy mauve carpet of the rostrum; which Sunny thought smelled of rubber and glue and tasted like a fuzzy balloon). Sunny heard several sets of steps spring across the chamber. He felt McNulty's knees pin his shoulders, one of his hands press the back of his head while another—the right one, Sunny guessed—bristled with the switch and slide of his own Walther. A score of aldermanic asses plopped on the floor behind their desks. Joints snapped, shoes thudded, chair wheels squealed, seats banged into the desks behind.

Daryl Lloyd shouted: "This is how the Chicago Police Department serves and protects! Any *fool* can walk in to City Hall with a lethal weapon!"

Four uniforms had sprinted down from their posts to advance on Daryl, one in front of where he stood behind his desk, but three others behind his back. Their guns were holstered. The police held their arms out, visibly empty, at the height of a man's neck. Daryl's gun was flat on his desk, but within his arm's grasp. Department training taught them that putting a gun down within reach was a sleight of hand, not surrender. The sergeant who was in front of Daryl leaned carefully toward his desk and gently said, "I'm just going to pick that up now, Alderman." But before the three uniforms behind him could hurtle into Daryl's shoulders, twist his spine, and wrench his arms behind his back, Alderman Lloyd reached into the right pocket of his trousers and extracted something with a high metal gleam and a black handle.

The uniforms froze in their crouches. From atop Sunny's shoulders, Sgt. McNulty called out excitedly—there was no mistaking his exhilaration—"I've got him." Then a more humdrum voice, as if pointing to a fly trapped in a corner: "Got him."

A voice arose from the second row of the chamber.

"Hold your fire!"

It was Tommy Mitrovic of the 21st, bellowing from below his desk, wrapping his arms around his head like a boy hiding under a bed. "Hold your fire!" he repeated, and then, on the chance that this was just a phrase from American war movies, Tommy rasped, "Don't shoot! There are *eee-no-scent* people here!"

"Innocent?" cried Linas Slavinskas. "We're *aldermen*!"

Astrid Lindstrom of the 28th ward put her head above the edge of her desk, or at least the top half of the chunky blond wig she had worn for the past nine months of chemotherapy on thirteen little nits of cancer in her left lung. She and Daryl got along. Astrid was chesty, feisty, and represented a ward that, at a hundred blocks north of his, was practically Nunavik to Daryl. He called her Momma. She was the mother of four boys and three girls, and accepted the name as factual and genially flirtatious. Astrid and Daryl served on the Committee on Health. Shortly after she had begun to lose her hair, Daryl had put a small gold foil box of Belgian chocolates and a Cubs cap at Astrid's place at the committee table; she was touched.

"Where the hell did you find a Cubs cap, Daryl?" she asked. "So far south on Cottage Grove."

"Salvation Army," he glared.

So now Alderman Lindstrom risked raising her head just high enough for her mouth to clear the lip of her desk and implored, with the matchless moral authority of a mother of seven, three-term alderman, and battler against terminal disease, "Don't be a dick, Daryl."

Four uniforms hit him at once. The officer in front drove his head into Alderman Lloyd's solar plexus, sending the alderman back onto the hard slab top of Alderman Alonzo Guttierez's desk. Another officer took hold of Daryl Lloyd's left hand and pulled down from his shoulder, as if trying to pump the first cough of water from a well. Another hooked his elbow below Daryl's chin, and began to pull, as intently as a four-year-old trying to disconnect a doll's head from its neck. The fourth officer brought a knee down on Daryl's right arm, slamming, smashing, and cracking it against the edge of the desk.

The gleaming object in Daryl Lloyd's hand slipped to the ground with disconcerting slightness. It was a Cook County deputy sheriff's badge.

Newspapers would report the next day that Cook County Sheriff Elroy Mitchell had issued deputy sheriff's badges (the final number would turn out to be more than a hundred) to contributors, friends, and supporters, including Alderman Lloyd. The badge gave them license to carry a gun. Daryl often carried large sums of cash in his car between his south side dental offices and worried that he was prey for armed robbers.

Alderman Lloyd disdained the city's law prohibiting private citizens from owning handguns. He denounced it as the Anti-African-American Self-Defense Act and used to thunder at Kiera Malek of the 43rd, "Well maybe when *you* call the police in *Lincoln Park*, they pull up in *ninety seconds*. But down on *Dr. Martin Luther King Drive*, they don't come *at all*! You don't like cheap handguns? Well I don't like that cheap Navajo jewelry you wear, Kiera. A cheap handgun is a home security system. My folks can't *afford* to get their apartments wired like a Paris art museum, like folks in Lincoln Park do." When Kiera would wearily point out someone's statistics that a gun in the home was more likely to cause an accident than deter a crime, Daryl would become most aroused. "Why don't you let us worry about that? What is it, Kiera—*you just don't trust poor black folks with guns*? You think we're coming for you and your Mercedes?"

(Daryl owned a Range Rover and several pieces of jewelry that were each more luxurious than the doddering and temperamental Toyota that Kiera drove to teach her law school classes.)

The officers loosened their grip on Alderman Lloyd; after a moment, they propped him up on Alderman Guttierez's desk (Alonzo, who ran currency exchanges on Harrison, Roosevelt, and 16th Street, had seen plenty of guns waved in his face, but usually behind thick plate glass. He stayed flat on his ass below his desk). A paramedic crew dashed onto the council floor and certified for Commander Green that Daryl had to be taken to a hospital for treatment of his bruised and maimed right arm. Commander Green would have preferred to have the alderman taken out in handcuffs, if not chains—heavy chains, that would bite huge crimson welts into his chest—but agreed because Daryl held up that right arm with heroic flourish to announce that bearing up under ruthless and vicious assault was the special fate of prophets and truth tellers, from Jesus to George Jackson to Martin Luther King.

"Don't forget Meir Kehane!" Jacobo Rapoport Sefran shouted from the last row in the chamber. Commander Green told the paramedics to quickly strap Alderman Lloyd onto a trundle and deliver him to Northwestern Memorial; squad cars would follow. Daryl waved to the gallery from his stretcher; cheers and *whoof-whoofs* rang out, as at a basketball game.

Alderman Lindstrom thought that Daryl had been a dick. But she also knew that his last two wives had left him, his children called him only when they needed money, and that she couldn't recall him seeing a woman for more than three dates. So she slung her deep canvas bag over her shoulder and followed Daryl's stretcher.

Christa Landgraf came down from the rostrum and whispered grimly to Commander Green that the corporation counsel had called even as they took shelter under their desks. He reminded her that under an 1872 statute aldermen were designated as peace officers.

"You don't mean," Green began more loudly than he wanted, "I mean really, *seriously,* that the son of a bitch can't be charged for walking onto the City Council floor and *waving a gun?"*

Christa turned up her hands in a gesture of helplessness.

"Apparently, he's a peace officer."

"Piece of *something*," said Commander Green.

Meanwhile Sunny had been let up from the floor by Sgt. McNulty, who dusted him off without comment, as if Sunny had only walked under a painter's scaffold. Aldermen began to get up on their haunches, scratch their heads, shake out their shoulders, and walk in groups. The council floor looked like a natural history museum diorama of hunters and gatherers. Sunny moved back toward the mayor's massive mogul's chair, ran a palm over his hair, and cleared his throat.

"The council will please come to order," he said.

Sunny looked down on the third row and saw Keith Horn of the 36th, who had sclerosis and was in a wheelchair, and Vernetta Hynes Griffin of the 37th turn around and look back at him in the rostrum; they just went on talking to each other.

"The council will *please* come to order," Sunny repeated, stressing the appeal but not, he hoped, making it a plea. Vera Barrow caught his eye from the first row, or at least caught something in his face. She turned side to side, speaking in soft undertones to Dorothy Fisher of the 3rd, Wanda Jackson of the 4th, and Grace Brown of the 6th, and as if on Vera's signal, they sat down, queens slipping back to their thrones. Sunny *ahhhemmed* into his microphone once more as John Wu of the 15th, Shirley Watson of the 16th, and Evelyn Lee of the 16th sat down in the second row, and then Emil Wagner of the 32nd, Patrick Tierney of the 33rd, and Regina Gregory of the 34th in the third tier of seats.

"The council will please come to order," he said in sudden silence.

"I see that the aldermen of the Ninth Ward and the Twenty-eighth Ward have left the chamber," he continued in a level voice. "I think that Alderman Lloyd had reached his conclusion in any case," and at this, Sunny pretended to begin a new sentence but let it be turned back by the abrupt exhale of laughter.

"The chair . . . the chair . . . will reserve the right of both aldermen to address the council when they become available." And then, as if turning the page of a familiar menu to look for the everyday list of desserts, Sunny said, "The chair recognizes the alderman of the Tenth Ward."

J. P. Mulroy had a doughy, unbaked face and dark raisin eyes that suddenly widened in surprise. He owned a real estate agency in Hegewisch, where the belly of the city's south side began to flop over the Indiana beltline. Months passed without Alderman Mulroy uttering anything beyond aye, nay, or present from the council floor; even that could be delayed by the need to look two seats down for a signal from Linas Slavinskas. Alderman Mulroy knew only one speech, but he knew it well. Every May he read the poem he had composed as a student at St. Francis de Sales commemorating Molly Weston and the Irish women patriots of 1798. "Molly rode at the English, swathed in outlawed green/ barefoot farmers following the sword of Colleen." By now, most aldermen could recite along.

When J. P. was taken aback, Jaco Sefran's voice rose up from the last row.

"Mr. Chairman," he called out. "Mr. President Interim Mayor. What's happened—I think many of us just feel the need to talk about this. Perhaps we need a break. Call our families. Let them know we're fine. Are we fine? I don't know."

"The alderman is right," Arty Agras volunteered from the first seat in the chamber. "Some of us could suffer from post-dramatic stress syndrome."

"I think we are fine," Sunny said after a pause. "Aldermen are certainly free to leave the floor and call their families. I will do so soon." He nodded his head gently toward the cameras in the chamber, taking care not to move his shoulders. "But I'm pretty sure they already know that we are unharmed. I feel the need to let the city know that we are *at work*."

Over a moment, Sunny could hear pens scratch against pads of paper, stifled coughs, and chair springs squeak. J. P. Mulroy rose slowly, tucking his black tie under the middle button of his gray suit.

"May I have the floor, Mr. President?" His voice quavered, but he was standing, hands folded at his waist, rubbing his thumbs, as if to crank a small engine.

"The chair recognizes the alderman of the Tenth Ward," said Sunny, and J. P. Mulroy kept his eyes locked on Sunny as he began.

"A great—another great—patriot, Brian Boru, a Knight of Munster, led the Irish against the Norse invaders. And in so many ways was the mayor a knight among men. . . ."

Sunny saw J. P. through his remarks, then Fred Sandoval. He sat through Linas's comments—he had been less stilted, and more plausible in private—and then Brock Lucchesi, before recognizing Collie Kerrigan, summoning Don Stubbs back to the rostrum to preside, and slipping back to the conference room, borne between sergeants McNulty and Butler, to make some calls.

"I'm fine," Sunny declared when Rita's mobile phone rang through to her mailbox. "Really, darlings, just fine. I'm here. I love you." He envisioned her phone, trilling some Anil Kapoor song inside her beige school locker, asphyxiated by the babel of a thousand teenage voices and the tweeting of their rubber soles squishing past.

Vera Barrow waited just in front of him, tapping a sleek black ball pen on the pointed toe of a silk shoe. Eldad hovered with more names on a pad, and the voice of the president of Malcolm X College squeaking in the earpiece of a phone he held against Sunny's ear. "And Alderman Wu," he murmured behind his head. "On his way back." On the council floor, Mitya Volkov acclaimed the mayor as a rare gem, and Janet Wantanabe cleared her throat in preparation for her own praise and despair. Sunny slid his phone into the waist of his pants.

Rula called back while Sunny was on the phone with a federal judge who had recessed a major tax fraud case to return his call. His Honor was detailing features of what made the trial complicated and important when Sunny heard the small beep, saw his daughter's name flash across the small screen, and waited for a pause—even a semicolon's worth of an intake of breath—to ask the judge to excuse him while he spoke with his daughter. But the judge's articulation was dauntless. By the time Sunny could make apologies, his daughter had been switched into his mailbox. By the time he heard another beep advising him of a message, he was on the phone with an expensive defense attorney. Wandy Rodriguez was rolling his hands, like a referee trying to speed up a game, and whispered urgently to Sunny, something he couldn't quite understand. By the time Sunny could hold up his hand to Eldad to say that he had to check his messages, the universal digital voice told him that he had twelve. Sunny had his eye on a screen showing the proceedings in the chamber. Ivan Becker of the 41st was comparing the death of the mayor to Abraham Lincoln's assassination. Lincoln had died trying to preserve the Union, Ivan informed the council, and the mayor had always supported unions. For that and a dozen other reasons, Sunny groaned.

He got back onto the rostrum at one-twenty, just as Jacobo Sefran of the 50th, in a resourceful flight of lamentation to prolong the memorials until Sunny could return, pledged to scrawl the mayor's name into a crevice of Jerusalem's Western Wall.

"What a fitting remembrance," he said. "For this man who loved his city. This man who loved his party. This man who loved all partiers. Democrats, Independents, Perotists, or even Republicans, and the privileged few they so ably represent. This man who loved his neighborhood. This man who loved all neighborhoods. This man who loved all voters, living and deceased, those who voted for him, and those who didn't—that tiny minority, really, though he loved minorities, too. This man who loved his *White Sox*," said Jaco, who knew he was beginning to flail, and was glad to see Sunny slip back into the mammoth chair.

"This man who loved our beloved Israel," he said, finally, sincerely, and solemnly. "And who believed that the lion should lie down with the lamb, the goat with the chicken, the Arab with the Jew, although of course only Israel should get to lie down with Jerusalem. 'He who creates peace in His celestial heights, may He create peace for us and for all Israel; and say, Amen,' "

"Amen," Linas Slavinskas echoed, and caught Sunny's eye with a wink. Sunny rose from the chair, and began quietly.

"I thank Alderman Sefran, and all aldermen, for a dignified memorial for our mayor. Finally, I would like to share my own thoughts." Sunny paused as he ran his fingers around the edges of another index card.

"I remember an afternoon about three or four years ago. A few of us had accompanied the mayor to the regional transit board. The commissioners had decided to reduce service times for the number twenty bus on West Madison. Ridership was down, and they decreed that instead of having a bus depart that route every twenty minutes after midnight, it should be every forty-five.

"I see Aldermen Lee, Kowalski, and Guttierez shaking their heads now; you remember this, too. When the mayor spoke, he took a last look at the service report, then flung his reading glasses aside, as if he could bear no more. 'Ladies and gentlemen, I have been poring over some of these findings,' he said. 'I wonder if any of these numbers can tell you the story I see herein.' "

Sunny was a gifted mimic. He had grown up imitating unctuous teachers with clipped British tones, BBC World Service announcers whirling regal *rrr*'s, Sean Connery's rolling *brrr*'s, the cricket clicks inside the Tamil language, and the cadenced chime of Punjabi. So when he recalled the mayor's monologues, he borrowed his unfiltered bourbon baritone.

" 'Who's riding your suburban commuter trains late at night?' the mayor asked. 'Senior partners who may have imbibed a tad too much at a dinner they charge to a client. Vice presidents giving *dic*-tation to their secretaries'—the mayor drew out the emphasis—'late unto the night.' "

Sunny let the little flares of laughter flicker and fall before going on.

" 'Do you know who's taking the twenty bus after midnight?' the mayor asked. 'Cleaning ladies and maintenance men. Ladies from Haiti who swam an ocean brimming with sharks just to wash up on a beach here. Grandfathers from Poland who stared down Communist tanks to get out. Salvadorans, Koreans, and folks from the hollers of Kentucky.

I know about these folks, ladies and gentlemen,' he said. 'My mother was a cleaning lady. She scrubbed your floors and toilets with the hands that fed me. She saw your walnut-framed degrees and Florida vacation pictures and said, "I want that for my son. He's as good as they are." And I sit among you today.'

"And here, the mayor began to tear. Anyway, he held his shirt cuff up to his eyes. And then he said, 'My momma's gone now. But gentlemen: I don't believe that *anyone's* momma should have to wait more than twenty minutes in the cold, snow, and peril of the streets to catch a bus. *Do you?'* "

Sunny rocked back on his feet, to suggest pinstriped commissioners getting thrown back in their plush leather chairs. When he resumed speaking, it was in his own softer soprano.

"A few days later, we met about something else. I suddenly remembered—I said to him, 'Wait, Mr. Mayor. I thought your mother left home when you were nine. I thought your aunt raised you. The schoolteacher.' The mayor lifted his eyebrows and asked, 'Where'd you hear that?' I said, 'From *you*. It's what *you* told a hearing of the state Children and Family Services department.' "

"And the mayor looked up from his desk and said,"—and here Sunny coated his voice with gravel again—" 'A good memory can be a curse, Sunny. You'll find my mother did a number of things in this city of boundless opportunities. I think the Chinatown Civic Association believes she worked a cart at the Maxwell Street Market. I believe the governors of the Chicago Board of Trade have the definite impression that she hauled carcasses in a packing plant. I believe I even left the president of Ukraine with the definite notion that she may have hailed from Kirovograd. I don't know a blessed thing about my mother, Sunny. But thanks to me, she has had a valuable career in public service.' "

Flabbergasted laughter burst out in the chamber, like spray from a fractured water pipe. Sunny let it run. He turned his chin down, almost prayerfully. But quiet was quickly reasserted as aldermen reminded themselves to be solemn.

"That voice," Sunny concluded. "That wit. Such fun. The utter audacity. His loss is incalculable.

"I am informed by the corporation counsel," he moved on with just the slightest hastening, "that as presiding officer, I have the privilege of offering legislation. I ask the council to suspend the rules to immediately approve a commission to investigate the mayor's death and any and all related issues."

Sunny saw Linas Slavinskas sit forward suddenly with unflustered attention, John Wu release a slow, subtle smile, and Vera Barrow hunch below the collar of her black suit as Sunny drew another index card from his pocket.

"I propose that the commission be chaired by Peter Mansfield, the distinguished professor of international law from DePaul. His co-chair will be U.S. District Judge Emmett Sullivan. The other members will be Dr. Ellen Watkins, the president of Malcolm X College; Professor Carlos Nieto of the Northwestern Law School; and Paul Freeman, a former federal prosecutor." Sunny hesitated as he contemplated adding, "whom you may remember from prosecuting several members of this council," but decided to go on before the name could register too deeply. "He is now a partner at Altgeld, Ogilvie, and Stevenson. I would suggest that this commission receive a million dollars to begin their inquiry immediately and deliver a preliminary report—six months from today."

"I move for immediate consideration, " Vera called from the first row before a chorus of confused, sputtering voices began to shoot up from the floor. Sunny brought the heel of his hand smack down onto the lectern to declare, "Evidently a sufficient number. I hear a motion to adjourn," and Sgt. McNulty and three uniforms stood at Sunny's arms as he left the rostrum and dumbfounded aldermen scrambled to their feet, shouting and waving for recognition like shipwrecks.

He slipped out to meet Peter Mansfield for lunch at Fannie's on Jefferson, just before they closed at three. Surgically bright lights screamed down over steam tables groaning with ruddy rumps of smoked meats, peppery and dripping. The men and women in white smocks behind the counter took care of Sunny—a couple were Guatemalans from the 48th, and a couple more lived in Adam Wojcik's 45th, but were from Kerela—and winked as they put a chicken pot pie on his tray, the top crust blistered with crisp brown bubbles. They carved corned beef thin enough to read baseball scores through the slice, but piled it high and dredged his onion roll in the warm drippings, softening the white bread into a kind of oniony cake.

"I like this place," said Peter Mansfield, who flicked the four glistening strips of crisp bacon off of his spinach salad as if they were caravans of ants. "It's so authentic."

"As coronary blockage," Sunny agreed. He had a superfluously dietetic celery tonic fizzing alongside. They sat at a plastic table scoured by spills of sugar, salt, and the scrapes of trays. Sgt. McNulty pulled up just behind them. Two uniforms joined him, never so much as unbuttoning the top button on their blue leather service jackets. Sunny's security detail looked about as inconspicuous as rhinos in a fragrance shop.

"Ellen Watkins is a fruitcake," Peter announced. "She sees a horse and calls it a zebra—everything is black and white."

"Well, if you're in a zoo . . ." said Sunny.

"And Carlos Nieto is a Republican."

"So was Lincoln. So is half the country. Please, Peter, you've played kneesies with Yasser Arafat and written constitutions for war criminals."

"Well they're not *Republicans* . . . Judge Sullivan isn't even in Chicago."

"Technology is amazing these days," Sunny told him. "It's like you're in the same room. Teleconference with Ellen Watkins, if it helps you get along. You know Paul Freeman?"

Peter Mansfield leaned forward and muttered from behind the heel of his hand.

"He sold dope to me in law school."

"So you already have a professional relationship."

Sunny parted the crust of his pie with a fork; a blast of steam shot up, then an ooze of peas, carrots, and pearl onions.

"Two blacks, a Hispanic, two whites," Peter totaled it aloud. "A woman, a Jew, a Cuban, a Republican. I don't think I've made out a grocery list quite so quickly."

"Your name helped," Sunny conceded. "I prefer to see it as a host of independent talents led by an intrepid scholar who owes nothing to the entrenched powers in this city."

"Except to wife," said Peter Mansfield, the boyish forelock he sprayed into place over his left eye bobbing as they both laughed.

"We all owe someone," Sunny told him. Peter Mansfield put just enough blue cheese dressing into a spoon to cover the bristles of a toothbrush and combed it through his salad.

"Okay," he announced. "First and last time I'll bring this up, but . . ." Peter set aside the salt, shook a jolt of pepper onto his salad, and met Sunny's eyes with his own.

"Are you fucking me?"

Sunny sensed that a quip—"Thanks, Peter, but I have a busy afternoon"—would not suffice and was not deserved. He finally just reminded him, "If you fell on your face, it wouldn't do me much good."

"That schedule you pulled out of your ass today—we would issue our preliminary report just as the campaign begins."

"Deadlines focus the mind."

"What if we're both running?" Peter asked.

"*We* won't be," stressed Sunny.

"You've decided not to?"

"I don't know. But even if I do, both of us won't last six months. In four or five, I won't have enough money, or you won't have enough support. I hope your advisors have told you as much. At those prices . . ."

Peter Mansfield ran his fork through a spinach leaf as he fidgeted against whatever was the stickiness in the well of his orange plastic seat.

"Is that what the mayor figured out?" he asked finally.

"We'll never know."

"He wanted us both to run," said Peter. "I don't know if he wanted either of us to win. He would have liked having me out of town." Peter Mansfield ducked his head slightly to halt a trickle of vinaigrette threatening his chin. "He would have *loved* having Dolores out of town. But he would have missed you. He loved you, Alderman Roopini. Surely you knew that."

"We were useful to each other," said Sunny.

"That's not love? He wanted to set you up—the right way—after . . ."

"After what happened," Sunny finished the sentence with his own genteelism.

"Introduce you to people who could help you," Peter Mansfield ventured a few words on. "Make you comfortable when you need it most."

Sunny used his fingers to pluck a splinter of coppery crust from the rim of the pie tin and a black curl of onion from the crust of his corned beef.

"With two daughters," he said. "I'm already rich in all the things that count," and the two of them laughed so heartily and unexpectedly that Sgt. McNulty sat upright and alert at the kaboom of cackling.

Sunny caught himself before he could advise Peter Mansfield that he might discover in politics that you sometimes laughed more with your opponents than your supporters. Your opponents didn't harbor so many noble expectations.

A message in Rula's voice waited for Sunny when he returned to his office at the Hall. Eldad had gone home to sleep and to change more than his earring. Sgt. McNulty and the uniforms affected to seem distracted as they minutely examined Sunny's rampart of pictures, citations, and plaques, and Sunny listened to her message.

"It's us," said Rula. Her voice struck a pose; she must have had an audience. "We're fine, too. Glad to know you are. Wow. Some day it sounds like. Bloody hell. We're here. Oscar has made us faloodas"—a rose-flavored ice cream drink—"and badam kheers." Ground almonds swooshed with milk and saffron. "Muriel and Virginie"—wild, pretty friends of the girls; the sort of girls, with deep Brazil nut eyes and untamed swells of hair, who Sunny used to dream of as a teenager and now dreaded as a father—"found the badam kheers a little heavy. We're off. Catch you later," she rang off.

Sunny was about to leave his own message (*Tell Muriel and Virginie I think their ankles are a little thick* occurred to Sunny) when the police chief came in with a heavy tread to explain how it was that Daryl Lloyd had managed to take a gun onto the City Council floor and hold it above his head like the Stanley Cup.

"That would seem to be the question," Sunny agreed.

Chief Martinez had pushed his blue cap back by the black-and-yellow checkerboard pattern across its brim and gave a slight tug to the clip of his tie.

"Shortly after two last night, I phoned Sam Stanky. You know him?"

Sunny wiggled his right hand to signal minimal recognition.

"Chief engineer at the Hall?"

"And by the way," Chief Martinez agreed with a nod, "one of Alderman Agras's best precinct captains."

"He wouldn't hire a bad one."

City Hall's day-to-day operations came under Arty's Budget and Government Operations Committee.

"I told Sam there would be a special council session at ten," said Chief Martinez. "so he should get the metal detectors we always set up in place A-S-A-P."

"Which means?"

Sunny let the chief sit back and begin to thrum the fingers of his right hand over a couple of his brass buttons.

"As soon as his crew chief could get in from Oriole Park," the chief said. "Which he couldn't until seven because he had to wait until his wife got home from her shift at Good Samaritan a little after six. Which was fine with Sam because to call in the crews to set up the metal detectors any earlier—they're not pop-up toasters, after all— would mean four hours overtime for twelve people. They're all Local One of the Service Employees Union. Now Sam runs a precinct for Arty, of course. But a couple of the guys on the crew—one is a woman—were recommended by Alderman Suarez's Hispano-American Citizens Action Foundation. Three are members of Alderman Sparrow's Jesse Owens Athletic League."

"Citizen participation is the foundation of democracy," Sunny reminded him.

"Sam says that his overtime budget is already shot to hell from December. He had to have crews clean up after Alderman Suarez's Yuletide party, Alderman Siegel's Festival of Lights, Alderman Sparrow's Kwanzaa party, and Alderman Walker's Wicca festival."

(Sunny especially enjoyed Harry Walker's gatherings: White candles dripped, half-wheels of chalky brie cheese oozed over black plastic plates, and boxes of astringent white wine warmed next to a radiator while Harry, with his white Neptune's whiskers, implored some demiurge, "The dark caresses me like a mother's womb. I am at peace with the wicked world. The Sun King is born! The Sun King is born!")

Sunny also knew, as Chief Martinez had to, that Arty devised the munificent overtime payments of December to steer a bonus to City Hall maintenance workers. They kept the Hall immaculate (Sunny remembered the mayor of Philadelphia once telling the mayor, "I had a pelvic laparoscopy at the Einstein last year, and the *operating room* wasn't as spotless as your stairwells!") and besides: as Arty put it, "Why should only *corporate magnets* get Christmas bonuses?"

Chief Martinez rolled his eyes and tugged on both ends of his mustache.

"So the metal detectors weren't up until nine. Alderman Lloyd came in through the Finance Committee conference room at about eight-forty."

Sunny winced at this and stamped one of his brown brogues against the carpet as Chief Martinez continued.

"I said, 'Sam, Sam! A special session! The mayor was dead! Why didn't—' and Sam stopped me cold. 'Chief, I had to have twelve people work overtime to dismantle the goddamn detectors today after Daryl's little stunt. Who's going to pay for all that overtime? Are you?' "

They laughed. Raspy, coughing, smoky-throat, wipe-your-chin bellows from two men who were sixteen hours into a day on two hours of sleep. Their neck muscles stung when they held up their heads.

"It's been my experience, Alderman," Chief Martinez finally said, "that sometimes your wiliest adversary isn't Al-Qaeda or La Cosa Nostra. It's Sam Stanky."

The police chief sighed and went on to detail more quietly that both Frank Conklin and Mrs. Bacon had been cleared of suspicion. They had tossed Quattro's "like a Caesar salad," as the chief put it, and found nothing of consequence. As to Collins Jenkins—they were still pulling out threads.

"He kept a lot of secrets."

"So do priests."

"A love-struck e-mail—a lunch proposition—can all mean something else when it comes from the mayor's right hand."

The chief sat forward to stand up from his chair, but stopped with his hands still on his knees.

"Do you want my resignation?" he asked. Sunny paused so that he could be seen pondering it openly.

"No," he said finally. "But I wouldn't suggest that you wait until the next mayor asks—whoever she is. You'd be impossible to replace now, but impossible to keep after Monday. I know it's not fair. You've caught people before they could blow up Sears Tower or sprinkle cyanide pellets in the Clark and Division subway. Then something ridiculous happens. A pizza. A stunt. I'm, sorry, Matt. You're a good man and a fine policeman. But politics . . ."

"She'll have it," Chief Martinez said instantly. "I'm as angry as anyone. I believe in taking responsibility."

Sunny cast an eye over to the doorway, where he could see Sgt. McNulty's elbow just inside the frame.

"You know, I've heard—just today, in fact—that they've been searching for a top-drawer security executive over at the Yello Corporation," Sunny said as if some needling, nagging thought had just surfaced. The company was building a world headquarters on South Dearborn. "Your name came up."

"My name has been thrown around a lot today."

"Some damn outpost in the Middle East," Sunny went on imperturbably. "The position would pay—I don't know—three times what a man can make in public service. And you never have to deal with aldermen."

"Glittering incentives," the chief agreed. "Must be Iraq."

"Dubai, actually. That place is sizzling, you know. Amazing things going up each day. They're building five hundred skyscrapers, including one underwater."

"I'm an air-breathing mammal," said the police chief.

"You know, it's possible that your name could be linked to that search."

"A-S-A-P," Chief Martinez agreed. "Which means . . ."

"I might know someone who could make a call to those two young genius brothers who run Yello," Sunny suggested. "You owe it to yourself, Matt. To your family. Corporations are crazy, Matt. Bonuses, housing, travel—the more you make, the more freebies. And if their interest gets into the news, you'll hear from other places, too."

Chief Martinez got onto his feet, clapping his heavy checkered superintendent's cap against a leg.

"I'll keep you informed, Alderman."

"You deserve it, Matt," and as the police chief began to leave, he turned around and spoke over the braid on his shoulder.

"Before I forget. Richard J. The cat. He's been found. Months ago, Collins gave him to Terrill Layne, who works in Human Services. He's fine."

"Well there's a puff of good news," said Sunny. "Maybe events are finally moving our way."

Then Claudia McCarthy came in, clenching sheaves of paper against her chest, waggling a small folded sheet from her fingers.

"Here's where the U.S. attorney wants to meet," she said. "They pulled around a car for you."

Sunny stared at the unfamiliar address, as if something more recognizable must surely swim into focus.

"Of all places," he began.

"Maybe he figures no one will see you there."

"Alderman Slavinskas told me once that he takes his lunch dates to the Drake. He said, 'If someone sees me in the lobby at the Drake, they think I'm meeting with Donald Trump. If they see me at Mums-the-Word Motel on West Jackson, they call the papers.' "

Claudia McCarthy put a folder against her mouth as he laughed.

"I think he invited me to lunch at the Palmer House." She held up the thicket of papers. "These are bills," she explained. "All passed by the council. You sign them. They don't even say 'interim acting mayor.' "

Sunny found himself unconsciously smoothing his tie with his little finger, pulling up the knot, and inconspicuously crossing his brown suede shoes below his table.

"Shouldn't they wait for the new mayor?"

"Law says they have to be signed before the next council session, which is now Monday," Claudia explained. "And then there's a whole slew of citations that have to be read at funerals or banquets this weekend."

She ran a gently flaking red nail over the edges of thick paper and stiff card stock.

" 'Citations honoring Chicago Firefighters Kevin Wirtz, Mike Uczen, Michael Agostinelli, and Brian Kehoe. Congratulations to Jeanne Reckitt, Pat Biernat, Carl Gies, and Richard Sachaj for Performance Plus Teacher Awards.' " Claudia vocalized the titles without emphasis, as if reading off the spines of abandoned books on a shelf. " 'Approval of property at 255 N. California as Class 6b and eligible for Cook County Tax Incentives.'

"Alderman Slavinskas' resolution," she explained, with the tinge of a smile.

"We voted on all these?"

"Monday," Claudia answered without lifting her head. " 'Congratulations to Adrian Martinez and Jose DeDiego Community Academy on winning Manuel Flores Excellence in Reading and Writing Award. Approval of contract with Earth First LLC for recycling services. Tribute to late United States Marine Corps Sergeant Edward Davis.' "

"Ohmigod, where?" asked Sunny.

Claudia McCarthy seemed puzzled for an instant, then moved her eyes over the papers.

"Henderson, North Carolina," she said with some relief. "He was retired. 'Tribute to late Honorable Ruth Gruber,' " she continued. "Congratulations to Reverend Jeremiah Boland on Silver Jubilee Anniversary of ordination. Congratulations to Shirley Forte on retirement from Gunsaulus Scholastic Academy.' "

"Do I need a special pen?" asked Sunny. "Sealing wax?"

"Any pen. A crayon."

"I suppose it's the one thing I'll do. Can I take them in the car?"

"They're not classified," said Claudia, evening the edges in the folder with her fingers and gently putting the pages in front of Sunny. "The mayor used to hand them back with splotches of clam sauce."

Sunny began to get out of his chair but stopped, brought down as much by his own exhaustion as with the thought in front of him.

"My god, Claudia, this is a helluva day for you, too. Thank you."

Claudia opened her mouth to speak, and then seemed to hesitate about bringing something out in words. She had crossed her legs, and the gray woolen tights she had pulled on in haste at two in the morning puckered at her knees, like small frowns.

"Mr. Roopini," she said and held up for a moment. "Do you think any of the rumors about the mayor are true?"

Sunny inclined his head.

"That he had AIDS," Claudia explained. "That Mr. Jenkins helped the mayor die the way he wanted to go—in his office. Then Collins killed himself to keep the secret. Or because he couldn't live with the secret."

"I guess I've been pretty isolated today," he told her. "Missed out on all these news flashes."

"Alderman Rodriguez says that south side gangbangers and international terrorists killed the mayor because the Chicago police shut down their drug markets. Collins helped them, to make the police look bad before their next contract came up, then killed himself."

"Well, that ties it all up. But what about the Jews?"

"Left out again, I guess," and they both smiled. Claudia's ex-husband was McCarthy, who had worked in the corporation counsel's office. Sunny knew that Claudia had been born a Hauser in the 49th Ward.

"Did the mayor hoard millions of dollars in Anguilla?"

"A plush retreat guarded by alligators and Dobermans? If so, he never saw it," said Sunny. "The mayor said atmospheric pressure got to him outside the city limits. If he had a hidden treasure, he never used it to so much as buy a wristwatch that didn't come from a drugstore."

Claudia ran a hand through tines of dark hair that had fallen over her forehead.

"*Did* he have AIDS?" she asked with sudden whispered hoarseness. "I heard that from a friend who had a friend who saw the mayor a couple of years ago."

"Not even syphilis," said Sunny. "Not even diaper rash."

"I heard that he had Tourette's. Specialists worked with him to say 'antediluvian' when he meant something . . . more colorful."

"Well, the treatment was sure incomplete," Sunny said. "The best-known man in town and the most mysterious. People filled in the blanks with the mayor, Claudia. I guess I did, too."

Sunny sat back, his chair creaking like a twig snapping in the vacant hallways. He began to punch in Rula's number on the blue face of his phone. He had gotten through 7-7-3 when Claudia asked, "Alderman, I know that Ms. Fite"—the city's commissioner of special events—"is handling the mayor's memorial. But I wonder if someone really close to him shouldn't be involved, too."

Sunny halted his fingers.

"I thought of Alderman Barrow, but . . ."

"She's busy."

Sunny stopped to think of people who were close to the mayor; he ran out of names within a moment. Then he brightened.

"Do you have a home number for Mrs. Bacon?"

He pressed in the rest of Mrs. Bacon's number, digit by digit, as Claudia McCarthy inscribed it on the edge of the folded sheet of paper.

Brooks Whetstone, the U.S. Attorney for the Northern District of Illinois, sat in a blue vinyl booth behind lane 23 at the Star of the Nile Bowling Lanes on Western Avenue, a blue and red striped tie, a button-down white shirt, unclasped black snow boots, and a tweed jacket. A thread snaked out of his lapel, as if charmed out by a flute. When Brooks stood up, reached out to Sunny and smiled, his teeth shone like a row of runway lights.

Each afternoon, the lanes declared Cosmic Time. All overhead lights were extinguished or dimmed; ultraviolet lights were snapped on. Balls thumped in the dark center of lanes lit in screaming lime green. Luminescent violet-white pins clattered, music videos thumped like baritone jackhammers. Clusters of balls glowed in electric Jell-o colors of orange, green, yellow, and grape. Sunny looked down at his own extended hand to see his cuff buttons aglow, then his shirt buttons, then the stitching in his jacket, as if his own skeleton had been plugged into a wall socket.

"I recognize you from the news," Sunny told him.

"Same," said Brooks Whetstone. "And your trustworthy protector. He's *really* famous." Sgt. McNulty had taken up a position alongside the glass entryway, just below a line of signs about league nights, mixed teams, and Ball, Bag, and Shoe Night.

"Do you conduct a lot of business here?"

"You never run into a lawyer or a reporter," the U.S. Attorney explained, and pointed to red letters glowing on a sign overhead: WI-FI INTERNET ACCESS.

"Plus that."

The music videos seemed to be of all varieties, and as Sunny took his seat in the booth, Indian women on the screens overhead spun, swiveled, and shook sultry bare shoulders.

"Do you have any idea—"

"I know about a hundred words of Hindi," Sunny volunteered. "I can tell you that they're not ordering onion pakodas."

Sunny and Brooks Whetstone amiably established that they had never met. The U.S. Attorney usually met politicians only in depositions and courtrooms and politely declined invitations to those very civic events—the Polish Day Parade, Cinco de Mayo, the Gospel Music Festival, or lunch with the Reverend Jackson—that politicians coveted.

Under normal light, Brooks Whetstone was shampoo-ad handsome, with sandy hair, silvering gently and curling behind his neck. He sometimes went two or three days without shaving, raising a field of coppery thistles across his chin that, together with his lengthening hair, left a perpetual suggestion of windblown daring.

Brooks was simply driven: unmarried, unmated, and indifferent to all but the law and, occasionally, baseball. He often slept in his office, showering at the New City YMCA, dragging a plastic razor across his chin for five shaves, then not making the time to buy another and lacking the inclination to dispatch a staff member. To protect his appearance for courtrooms and press conferences, every few weeks Brooks's staff would schedule an appointment away from their offices. When he had buckled himself into the rear seat of his official sedan, reminded his driver to observe all speed and parking laws, and not to use his cell phone without an approved headset, his staff would exhale as he buried his nose in an expanding file, and deliver him into a barber's chair.

Illinois's Republican senator had recruited Brooks Whetstone. He believed that an honest, aggressive prosecutor could clean up corruption and, in the bargain, bedevil the mayor's Democratic organization with indictments, prosecutions, and rumors of indictments. Brooks had an outstanding record with the U.S. Attorney in San Francisco, prosecuting the leaders of the Joe Boys Chinese street gang in Richmond, Sunset, and Daly City. (Brooks was known as Butt Boy among San Quentin's residents) His father, a nominal Republican, was a Marin County board supervisor.

Brooks kept his own political convictions concealed. Not just from his staff, but from his mother, father, sister, and old girlfriends, who said that he probably lifted his eyes from a brief a week after they left and wondered where they had gone. No Marin or Stanford classmate, or any officemate, could recall Brooks, who was now forty-four, ever uttering an opinion about abortion, gun control, gay marriage, medical marijuana, or flag burning. Some wondered if he had convictions or merely sought them for others.

Brooks had inscrutable allegiances even in baseball. One of his assistants asked, as he followed a Cub game droning in the late afternoon, "If you don't mind my asking, chief, are you a Giants fan or an A's fan? Any feeling for our long-suffering Cubbies? Or what about—" Brooks halted her with a glance that could have backed up traffic.

"I root for whoever follows the rules," he told her.

Yet Brooks Whetstone wanted to run for office someday. He had just enough experience in politics to believe he could do better. He had a reputation to spend and access to funds from his family and old school ties. But Brooks's ambitions resided in California, safely removed from those of the senator who had recommended him and from the repercussions of his trials. A prosecutor could make his reputation by sending Chicago Democrats and their donors to jail, but he would find it hard to raise money to support his own run in the same state.

As the mayor once said, "The son of a bitch can't poison the well and expect anyone here to buy him a drink."

A country video began to play—Sunny had an impression of guitars, cars, and longing—as Brooks Whetstone leaned in to speak over the din.

"I've been here just about three years," he began. "And I've really gotten very fond of the city. I guess we sometimes think of this as flyover country—landlocked and dreary. But the lake is dazzling. Music, theater. And the politics, I don't have to tell you, is high drama indeed."

"I'll tell everyone down at the Hall, 'Good show,' " said Sunny.

"I know you and the council have an important job to do over these next few days. I admire what *you* did today—talk about drama."

He paused as if for Sunny to refuse or accept a compliment, but Sunny merely nodded up down, and then sideways—*that maddening Indian rain dance*, his daughters called it—and knitted his forehead. Brooks Whetstone went on.

"Architects can plant vines," he said. "Politicians appoint commissions. A group that distinguished might help you keep a lid on silly speculation. It must be difficult when emotions run high. I don't know if what I have to tell you has any bearing. The mayor's death comes at a time when we were taking a look at several things. Let me put it that way."

Brooks sat back and held his hands a foot apart, as if trying to fathom what would fit into a travel bag.

"You know, alderman, I have my side of the street to work. But I knew the mayor a little. Charming, intelligent. Resourceful. I just wish that he hadn't been such a"—he hesitated over what word to load, only hours after his death—"*rascal*," he said finally, and Sunny had to admire the choice. *Rascal* cast the mayor as a tomcat, innocent to resist his own mischievous nature.

"That's the nicest thing I've heard even his friends call him," remarked Sunny, and the prosecutor smiled.

"He certainly helped his friends," said Brooks Whetstone.

"He should have helped his enemies?"

"The law is clear, alderman. Jobs go to the people who are most qualified."

"I suppose I'd be comfortable with that, too," Sunny replied. "If I had gone to Stanford Law School."

The U.S. Attorney smiled. The zest of contention had led him into law, and Brooks encouraged his subordinates to dispute him. It's an adversarial system, he reminded them; we have to prepare for attack from any quarter. But when junior lawyers did so, their deference—"If I may reluctantly point out, chief . . ."—could be cloying, as diverting as throwing an old tennis ball against a garage wall.

"You and I will always disagree about this, alderman," he told Sunny. "History moves on, too, you know. The days are past when the politicians opened bathhouses for the unwashed. People have rights and expectations now. They don't have to depend on"—he hesitated again, probably choosing not to personalize the sentence for Sunny— "*anyone* for favors."

"All the people hired have to work hard. It's no favor," Sunny replied. "Look around. You ever seen a city better run than this one?"

"No," said Brooks, which was true. "Which is why a man in my position wants to understand how you manage it. So last summer—when your committee gave the Parks Department authorization to hire— what was it—a dozen new employees to pick up litter in the parks and sweep leaves? They were all the most qualified?"

"Most qualified to spear tin cans, spent condoms, and paper cups from the grass?" Sunny asked almost wearily. "Let's just say we don't see a lot of resumes from Stanford men. It's the job you try to get when you can't get any other, shit-shoveling included. So we post the job, and say, 'First come, first hired.'

"And then you make sure the people you want to hire are lined up by six a.m.—before anyone else can get there?" Brooks remembered at the last instant to lift his voice into a question.

"We reward initiative," said Sunny. "They work hard, and they're accountable."

"Especially to put up posters during election campaigns." Brooks made no effort here to leave the impression of a question, but Sunny was prepared.

"We don't discourage citizen participation, if that's what you mean."

Brooks Whetstone smiled, as if turning the page of a treasured book to a favorite section.

"You have a campaign fund. . . ." he began.

"Of course. I'm a politician. Not a rich one. I can't just have my father-in-law write a check."

"I don't need a local phrase book to translate that," said Brooks. "Your fund has—"

"Something like two hundred forty-five thousand dollars. We declare it to the dime."

"A lot of money to run for alderman."

"And not enough to buy a broom closet on Lake Shore Drive," Sunny answered and stopped. It was the equivalent of declining to take a new card in a game of chance.

"Those prices are crazy," the U.S. Attorney agreed. "You know, alderman, we have people go over the quarterly campaign reports. The way the CIA goes over satellite photos."

"Then I'm sure you found nothing out of order."

"Absolutely not. *Ab-so-lutely not*," Brooks emphasized, shaking his head as if to empty it of all suspicion. "But a few interesting items. Do you know Avi Cohen for instance?"

Sunny wrinkled his forehead, arched his brows, and held his chin in a frown, as if he'd been asked about an old, abstruse German philosopher.

"The name . . ."

"He's twelve," Brooks explained helpfully. "Seventh grader at the Ogden School. Imagine—deposing a twelve-year-old. He's so bright, knows all fifty state capitals, though he sometimes forgets Columbia."

"South Carolina."

"Not Missouri?"

"That's Jefferson City," Sunny told him, a bit too proudly. "A common mistake. But you remember such things when you have to take a citizenship test, instead of taking it for granted."

"Avi gave seven hundred fifty dollars to your campaign," Brooks informed him.

"He sounds like a splendid young man."

"Do you know Billy Leavitt?"

"Politicians know lots of people."

"Billy is thirteen. He's a crossing guard at Morgan Park Academy. He gave seven hundred fifty dollars too."

"Do you know what some thirteen-year-olds spend on baseball cards?" Sunny asked, but Brooks Whetstone had already proceeded.

"And there's a sixth-grade big spender named Joy Wassell on your donors list. She's in accelerated math at Francis Parker. Geometric probability and theoretical and experimental probabilities—amazing what they teach youngsters these days. She gave seven hundred fifty dollars."

"And to think," said Sunny. "That's seven hundred fifty dollars she could have spent for drugs on the playground."

"Do your young contributors get to bring you in for show and tell?" asked Brooks Whetstone, and both men sat back a few inches from the edge of the small tan table between them, glad to laugh.

"Every campaign wants the youth vote," said Sunny. When Brooks continued, his tone had grown softer and less pointed, as if he were speaking distractedly about the fine print in a car rental contract.

"So if Billy Leavitt gives you seven hundred fifty dollars, his mother gives you seven hundred fifty dollars, and his father, David— don't want to forget him, he owns Leavitt Tube—"

"Him I know," Sunny interjected.

"—gives you a thousand dollar contribution, suddenly the Leavitt family has given you twenty-five hundred dollars. Which is above the legal limit for individual giving to a congressional campaign."

"But eminently legal for three members of a family," Sunny pointed out.

"Still, if that kind of thing got into the papers . . ."

"Yes, I might have to volunteer to give it back," Sunny said with a show of indifference. "Leaving my campaign fund with what—two hundred forty-five thousand dollars? People give money in their children's names to build libraries and museums. You act like making a political contribution turns kids into child soldiers," said Sunny. "Bloody hell," he said, fighting a smile—he must tell Rita and Rula that their argot had become infectious.

"It violates the spirit of the law," Brooks pronounced slowly.

"I didn't know you could prosecute spirits," Sunny said. "It must be difficult to keep handcuffs on them." He began to stand, suddenly thirsty, to signal a server, his hands liquid and wobbly.

"You put roadblocks up on a highway," he told Brooks Whetstone from his feet, "and you can't blame people for finding side streets. Do you want anything? To drink," he stressed.

A young woman in glowing blue-white pants came over with a tray, the blond highlights in her pigtails flashing light like foam in a waterfall. Brooks ordered a Diet Dr Pepper. Sunny would have preferred a beer—he had been up a long time, and all signs indicated it was a specialty of the house—but he was not about to order one in front of the U.S. Attorney; so he merely seconded the motion. When their waxed cups had been thumped down in front of them, Brooks inclined his toward Sunny so that their plastic lids glanced against each other.

"To the mayor," said the U.S. Attorney. "To the city. And good luck over these next few days." They sucked at their straws briefly, bubbles gurgling.

"Alright then," Brooks asked finally. "A strictly social question. Do you smoke cigars?"

Sunny permitted himself to look annoyed, put upon, and amazed.

"As far as I know, you can still light up in the middle of Montana at three a.m.," he said, then added, "Only every time the Sox or Cubs win the World Series."

Brooks Whetstone chose to share Sunny's chuckle.

"I'll mark that as 'rarely.' You have friends—two ladies—who run the Love Muffin."

"Marti and Terri Gieger-Soriani."

"Sisters?" asked Brooks. Marti was dark-haired, round-faced, cream-complexioned, and decisively Irish. Terri had sienna-reddish hair and an oblong face, freckled and markedly Italian. Sunny didn't care for Brooks's profession of blank-faced naiveté.

"Halsted Street marriage has become the term. They're a few blocks down from my ward office on Broadway. They've opened an adjoining restaurant next door, too, called Martina Serves. If you ever want a good marinated tempeh with broccoli rabe. If that's possible."

Brooks Whetstone pursed his lips into a sour smile.

"They applied for a liquor license last year."

Sunny smiled back in recollection.

"And yes, there was a problem. They rented a storefront that used to be Li Kim's Marmara Sea Diner. Li never served alcohol. Marti and Terri wanted to. But the door of the restaurant turns out to be within ninety-four feet of the Yeshiva Anshe Lwow. It's against state law to serve liquor within a hundred feet of a house of worship. So they came to me. Rabbi Zemel at the yeshiva didn't mind the restaurant. Marti and Terri keep him in pumpkin carob chip muffins. 'Hell,' he said, 'all those tough girls in leather jackets keep the neighborhood safe.' I told them all, 'What a farce—a law nobody wants for a problem that doesn't exist. In the old days, a couple hundred dollars in a handshake would have made everybody happy.' Yes, I said that. Maybe you've heard; I'm known for my disarming wit. So we drafted a special bill to exempt the space from 4801 to 4819 on Broadway from that provision of the liquor laws. It was for everyone's benefit. It's what an alderman should do."

"They were grateful?" asked Brooks

"They care about their community."

"A thousand dollars' worth?"

"They usually care the legally maximum amount. I accept it humbly. I like to think I'm an effective representative of their interests. Theirs and a lot of other people's."

"Indubitably," said Brooks, turning his head down as if in contrition and shaking it from side to side. "Did they express their gratitude in any other way?"

"They run a *muffin shop*," said Sunny, more sharply. "A bakery and a forty-seat restaurant. Do you think that's a fast track to riches? It's month-to-month. It's five a.m. to eleven p.m. *I know*. Most of their money is tied up in organic flour, for goodness sakes. They always have dried dough under their fingernails. They have to worry about mice eating the inventory. Do you think they have a private plane on call to whisk a raft of politicians away for a weekend of don't-ask-don't-tell debauchery at the Kentucky Derby? Sorry. That's your Stanford mates."

But the U.S. Attorney, with a comic gift that surprised Sunny, held a phantom smoke in the crooked fingers of his right hand, and pretended to puff, puff, puff. Sunny had to laugh.

"I believe they gave me a box of cigars," he said finally. "Cohibas, marked *authentico Cubano*, to anticipate your next question. The Lanceros, seven and a half inches. Should I have made a citizen's arrest?"

"A box of Cohibas must cost. Certainly above the fifty dollar limitation for gifts to a public official."

"I suppose," said Sunny. "*If* they were *authentico*. The streets are awash with counterfeits. A scandal. The U.S. Attorney's office should look into that. But alas, it would be hard to locate the evidence in this case. It's all ashes by now."

Sunny smiled and crooked his own fingers as if to clasp a Lancero and cupped his mouth to blow a smoke ring across the table. Brooks Whetstone's face stayed impassive, but he quietly raised a hand and waggled it twice, to wave away imaginary vapors.

"Justice is served," the U.S. Attorney announced, and waved his hand a few more times. Both men laughed. Five young men on the video screens approached one another with chains and bats, but Brooks Whetstone looked across the table to find Sunny's face again.

"Look, this is not an official inquiry. It's just to let a couple of public officials do their jobs. You tell me now that you carried Mohammed Atta's bags to the plane, or helped Charles Manson write Helter Skelter on the wall, and it doesn't matter. Free pass. Gift certificate. I'm just trying to learn."

"My daughters don't think I have much to teach them," said Sunny. "I don't know what interests you." The back of his neck felt his muscles becoming dense and mulish around his shoulders. "Isn't it about time for you to tell me something?"

"I have. A lot of people would like the kind of peek at their credit report I've given you."

"Something I don't *know*," said Sunny with real heat. "Something to convince me that I need to be here, playing badminton with you, rather than doing the million and one things I have to do to mislead the public as acting interim mayor. Or trying to manage a pathetic five-minute conversation with my daughters."

"How did the Yello Corporation happen to make their headquarters here?" Brooks asked suddenly. Sunny took a short, loud draw from his waxed cup, gurgled his displeasure, and twitched his brown suede brogues below the table as he prepared to stand up.

"We have five hundred major corporate headquarters. Why are any of them here? Location, location, location. The city sparkles. It runs like a Rolex."

"A gold Rolex for some," said Brooks, and Sunny decided not to overlook the interjection.

"Yes," he said evenly. "And like mere stainless steel for many others. And cheap crap that breaks down for others. But this city *works*. The streets are clean, crime is down, the schools are getting good, the culture is terrific. The food is fantastic. No earthquakes, no hurricanes, and city workers aren't always on strike, like in Mumbai or Paris." He smiled as automatically as a red light on a vending machine. "The elected officials are accessible and caring. Hell, Mr. Whetstone, you live here. Why would anyone put their headquarters anywhere else?"

Yello was an Internet company that had been founded, as casually as a lemonade stand in the legend, by the Nygaard brothers, Ben and Barry, in their upstairs bedroom in Marquette, Michigan. They had made millions, taken their company public, and become billionaires.

Yello was founded on the idea that people in separate dots of light scattered over the universe could work in effortlessly close connection through Yello technology. The brothers believed that nothing would signify their success so dramatically as a soaring world headquarters to bring their far-flung work force together under the same solar-powered roof. Eighteen-hour days would be fueled by coffee, candy bars, and herbal diet pills, while workers could avail themselves of on-site day-care centers, day spas, alcohol, drug, and domestic relations counselors, dentists, eye doctors, basketball courts, ballet studios, chess lounges, chiropractors, yoga studios, and cafeterias serving organic produce grown within a two-hour drive.

Yello's lawyers and lobbyists had deployed around the country to solicit bids. New York, San Francisco, Seattle, Denver, San Antonio, Newark, and St. Petersburg all made offers. (Newark's proposition was generous, but the brothers said that they did not make billions to build their headquarters in New Jersey; they hoped only that New York would match it).

"I asked for a speech," Brooks Whetstone told Sunny. "Yours was good. But a man in my business—yours too, for that matter—looks for mutually fulfilling relationships. Were any promises made? Them to you, you to them?"

"Are you six years old?" Sunny asked. "Of course. It was *courtship*," he said. "Preening, fanning feathers, drones dancing for the queen. They promised to bring billions of dollars and thousands of jobs to the south Loop. We promised not to take too much of it away in taxes for the first ten years. So did every other city. Everything else was candy and flowers."

Sunny had not been along for the candy and flowers. Magnates didn't spend time with aldermen, and the mayor liked it to be known that in the city's rich democracy, Yello would need to account for only one public official's opinion. The mayor and a commission of civic notables took the Nygaard brothers and twenty of their executives to the Chicago Symphony, the Joffrey Ballet, the Steppenwolf Theater, Topolobampo, and the Lyric Opera. The brothers got their pictures snapped with famous stars and celebrity chefs and were mercilessly lampooned on the stage of Second City by the brightest stars of tomorrow. They sat, laughing gamely, at the small black tables in the first row. Bill Murray joined them for a drink. There were tickets to Oprah's show, and dinner with Jerry Springer (the Nygaards told him that they loved his show, and more: "It's a touchstone for popular culture.") The city sent Yello executives gallon buckets of Chicago mix (caramel and cheese) popcorn, and five-pound boxes of Dove chocolates and Frango mints. They got stuffed bears embroidered with the names of their children, and crystal models of their proposed headquarters, laser-etched with the city's motto: *I Will.*

When the Nygaards arrived back in leafy Marquette, there was a stout brown box waiting. It held two red Chicago Bulls jerseys with the white numerals 23, and BEN and BARRY embossed on the back. The gift card was signed in small, elegant script: "Looking forward to being teammates. Michael Jordan."

Sunny recalled the mayor describing the box and its contents, checking the time, rubbing his hands, and waiting for the brothers to call.

"Match that, New fucking York," he said.

"I'm interested in a pattern," Brooks Whetstone continued. "Not a one-night stand, but an ongoing enterprise. A lot of Yello executives have made contributions to the mayor."

"And to the symphony, the opera, and Northwestern's cancer unit," said Sunny. "And Provident Hospital, fifty local theaters, and the re-construction of the Pilgrim Baptist Church. Rich people shed dollars. That's why we want them here."

"A number of them have also shed a few dimes to you."

"So have a lot of cab drivers and fry cooks. Government would be so much easier if we could just get rid of all this campaign nonsense, wouldn't it? Just have the academic committee at Stanford choose. But as you say, it's the law right now. What can you do? Until we come to our senses, the votes of folks here in Humboldt Park and Pilsen count just as much as the ones in Marin County."

Brooks Whetstone took a long draw from his cup, rattled such ice as remained, and took another, scrunching his face as if peering through a screen. When he spoke, Sunny was impressed by his flat voice; indeed, he even seemed to keep a chord of friendliness.

"I know someone like me will always seem insubstantial to you, al-derman," he began. "If you're interested, my father ran an ad firm. But he didn't own it. He was a county supervisor, not a pasha. I was a life-guard in Santa Rosa and a cab driver in San Jose. Three passengers robbed me at gunpoint. I worked all through law school. I live on a government paycheck. I buy a dozen white button-down shirts once a year, on sale from a catalog, and I never, but never, let anyone pick up the check. Please don't try to play class games with me. I've worked as hard as anyone you ever gave a city job to, I'm sure."

Then, without so much as unfolding his fingers from his cup, Brooks delivered the dart he had tucked away until he was quite certain that Sunny knew nothing of it.

"At the time of his death, the mayor of Chicago had turned state's evidence," he announced. When Sunny simply held his gaze, he went on.

"Do you understand what I am saying, Mr. Roopini? The mayor was furnishing evidence to us that would have been—that still will be—used to prosecute city officers for corruption, bribery, conspiracy, and mail fraud."

"I don't believe it," Sunny said finally. It was all he could manage without clearing his throat, or risking a quaver. He felt as if a plug had been pulled on his right heel; he could feel blood draining to his toes. He stamped his right foot three times, but regretted it as soon as he heard the sole of his shoe slap the black industrial carpet. It sounded like a spoiled child pouting, "No, no, *no.*"

"Then don't," said Brooks.

"Whether or not he had anything to give you," Sunny finally managed, "and I don't think he did, it would have been against every fiber in his soul."

"The mayor I knew," Brooks Whetstone said softly, "would spend every drop of his blood to stay mayor. I've prosecuted mobsters, gangbangers, and drug addicts who have sold their baby's shoes to get a fix. Believe me, Mr. Roopini, they're all better friends than politicians."

Sunny needed to go to the bathroom—to stretch his legs, wash his hands, and splash his face with cold water, as much to expel the two cups of tea, diet soda, and ice water that now seethed in his stomach like solvent. But he sensed that would be mistaken for fleeing the scene. Instead he pressed his knees together and leaned forward slightly, so that his jaw was above Brooks's elbow.

"Did you go to him, or did he—I find this inconceivable—come to you?"

Brooks shrugged, to signal that he might choose to act amused by the answer.

"Who says 'I love you' first? We turned over a few things. We found traces of his fingerprints, okay? We met. We made our case. We did business."

"Whatever he told you—whatever you *think* he told you—doesn't seem to have resulted in much."

Brooks Whetstone turned both palms up from the table, as if to show that a coin had disappeared.

"Well I don't have anything to hide," Sunny said forcefully, and at this, Brooks Whetstone actually pushed back on his chair and laughed.

"Well *I* sure as hell do," said the U.S. Attorney. "Everybody does. This is why I've lifted the flap on our tent, Mr. Roopini. Did Collins Jenkins know what the mayor was doing, realize that he had been left in the cold, and set something in motion? Or once someone else had taken care of the mayor, did Collins suddenly realize that he had been left alone and couldn't face it?"

"Or . . ." Sunny suggested.

"Or," Brooks Whetstone agreed. "Something to put in with all the other plots, nonsense, and peril that you have to worry about these days. Well, you have work, I'm sure," he announced, finally standing up from the table. A platinum blond was winding a snake around her neck on the overhead screens, while men reached out for her and fell back as she dispatched them with a lethal flick of bullet-sharp finger-tips. Chains climbed her legs. Sgt. McNulty could see that both men were on their feet and moved toward them as he buttoned his jacket once more around the line of his holster. Brooks held Sunny's hand-shake for a moment and brought him in close.

"I've heard the local creed, alderman," he said softly under the din of snakes hissing, lights sizzling, and pins clinking. "A little cheerful corruption nourishes the soul. It keeps people interested. No one minds if you pick up a few crumbs that fall off the cake as long as they get their slice. But I can't see it that way. I've seen too much. One day, a bolt in a tunnel gives way because somebody cut the concrete with water to skim a little for himself; a slab falls and smashes a family. The brother-in-law of somebody that you hired for a job at the rec center turns out to wave his genitals at children. The cracks in the levees you let go from year to year, because it's more rewarding to spend the money on contracts and jobs, start leaking. One day, they get smacked by a storm, and a couple hundred thousand people have to swim for their lives. I have as little use for piety as you do, Mr. Roopini. I'm just being practical."

He reached down for the check for two diet drinks.

"My treat," he said, and as Sunny mechanically reached into his pocket to leave a twenty for the girl with gushing electric pigtails, he put a hand on Brooks Whetstone's elbow.

"Did Collins Jenkins know?" he asked.

"Not from us."

"You weren't working with him, too?"

"No."

"Did the mayor give you Collins?"

Brooks Whetstone wavered.

"No comment."

"I'm not the *Tribune*," Sunny reminded him. "Impossible as it seems, I'm an elected official with responsibilities."

Brooks held back a moment longer. "Nothing we recognized as such," he said finally. "A thing like that—there's no yes or no."

"And you've informed the police chief?" Sunny asked.

"Yes," Brooks affirmed, and then the corners of his mouth rose slightly. "In his fluent Arabic." And then as Sgt. McNulty leaned into one of the glass doors that led onto Western Avenue, the blare of music was matched by the gassy blather of rush-hour buses grinding past.

"What happened to you—to your family," Brooks said. "I'm sorry."

Sunny nodded. His head was beginning to feel so leaden, his chin brushed against the knot of his tie. He could see his feet, those embarrassing brown brogues at the bottom of his pinstriped legs, plodding like otters over the pavement.

"The two men—" Brooks began.

"Stateville."

"Yes. I remember. One of them was out on parole. A gun charge."

"Yes," said Sunny. "But your office was probably busy trying to find my cigar ash."

Sunny knew that it was the kind of blow a man lands in retreat, more for self-respect than result. The gray sky had begun to deepen while they were inside, and minute glints of snow pranced like gnats in the silver streetlight floating across Western Avenue.

"You're free and clear, Mr. Roopini." Their two black government sedans were parked at the curb, engines running, window wipers squeaking and slapping, wisps of smoke puffing from the tailpipes. "I'm not about to try to make a case over lunch money from a few grade schoolers. As far as I know—and I *know*—you're as virtuous as politicians get here. But you would know—if there's cigar smoke, there's fire."

A younger man in a darker tweed opened the back door of Brooks's car just enough for the bell to ding and the inside light to snap on. Brooks had no gloves and had shoved his hands halfway into his coat pockets, which splayed his elbows awkwardly to his side, as if he were about to flap his arms.

"If you ever want to talk, alderman, I'm a good audience," he told Sunny. "And I know how to show my appreciation."

Eldad Delaney was inside Sunny's car, where the heater was on high and Eldad had shucked his overcoat and sat in rolled-up sleeves, sipping from a dark green beer bottle.

"This is why people run for mayor," he said to Sunny. "Not just borrow the office for a couple of days, like us. A warm car on a dark night, cute cops to go, and cold beer. Your men insisted," he quickly informed Sgt. McNulty. "I believe there's more in the trunk, when duty ends."

The sergeant had scrunched himself in a fold-down seat across from Sunny and knocked twice on the thick dark glass screen that divided the driver from passenger sides. Sunny felt the car begin to move.

"No siren," McNulty called through a starburst of small holes, and turned back to Eldad. "You never know when a security shift ends, so we prepare for the worst," he explained.

Eldad held out a beige folder to Sunny.

"Granville North Side Neighbors," he said. "B1–2 versus B1–3. Smackdown of the century tonight." They were bills proposed to regulate the height of residential buildings along north Broadway.

"Oh, shit," said Sunny. "I forgot. Can't I be a little late? Under the circumstances."

"Under the circumstances, especially not," said Eldad. "They'd think you've gone Hollywood," and when Sunny was visibly baffled and frowned, Eldad explained, "Your one day under the bright lights."

"I was hoping to stop home," said Sunny. "Can I at least call my daughters?'

"Of course,' said Eldad, and as he lifted a worn red folder from under his arm, Sunny groaned. It contained the names and phone numbers of about two hundred people. A hundred of them, more or less, had contributed at least a thousand dollars to at least one of Sunny's last three campaigns. The rest were the names of people those donors had suggested would be receptive to cultivation.

Every day, Monday through Saturday, Eldad selected five people for Sunny to call. Sunny was a skilled conversationalist. He could keep the call skimming between inconsequential confidences and the noncommittal solicitation of advice. Sunny would tell them about what was coming before the council ("Now 965-46—what we're calling the Renter's Bill of Rights—should make the conversion of those units on North Malden easier. . . ."), and pause for their reaction; sit still for their advice, remarking only, "Yes, I see . . ."

Sunny was careful to pass along—it was the lollipop following the flu shot—at least one sharp, farcical, and essentially superficial anecdote from city council life that Sunny's donors could share at dinner parties, client lunches, or foursomes (Arty Agras stories were abundant; and citations from the mayor were practically legal tender).

Sunny almost never actually asked for money. It would be boorish— "Like asking for a blow job over the bread basket," said Linas Slavinskas—and risked snapping the mutual illusion that their worldliness alone accounted for the alderman's assiduous interest in their opinions. If a politician was sensitive, it was also unnecessary. "Like asking for a blow job over the brandy," is how Linas put it. "If you haven't talked your way in by the budino al cioccolato, no amount of begging will get you there."

Eldad Delaney wriggled the folder at Sunny as if he were trying to signal a passing plane.

"We can't skip a night? Under the circumstances . . ."

"Under the circumstances, I think they'd be even more eager to hear from you. A phone call now is worth five or six a few weeks from now."

Sunny sighed as Eldad dialed up the number of Mendy Huster, a securities analyst on Wacker. Sunny remembered his oaken office along the green river, the bridges in his prodigious windows yawning open slowly for barges, and a grove of frames standing on his credenza showing the smiles of four daughters, two stepsons, two sandy-haired wives, and a white-throated Bernese mountain dog.

Mendy Huster was a busy man. They were still open for business in San Jose. They were still trading commodities in San Francisco. They were making plans for Monday in Tokyo. He came to the phone for Sunny's call within a moment.

"Alllderman Roopini," he said with unusual formality. "You must be a busy man." It was his highest accolade.

"Thank you for taking my call," said Sunny. "I appreciate it."

Eldad was already pointing to the name of Hannah Williams, a trial attorney in Sears' Tower who was next on his list. *Worried about proposal to make Sheridan one-way west of Clark,* he murmured into Sunny's uncovered ear.

"I know how hectic Fridays are for you, Mendy. But first, how is the family?"

15

FRIDAY NIGHT

The Granville North Side Neighbors met in the basement of a Methodist church in which Sunny had also attended meetings of the Concerned Citizens of Andersonville, the Edgewater Watch Auxiliary, and the Margate Park Native Seeds Association. He recognized the tall, tarnished coffee urn that the Reverend Sillitoe kept simmering at the back of the room as well as the one in his own kitchen (though Reverend Sillitoe kept only hot water roiling in his urn, which attendees could use to moisten herbal teabags, powdered decaffeinated coffee, or dietetic hot chocolate).

People sat in folding chairs under tawny yellow light, the sleeves of their nylon snow jackets sliding as they squirmed in their seats, the suction *smack!* of wet snowshoes pulling away from the slick floor. Sunny could see posters from his seat: WHO WOULD JESUS BOMB? GO SOLAR, NOT BALLISTIC, and IMAGINE ALL THE PEOPLE, SHARING ALL THE WORLD.

"We are so glad that Alderman Roopini could make time for our humble community meeting," said the reverend. "We know he is now concerned—we see it on TV—with so much loftier issues."

Sunny spotted the tartness in the reverend's thanks and began by springing to his feet and holding his hands at his waist.

"Thank you for your warm welcome," he said. "And now I ask that we all observe a moment of silence in honor of our late mayor."

The room rose, sorrowfully and dutifully, sleeves scratching, snow-shoes clopping, and faces downcast. The reverend could see that Sunny had gained a tactical advantage with his reminder of his close association with the mayor. He stewed through half a minute of reverential silence before moving to recapture the room.

"We thank thee, oh Lord, for the late mayor's commitment to sustainable neighborhoods," he said, his eyes fastened in prayerful communion. "Thy creatures know that taller is not better, that bigger is not more beautiful, and that responsible planning, rather than unchecked development, can make His earth in this ward into Eden once again."

(Reverend Sillitoe was in favor of a proposal to limit the height of new buildings along a newly leveled block of Broadway to six stories.)

But before murmurs of "amen" could move around the room, Dennis Pietrzak, a realtor who owned four buildings on Glenwood, added his own supplication from the third row.

"And remember, oh Lord, as Thy mayor always did, that sustainable neighborhoods require vital local enterprises at street level, and that commerce is also a part of Thy kingdom. Thy will be done!"

(Dennis favored an eight-story height limitation on that block, to encourage small stores on ground floors.)

The meeting wound on an hour and forty-six minutes. Sunny, who explained that he was there to listen and learn, kept his eyelids open, but only by blinking very hard, as if he were casting out sand.

Proponents of the six-story height limitation said that if eight-story buildings were built, those two blocks along Broadway would soon look as cold and forbidding as the crags of the Khyber Pass. Eight-story buildings would choke off all sunlight. They would massacre all greenery. Could city pigeons even twitter in such a ghastly landscape?

But supporters of eight-story buildings said they were necessary so that hardware stores, shoe repair shops, and independent coffee houses could abound on the ground floors, each staffed by knowledgeable, personable proprietors. Otherwise, the streets would be lonely, dangerous, and desolate. Unemployed young toughs would gather in gutters to mug grandmothers and exchange infected heroin needles. So the debate bounded back and forth.

"We don't want our streets to look like canyons!"

"And we don't want a whole block of Broadway to look like a bunch of army barracks!"

"You want to live like the folks on the Gold Coast? Four-million-dollar condos, and you can't buy a stick of sunlight!"

"If I had a four-million-dollar condo there, I'd go to Miami every year for a little sunlight!"

"Look how developers leveled lower Manhattan!"

"Developers!" gasped Floyd Porteus, who ran a stationery shop and newsstand on Sheridan Road. "That was terrorism!"

"By the U.S. government!" shouted several people from their seats, and when a few more voices bellowed back, Jack Merritt, who was an information technology teacher at Senn Academy, rose with a rolled-up newspaper in his hand to emphasize, "The FBI and Enron wanted to suck the American people into war. Just like Pearl Harbor!"

"That's nuts!"

"You don't know that Roosevelt planned Pearl Harbor?" roared Jack. "Then *you're* nuts."

"I deeply respect this exchange of views," the Reverend Sillitoe stepped in, hands waving. "But just in the interest of time—can we keep this discussion a little more focused?"

"If you're not part of the exposure, you're part of the cover-up!" Jack rasped.

It was two hours before Sgt. McNulty could convey Sunny back into their long black car and pull away from the church, wheels crunching and whining in the thudding snow.

"Such a wide-ranging discussion, alderman," Sgt. McNulty told him after they had dropped Eldad Delaney at home, just a few blocks away. "Down in Alderman Corcoran's ward, we don't hear quite so much of that world perspective."

Sunny smiled sourly. *World perspective* sounded like receiving a compliment for your child's *feistiness*.

"The *Grrreat* Forty-eight," Sunny reminded him. "I remember one night when a proposal to extend weekend parking on Sheridan Road turned into a debate on nuclear power. What's the story of America? The farmers and the ranchers. What's the story of urban development? The families and the single people. Any debate about housing and zoning, and you can match up sides like that."

"I noticed that you didn't express any opinion," said the sergeant.

"Vehemently so," Sunny agreed.

They came to a block of North Clark Street that was nominally identified with Swedish immigrants. But that lineage lingered only in the names of a few bakeshops. Greek and Persian families had moved in a generation ago. Blue and white striped flags were taped into deli windows, next to Farsi language ads for shampoo and cigarettes. The newest arrivals were gays—and their families. The newer restaurants they opened had loudly Italianate names, like Fredo's, Lucca's, and Fat Clemenza's. The newer bakeries had signs blaring LOW-FAT CINNAMON RAISIN SCONES, not cinnamon rolls.

Sunny had gotten a message from Rita and Rula, the two of them crowding the mouthpiece and alternating sentences.

"Why don't we, Pappaji—"

"We're down on Lincoln, it's on the way—"

"—meet at Big Ern's."

Big Ern was a tavern that, its current owner claimed, had been opened as a speakeasy in the late 1920s. Big Ern (who was less so after having a triple bypass operation at the age of forty-six) kept the front door with the peephole and small grate, which now was shoved aside only so that the Budweiser man could shout, "Delivery, Ernie!" Boasting of an outlaw pedigree was an attractive word-of-mouth promotion in Chicago.

Big Ern insisted that the bar had been built to resemble one in the old French ocean liner *Normandie*, so that people who could not afford to cruise could have a cocktail in comparable surroundings. The tavern had low ceilings, snug red booths, and porthole windows that looked out onto the salty spray of Clark Street. When someone pushed open the door, the hinges creaked, light from the streetlamp flashed off ship's brass bells behind the bar, and Big Ern sang out, "Hi, neighbor!"

Sunny and Elana used to end their nights out there, on a slumping red velvet couch in the back, under an old neon display of a fish dancing on his fins and holding out a martini glass in some underwater toast.

"A pickled herring," Ern explained.

Sunny usually nursed a brandy and coffee, Elana one more glass of white wine. When Ern began to sing along from behind the bar: "When the moon comes over the mountain . . ." it seemed to remind Sunny to complain that their daughters no longer needed him.

"Only to leave a twenty on the table in the morning," he said, usually running an index finger around the smooth rim of his brandy glass. "You can tell them about sex, college, smoking—not smoking. Boys—no boys. What could they possibly find out from me? Whole continents have emerged from the sea since I learned anything. Stars have been discovered, diseases conquered. What value is there in knowing how many onions to order every week, or how to get a tree stump removed from Ainslie? They think that running a restaurant is squalid. They think that politics is stupid. They think . . ."

"They love you," Elana pointed out—not always gently.

"They're convinced that Salman Rushdie or Antonio Banderas must be their real father. They think anything I might know a little bit about isn't worth knowing."

"I would never have anything to do with Salman Rushdie," Elana would smile (Sunny changed the name of his example every few months).

"Remember when they were little?" she asked, her long dark hair swishing sensationally over the lip of her long-stemmed wine glass. "All the giggles at Pappaji making faces, squirting water out of his nose, and talking like Donald Duck? God it irritated me! *I* wiped their asses. *I* pulled the pants over their little puffy squirmy sausage arms and legs; it was like trying to put pantyhose on rabid dogs. I'd pack their little juices and snacks. And they'd act like little memsahibs—"

"Schmucks," Sunny amended.

"—barking that they wanted milk in the blue cup, not the red one, and throwing it across the floor, like Henry the Eighth flinging a chicken leg. Then *you'd* step through the door, and I'd hear the goddamn giggles. That's what people in love really want to hear—anyone can learn to say, 'I love you.' The girls and I are just making up for lost time, Sunny. They'll rediscover you, too."

"I'd give five years of my life," Sunny would say, drumming his right hand along the small, smooth table. "Just to have them back like they were when they were five and three. Just for ten minutes. Shit, I'd give ten years."

"Don't you dare," Elana would tell him, running a long finger across the top of his closed hand. "Those years are for me."

Sunny stopped going to Big Ern's after Elana died. Ern left a few messages over several weeks. "Aren't you thirsty? I have a bottle of Baron de Sack-o-shit or something on the back row that's getting dusty," and when none of those tender and considerate invitations prompted Sunny's reappearance, Ern left something sharper.

"You lost your wife, Sunny," he said. "Not your friends."

Sunny finally came in with his daughters on a Sunday night. The Bears were six points behind Green Bay on the screen behind the bar, and Russ Morgan's wah-wah trombone whined through "Dance with a Dolly With a Hole in Her Stocking."

"Nice to see you, alderman," Ern sang out, taking care not to turn his head from the rose-colored Cosmopolitan he was straining from a beaded shaker. "But we already paid you off this month."

"I've heard that your bar sink lacks a second tube for proper evacuation," Sunny told him with elaborate composure. "It'll cost you another fifty to overlook that code violation."

"Hey, alderman. I'm just a small businessman trying to survive," said Ern.

"Me, too," said Sunny, and the laughter of drinkers tinkled up and down the bar. Big Ern came around as he showed Sunny and his daughters to the drooping red couch below the dancing fish.

"I can see why you've been keeping these beautiful young women away," said Big Ern.

"We're old enough to drink," Rula told him. "In truly civilized cultures."

"This is the Forty-eighth Ward," Ern reminded her. "I make something—a touch of cola in 7Up—that looks just like Glenfiddich and a splash on the rocks. I'll set it up for you."

"Could I have an orange slice in it? Cherries, too, please," Rula asked.

From that night on, Sunny and his daughters usually met at Big Ern's one night a week, the girls sitting on the frowning red couch, Sunny settling in a seat across the way.

It was neutral territory for Sunny and his daughters. Elana still lingered in their apartment, her skirts and shirts still hanging in their closets. He still hadn't brought himself to remove or use her towels from the rack in their bathroom. They still drooped down, wrinkled, frowning, and sagging, when he snapped on the light in the middle of the night. Sunny and his daughters just couldn't talk around their mother.

They were arrayed along the red couch when Sunny and Sgt. McNulty rocked open the door to Big Ern's, and they sprang to their feet, red scarves encircling their necks in the way Elana had taught them to wrap themselves against the cold.

He brought both girls into his arms. Rula put her head onto the right shoulder of his topcoat. Rita kissed the left side of his neck.

"Pappaji . . ." It was Rula, alongside his ear.

"Poor Pappaji," Rita added from under his chin. They helped him into the couch, swinging his legs to fill one side, and took chairs across from their father. Ern appeared above them.

"Hi, neighbor. Good to see you intact, Mr. Acting Interim," he said. "Your girls have been passing out ambassadorships."

Ern swept an arm toward the screen behind the bar, showing long lines of people with bowed heads and slumping shoulders standing noiselessly along Randolph Street, waiting for the mayor's casket to be borne up the steps of the Cultural Center.

"Quiet tonight," he added softly. "I turned off the juke. And I hear—" Ern threw a thumb over his shoulder, up toward the screen— "that the south side is a ghost town . . ."

There were two white restaurant boxes on the low table in front of the couch, which Rita and Rula popped open to reveal a beige lagoon of baba ghanoush, speckled with smoky bits of charred eggplant, and a creamy pink lake of taramosalata.

"Anmar sent it over," Ern explained. The Békaa Gardens was just across the street. Rula and Rita reached over with crusty spades of pita, while Sunny struggled up from the cushions to stand to shake hands with a short, dark woman who had appeared alongside Sgt. McNulty.

"Sgt. Andrea Jelsen-Gidwitz, sir," he explained. "You rate an overnight shift now."

The sergeant with the hyphenated name had wavy dark hair, almond eyes, and commanding hands. She wore a long black coat and heels that gave her an extra inch of height.

"Whenever you're ready, we bring you home and sit outside on Lawrence," she said. "Sgt. Gallaher—I believe you know her—takes over tomorrow morning."

Sgt. McNulty had reached over for Sunny's hand to say goodnight, but Sunny ran his free hand up the sergeant's arm to clutch his shoulder. At first, Sunny was moved to take the sergeant into his arms, but caught himself. McNulty had probably worked around enough politicians to know that they hugged people the way that chimps hung off tree limbs. So Sunny settled on the shoulder clasp, and the steady—so he hoped—look into his eyes.

"You saved my life."

"Not even close," Sgt. McNulty reassured him.

"Are you off duty?"

"As soon as Sgt. Andi shook your hand."

"A bon vivant like you must have places to go," Sunny told him. "But a man saves my life, I ask him what he drinks."

Sgt. McNulty looked around the room before breaking into a smile.

"One for the road then," he said, before sitting down on a bench across from Rita and Rula.

"Johnnie, rocks, please," he said to Ern. "I'm not a fancy guy."

"Blue label, please, Ern," said Sunny, sitting down on the rim of the red sofa's cushions. "I beg to differ."

"I know you," Big Ern told the sergeant. "I saw you all day. They've been playing your big scene over and over, like JFK in Dallas. Better ending, of course."

"Think what Sgt. McNulty could have done for Lincoln," said Sunny.

"What would you have done if the guy reached for his piece?" asked Ern, presenting the sergeant's drink, ice cubes crackling and elegantly tinkling.

"My job."

Ern whistled admiringly, as if at a sleek car.

"I protect the acting interim mayor of Chicago," Sgt. McNulty explained.

Sunny raised his glass and the sergeant, Rula, Rita, and Ern followed with their own, clinking.

"To the mayor of Chicago," Sunny declared. "The one and only." Sunny's voice broke and his eyes simmered. He was so worn out that he couldn't seem to blink back the tears, and feared that he was getting weepy. Several voices up and down the bar pealed back, "The mayor . . ."

Rula and Rita scraped their chairs around Sgt. McNulty, clearly intrigued with his rounded rower's shoulders, his short, sandy hair, his blunt sentences, and impeccably straight sideburns.

"Would you have *shot* that alderman?" asked Rula.

"Let's just say he's lucky to be home tonight, flossing his teeth with one arm."

"Would you have *killed* him?" Rita asked more softly.

"I would have dropped him," the sergeant said flatly. "We don't go in for dramatic language."

"*Dropped* him?" she asked.

"At that distance, it would have been like putting holes in a sofa. Drop—like a watermelon from a window."

Rula mashed the palm of her right hand down on her knee.

"Splat!" she said. "How many people have you *dropped*?" Sunny noticed that his daughter had absorbed her mother's custom of swirling the ends of her long hair over the rim of her glass.

"None," said the sergeant evenly.

"How do you know you could?" asked Rita.

"You just do."

"Do you have a girlfriend?"

"No."

"Don't want to be tied down?"

"I don't have girlfriends," said McNulty, and Rita slapped her forehead into the palm of a hand as Rula blurted, "Oh bloody hell," a gobbet of baba ghanoush clinging to the line of her lip.

"It's true what they say," she declared. "All the good ones are already taken, or gay."

"Who the hell says that?" Sunny asked with alarm, and his daughters laughed as if their father had just blurted out the most ridiculous and endearing thing. They stood up to take a couple of stools at the far end of the bar to watch the TV screen. There were long lines of people standing soberly in heavy boots outside of the Cultural Center, flurries frosting their arms and shoulders. Sunny could hear sobs from the screen, cars crunching past slowly in the snow, and the muted voices of announcers. Rula reached her right arm across Rita's shoulders. Rita leaned her head against her sister. Sgt. McNulty leaned in closer to Sunny, speaking just to him.

"That must be nice to see, Mr. Roopini."

"They could just as easily dig their fingernails into each other," he told him. "But, yes. Especially now."

"What happened last year," the sergeant said cautiously. "I'm sorry."

"Thank you," was all Sunny could ever seem to say.

"It was on my mind today. I didn't want . . ."

"Yes," Sunny said simply.

"May I ask—what happened?"

"Oh. Well, the two guys took a plea."

"I meant your wife," the sergeant stressed. "The guys—I couldn't care."

"Oh," said Sunny. He folded his hands over a knee and wondered how to state it once again. "Well. She was in the currency exchange to buy phone cards. She got them every few weeks so the folks who work in our restaurant could call back home to El Salvador, Greece, Hyderabad, whatever. She was putting the cards in her bag when those guys came in."

McNulty shook his head with every other word.

"I wish I'd been there that day, too," he said.

Sunny could not seem to turn his eyes off. Rula and Rita could overhear their father getting choked and teary and moved back toward the sofa and their seats.

"Sheldon misses you, Pappaji," said Rula, reaching around his shoulder. "He saw the TV and was worried."

"Me and Sheldon both."

"Do you protect Sheldon, too, Sgt. McNulty?" asked Rita.

"Our cat," Sunny explained.

"I guessed," said the sergeant. He turned up his glass and took a solid swallow. "You bet," he announced. "Nobody gets the drop on Sheldon."

"He hasn't been declawed," Rita said teasingly, drawing her tongue across her lips. Sunny hadn't liked seeing the expression since she was six.

"Me neither," said the sergeant. "We're a good pair."

"Sheldon loves our father," said Rula, moving onto Sunny's left knee. "Two of a kind, we say."

"There is no need to finish that thought," said Sunny with an urgency that surprised him; but Rula went on.

"The two of them scratching themselves, watching TV and falling asleep on the sofa." Then she noticed Sunny's light brown suede brogues at the end of his pin-striped legs, and leveled a finger at them as if she were pointing to lichens glowing at the back of a cave. She leaned over to kick her father's right foot.

"Oh Pappaji," said Rita. "Poor Pappaji. You look like such an *alderman*!"

16

Aldermen were considered the comic relief of politics. Chicagoans liked their mayors to be pugnacious and effective. They rarely cared if a mayor rewarded his or her allies, as long as those enriched could build the buildings, run the trains, sweep the snow, haul the trash, catch the muggers, and stand back to let people make money. They could even tolerate officials who ached to be statesmen; they had put up with the likes of Lincoln and Stevenson, if a long time ago.

Most people recognized only a few aldermen by name, but tended to associate almost all of them with a series of traits. Aldermen mangled language. Unless disciplined, they behaved like four-year-olds trying to catch candy spilling out of a piñata. They would tell a blind newsstand clerk that a five-dollar bill was a twenty. They might be occasionally entertaining, in the way that Roman emperors kept young children at their banquet tables for amusement. But you wouldn't want your sister, your daughter, or nowadays, your son, to marry an alderman.

Sunny knew that he benefited by contrast. He was well spoken and immaculate (he was especially careful to attend to his hands; slapping dough onto the rough clay side of tandoori ovens made him scarred and hairless on the back of his hands). He knew that his faint English accent conveyed a note of sophistication to Americans, and he worked to keep it, after more than thirty years in the city. Once, a reporter caught Sunny carrying a copy of *The Economist* under his arm. He reacted with exaggerated surprise, as if he'd just seen an orangutan wearing velvet slippers. It was enough to earn Sunny a reputation in the council for being some kind of Disraeli or Vaclav Havel.

In fact, Sunny was probably less well educated than most aldermen. He had left Truman City College in his second year after the death of his father, Sidhan. His brother, Vendan, was already a premed major, so the future of his family's restaurant fell on Sunny. He buried his father with remorse, but ended his academic career with relief.

Yet two decades in the chamber convinced Sunny that there were as many certifiably smart aldermen as those who were embarrassingly stupid. Linas Slavinskas was not only an astute lawyer. He surprised Sunny with cosmopolitan observations about opera, literature, and art. (Linas explained away such fluency by telling Sunny, "You don't impress the girls who work the makeup counter at Saks by talking about our sewer rebate program.")

Vera Barrow and Kiera Malek were poised and informed on weekend interview shows. The mayor usually dispatched them to represent the city at international conferences that wanted a look at a real Chicago alderman. Vera would return and report, "They kept waiting for me to drool."

Once the mayor had posted Arty Agras to an urban land use conference in Athens. "I'm so glad to be in the land of my forefathers, who have given so much to civilization," Artie told his hosts. "The Acropolis, the Coliseum, and the right of affectional preference among men."

But even Arty, who was certainly more what the delegates had in mind, had spare moments of such lucidity in reading the small, numbing print in a city budget that Sunny had wondered if his malaprops were part of some prolonged act. "You see, Sunny," he would say as he drew back one of the blue vinyl covers and let the pages fall, "a printed budget is a little like a fan dance. The small part that shows makes you think you're seeing more than you are."

Cyril Murphy of the 40th was the Irish Republican Army's legal counsel in Chicago and could draw the minute lines of a redistricted ward as if he were deveining shrimp. Rod Abboud was an ass, but no fool. He had been to the University of Chicago's law school with Linas

Slavinskas (but unlike Linas, couldn't seem to make an observation about parking restrictions along Western Avenue without quoting "the distinguished scholar, my fellow Maroon . . ."). Evelyn Washington was a second-grade teacher at the Cyrus Colter School. Reasoning with seven-year-olds, she said, prepared her to mediate with aldermen.

Sunny didn't want to devote too much of his life listening to Arty Agras retell old goodfellas stories, or swallowing a grimace that could be confused with a smile at one of Collie Kerrigan's jokes. But he didn't regard the time he spent with his colleagues as personally disagreeable, and certainly not beneath him. Politicians tended to be friendly, aldermen especially so. They collected funny stories. They wanted to be liked. Hell, they wanted to be loved and asserted themselves desperately and gracelessly, like ducks trying to make love to a football.

The Roopini name had been the object of joking ("Dark as you are, you must be from Calabria,") since the family arrived in Chicago in the first great wave of East Indian emergency room doctors and grad students. One day Sunny found an Italian cookbook left in a booth. He thumbed through it and began to think. Within a few weeks, he offered spaghetti with lamb meatballs on the menu, mostly to feature something for Chicago children who still wrinkled their noses at the idea of lentil dal and sag paneer. Within a few more weeks, a neighborhood newspaper made admiring, humorous mention of Sunny Roopini's Italian specialties—and Sunny was obliged to concoct several more. Sidhan had opened the restaurant to Indian community meetings on flat Sunday afternoons, when football and baseball games usually made business slow. Sunny reached out to bring in Dante Alighieri clubs, Kiwanians, synagogue groups, realtors, undertakers, and a swinger's club (for, as Sunny reasoned, people who favored orgies would certainly enjoy their three-course buffet). Within months, there were wedding rehearsal dinners, bat mitzvah luncheons, and happy hours with samosas and chapatis. For greeting the disparate groups of people, Sunny began to perfect witty little speeches about being an Indian in America, but not an American Indian. Looking back, it was his beginning in politics.

But after twenty years in the council, Sunny Roopini felt increasingly spent and dull. All the irrecoverable hours he had spent at meetings, rallies, and citizen forums, absorbing breathless banalities and policy babble like a sponge at the bottom of a pail. All the cynical courtesies he had awarded uncaring adversaries, all the tinny excuses he had offered disappointed friends.

There were times that even as Sunny opened his mouth to make some pledge—to balance a budget, slash taxes, or keep Chicago clean!—he mentally prepared to explain, a few months hence, why it was not possible. The state legislature blocked it; the federal government wouldn't fund it; powerful antediluvian forces crushed the will of the people like a paper cup in the street. The next campaign came, and politicians would still send new promises into the sky, like balloons, to drift away.

The predictable rotation of promises and excuses made people cynical. But Sunny sometimes told friends, "A campaign promise is like shouting out 'I love you' during orgasm. You mean it. You mean it *absolutely* in that moment. But any adult should know that you might not be able to mean it next week."

Increasingly and uselessly, Sunny imagined ways that he might have made more money, seen more of his daughters, met Salma Hayek, or at least have been the best at some craft or business. The issues with which he was identified—gay rights, school reforms, and immigrant issues—had mostly prevailed. Sunny didn't fool himself that he had made the difference. But there were times when he wondered why, if the goals had been gained, he was still on the field?

But a politician wasn't a priest. A professional had to find new things to believe in.

Sunny found that he still enjoyed the chance to accomplish something actual and concrete—to make a call and get a dead tree cut down, a traffic light put up, or a parking ticket dismissed for a senior citizen who had confused Tuesday and Thursday. He was glad that the right note or phone call—the right small joke in the ear of an overburdened city bureaucrat—might get an autistic child into a good program. He took pleasure in writing a recommendation for the Alferez girl to get into Annapolis, or for the father of the Schweppe boy to get early parole. He was happy to hear people say, "All that snow, but I could get to work because the thirty-six was running. Alderman Roopini makes sure the plows are out before the first flake."

Sunny hadn't had a serious opponent for years. But he was still surprised by the number of people so eager to compete for a prize that was so widely mocked.

Some still saw the chance for financial reward in a council seat. "Never take a dime," Linas had famously advised. "Just hand them your business card." But forty years of reforms had heartlessly curtailed the ways in which an alderman could avail himself of opportunities.

Some who ran hoped the council might confer enough fame to help them run for higher office. But Sunny thought it was an undependable stepping stone. A voter might forgive a congressman for voting for or against war in Iraq, the medicinal use of marijuana, or expanding gun controls; but never an alderman who had opposed installing a traffic light on the corner of Ashland and Wrightwood.

Yet running for the city council was still an affordable exercise of citizenship and ego. The excessive number of wards meant that the city's political map was broken down into fifty accessible enclaves; Sunny could walk the length of the 48th in fifteen minutes. An aldermanic candidate could forgo the spectacular costs of buying television ads to charm, scare, or intoxicate millions.

One night, the mayor had asked Sunny to watch a reel of his political commercials. Horns soared; strings swelled. The camera swept quickly over glossy skyscrapers glowing in the morn. A female African-American crossing guard in an orange belt warmly waved on a waddling flock of six-year-olds in a multiplicity of hues. Office workers strode purposefully over bridges, their faces intent on the future. Well-proportioned construction workers struck poses of casual prowess against a pile of red girders and construction cranes. A man with a handlebar moustache (he could be Greek, Italian, Mexican, Lebanese—he could be *Icelandic*—but in fact was an Australian actor of Scottish ancestry) playfully pummeled dough in his beautifully bricked restaurant kitchen. *Ola! Opa! Mangia!* A white woman in a pinstripe suit toting a portfolio against a slender hip talked on her mobile phone as she stalked a busy street. A diversely complexioned crowd in short-sleeved shirts rose from ivy-walled bleachers. A chorus sang:

Chicago breaks new ground! Chicago reaches for the sky! It's the city that astounds! On that you can rely!

The camera finally settled on the mayor in Daley Plaza, his broad shoulders admiringly encircled by nine photogenic youngsters in various heights and hues.

"I remember when you could get by with just four kids," the mayor told Sunny. "Black, brown, white, and yellow. Now, they got to add a beige one. Could be Indian, Assyrian, or Brazilian. Soon you'll have to add a kid in pink socks, so you think he's gay. Good ad?" he asked as the screen blinked back into the dark.

"Jewish guy from LA?" Sunny asked. The mayor shook his head.

"Jew in Sydney," he explained. "We wanted something fresh. Know how much that cost? To make, to run?"

"A million." Sunny blurted the first round number that occurred to him.

"Try seven," said the mayor.

"And gone before you can get up for the bathroom," said Sunny.

"That's the idea," the mayor explained. "I asked the consultants if we could make one that runs sixty seconds. Say a little something about issues."

"And they said?"

"'Do you want to run for reelection, Mr. Mayor, or make movies?'"

"Seven million dollars," Sunny said slowly.

"That's why you hire consultants, isn't it? To keep you from doing the right thing. Plus I'm buying radio, polls, newspapers, phone trees, popup screens, pooper scoopers with my name on the handle, and enough window signs to cover the moon. And I'm running eighty points ahead of a bunch of dented bean cans."

The mayor meant the assortment of Prohibitionists, Trotskyites, and people named George Washington who managed enough signatures to appear on the ballot.

"Seven million dollars," Sunny repeated. "How many phone calls does it take to raise that kind of money, two thousand dollars at a time?"

Silently, both men tried to do the math. They burst out laughing.

"Too fucking many," said the mayor.

The natural orbit of aldermen around the city's mayor had been in ebb since the disco era. Hiring laws had become so depressingly sincere that the mayor had once exclaimed, "What's this city coming to when you can get a job for a total stranger more easily than for an alderman's brother-in-law?"

Mayors and senators met with the French ambassador, the head of the World Food Program, or Bill and Melinda Gates. But aldermen were considered household appliances. People expected them to work at the touch of a fingertip. No one believed that an alderman had anything more urgent in life (no excuse short of kidney dialysis would do) than to sit through a community meeting about making Buena a one-way street between Broadway and Marine. And if Sunny spent two hours absorbing the anxieties and gripes of the Andersonville Neighbors Association, how could he tell the Edgewater Council that he was too busy on Tuesday?

If heavy rains in the middle of the night made a gutter overflow along Ridge Road, the phone in Sunny's pocket would warble like a trapped bird.

Sunny began to believe that the ceaseless drip of demands were what made many aldermen amenable to bribes. They began to think that a few bills taped under the bar to assist a small change in a zoning ordinance were a fair gratuity for all the uncompensated hours politics took from them.

Sunny knew about epochal corruptions. But few aldermen could award the kind of favor that would warrant a wire transfer into a Cayman Islands bank account. Most of the bribes to which he had seen his colleagues succumb were embarrassingly small change: box seats to a Cubs or Bulls game, a set of snow tires, or, as with old Hatcher Gutchess of the 25th, a couple of hundreds in an envelope that he didn't use to buy drugs, play horses, or pay hookers, but buy basketball shoes for his grandson.

Reformers were Sunny's natural allies on many issues. But he often felt uncomfortable around their meticulous righteousness. They forbade their housekeepers to shop at chain stores. They wore blue wristbands to stop global warming. At least people who left room for a little corruption in their souls could be modest about their virtues. Sunny found them easier to be around.

Sunny had never taken a bribe. He had never really been offered one and wouldn't even quite know how to ask. So he wore his virtue lightly, like a man in a clean white T-shirt at a spaghetti dinner.

Besides, how could people trust someone who was incorruptible? It was impossible to tell what was in the person's heart.

Despite his exhaustion, Sunny still had occasions that made him glad for his seat in the council's back row. Just a few months before, Sunny and the other aldermen had filed into their chamber for a morning session and saw a photo of a young policeman sprayed onto the white marble space above the mayor's high-backed chair. It was Vicente Romo, who had been twenty-six, and a patrolman in the Wentworth Avenue district. They knew that Officer Romo had been off duty one morning and brought his daughter to school when people came running over from Twenty-third Street to say that an apartment house was burning.

Officer Romo put the soft left hand of his little girl, Vanessa, into the hand of a teacher on the playground and ran toward the building. Children on the playground began to cry and shout, "Vanessa's poppy is going to the fire!"

When Officer Romo pulled up on foot, Chinese families stood in the street, pointing and spilling out words he could not understand. One young woman took hold of his arms and said, "Ye-ye, base-men! Ye-ye, base-men!" He hitched his sweater over his nose and mouth and ran into the building's open door. Blue clouds already boiled out of the windows.

By the time fire trucks arrived, Vicente Romo had staggered out of the building with an elderly man in his arms and laid him gently onto the hard black tar of 23rd Street. The man was sixty-seven-year-old Wen Wuan Cheng. But when Officer Romo tried to stand, he fell back. His head hit with a gruesome splat that was buried under the sound of sirens.

Heroic is a word often thoughtlessly applied. For Vicente Romo, no other word was apt.

At the time of Officer Romo's death, construction crews rushed to complete a new public library on Wentworth, on the side of Cermak Road where Spanish-speaking families lived. The city had piled ballots in churches and convenience stores, inviting the public to choose the name of the new library from an extensive list that, in a mishmash of inclusiveness, ranged from Minnie Minoso to Che Guevera to Raquel Welch.

A small local group, El Frente Popular por Lolita LeBron, got organized. Their ten members found the mounds of ballots as they were distributed, loaded sheaves into their arms, and marked them for their namesake. When the ballots were totaled, Lolita LeBron was the choice of about 6 percent. No other name won more.

"Lolita LeBron?" the mayor inquired from the couple of aldermen he called to his office.

"A figure from history," Jesus Flores Suarez of the 22nd explained, shifting from side to side. "She won beauty contests in Puerto Rico in the forties, then became a nationalist."

"I am a student of history, Jesus. I know who Lolita LeBron is. I just don't want to name a library after someone who opened fire on the U.S. Congress."

Harry Walker, who was chairman of the Cultural Affairs Committee, held the wedge of his beard judiciously.

"She felt they were imperialists assisting the continued occupation of her homeland."

"She shot three Democrats!" the mayor thundered.

"She was let out of prison by Jimmy Carter," Alderman Suarez pointed out, but the mayor snorted.

"I don't have a peanut farm to go home to, Jesus." He pawed the top of his vast desk. "Every time *del pueblo* votes down there, the independence line can't get four percentage points. You *chuckleheads* put Lolita LeBron on the ballot up here and she gets six, 'cause people think she must be a porn star. Why didn't you put John Wilkes Booth's name on the ballot, too, Harry? Folks know that name."

The meeting continued in that mood for a few more minutes, with both aldermen squirming as if the mayor had installed gas burners below their chairs. An ordinary leader might shrug and concede that the same democratic processes that elected him now had him backed into a corner. But the mayor was a man of vision. He could see, where others could not, how disconnected events could be realigned.

As the council session opened, the Romo and Cheng families occupied honored seats on the council floor. Little Vanessa was an especially affecting sight, a black lace scarf stretched across her head to match her mother's. Her tiny hand flashed small, pink, freshly painted nails, enfolded with her mother's, reminding all that a little girl could no longer hold her father's hand.

The mayor began his remarks slowly, gravely, like a great train pulling a great load.

"This was a young man," he said, "who got up on his day off, expecting just to take his little girl to school. And later, tuck her into bed."

His voice had become soft, but had a charge of magnetism in it. The aldermen lifted themselves forward to hear.

"Maybe to read *Goodnight, Moon*. '*Good night, bunny. Good night, light.'* But God gave him an emergency call. This fine, young, strong man," the mayor said, and raised his voice in measured steps as his words gathered steam. "And when humanity called, he didn't walk. When *du-ty* called, he didn't stroll," and here the mayor put his two huge hands to his hips with exaggerated daintiness. "*He ran* into a burning building. He didn't say, '*Sor-ree,* I'm off duty.' "

The mayor turned his great, weighty jowls toward the Romo family. Vanessa and her mother tightened their hold of one another.

"The name of your husband," he said and paused so his voice could catch. "*Your daddy,* will rest forever in our hearts." Then his face softened, as if beholding a new grandchild.

"A new public library is being built on Wentworth Avenue," he said. "Generations will grow up with the name of that library on their lips. I propose that when that library opens, the name incised above the entrance will be—" He drew in breath, then barked each syllable: "*Vi-cen-tay-Ro-mo-Pub-lic-Li-brary.*"

Explosions of applause burst on the council floor. Sunny found his eyes brimming and his hands stinging. About thirty voices shouted out, "Call the question, Mr. President."

"The motion has been moved," the mayor declared solemnly, as if he were a disinterested witness. "The question has been called. All in favor?"

A thunder of, "Aye! Aye! Aye!" pealed through the chamber.

"Do I hear—" the mayor began, and then Jesus Flores Suarez, who saw that he had better not be the last man clinging on to Lolita LeBron, called out, "I move to make the motion unanimous."

The mayor brought down his gavel hard.

"With*out* objection," he stressed. "I ask aldermen to come to the front of the chamber and offer thanks to the Romo family."

Mrs. Romo was short, sweet-faced, astonished, and sad. Her eyes were dewy under her black shawl as she nestled Vanessa against her knee and mouthed "Thank you," as Sunny passed. He raised his hands in front of his face, and touched his thumbs and fingers lightly.

"*Namaste*," he told them from behind steepled fingers. He could hear his voice struggling to speak above a whisper. "In Hindi, it means, 'I am humble before you.' "

The Cheng family stood several feet away. They looked respectful, thankful, and deeply moved. But awkwardness was apparent, too, in the way they held their eyes down. Their grandfather was alive. Yet the life of a fine young man—a father, a husband, a protector of his city— had been lost to save him. What grandfather wouldn't say that the sacrifice had gone in the wrong direction?

Council members drifted over to offer their hands. Their grandfather nodded feebly. One of his grandchildren, a girl of about ten, stood at his shoulder to translate as he stooped forward to hear soft words from the aldermen. Sunny pointedly took the old gentleman's hand and spoke into his face.

"Your family is also making great contributions to this city," Sunny told him. "We're glad you're here."

The mayor had come down from the rostrum to oversee the city's expression of grief. Jesus Flores Suarez tried to slink inconspicuously back into his seat in the second row, but the mayor beckoned him over with his arms. He took Jesus by his shoulders and said in a forceful voice that carried into the chamber's galleries, "Thank you for your statesmanship, Jesus."

Then the mayor drew him into an embrace, and administered three manly pats on his back. When Jesus' left ear was over the mayor's shoulder, he uttered private words of counsel.

"Be careful going home tonight, Jesus. Those folks in the Lolita Le-Bron Society don't take disappointment lightly."

The aldermen filed back into their seats, heads still bowed. The mayor moved back onto the rostrum.

"The wife is pretty," Luis Zamora, who sat just in front of Sunny's row of seats, remarked in a loud whisper. "The daughter's cute. I say the widow Romo remarries in a year."

"Another cop," suggested Jacobo Sefran, sitting to Sunny's left. "Some 'friend' of Vicente's who's probably always had his eye on her."

"In the meantime," said Luis Zamora, "I believe señora could use some comforting."

Wandy Rodriguez of the 30th turned and said in a low murmur, "She's Puerto Rican, Luis. Stick to your own kind."

And when she could hear low laughs in their throats beginning to break through, Jane Siegel hissed from the third row behind them, "Be respectful, will you? Shut the fuck up."

SATURDAY MORNING

By the time Sunny made it to his restaurant's kitchen the next morning, the staff was already setting up for lunch. Oscar and Wilmer had filled the small steel tubs near the door with brick-red tomato chutney, burgundy tamarind, white cucumber sauce flecked with green, and the beaming emerald mint sauce. From around the corner, he could hear Matina and his daughters laughing with a visitor.

Only Sgt. Gallaher stood when he turned the corner into the kitchen, tugging a long black whip of hair behind her neck. Her hair was pulled more tightly behind her head than yesterday, and tied with a small white scarf. She wore a red rose on her left lapel—over the heart—of her long black coat.

"We've been getting acquainted," she explained. Rula turned her head around from the small steel table where they sat.

"Sergeant McNulty mentioned the tall, pretty one."

"Sergeant McNulty is awfully pretty," Maureen Gallaher pointed out.

"But not so tall. And he told us that he doesn't have girlfriends."

"You *did* become friends."

"Do you have boyfriends?" Rita asked, and before Sunny could interpose himself in the conversation, he thought he could see the sergeant's face bloom.

"I work strange hours. I wear flat shoes," she explained.

"But you have such beautiful eyes," Matina told her.

"And you're armed and dangerous," said Rula. "Men must find that interesting." She hesitated over the last word, as if trying to identify an ingredient in a stew.

Sgt. Gallaher widened her smile and let out a schoolgirl's giggle.

"I've been proposed to three times," she said. "By men I was cuffing. Putting into handcuffs," she explained, when she saw Rula's eyes swell. "And I once got flowers from a man named Nick who held up a donut shop on Thorndale. I laid him out with my service flashlight when he ran out of the store, waving a piece. 'He saw stars,' is how we put it."

The sergeant turned down her chin, so that only the huge, blue lamps in her face could be seen across the table. Sunny decided to step in with a distracting observation.

"It won't get above twenty today," he told them. "But the flurries will stop. I heard it on the news, which is all about the mayor. The Bulls signed that guard from Argentina. Some French guy is swimming the English Channel and towing a trash barge by his teeth. O'Hare was ahead of Hartsfield in departures last year, but it was close. The Reverend Jackson will give the mayor's eulogy. It should be historic."

"It must be, Pappaji," Rula said, casting an eye and taking a slurp over the wide blue edge of a coffee mug. "You're not wearing your clown shoes."

Matina leaned over with more coffee and embraced Sunny wordlessly. He was wearing a blue blazer, his darkest charcoal slacks that still possessed the semblance of a crease, another silver tie, a white pocket square, and black brogues. Sunny's grassy cologne cut through the morning smells of coffee cooking against the side of the pot and white rice flour fermenting in a steel tub near the back.

"Has everyone had breakfast?" he asked.

"Mango ice cream and cold bondas from last night," said Rita. They were fried dough balls filled with potatoes, onions, ginger, chiles, and coriander leaves.

"Those dough things were delicious," said Sgt. Gallaher.

"I'll make you a dosa," Matina informed Sunny, pushing back her chair.

"Coffee is fine," he protested, but stayed seated as she moved over to the griddle. Sgt. Gallaher stood up again, too, and began pacing and guessing the ingredients in white bins along the kitchen's wall, touching the edge of her long index finger along the rims.

"Raisins, cloves, cardamom seeds. These green ones?" she asked.

"Fennell," said Sunny, who didn't need to raise his head from his coffee.

"The orange one has to be chili pepper. The dull green is cumin. I used to wait tables in a Mexican place. But these two . . ."

"Tumeric and coriander powder. You'll never guess the bottom shelf. No one does."

There were white powders, bright white and dull bone.

"They sure look like the kind of stuff you stop at Customs."

"Moong dal and lentil dal," Sunny revealed after a pause. The griddle behind Matina hissed as she splashed a handful of water onto the top, and the bubbles skipped and sizzled.

"Be nice to Sgt. Gallaher," said Rita. "She took us across the street to get phone cards this morning. We told her you weren't up yet and that you never let us do it alone."

Sgt. Gallaher truly blushed now and waggled the finger she had once used to wield a flashlight on the skull of a man who robbed a donut shop.

"I left my post. I shouldn't. But I made a judgment. The phone cards are important, I know."

Sunny said only, "Thank you, sergeant," as Matina sprinkled chopped onions and potatoes into the soft center of Sunny's dosa, where they hit the small, winking bubbles with a squashy plop.

The mayor's memorial service was the largest outpouring in the history of the city.

A million and a half people pressed into Millennium Park, surged over into Grant Park, and filled Michigan Avenue from the bridges along Wacker Drive, which were raised for a minute in tribute, down to Monroe and Adams. Tugboats, fireboats, and police boats plied along the river, shooting sprays in salute. All cars stopped as the hour of the mayor's memorial service approached, making the city harshly quiet. A hundred thousand people stood in the gloom and gripping chill to look up at huge screens raised in front of Picasso's ambiguously Trojan Daley Center sculpture and spilled out into Randolph, Washington, Dearborn, and Clark, their breath seeding a low sky of clouds across the streets and plaza. Another hundred thousand people huddled under the elevated tracks of the Green Line to look for the special silvery transit car that would convey the urn holding the mayor's embers from the platform at Lake Street, south to 63rd Street, where a convoy of motorcycle police would receive his cinders and escort them to the Jackson Park lagoon.

Doris Bacon would scatter his ashes into the water (the Parks and Recreation Department had turned tall heaters onto the lagoon overnight, so that the mayor's powdered remains would not simply skip across ice and blow away), as Buddy Guy sang "Sweet Home Chicago" as a dirge.

The mayor's memorial was held in the city's ornate old Cultural Center, formerly the public library. The gray light of the grim day toned down the dazzle of the green, gold, and turquoise tiles of the dome and surrounding skylight. Sprays and wreaths of white carnations, plump as children's heads, and yellow-eyed daisies were piled onto a small stage, flanked by the flags of the City of Chicago and the United States.

The most striking display was a white heart of daisies, slashed by a sash of red roses. The card was signed, "Mr. and Mrs. Linas Slavinskas."

A small table held the onion-shaped bronze urn that contained the mayor's ashes. Engravers had hastily inscribed it overnight with the refrain that Mrs. Bacon remembered from the mayor's favorite hymn: "Take Me As I Am." Linas, who sat in the second row of seats alongside Aldermen Barrow, Agras, and Sunny, put a hand gently on Vera's shoulder and leaned over to whisper, "On the other side it says, 'Or Else.' "

Rita and Rula, reflecting Sunny's fleeting new status, were seated to Sunny's left, Rita in a high-collared gray sweater and black coat, Rula in a black pinstripe jacket. Sunny knocked his heels together softly. His daughters looked down, risking mild smiles of endorsement at his black shoes. Sgt. Gallaher stood at a kind of attention at the front of their row of seats, her hands at her side and her long, black coat parted to reveal, for those who knew where to look, the polished leather holster that held her radio at her belt and her gun under her left arm.

Young men and women from the Moody Bible Institute choir, swishing the folds of their burgundy robes, began to sing with soft intensity:

> Yes, we'll gather at the river,
> The beautiful, the beautiful river;
> Gather with the saints at the river
> That flows by the throne of God.

The burgundy robes stepped down silently from the stage. Black and gold robes from the Pilgrim Baptist Church choir began to climb on. Heels clipped, throats cleared, and wooden planks creaked in the stillness. Sunny turned to take in those assembled behind him. He could make out the governors of Illinois and Indiana, the U.S. senators from Illinois, Wisconsin, Michigan, and Indiana, the president of the county board, a collection of congresspeople, and a medley of state senators and representatives.

A senator from California, a silver-haired woman in a charcoal suit who was running for president, scrambled to locate a seat; a couple of aides stood by with their hands opening and closing uselessly for folding chairs. She had been brought along by one of her major contributors, the chairman of the Chicago Bulls, who whispered gruffly and unsuccessfully to guards in blue suits. A former governor of Rhode Island, who had once been the Democratic nominee for president, had found a seat just behind a pink stone pillar. The high, dark pompadour that had become so famed for several months had now silvered and flattened. Gravity was beginning to tow his well-born granite jaw south, making the governor look more than a little equine (Sunny remembered that the mayor had disdained him as both humorless and unserious. When he saw clips of the governor campaigning, waving from a platform like a marionette who had just suffered an electric jolt, the mayor often turned to those around him and announced, "Glue truck is a comin',"). The governor now sat nobly alone behind the pillar, looking deeply moved.

Sunny glimpsed the president's secretary of Health and Human Services; the comptroller of New York; the mayor of Los Angeles, looking bleary and teary after an all-night flight; the mayor of Boston, looking ruddy and distracted; and the fire commissioner of Miami in his dress blacks, who had once been a deputy chief in Chicago. The mayor had passed him over for the chief's job after learning that the deputy was an accomplished amateur jazz violinist.

"I can see the photo now," he told Sunny grimly. "'Chief Fiddles while High-rise Burns'. I'm not doing that."

A man with a dark face and blistering brown eyes, rimmed red with drowsiness, caught Sunny's gaze and offered a half-bow with his head. They had met once. He was the deputy mayor of London. His name was Mansukhani. Sunny put his arm around his daughters and they all nodded back.

"Sindhi," Sunny explained to his daughters, and once the Deputy Mayor had turned away, Sunny raised his index finger slightly above his nose.

"Haughty," he whispered.

Rita's eyes fastened onto the mayor's urn, and she began to cry, leaning forward to grasp her knees. Sunny ran his hands over her back and shoulders and kissed her lightly between the shoulder blades.

"He was so nice to us. . . ."

Rita held her sister's hand, her own eyes stinging. The boys and girls in black and gold robes had begun to sing:

Helpless I am, and full of guilt
But yet for me Thy blood was spilt

And Thou canst make me what Thou wilt
And take me as I am.

Six pallbearers took up positions around the mayor's bronze urn. There were lieutenants in dress blues from the Chicago Police and Fire Departments, another dressed in the pressed working blues of the emergency medical services, another—Santiago Rivera, a 48th Ward constituent; Sunny made sure of that—in the green service uniform of the Chicago Park District, and a nurse in working whites whose arm patch bore the name of the hospital named for the mayor. The sixth pallbearer wore the gray-striped coveralls of the city's official maintenance crews. Sunny glimpsed Chief Martinez winking before he could make out the name on his breast pocket: *Sam Stanky*.

A seventh man in a stretchy gray suit and slumping shoulders nodded and murmured, and at his direction the pallbearers assumed seats. When the man turned around, Sunny recognized Frank Conklin and looked to catch the police chief's eye once again. He was glad to see that the mayor was not totally surrounded by strangers.

An elderly, bespectacled man with a half-moon of gray hair stepped behind a lectern embellished with the city's emblem and began to tell sweet stories about the mayor in a quiet, musical voice. He recalled that when the two of them were boys, they feigned tummy aches to be sent home from school and snuck into Comiskey Park to watch the White Sox take batting practice. Minnie Minoso threw them a ball as he trotted in from the field (Sunny remembered that in the mayor's rendition, Huck and Tom also filched cans of Hamm's beer from pallets in the loading docks). The man had recently retired as principal of the Ludwig van Beethoven grade school.

"Every time I ever had a youngster brought before me for ditching class," he said, "I'd tell him that story. I'd say, 'Now you can turn things around and become a mayor. A teacher, a lawyer, a policeman, or a principal. Or you can spend the rest of your life waiting for people to throw little bitty favors at you.'" When he finished, the principal stepped from behind the lectern and ran his fingers lightly over the top of his old friend's urn.

The Reverend Jackson stood up slowly, and took stately steps toward the lectern, with the slow pace of a processional. Masses of hands went up, snapping photos with cameras and phones. The reverend paused for several moments, as if to offer his unimpeded profile, before reaching into a vest pocket and extracting the elegant gold frames of his reading glasses.

"Take me as I am," he began softly. "Thou canst make me what Thou wilt. And take me as I am. . . ."

By the time the Reverend Jackson finished, most of the mayor's adversaries had succumbed to tears, and his supporters were beyond consolation. He came down from the lectern with the quick, clever step of an old quarterback and worked his way through the outstretched hands from the first row; the reverend had to catch a flight for Athens or risk missing his connection to Amman.

He put each of Sunny's daughters under an arm and kissed the top of their heads.

"Be sweet, baby," he told them. "Be strong."

He took both of Vera's hands in his own and planted an austere kiss on her cheek, as gently as he might on the forehead of a sleeping child.

"Moving on up," he told her, and withdrew one hand to squeeze Sunny's shoulder.

"Mr. Acting Interim," he hailed, while extracting his other hand to grasp Arty Agras at his elbow. "Hey, buddy," he told him.

Linas Slavinskas made a point of putting forth his own right hand. When the Reverend Jackson took it, Linas enfolded his left hand around their handshake like a clasp.

"That was very moving, reverend," he said. "I hope you'll do the same for me some day." The reverend emitted a tight smile.

"I'll look forward to that," he told Linas. "Real soon."

The Reverend Jackson had worked his way three seats down and was kissing the top of Wanda Jackson's hand in a fleeting farewell, aides dashing and guards converging, when he looked back at Linas and called, "I'll fly back from *Khartoum* if I have to."

Sgt. Gallaher and two uniforms moved to surround Sunny and his daughters as soon as the last clergy onstage had uttered his final amen. Borne along in their quick procession, Sunny reached out to snag Chief Martinez at the elbow. The uniforms hung back to stand just in front of Sunny, while Sgt. Gallaher stayed a few strides ahead with Rita and Rula.

"You talked with our friend from California?"

"I listened," the chief answered, staring ahead with a discernibly unimpressed expression.

"Any bearing on your investigation?"

"I suppose it narrows the list of suspects to eight million."

As Chief Martinez turned back to his own circle, Sunny saw Arty Agras's short, slumping silhouette from behind and put a hand softly on his shoulder.

"A dignified and moving affair that refracted the city that loved him, don't you think?" Arty asked. "The kids in blue sweaters who requited the Sandburg poem? From our Sabin Charter School on Hirsch."

"Outstanding," Sunny assured him. It seemed to Sunny that at least half a dozen batches of youngsters in school sweaters had recited Sandburg poems at the service. He got all the "hunched and humbled shoulders," the haunted and huddled multitudes riding the Halsted streetcar rather confused. "Inspirational," he added.

Sunny kept a friendly hand on Arty's shoulder and leaned down close to his left ear.

"Arty, they brought me the bill to approve the new contract with Earth First. I didn't sign it."

Arty drew back, the rusting curls of his toupee sticking to the slickness on his forehead in the heat of the crowd and lights.

"Sunny—that's paramount to a veto."

"I took a closer look, Arty," he explained. "Not just who was for it, who's not, and who's holding the laundry bag. The numbers, Arty. The contract with Earth First pays three hundred and forty dollars a ton to collect recycling. It costs about a hundred and fifty dollars a ton to collect trash. That's more than twice as much per ton. And we've got seven thousand tons a day. That gets to . . ."

Sunny had to pause to recall the figure that Claudia McCarthy had worked out for him on the small calculator in her purse.

" . . . million dollars of difference a year, Arty."

"Progress has a price, Sunny. We can't say no to the future."

"Encourage your friends to bring down the price of the future."

Arty reached a hand over to Sunny and tightened his thumb against his forearm; his voice tightened in his throat, as if he were struggling to speak underwater.

"Sunny, you *voted* for that contract."

"As an alderman."

Sunny let one of his own hands slide up to Arty's shoulder and squeezed it lightly. A passerby might see Arty's face flushing, Sunny's hand clasping his shoulder, and conclude the old friends were commiserating.

"Recycling is a religious conviction in my ward. I could hardly vote against it. I believe in it," said Sunny. "But for a couple of days, I've got to worry about making laws, not just campaign promises. That made me pause. You can't make a trashy deal smell like roses just because you stamp *'All Natural. Organic. One Hundred Percent Recycled!'* on the can."

"Landfills are a cancer, Sunny," Arty said urgently. "They contaminate our precious groundwater. They agitate global warming. We don't want to wake up one morning and see buzzards circling Millennium Park."

"They're recyclers too, Arty," Sunny suggested with premeditated lightness. "I'll bet they'd work for less than the buzzards at Earth First."

"Sunny—"

"*Urbs in Horto,* Arty." Sunny began to turn and caught Sgt. Gallaher's eyes to proceed. It was the city's motto: *City in a Garden.*

Arty took a step back and turned his chin down. When he spoke, his voice seemed to stall between a whisper and a moan. Sunny had to turn back and lower his head to hear, until it seemed to him that he was standing over Arty the way he used to stand over his daughters as they explained why certain teachers didn't understand them.

"Sunny, please. These are important people. *Very important,* Sunny. These people are urgently concerned about global warming and arctic preserves. These are people who say we can't let anything—*anyone,* Sunny—stand in the way of protecting our environment."

When Sunny spoke, he shook his head indulgently. "Remind those grown men with third-grade nicknames that it's hard for me to sign a bill with broken knuckles. I'm just walking the city away from a bad offer, Arty. There's a firm in St. Paul that does the job for a hundred and eight-five dollars a ton."

"St. Paul!" Arty gasped. "That's only half a city."

"And a firm in Toronto who can meet that."

"Sunny, we can't subcontract our recycling security to foreign interests."

Sunny began to take several deliberate steps away from Arty, nodding slightly to Sgt. Gallaher in a forward direction.

"I can see going to two hundred dollars a ton. As you say, Arty, we're not half a city. Your friends can take credit for being good citizens. If I don't sign the bill, they'll have to try to override it with the next mayor. Even if that's you, Arty—especially if it's you—there'll be a lot of questions. A lot of looking into Earth First."

The folding chairs snapped up behind Arty, like yawning alligators.

"Sunny, it was moved! It was voted! It passed!"

"And now it needs the mayor's signature," Sunny stepped toward the staircase. "Even one just filling in."

"Sunny! It was tied with a ribbon! It's the will of the people! *Sunny!*" Arty implored as Sunny flicked his right hand to motion Sgt. Gallaher to take the first step down the staircase. "Sunny! *You can't be a leader unless you go along with the majority!*"

They were out on Randolph Street, walking toward the beetle-black car Sgt. Mayer had kept running and burping steam, before Eldad Delaney turned to Sunny and asked, "What did I hear Alderman Agras say?"

Rita and Rula had had enough of mourning and memorial and decided to run along to the State Street stores, which would reopen after the memorial service. He peeled five twenties into their hands, then a couple more, and finally a credit card.

"I don't need anything. *You* don't need anything. Get whatever. Just don't say you were looking for me."

"You can always use a dozen handkerchiefs."

"All of the stores that you go in have mannequins with rings in their noses."

City Hall was just five blocks away, and Sunny's instinct was to walk. But Sgt. Gallaher said that the mourners would be teeming in the streets, and persuaded him to ride. Eldad sat alongside him in the back, the sergeant just across from them. The throng of cars was so thick that Sunny doubted they moved more than a foot a minute. Every now and then, a red face under a ski cap, flaring steam from his mouth and nostrils, would press against a tinted passenger window and demand, "Who the fuck is that?"

Eldad announced, "The alderman and I need to talk, sergeant."

"I need to be right here," she said. "But I don't hear a thing."

"Nothing mysterious," he hastened to explain. "But politics can sound harsh."

"I'm a cop," she reminded Eldad, and then, when his eyes hardened, she flicked her fingers against her head.

"Went swimming this morning," she assured him. "Water in my ears."

Eldad told Sunny that all phones, pagers, and message systems had been turned off during the memorial service, so the forty-some aldermen sitting behind them had scrawled messages on scraps of paper and tossed them, sometimes rows away.

"It looked like the worst sixth-grade class you ever saw," he said.

"A heartening display of aldermanic literacy," said Sunny, who found himself looking for Sgt. Gallaher's eye. "I would have guessed that we could only throw twigs and stones."

Eldad explained that the nineteen votes they had predicted for Vera seemed correct. She might be able to pick up six more in the second round from among aldermen who would cast their first ballots for Arty Agras; and even a couple inclined to vote for Linas. But such hope soared on the idea that Vera would begin to look inevitable. Aldermen voting for someone else would conclude that there was no reward in losing, and distinct disadvantages in opposing Vera. Some spoils might even be earned from being one of the last votes to make Vera Barrow mayor.

But she needed to win early, or votes would begin to fall away like loose shingles. This was exactly the circumstance hoped for by Daryl Lloyd. He could not win enough council votes to become mayor. Yet if he could win enough to thwart Vera, he had a chance to position himself as the preeminent African-American candidate to run against Linas next year.

Linas, for that matter, preferred running against Daryl to Vera. He and Alderman Lloyd shared the conviction that the other made him look more plausible.

"So now Daryl is making noises like he won't wait," Eldad told Sunny. "He might just jump."

"On a platform of pulling a gun on the council?" asked Sunny. "That could be popular."

Eldad said that Dorothy Fisher of the 3rd had let it be known that Daryl had assured her of his support for a zoning change.

"She wants to permit construction of a thirteen-unit condominium building on south Drexel," he explained.

"Housing is good," said Sunny. "Everyone from the Holy Father to Dr. Kevorkian is in favor of housing. But sales, not rental, on that block? Does Dorothy have any other interest?"

"I'll check. Miles Sparrow wants to create a TEZ to turn a vacant lot at Seventy-ninth and Halsted into parking for a new block of doctor's offices."

TEZs were a city program devised by the mayor called Tax Enhancement Zones. It permitted the city to declare a parcel of land as being off the property tax rolls, to induce someone to buy, develop it, and create jobs in neighborhoods that might otherwise be forsaken. But the mayor and council had creatively reinterpreted the program. There were now posh hotels, day spas, and co-ops on several TEZ zones, too. Sunny sat up at the utterance of the initials.

"He says you won't have doctors down there unless you give them parking," Eldad explained.

"Their Cadillacs too good for a public lot?"

"It's for patients. Public lots get full. They cost. You don't want a patient to have to choose between parking and filling a prescription."

Sunny rubbed his index finger in small, slow circles over his chin.

"Donald Trump isn't coming to Seventy-ninth and Drexel," Eldad pointed out. "Vacant lots are the devil's playgrounds. Parade grounds for prostitutes."

"And garages become shopping malls for hard drugs. What did Vera tell him?"

"'We'll see.' "

"I'll ask. Maybe she smelled a rat in the garage. What's the projected cost?" Sunny asked.

"A million and a half," said Eldad.

"That's a lot of digital rectal exams."

"Those aren't the fingers to worry about," Eldad replied, flexing the digits on his right hand. "Miles doesn't miss many targets of opportunity. Speaking of which . . . Luis Zamora wants a TEZ for Breslau Brewing's old warehouse. To expand their adult learning center. He's with Arty out of the chute, but . . ."

The 31st Ward alderman ran a beer distributorship, delivering nine different brands from national brews to Pilsen Pilsner to restaurants and taverns.

"On Fullerton?" asked Sunny. "I saw a coffee bar nearby just a few months ago. That's usually the first sign. Then a wine shop, then an organic grocer, then next thing, Hilton wants the warehouse."

"But until they do," said Eldad. "The brewery keeps the building off the tax rolls."

"Christ, that's clever," said Sunny. "I guess that's why some of us drink beer, and others own the breweries."

Their car was moving as slowly as if two men were pushing it through heavy snow. They were only now approaching State Street, and the short arm of the old green Field's clock was rising toward one in the window over Eldad's shoulder. Sunny sighed, smiled, loosened his maroon muffler, and touched a button at his right elbow to lower the tinted window just enough for cold, fresh air to whistle into the car.

"Making an empty warehouse into an educational center. Jobs. Adult classes. Immigrants holding jobs and learning English. I could vote for that."

"He votes for ours," Eldad reminded him. The site of an old auto body shop on North Clark had been declared a TEZ, and the block now held a chain bagel shop, a franchise coffee shop, and Clarabelle's Preschool.

"Maybe we should remind Luis that he can waste his vote on the first ballot," said Sunny. "But on the second, he has a chance to bring Mayor Barrow into office, and Mayor Barrow knows how to express her appreciation."

(Sunny was appalled to hear Brooks Whetstone's expression emerge from his own mouth.)

Eldad said that Vernetta Hynes Griffin of the 37th was a sure vote for Vera on all ballots, but she had a concern.

"She wants to delay implementation of Eleven-B."

It was an ordinance, set to take effect in March, which required trash compactors for all buildings that produced fifty or more cubic yards of garbage a week.

"It's been a year," Sunny pointed out. "They should be ready."

"Fuel prices," Eldad reminded him, raising a hand from the middle of his chest to just above his forehead. "Vernetta says that the landlords on Austin Boulevard are locked into leases. They can't pass on the costs. They've had to take money they were going to spend on trash compactors and pay for heat."

"We had a trash smasher installed at the restaurant," said Sunny. "It's a thousand, fifteen hundred."

"But apartment buildings on Austin Boulevard?" asked Eldad. "Do we want them to choose between giving heat to residents and squeezing trash into bunny pellets?"

"That's why we pass laws," Sunny said, squirming at the slow pace and blasting heat. "They're not supposed to choose. Trash compactors keep rats away. If Vernetta's landlords think trash compactors are expensive, they should weigh the costs of paying a settlement to the parents of the first sleeping child that gets bitten by a rat on March second."

Sunny drummed his fingers along an armrest and tipped his head on the back of the long black seat.

"She wants a delay, alderman, not a suspension," Eldad said just above Sunny's drumroll. "Just to give the landlords a couple of warmer months to catch up. April and May. She's with Vera. But she says that friends have to know that friendship is worth something."

Sunny rolled his muffler over and over in his hands, as if wrapping something fragile, then stretched it out with an audible snap.

"Maybe three months isn't so bad," he said finally. "Blame global warming. Unscrupulous oil companies."

Eldad squeezed two fingers into his pants pocket and pulled out a scrap of card stock.

"Sanford Booker," he announced. "Has two people who want jobs in the Bureau of Forestry, cutting down trees. He says they're the best qualified. He knows them—they've worked for his contracting company. That's why he has to stay away from writing a recommendation."

"It's also why we do. A letter, a phone call, this close to the special council session—stupid."

Eldad pressed the scrap of paper against his chest with a finger.

"Why don't we tell Sandy that *Mayor* Barrow will be pleased to work with the alderman on seeing that the best possible public servants are hired in the city of Chicago? The only recommendation that Dr. Daryl Lloyd will have the authority to make after Monday is to floss nightly."

Eldad tented his fingers over a knee and brightened.

"I almost forgot to tell you: Vernetta says that Daryl offered to do a dental implant for Emil Wagner." The 32nd Ward alderman was a home security consultant with a heavy red rump roast of a face. Eldad waggled the scrap of paper until it made a flapping sound. "I even wrote down the particulars: tooth number five, upper right. A lateral incisor."

"Daryl once offered to a repair a crown for me," Sunny recalled. "But I thought he'd only steal the gold filling."

The car had finally pulled to a stop on Randolph Street. Officer Mayer had softly told Sgt. Gallaher that it could take another fifteen minutes to pull around to the LaSalle Street entrance of the hall, but she could observe Sunny's impatience and fidgeting and asked if he would like to make the walk from there.

"Thirty to forty steps," she said. "But, with these crowds, sir, I'll have to ask that you wait until I can get two uniforms out in front." She leaned into the door while speaking into the radio on her belt and rocked open the door long enough for a blast of wind to blow the tassels of Sunny's muffler against his ears, tickling. When the car door had snapped closed and silence had returned, Eldad sat back and just said softly to Sunny, "Ivan."

The 41st Ward alderman ran a neighborhood credit union.

"Arty."

"Yes. But. He wants traffic on runway fourteen R-thirty-two L cut after eleven p.m."

Sunny had unwound his muffler and now stretched it between his hands.

"Every few months we go through this. You've got long-range jets coming in from Hong Kong, Tokyo. You've got—"

"He's got constituents who say the sound depreciates their property."

"Did they think that the northwest side was an old growth forest? There's the whole state of Maine for those who want the quiet life. He can't get Arty to sign on?"

"Alderman Agras apparently shares your analysis. As well as bedbugs with the Air Traffic Controllers and the Transport Worker's unions."

"Losing a couple of hundred jobs on a shift at the airport depreciates property, too," said Sunny. "A few homeowners are getting their windows rattled. The people who work there—apartment dwellers—can lose their jobs. An international airport has to be a twenty-four-hour operation. Otherwise, they'll start building them in Nowheresville, and nobodies get the jobs."

"Homeowners stay put and vote," Eldad reminded him. "People who lose their jobs can wind up moving to—*At-a-lanta*." He pronounced the name as if it were one of the smallest of three hundred volcanic isles of the Aleutian Islands.

Sgt. Gallaher opened the door about a foot wide and leaned down to declare, "Whenever you're ready, alderman." Sunny saw small grains of snow dance and melt in the wind sluicing into the car and leaned over to tap Eldad's knees with his ungloved knuckles.

"I wonder," he said. "Put in a call to the general manager at the big arena right across from the runways at I-90. That arena changes names more than a porn star. They've got basketball games and beauty pageants there all the time. I never once heard somebody say, 'And I couldn't hear Miss Naperville sing, 'Raindrops' because they've got planes landing and taking off.' "

Eldad turned his head up with sudden new attention.

"They must put soundproofing in the rafters and walls," said Sunny. "Let's find out what it is—brand names, retailers. I'll explain to Ivan that you can make a major motion picture quicker than you can get the federal government to authorize new landing restrictions. You'll have everyone from AARP to the International Criminal Court file impact statements. But by the end of the year, we can get a bill authorizing payments to homeowners to install soundproofing. Ivan can put checks into their hands."

Sunny pushed his shoulder over to the car door and paused for Eldad to put his feet forward and pull himself out. By the time Sunny stood up on the Randolph Street sidewalk, Sgt. Gallaher's dark hair was adorned with icy white flurries.

"I'm sure the mayor's conversations were a lot more colorful," he said as he fell in behind her long steps. "All our talk was about parking and trash."

"Politicians love to talk trash," she called back. "Food, roads, and trash." Two uniforms had snapped open a door next to the revolving one that other people—including Sunny until recently—had to use, and they stepped into the quiet of City Hall on a Saturday. Small threads glistened as the flurries melted and slid down the sergeant's dark hair.

"It's actually getting rare to hear politicians talk politics," Sunny told her in a low voice. "Politics is being outsourced like everything else. You hire professionals to ask for money, the way you can pay someone to talk dirty to you on the phone. Politicians used to hire a campaign manager—some old school chum or business partner that you could trust to be unscrupulous on your behalf—to run the campaign while the candidate took positions. Now, politicians consult consultants the way Hollywood stars confer with their psychiatrists and astrologers. Won't go to the bathroom without them."

The empty brass cab of Elevator One waited for them in the dim, hushed halls.

The police superintendent of Chicago also waited, his blue coat folded into a side chair and drizzling onto the rug of the conference room that had been appropriated for Sunny's use. Chief Martinez turned at the sound of Sunny's approach and dipped his head slightly to signal Sgt. Gallaher to stay nearby.

"Don't dribble on the carpet, Matt," Sunny told him. "They might charge a damage fee on my way out."

"Two people are being held in connection with the death of the mayor," Chief Martinez announced. Sunny drew in a small, stunned breath.

"It may amount to nothing. But . . ." said the chief. "They're both service people at Quattro's. The first goes by the name Carlos Ponce. He has also been Zambrano, Reyes, Rios, Contreras, Alomar, and Uribe."

"I know those names. . . ." said Sunny, and the police chief smiled curtly.

"Baseball players."

"Ah yes. Well he's smart enough not to try to pass himself off as Ichuri Suzuki."

"A real criminal mastermind," the chief agreed. "We found him with a change of clothes and almost a thousand dollars packed in a laundry sack, hiding out in a garbage trough under Wacker—knowing that Streets and San wouldn't be through until Monday. He's wanted in Guanajuato, Hidalgo, and Mexico City. Drugs, smuggling, money laundering—the whole combo platter."

Sunny shucked his own tan coat, spattered with snow and suddenly as heavy as a grocery sack, and held it out until a uniformed man took it in his arms.

"I'm glad you got him before he could run off with my daughters. Still, Matt, how do you go from any of that to something like this?"

"Someone could have threatened him with exposure," the chief ventured. "'Do this, we wipe your debt off the books.' Or he could have a stash of doubloons waiting for him somewhere. He had proximity to the poison and the pizza. When word leaks, I'd rather have him locked up than at large."

"Holding him on Mexican warrants?"

The chief nodded almost imperceptibly.

"Mexico City detectives arrive Monday. I told them that I know Sunday is a day for faith and family among we Mexicans. Their prisoner can enjoy the hospitality of a holding cell on North Larrabee until then."

"Which gives your folks at the Eighteenth District—"

"—about forty hours."

Sunny squirmed in a side chair, and knocked his muddy heels together before replying.

"Well, be hospitable indeed. And the other?"

"Kambiz Said. Twenty-six, and, conveniently for us, working on a counterfeit green card," Chief Martinez explained. "He fled the restaurant, too, and when the mommy and daddy tracked him to a basement apartment on Kimball, they discovered that he is a frequent visitor to a white supremacist web site. Forty-something times in recent weeks."

"His name sounds . . ."

"Iranian. By way of Jordan. The group in question is called the National Vanguard." The police chief looked down at a cluster of printed pages, and seemed to trace words with an index finger. "Although they say: 'Persons of Jewish descent, homosexuals or bisexuals, persons with a non-White spouse or sexual partner, or persons with more than an undetectable trace of non-White ancestry are specifically barred from National Vanguard membership.' End quote," the chief emphasized.

"Good Christ. And he didn't think that meant him?"

"Maybe he came to the site just to be appalled. Or for the music— they play something called White Power hip hop. Or maybe he thinks Persians are descended from Aryans, and they mean everybody but him."

"Like Kashmiris," Sunny suggested.

"Look, Mr. Roopini, both you and I know that bigots come in all tints."

"Like idiots," Sunny repeated. "And he's being held—"

"At the Fourteenth." The Shakespeare Avenue district. Sunny's voice subtly changed pitch.

"Matt, how did you folks discover his surfing habits?"

"His laptop was on the toilet seat."

"Along with a court order?"

"Plain view. Obvious and germane. The mayor had been murdered. The subject had fled. He had access to the means of murder." Sunny noted that the police chief would not deign to identify a pizza as a weapon. "Mr. Jenkins had done his Dumpster dive. Our officers had to assume the computer could contain clues."

"No time for a warrant?"

"In theory. But practically, that would take an hour. There was an ongoing situation. Evidence could be destroyed. Lives could be threatened. In an hour, someone on the north side could be in Milwaukee. Someone in Milwaukee could be . . ." Chief Martinez hesitated over an example. "In *Wauwatosa*," he declared finally, then warmed to the word. "Someone in *Wauwatosa* could be in the woods. Someone in the woods could hide for years among bears and woodpeckers."

"You might have to tell a court how nature works," Sunny advised, and the police chief tipped back in his chair and lowered the brim of his service hat over the back of his head.

"I'll gladly explain that our officers acted aggressively to protect the people of this city," he said softly. "They didn't flinch because a lawyer might try to take them down later. I'd rather explain a procedural error than another murder."

Sunny smiled.

"You'll be sipping rum punch in Dubai when that happens, Matt. Or whatever they drink there."

"Orange juice, I believe," said the chief.

"Any ties between the two?"

"So far, only that they swabbed the same floors and set the same tables."

"And you're sure we're not looking at a couple of wet matches here and seeing weapons of mass destruction?"

"We're sure of nothing," said Chief Martinez. "That's why I don't want to let them out of our grip until we are."

"You found a thousand dollars on Roberto Clemente—whatever he calls himself?" asked Sunny. "Not top dollar for a paid assassin."

"But just enough to get to—I don't know—Trinidad and Tobago," and when Sunny rocked back on the rear legs of his chair, the police chief said with pointed gentleness, "You know, sir, it doesn't take a Leonardo or an Einstein to kill someone famous. Look it up in the history books."

The men let the chief's observation float between them for a moment; Sunny returned the front legs of his chair to the floor, squishing softly as they heard a shrill twitter from a police traffic whistle outside.

"And you've ruled out any possibility with Collins?"

The police chief hesitated only slightly and plucked the white gloves of his dress uniform out of a deep side pocket and balled them against his chin.

"Nothing is ruled out. But Collins . . ." Chief Martinez let the fingers of the gloves fall over his chin. "I suppose no man looks very appealing when you have to gut his life open. He told some people that the mayor was a corrupt bastard who spouted populist rhetoric but kissed ruling class ass and repressed the people with a political machine. He told others that the mayor was a shrewd, selfless public servant who dared to fight special interests and antediluvian forces everywhere. Depending."

"On?"

"Who he was trying to impress."

"No funny money?" Sunny asked, but the chief was already shaking his head.

"Trust fund baby unto death. Every month, interest just accrued. He couldn't be bothered. Holes in his black nylon socks. Didn't even open the copies of the check deposits. No red flags. The mayor however . . ."

Sunny sat up, and for the first time, the police chief allowed a grin to stretch across his face.

"A model of frugality," he explained. "Bank records say that he spent just twenty-three thousand nine hundred five dollars all of last year."

"Is that possible?" asked Sunny. "Apartment, food, clothing . . ."

"A place on Milwaukee Avenue gave him suits and shoes," said Chief Martinez. "A market on Hyde Park Boulevard sent over milk, peanut butter, coffee—a whole smoked turkey, if he wanted. A place on Rush sent over bottles of Maker's Mark and Gayle's root beer. A drugstore delivered toothpaste, soap, shampoo, razor blades, ointments, creams, and jellies that, even in death, should remain private. Never a charge."

The chief shook his head, like a parent beholding the scrawls of a six-year-old on white walls.

"Brazen. Blatant. And of course as we now know, the U.S. Attorney practically co-signed his tax returns."

"Then how did he even spend twenty-three thousand dollars?" asked Sunny.

"Tips," the chief explained after a pause. "Near as we can tell. He'd let the owner—expect the owner—to pick up a thousand-dollar dinner check for four. Smoked Irish salmon, sixty-four ounce porterhouse, garlic sautéed spinach, macadamia turtle pie, a fine cabernet. Then he'd leave five hundred dollars in cash for the wait staff—and walk out to applause."

"A man of the people," said Sunny, who then added quietly, "I had the porterhouse."

"Chicken and peppers for me," said Chief Martinez.

"Hard to hate a man like that," said Sunny.

"Well, somebody managed," the chief reminded him.

The splat and trill of traffic whistles outside reminded Sunny to turn to his wrist: It was just a few minutes before four.

"It was good to see Frank Conklin with the mayor. He really did love him. And the mayor loved him. Remember? 'My Irish Wolfhound.' I gather everything with Frankie is in order?"

"For us. Not at home, though," and when Sunny arched his eyebrows Chief Martinez understood that the acting interim mayor did not want to be spared any seamy details.

"Let's put it this way," he began. "Frankie won the Claudia McCarthy Open."

"No! The dog. The cad. The lucky bastard. His wife?"

"He left home a few weeks ago. Wife *and* kids."

"Then I'm sorry for everyone," said Sunny.

"They're trying to do it as honorably as these things are done," said the chief. "We had to speak to Frank's wife, of course. There were a few phone messages and emails. 'I want to cut off your balls, I want to wring her fucking neck.' Nothing you wouldn't expect. And nothing that gets to the mayor."

"Frankie fucking Conklin!" Sunny rolled the words out like the bark of a football cheer.

"She had a boyfriend, too. A *barista* somewhere on Wells."

Sunny held his hands up in mocking incredulity.

"But there's something about a man in a CPD uniform," said the police chief, straightening himself into a parade stance. "Even plain clothes."

The chief had seen Sunny sneak a glimpse of his watch and began to fasten the six brass buttons on his heavy coat. Sunny drew near and put a light hand on the gold stripes that ran across his arm.

"I'm glad you're here, Matt. These next few days are critical."

The police chief reached his third button. "Well, for a little while," he amended, and resettled the coat along his shoulders.

"But you can be confident about your future, Matt," Sunny went on in a low, level voice. "You're just a month away from blue waters, sugary beaches, and enough zeroes in the bank to send your kids to Harvard. What you've just laid out: it could be nasty. The chance of a racial assassination. A couple of immigrants—from places like that, too—in custody but not charged." Sunny shuddered willfully. "That's why we need to get ahead of rumors. You can afford to have absolute autonomy, Matt. No politician, newsman, or prosecutor can touch you. Observe all the rules, chief," Sunny advised him. "But remember the stakes."

"Utterly clear, alderman," the chief said, with a small, stiff, nod of his head under his heavy cap, and departed the conference room, blue uniforms in snow-slick coats in tow.

Sgt. Gallaher stood up to tell Sunny she would be right outside the door. Her blue eyes were unblinking; she kept her hands thrust deep into her pockets.

"Are we going to pretend that you didn't hear any of that?" he asked.

"Yes sir. Unless you ask me a direct question," she smiled, and went on to spare him the silly discomfiture. "From what I heard, it could be significant. Or it could be nothing."

Sunny had returned to his chair and ran a hand over an arm, knead-
ing something every few inches.

"You've learned how to talk like a pol, sergeant," he told her. "We
arrange sentences like paint and tile swatches, any way you want.
'We must not negotiate out of fear, but we must never fear to negotiate. 'We must abandon the old and worn, but embrace the tried and
true.' 'Observe the rules, but remember the stakes.' " Sunny put his
hands on his knees and began to rub his palms along the pinstripes.

When the sergeant chuckled so unexpectedly that she put a gloved
hand to her mouth, Sunny chanced to tell her, "Thank you for taking
the girls to get phone cards."

"I knew they're important."

"You can't imagine."

"I can *only* imagine," said the sergeant; and when Sunny just sat
back, turning up the souls of his shoes, she added softly, "You know, sir,
anyone assigned to your watch reads the case file."

Sunny slid back into his chair—more resigned than relieved,
thought the sergeant.

"Then you know about as much as I do," he said. "Dusk on a November afternoon. Santa Clauses and red-nosed reindeer in the windows of all the Indian and Kosher delis. Two guys on the street, who
had records from the age of twelve. It was getting late in the day and
they needed to score. So they went to where they thought people kept
money. It could have been a donut shop; it wound up being that currency exchange. They waved their guns. Mr. Yawar, who runs the place,
told them all the cash now goes directly down a hole. Into a safe that
only opens on the other end in Mongolia. That's what everybody does
nowadays. Everybody knows that—but those two. Crackheads. *Crap-
heads*. They fired into the glass. But that kind of glass is thick, you
know? They couldn't score. Their blood was boiling. They couldn't pull
off an everyday stickup. Then, they couldn't even make a crack in a
pane of glass with a gun . . ."

Sunny caught his voice as it snagged; when he spoke, it was if he
had to steer his words up a hill.

"The Yawars said they thought she said something. They couldn't hear from behind the glass. Elana was on her feet. She opened her hands—twelve dollars and six phone cards. The two guys said they didn't remember what she said. On advice of counsel, I assume. She must have begged them to throw away the guns. Walk out while they still could. She must have said—maybe this was a mistake—'Let me help you.' She helped people sleeping on the street. She helped dogs and cats cringing under Dumpsters. She helped *me*. They said they remembered nothing. Can you imagine? Her last words . . ."

Sunny turned away in his chair, and then when he couldn't bring his arm down across the rest, he twisted his seat around in three small rasps against the carpet. The legs of the chair creaked like shinbones.

"You ask yourself what anyone might have done. That's a delusion, isn't it? A little guilt makes you feel less helpless. *If* we had run the Saturday buffet to two instead of three, she might have run that errand an hour earlier. *If* it had been Sunday. *If* there was a parallel universe. *Ifs* are superstitions—like saying it would have made some difference if you had worn red socks or a lucky hat. There are what, five hundred murders a year here? How many of them really have a why? Why does someone kill someone they don't hate—that they don't even know? No storm, no lightning, just out of the blue, some thunderbolt, some meteorite, comes down on the person who least deserves it. Sick and crazy can wipe out beautiful and worthy. Of all the things I ever wanted my daughters to learn, I wish they could have missed that."

A long police whistle trilled outside. The lights of the conference room seemed to buzz under the sudden, white-walled stillness. They heard an isolated shout from an alley. They heard the chuffs of a LaSalle Street bus, and the slick frizzle of tires crackling over melting snow. Sgt. Gallaher brought the ends of her coat around her, so that the short collar covered her chin.

"Yes sir," she began, then decided just to shrink down against the cold wall.

18

Sunny left the copies of city legislation, signed and unsigned, on Claudia McCarthy's desk. He and a flanking of uniforms, lead by Sgt. Gallaher, moved at a five-o'clock clip through the halls when they passed the glass-paned door stenciled PRESS ROOM. He held himself up for a step. Reporters were working on their stories about the mayor's funeral, summarizing his legacy, and speculating, with no specific or particular knowledge, about the succession. Sunny lingered for a moment; he wondered if he should pay a call.

Sunny had once been with the mayor when he decided to drop in early one afternoon, no warning to reporters or advance word to his guards.

"We'll catch the chihuahuas unawares," he told Sunny. "Pat their heads, give them a treat. Let them know you're coming, and they can look up who the president of Slovenia is, just before you walk in the door. Then they ridicule you for not knowing."

When the mayor had walked in, the midmorning babble of desultory phone calls into desks and editors, the strident reassurance that nothing of consequence was—or ever was—afoot, the raindrop spatter of fingers tapping keyboards, and the exploratory calls for lunch orders—"Wanna go Greek? A little Mex?"—had subsided at the first sight of the mayor's famous purple dinosaur silhouette materializing in such an unfamiliar place. The two men from the Tribune stood up in silent astonishment. A woman from the Sun-Times, the nominal dean of the City Hall regulars, stepped forward with an apologetic sweep of her arm at the tumble of decrepit desks, the birdcage litter of curling old newspapers, and the cemetery landscape of cold, old coffee cups.

"Good morning, ladies and gentlemen," said the mayor in a low, courtly voice. He stood in front of a boxy old television set that Arty Agras had cadged from the auctioneers overseeing a sale of used furniture from the Bismarck Hotel. The reporters watched it during afternoon Cub games, and on the morning the World Trade Center had been cut down.

"I've just come to pass along my regards in a neighborly fashion. Here we are, just three floors away, and we never get together for a cup of coffee and a plate of cookies, do we?"

"Would you like some coffee, Mr. Mayor?"

He took a sniff and launched a face of distaste in the direction of that morning's brew, which was beginning to bubble like road repair tar.

"No thank you. I appreciate the offer." The mayor turned his head and instructed an aide, "Send a pound down here of the Tanzanian peaberry that the Austrian consul general sends us."

The reporter from the Sun-Times wrung her hands.

"We had a tin of Christmas cookies somewhere," she remembered, "but I haven't seen it for a few weeks."

The mayor turned his head once more.

"And add some of those fine golden biscuit beurre that Audrey Tatou brought along for lunch last week." He turned his face back to the reporters.

"She's making a film here, you know. I meant to invite you folks in. But we were fussing about something that day."

The man from the Daily Southtown began to remember the fuss (a functionary in the City Clerk's office had told the jury at his bribery trial that he had been personally recommended for his position by the mayor), but the other reporters shrank back from their colleague, as if he had just put his hands on an electric fence.

It was then that the mayor's brown eyes grew suddenly flinty, and his smile hardened like a tire chain across his chin. One of his cam-

paign posters had been taped to the wall. It proclaimed CHICAGO'S
OWN in bold red capital letters across the top, bordered by the four
blue stars of the city's flag, all above a classic, smiling portrait of the
mayor (from six years ago, to be sure) looking vigorous, warm, and in-
domitable.

Five darts had been thrown into his picture, three in his cheek-
bones, one in his chin, and one in his scalp.

The woman from the Polish Daily News finally announced, "We do
that for every mayor, Mr. Mayor."

"Actually," murmured someone behind her, "it's a mark of respect."

The mayor let a pause grow large in the room.

"Clearly," he finally said.

The reporters urgently examined every inch and fissure of the tops
of their shoes.

"Let's throw a few," the mayor suddenly declared.

It took the reporters a few moments to absorb their amazement.
The lady from the Sun-Times at last stepped forward to begin pulling
darts out of the mayor's face.

"There was a time, when I spent more time in bars," he said affably
as she worked. "I made sort of a study of this divertissement and was
reasonably good at it."

The mayor unbuttoned his smooth gray jacket while the woman
from the Sun-Times handed the darts to him in a bundle. He beheld
their tips, counted them carefully, and appeared to blow dust from
their points before drawing back his left arm and throwing the first
dart with a quick, surprisingly smart flip (the mayor had been a star
high school third baseman, and sometimes startled onlookers with his
residue of physical grace—"like a polar bear diving underwater,"
Linas Slavinskas once said). The dart dipped at the end of its flight,
piercing the iconic mayoral chin.

"Good throw, sir!" the reporters shouted a little hesitantly, and
clapped with the insecurity of people at a modern jazz recital who
weren't quite certain when a set was done.

"Merely a shaving cut," the mayor growled.

The second hit just an inch to the right. The third dart was slightly wide, so that it clipped his right cheek. The mayor grunted softly, then drew his arm back, just over his shoulder. The fourth dart shot out, straight as the flight of a bullet, into the tip of his nose.

"Way to go! Way to go!" The reporters churned their arms above their heads and barked like fevered dogs.

The mayor whistled his last shot down, on a line below his nose, striking a few feet below the bottom edge of the poster. There was awkward silence as the reporters wondered why his last throw had gone so badly off course. Then they just as suddenly understood: The mayor had thrown the last dart into that unseen territory that, if the campaign poster had been full-size, would have been the mayoral groin.

Hoots and shouts rang against the large windowpanes looking down over LaSalle Street. The mayor shouted into the swell of sound, "I am impervious there! I am impervious!"

The mayor rearranged his jacket, settled it on his shoulders, removed his pink silk pocket square, and puffed it afresh into his lapel pocket as he waited for the din to decline.

"Well, we've had a delightful time in your clubhouse," the mayor began. "A welcome distraction from my momentous duties. But regretfully, I have to take my leave. I'm going back upstairs to my office now. I'm going to appoint a few city officials. I'm going to sign a few slips of paper that will spend a few million dollars of your tax money—fixing roads, repairing bridges, building six new schools. I've got phone calls to return. The head of the Board of Trade, the Chinese trade commissioner, the president of the United States. I've got to clear time to have a heart-to-heart with Roman Abramovich. Nothing like a rich Russian who wants to see his name in the sky. He sold a couple of soccer players to buy that site over on west Monroe. Now Helmut Jahn has designed him a one-hundred-and-eighty-story building. Tallest in the world. It was going to be a hundred-and-sixty, but someone in Shanghai said they wanted to build something bigger. I said, 'Roman, oh Roman, do we want the world to think that a bunch of slave labor gangs in China can build taller than our minority-owned contractors and union construction crews in Chicago?' Well, Roman

laughed and laughed. 'Right-inski you are, Mr. Mayor,' he said. So it's going to be one hundred and eighty stories. The tallest building in the world is coming back home. It'll cost two billion dollars. Maybe three. But as many people are going to be in that building every day as live in San Francisco. That building is going to be on postcards, calendars, snow globes, key chains, prophylactic foils, and movie screens. It will have the most recognizable profile since Rudolph Valentino. It'll be a symbol of the century. Your children will grow up pointing to it in the sky," the mayor told them softly. *"Right next to the moon."*

He had turned in the frame of the doorway to deliver his departing words.

"You boys and girls have a good time, too," the mayor told them as gently as he might read a nap time story to a class of third graders. *"Writing your little stories."*

Sunny decided just to keep walking.

SATURDAY NIGHT

Sunny asked to be taken to a small strip mall on a block of Racine Avenue in which painted signs seemed to scream back and forth as streetlights snapped on. ASIA QUAKE EMERGENCY FUND commanded one. ISLAM: MEDICINE FOR ALL EVILS bellowed another, while ADAM'S APPLE HEAD SHOP, KOLLEL TORAS CHESED, and 2,000 SONGS IN TAGALOG; 5,000 SONGS IN MANDARIN howled across the block.

One of the uniforms in Sunny's traveling crew pulled open the door of a storefront with windows that seemed to be covered with the slick white backs of posters.

"Don't like this," said Sgt. Gallaher, who for the first time thrust out an arm to hold Sunny back from a step. "Are you sure?"

"It's a restaurant," Sunny said as the sizzle of garlic began to reach them through the frigid air.

"A *secret* restaurant?"

"A *Korean* restaurant," he explained. "They believe that eating is private. Strangers shouldn't see strangers eating."

A bell on the door jangled as it snapped shut on a whoosh of wind. Edges of the posters fluttered as squirts of wind rippled the smiles of Korean film stars, models, and headstone-sized pictures of glimmering bottles of Green Soju, Jinro Gold, and Xozu.

"Alderman Roopini," Evelyn Lee called out from a center table. She swayed slightly in coming to her feet, a silvery woman on slender legs whose center of gravity had migrated. She held a cheek against Sunny and blew a kiss across his ear. A Mexican man carrying a small bucket of hot coals poured half a dozen orange, ashy rocks into a small hole in the center of their table and snapped a grill across the top. Sunny flattened his hands against the table.

"No, thank you," he said.

"You'll need your strength," Evelyn suggested. "If you've come to put an arm on me."

A Korean man in a white cap thumped knives and forks against the table, then dealt down a quick sequence of small dishes with almost blinding colors and biting smells, grunting as he turned to go. By the time Sunny turned to thank him, he was back on a stool by the bar.

"Something I said?" he asked.

"He was a medical technician in Sinchon," said Evelyn Lee, "who worked with radio isotopes. Now he's serving tiny little plates of panchan—appetizers—to a bunch of people like me, who used to be seamstresses and tailors."

The small bowls glowed like a science fair project, scarlet-orange kimchee, small hard brown sweet beans, lustrous green seaweed salad, dappled with toasted sesame, bone-white tempeh, pearl white slices of radish, white whittles of garlic, and pale green chips of cucumber.

"Is this one of those situations," asked Sunny, "in which a gentleman is expected to belch?"

"After, not before," laughed Evelyn, holding up two fingers for beer. While Sunny comically smacked his stomach, as if to coax something up, Evelyn held her head close to his own.

"I love Vera, Sunny," she told him as the beer was quickly set down. "But it isn't who would be the best mayor. Who would be best for me to vote for?"

Sunny took a small sip from his brown bottle.

"You could vote for Mickey Mouse, Evelyn," he said. "You could kiss a toad, rob a bank, and still get reelected."

Evelyn Lee let Sunny's praise evaporate before she replied. Their surly server had plunked down a dish of beef, raw, sliced, soaked in soy, sesame oil, and garlic, and rolled to resemble a bouquet of petals.

"I vote for Vera, Sunny, and I take a number," she continued. "Number twenty, from what I hear. I don't mind waiting my turn. I mind being taken for granted. I've carried some hot coals for the mayor on quite a few things. I heard a lot of, 'The size you want is on order, we'll let you know,' from him, Collins, and Vera. Our ward is swelling, Sunny. We need two grammar schools. We need an adult learning center. We need—"

Sunny shifted in his seat, and daubed a gray ash from the coals against his chin.

"Evelyn, you can't just snap your fingers, abracadabra, and pull out new schools," he said. "People want schools, roads, teachers, police, armies, doctors on call, and a chicken in every pot. But they don't want to pay for them. It's like reasoning with my daughters."

The Mexican man slapped rosy shards of chicken and ruby-red thick slices of beef onto the grill, the drips of marinade making smoke and flames sputter.

"That's smoke, Sunny," she said. "You don't need new schools. You can change the boundaries. You don't need three grammar schools in Shirley's ward."

The 16th was Shirley Watson's ward.

"Have you walked down Garfield Boulevard?" Evelyn asked. "Sixty-third? You see more boarded windows than after a hurricane. Three grammar schools within fifteen blocks? But the mayor wouldn't let them redraw the district lines because the mayor needed Shirley," she pointed out, gently tapping her elbow in emphasis. "The mayor needed the teacher's union. The teacher's union is filled with certain teachers who think they're going to lose jobs if their classes start filling with the children of immigrants, and their parents start getting active on school boards."

"Certain teachers?" Sunny asked with a tone of admonishment, but Evelyn Lee was prepared.

"Teachers who don't speak Chinese, Cambodian, or Korean," she said almost primly. "I hadn't noticed anything else about them—like color, creed, Cubs or White Sox fan—if that's what you mean."

Sunny raised his brown bottle and clicked it against his head.

"Your point, Alderman Lee," he conceded with a laugh. Evelyn Lee had laid out a lettuce leaf, swabbed it with soybean paste, and then laid in a slice of beef and a sprinkling of radish slices.

"Bloody hell, Evelyn," Sunny told her as she leaned over to take half of the loaded leaf into her mouth. "One of those schools is called Crispus Attucks."

Alderman Lee sat back to chew, then took a half-swallow of beer before clearing her throat in reply.

"I don't want to change the name to Reverend Moon, Sunny. Just redraw the boundaries."

Sunny picked up a set of chopsticks to seize a wedge of chicken and wrap it in the lettuce leaf with some charred motes of garlic and a springy chock of white rice.

"Shirley's folks always turned out for the mayor, Evelyn," he reminded her. "Your ward is a little less assimilated to our quaint local folkways."

Evelyn Lee sat back to laugh at Sunny's own artful construction. During the last elections, an independent reform candidate for state's attorney, Shin Rhee, an Evanston lawyer, had run almost even with the mayor's choice in Evelyn's ward.

"Sometimes you have to take your pillow out to the sofa to get a little more love," she explained as she rubbed the last dollop of lettuce leaf across her front teeth. "There's not much you can tempt me with, Sunny," she went on. "I don't need help getting elected. I don't need help to be any busier." It was another genteelism; Evelyn said *busy* where others would say *successful*. She had opened six dry-cleaning outlets and two Korean movie houses.

"Linas hasn't promised me any abracadabra," she said. "Just his direct line. He's good to his friends, Sunny. You're his friend. You know—he has every quality to make a great mayor."

"And more," said Sunny. "I don't worry about his qualities; it's the more."

When Evelyn launched an eyebrow as she laughed, Sunny said, "I wouldn't move to Canada if Linas were elected, Evelyn. But you know

Vera. She's got ideas that can match the size and drive of this city. She loved the mayor—we all did. But now she's her own enterprise."

Evelyn Lee put her chin on her right hand, then gently raised her left and shot up two fingers.

"*Maekchu*," she commanded the angry man who had whacked down their bowls and cutlery. As she spoke, Sunny saw him move his knees over slowly, as if he had been pinned beneath a crumpled car, before standing and shuffling toward the kitchen.

"I'm just one vote, Sunny."

"We need every one."

"You need six," she reminded him.

"People respect you, Evelyn," and while the alderman unflinchingly absorbed this established politician's flattery, Sunny added, "We make it known that you're voting for Vera, and Alonzo Gutierrez and Patrick Tierney might figure that you've added things up and join in before they get left out."

Their churlish server put down two more brown bottles, as if he were trying to stamp them on a scampering bug. Sunny tamped down his tone.

"Those schools in the Sixteenth are part of those neighborhoods, Evelyn. People have learned to read there, sing songs, play on the swings."

"Drug buys, drug busts, and drive-by shootings, too," she answered. "Neighborhoods change, Sunny. They've got a McDonald's in Tiananmen Square now."

"They've had tough times in the Sixteenth, Evelyn," he answered with a note of pleading. "The stores get boarded, buildings are abandoned; pretty soon the cops stop patrolling. Even the churches pack up their candles and leave. You can't take away their schools."

Gently, they clinked their two new brown bottles.

"Linas says you're thinking about cashing in and leaving the table," said Evelyn.

"Thinking, yes."

"About Congress?"

"Or the restaurant business," said Sunny. He motioned toward their waiter, now implacably planted on a stool and watching a game show. "I've got the perfect front man in mind. Lots of people can represent the Forty-eighth," he went on. "I'm the only person who can provide for my daughters."

"So you're trying to make time for them now, when all they want to do is get away?"

"I'm just trying to do a little better for them than I did for her," said Sunny. Evelyn Lee ran a lone chopstick around the edge of her dinner plate.

"Politics didn't kill your wife, Sunny," she told him heavily. "It didn't kill George." Evelyn's late husband had died from the lifelong saturation of cleaning chemicals into his lungs, clear down to his mustard-colored fingernails.

"Politics doesn't kill people, Sunny. It just suffocates them, little by little."

They sat back, the last wedges of chicken turning brown and brittle on the cold gray edge of the grill.

"Sunny," she began in a softer tone, "Vera can never be as grateful to me as she has to be to the people who are her core and soul. You know? It's not them or me. But if it's their wishes or mine, it has to be theirs. We've got competing grievances in this city. Our elbows are poking their ribs. I don't blame Vera. It's blood, it's family. If she walked in now, I'd throw my arms around her, drink with her, gossip with her. I'd want my brother to marry her. If I could shut a curtain and cast my ballot . . . But that's not how this works."

Sunny stayed still and silent. He sensed that Evelyn would have to answer any response with something rehearsed and prepared. His only small chance of moving her off her script would be to oblige Evelyn to fill the silence on her own.

"Sunny," she said finally, "my commitment to Linas is as total as it gets in politics. So we're not Romeo and Juliet, swallowing drams of poison in the last act. He's a professional. If it's just not breaking for him, I'll have to vote for someone else." She let the chopstick fall off the rim of her plate with a clang and roll toward the edge of their table. "Who can say what I'll do? That's the best I can do right now."

"I understand," Sunny said simply, and Evelyn took three strong gulps of water; the ice cubes inside had melted down to chips and chimed with each swallow. She wiped her mouth with the back of her hand, leaving a wide pink blot on her wrist.

"You can't leave the council," she said.

"It would be downhill from here," he told her. "Mayor for only three days, but I get my portrait hung alongside everyone else's, like it was three terms. And I don't have to worry about taxes, schools, jobs, the *Tribune*, or trash. Time for me to try something new. Why have an interesting life and still think the same things I did twenty years ago? I'll get the check from Mr. Personality," Sunny added, but before he could wave in his direction, Evelyn laid a strong hard hand over Sunny's palm.

"They don't serve that here," she said. "Leave a tip—a good one," and as Sunny fumbled in his pocket for two twenties, Evelyn Lee fell back in her seat in sudden mock astonishment and chagrin.

"You can't leave the council, Sunny," she said. "You're twenty-five percent of the Pan-Asian People's Congress!"

Back in the car with Sgt. Gallaher, Sunny smelled smoke in his sleeves, blinked smoky tears from his eyes, and saw small, soft puffs of chimney smoke scurry just above the streetlights in the dark sky as their car clipped past low brown buildings and flat roofs along Ashland Avenue. They passed a Catholic girls' school with a small white marquee sign above an entrance: TIME WILL PASS, it said. WILL YOU? Sunny lifted his forehead away from the tinted window and turned to the sergeant.

"You go to graduations or career days and students ask, 'Do you have to sell your soul to be in politics?' 'Sell your soul to be an alderman?' I tell them. 'That's a little grand. Selling a pint of your blood should more than suffice. In fact, just prick your finger—a few drops should do.' "

The police sergeant responded with a schoolgirl's chortle and shook out a thumb. Sunny smiled and turned back toward the window.

"At this point in my life, I've sold little slivers of my soul just to change a zoning ordinance," he said. "Or to get a man a job scouring fish feces off the docks at Burnham Harbor. I've sold chips of my soul at discount just to get someone a loading dock permit. I figure—I hope—that I have just enough splinters left to try to do right by my daughters for a while."

Sgt. Gallaher let another block of Ashland roll by—more Spanish, more red, and painted pictures of fruit in store signs—before she spoke again.

"May I ask a question sir? It's not strictly business, but . . . How did you meet your wife?" Sunny seemed to sit back with some relief. A preamble like the sergeant's usually led to a question about Elana's death.

"Oh, *that*," he said. "She just came in with some friends one night. The restaurant was smaller then. I had just put Sunny Roopini's Italian Specialties on the menu. We still can't have a liquor license—council ethics regulations, you know—but we'd send someone next door to get whatever they wanted. They ordered biryanis, with eggplant, shredded chicken, peppercorn, cinnamon, and cardamom. They ordered penne arrabbiatta, which has red pepper flakes. They wondered what wine I'd recommend. None, I said, beer would go better. And Elana—she looked up, I saw her brown eyes with little gray flecks, like pebbles—said, 'White or red beer?' "

"What had she been doing?"

"A media buyer at an ad agency in the Hancock building. Marked for success, until she met me. Sometimes, I'd catch her at night, going over our books with one hand, the girl's homework with another, and she'd say, 'I have a degree in integrated marketing from Northwestern so that I can count yellow onions and glue cotton pads in a shoebox to make a third-grade diorama of the Siberian tundra.' "

"She must have enjoyed the restaurant," said Sgt. Gallaher—testing, thought Sunny; it was the kind of observation that could be quickly turned away.

"Not the food part so much. I don't think she thought one way or another about that. But all the other things draw you in," Sunny explained. "You sure get to learn the price of milk, eggs, beef, and butter. You find out where Hidalgo, Gdynia, and Michoacán de Ocampo are. You know that every month you don't make a dime until you've taken in enough to pay rent, food, salaries, insurance, and electricity. Some months you look up and see that it's the twenty-fifth or twenty-sixth, and you haven't even made the rent. You get drawn into lives. A cook comes to work with a hacking cough, but he doesn't want to take a sick day because he needs to add them all together so he can visit his mother in Puerto Barrios. A server comes in late because his wife or boyfriend left. Or his girlfriend tested positive. Suddenly, those are your problems, too. You see people propose, confess that they're pregnant, declare that they're leaving, tell someone they're dying. You see that as soon as you've put out the trash, turned off the lights, and locked the door, there are people who come out of the shadows, no matter how cold, smelly, or wet, to scrounge through your trash. Your trash, their dinner. All of that—almost nothing to do with food. Everything to do with the city. That, I think she liked."

They had come to a stop on a small street a couple blocks off the main lane of Little Italy. Sgt. Gallaher noticed that this restaurant also had no sign, but was relieved to see that it at least had windows; they were gauzy with breath and steam. Even through the glass, she heard the clink of heavy plates, and the peal of throaty, scotch-soaked laughs.

"The uniforms knew right where to find this place," she told Sunny. "Prices must be good. They rave about the chicken limone with angel hair pasta."

"And they always send you home with a brown bag," said Sunny. "I notice that the officers never turn off the motor," he added.

"Standard procedure, sir," Sgt. Gallaher explained. "In case we have to pull away quick."

"I wouldn't worry, sergeant. The clam sauce here is pretty reliable."

At first, the sergeant's face seemed to stiffen with incomprehension, but softened as Sunny's joke snuck into her smile.

"Sgt. McNulty is right outside, sir, with outstretched arms and two new uniforms. I'll see you in the morning. I understand we're headed for church. I called my mother. She's delighted."

"A church, a Lithuanian festival, and a Chinese wedding," he said. "You can tell—Chicago the Sunday before a special election."

Sunny rapped on the thick window between the front and back seats and called out his thanks to the two uniforms, as Sgt. Gallaher rocked open the car door.

"And I hope we can find a Druid festival before nightfall," he told her.

Cold air surged into the car with a whistle.

20

Mama T's was filled with small children, squirming in their parents' laps as they slurped worms of spaghetti, and men and women in thick coats cracking loaves of crusty bread and pulling off great white hunks as they turned up their heads to keep track of that night's basketball game. The flocked walls were speckled with tea towels of Mt. Etna and the Strait of Messina, and graying photographs, illegibly signed, from Jack Nicholson, Jerry Vale, Spiro Agnew, Dolly Parton, and Frank Sinatra (who, according to local recollection, preferred a more posh spot nearby on Taylor Street—"Better broads," explained Terry Taliaferro, who ran the restaurant now—but sent his guards and gophers over to Mama T's).

Rita, Rula, Muriel, and Virginie were already seated. Sunny saw plates of crackling sausages and glistening red and green peppers, stuffed shells spilling white drifts of ricotta, and a yellowy pillow of eggplant parmigiana. A young man with buttery brown hair imperfectly bunched into a ponytail and a claret corduroy jacket above his blue jeans and boots stood up and extended his hand.

"Diego Pomeroy," he said.

"Yes," was all Sunny could manage. The name was familiar, but only recently. Sunny had begun to hear it emerge from Rita and Rula's detonating giggles, as if it was the name of a new pop star that Sunny couldn't possibly be expected to know. Sunny couldn't tell from their inadvertent accounts if one or the other of his daughters intrigued Diego the most; or if, as Sunny feared, both were some incomparable dual parcel to fuel an adolescent desire. For the moment, he was slightly mollified by the impression that the girls seemed to run in packs with their friends. The pride of the pack would deal with Diego if he threatened to reduce their circle.

A warm older woman with strawberry curls brought over Sunny's accustomed favorite, spaghetti with red pepper and brown curls of minced garlic blistered in olive oil. He inhaled the steam and twirled several strands on a fork.

"Remember when we used to come here as kids?" said Rula. "We'd stand on the chair and slurp noodles." She smacked her lips in loud, happy recollection. "We had contests to see who could slurp up the longest strand."

"They were noodles then, not pasta," added Rita.

"We'd get tomato splotches on our clothes," Rula remembered. "Back on the street, people would gasp. They looked like blood. Pappaji taught us to say, 'Jus' spisghetti, jus' spisghetti.' "

"A cover story to deceive the authorities," said Sunny.

"Pappaji," said Rita, "tell the Santa Claus story."

Each year during the Christmas season, the mayor spent a well-publicized couple of hours zipped into a red suit (no stuffing required) to play Santa Claus from a high-backed seat installed at the center of Daley Plaza. The mayor's seasonal throne was surrounded by a secular array of illuminated candy canes, reindeer, and glittering evergreens shipped in from Poland, Sweden, Lithuania, and Puerto Rico (the *Tabebuia haemantha*, which Sunny had not previously known to exist, and suspected had been cultivated only to assist the city's civic holiday celebrations).

Each alderman got to recommend five children from their ward to take a turn on the mayor's lap. Press coverage was extensive. So staffers from the mayor's office carefully pre-interviewed the youngsters to exclude any deemed likely to ask, "Can you find my daddy?" or "Santa, can you bring me some crack cocaine?"

"As the daughters of an alderman, Rula and Rita were preapproved," Sunny explained. "Anyway, there was a story going on then—"

"A scandal," amended Rita.

"Yes," Sunny allowed the revision. "Beyer and Beyer. An insurance firm. The mayor was accused of steering city business to the firm through one of their agents, who was the son of the president of the county board."

"Big commissions," Rula remembered.

"You should serve on a grand jury someday," said Sunny. "The story was on the news every night. 'Beyer and Beyer, Beyer and Beyer.' Every day, you'd hear the question, 'Mr. Mayor, what about Beyer and Beyer?' It was the mayor's first term. You were—"

"Seven and five," Sunny's daughters answered before he could turn completely around in his seat.

"So they settle onto his lap," Sunny continued. "Two happy little girls in red winter coats. This big man smiling down. So the mayor says to them both, 'My gosh, we have a couple of beauties here. Look like their mother, I'm pleased to observe. Sometimes God throws a pair of sixes in the roll of genetic dice. Not a drop of Daddy to blemish these two little innocent faces.' "

Sunny thought Diego seemed impressed by his deft mimicry of the mayor's mellow Old Granddad voice. He hoped it made the young man wonder, "How will he imitate me?"

"So the mayor turns back to the girls," continued Sunny. "He says, 'Lovely ladies, what can I do for you?' " And Rita and Rula—both of them, I swear—blurt out at the same time, 'What about Beyer and Beyer, Mr. Mayor? What about Beyer and Beyer?' "

The table laughed so explosively—forks ringing, plates bouncing—that people turned around, craned their heads and shifted legs of their chairs; a score of the Bull's game was drowned out. Rita flopped the folds of a white napkin over her head, as if to hide, and Rula put her head behind the wicker breadbasket. Diego turned back to Sunny.

"So when the afternoon was over—we had some hot chocolate; we had some cookies—we were brought backstage where the mayor was removing his boots and red suit. His cottony beard was hanging off one ear, so he could smoke a cigar. 'Sunny, I have been bitten in the bosom by an asp,' he said. 'And now I have been bitten in the ass by the daughters of my bosom friend.' "

"Bosom—what a comical word," said Rita. "Whenever I use it, I tell people that the mayor taught it to me."

"When—why—do you use it?" asked Sunny, but his daughters had already swiveled in their seats toward Diego Pomeroy.

"Whatever happened?" asked Diego.

"Precisely nothing," said Sunny. "The mayor thought it was hilarious. He told the story himself."

"That year, he gave us bicycles," Rula remembered. "Anyway."

"Or to keep you quiet," said Sunny.

"I mean what happened with Beyer and Beyer?" said Diego, and Sunny, who could feel a charred shard of garlic snuggle in a groove between two front teeth, snuck his small finger behind his napkin.

"Also nothing. Stern editorials, vows to investigate. In the end, no case."

"Fascinating, Mr. Roopini," said Diego. His ginger ponytail was beginning to unfurl, and fan out from behind his neck. "I tell Rula and Rita, 'How lucky you are. Some scandal breaks—you've had dinner at their house, you've played in the bathtub with their kids.' "

"Are you interested in politics, Diego," asked Sunny, pointedly attaching the boy's first name.

"Oh, plenty," he answered quickly, pumping his head up and down. "I just don't know if I believe in the utility of electoral politics."

"Yes. Well that probably makes fifty of us."

"Our mother hated politics," Rula said, throwing the words onto the table like a splash of water into a hot skillet. "Or was it just politicians? Except for Pappaji, of course," she said after a long—too long—pause. But Diego had a background of good manners.

"I'm sure it's a daily battle, sir," he said quickly. "For a man of integrity to resist sordid compromise."

"Well, that lets me off the hook," said Sunny. "What interests you, Diego?" he asked suddenly. "What do you think you'd like to do?"

The young man leaned in across his plate and lowered his voice.

"I'm torn."

"Between?"

"Becoming a teacher of autistic children. Or working in an AIDS hospice in Congo. Or . . ." He stabbed the last brick of eggplant parmigiana with a fork, and lifted it over Rita's plate of linguine with red devil shrimp. "Or getting my MBA at Wharton and become an international financier."

"Diego is a junior at the Latin School," Rita explained. "We met at a Ghost Trackers meetup."

"I was just there to see who else came," said Diego.

"Us, too," said Rula.

"Well, I hope you have the chance to do all of that and more," said Sunny. He put a hand across the table on Diego's folded hands and excused himself to visit the bar.

"I have to handle a few phone calls," he explained. By the time Sunny had turned and taken just three steps away from the table, he heard teenaged laughter behind him. Terry had a Rémy Martin waiting for him below the White Sox banner, ice pinging as it melted in the short, thick glass.

"VSOP," said Terry. "A step up, like you've taken this week. And because you may need it."

"Playing the fool for my daughters?" he asked. "The boy's not so bad."

"I mean your friend," said Terry Taliaferro, raising his eyebrows toward the television screen as he spritzed something into a glass.

The ten o'clock news had come on. Linas Slavinskas's carved red apple face filled the screen. Letters blared, "An Exclu-Two Report!" A video came on, in dim, grainy colors. A voice explained that it was a new bar on Western Avenue in the 12th Ward. There were hazy shots of Alderman Slavinskas, in one of his buttery cashmere jackets, a camel topcoat flagging his forearm, and an opulent magenta swash swirled around his neck, leaning over a polished bar to chat with a smoldering (even as seen, or especially as seen, from behind) flame-haired bartender. Her voice was gently flavored with the south, like a bourbon cookie. A small circle of light shone on a white envelope she had placed in the alderman's hand, her fingers lingering.

BARTENDER: *"This is something to thank you for all of your time and trouble, alderman."*

ALDERMAN SLAVINSKAS: *"It's no trouble. I always have time for you, gorgeous."*

A solemn, resonant reporter blinked snow from his eyes from in front of the bar and explained that the Good Government Association of Illinois was the clandestine owner. They called the bar the Oasis and wired it with hidden cameras and concealed microphones. They deliberately installed faulty ventilation and water pump systems to draw citations, so the Good Government investigators could document the many colorful corruptions with which a bar owner was required to comply. The bartender was a law student, Alison Parker Belle (co-editor, Duke Law Journal) who was also a GGA investigator.

(Alison had taken a two-week bartending course to learn how to handle speed racks, double sinks, ice bins, blenders, and soda guns with theatrical sincerity around customers. She learned how to mix a Beagle's Tail, a Blarney Stone, and a Slow Southern Screw—vodka, Southern Comfort, sloe gin, and orange juice—and was therefore slightly let down only to be asked for Jack on the rocks and Honker's Ale.)

The reporter gravely explained that the bartender had asked the alderman for help against the irrational demands of pitiless city bureaucrats. The alderman had assured her, "I'll take care of it."

They played the video once more, zooming in on the white envelope as if it were the winning kick of the World Cup. They sent bold letters marching along the bottom of the screen: 'OASIS' FOR CORRUPTION?

BARTENDER: *"This is something to thank you for all of your time and trouble, alderman."*

ALDERMAN SLAVINSKAS: *"It's no trouble. I always have time for you, gorgeous."*

Sunny's phone warbled inside a pocket. He let it jiggle. Overhead, there was a shot of Linas, wearing a more sober gray muffler above the same coat, speaking inside a circle of light and cluster of microphones in front of his home. Clouds of breath broke above him with each word.

"These charges are ridiculous," he declared, in a level, affable voice. "In fact, they're even *untrue*. I am assembling proof to refute this nonsense, and it will be my pleasure to meet you ladies and gentlemen in the second floor conference room at City Hall tomorrow morning at eight. So get your rest, and . . ." He began to turn away; a shouted question brought him back.

"Am I worried?" he repeated. "I'm an innocent man. They spent months on this so-called investigation. Let me have a few hours to reach some people and defend twenty-five years serving the people of my ward and city. Things will look a lot different by eight-thirty tomorrow morning. Tonight, I throw myself upon the mercy and sense of fair play of the people of Chicago . . ."

"He better not just rely on that," said Terry, as more chihuahuas' questions yelped and leapt at Linas' heels down the long walk back toward the glossy front door of his house.

Sunny's phone buzzed again in his pocket; he answered without looking for the number.

"I've got them, lordship."

"Linas!" Sunny turned away from the bar, and brought his mouth closer to his chest.

"There are shots that can bring me down," Linas told him. "Not this one."

"They're running it over and over."

"Who watches television? Psychos, shut-ins, and pimply teenage boys who just wait to jerk off when the girl who does sports comes on. Tomorrow, the same pictures will tell a different story. Stay tuned, your lordship."

Sunny could hear the click of another call and checked the screen. Terry, without so much as a nod of instruction, had topped off his glass; Sunny nodded in gratitude.

"Linas, is there—"

"I'm absolutely fine, lordship," he said. "I'm going to sleep the sleep of the just." Sunny heard a woman's giggling chime behind Linas. "After I spend about an hour licking Rosie's toes." The volume of the giggles climbed. Linas's wife was a smart, lissome blond woman—and attorney—named Rosemarie Fennell Slavinskas.

"Then good night, my friend," Sunny told him. "You're always the best show in town."

Vera's voice clicked on: she spoke in an urgent hush.

"You don't suppose, Sunny," she said, "that after all this time, Linas will be brought down by a redhead bearing gifts. He's too smart."

"It's the smart ones who think they're too smart to get caught," Sunny reminded her. "I was just on the phone with him, Vera. He really is amazing—sounds like he's just won the lottery."

"My phone has been beeping, beeping, beeping," she said. "I want to say something like, 'Alderman Slavinskas is a longtime colleague with whom I have worked despite many disagreements. I also respect the Good Government Association. All Chicagoans will be interested in what Alderman Slavinskas says tomorrow."

"Perfect," said Sunny. "Utterly useless. And the picture plays over and over."

"You were with Evelyn," she said.

"She loves you Vera. But until . . ."

"Could this be *until*?"

Sunny paused.

"John, Felix, Patrick, Keith, might feel they can't stick with him. Linas knows the numbers. If votes fall away, Linas won't play his hand. He'll fold and wait for next year. Arty may stick around. Daryl—it wouldn't matter. Arty—if we worked on him—might even be persuaded to put you over by acclamation. But you can't say *until* until."

"And if Linas is indicted?" Sunny stayed silent for a moment while the word smacked them both.

"I mean, it's on stage, screen, and video, Sunny," she said. "'*No trouble, gorgeous. I always have time for you.*'"

"He'll keep his seat," Sunny answered finally. "Linas could run and win from Death Row. But in this day and age, he won't be mayor—not even here. The state's attorney and U.S. Attorney will use this to get into his file cabinets. He'll become a professional defendant."

Sunny heard Vera Barrow blow out a long breath through her immaculate pastel lips; he wondered if she had decided to permit herself a cigarette.

"Strange. I'm almost sad," she said.

There was another chorus of clicks on the line, and Sunny told Vera that he would speak with her in the morning. The caller ID flashed: US-ATTY NODIST IL. It was 10:35 on a Saturday night, and Brooks Whetstone was at his office.

"This wasn't our story, alderman," he told Sunny. "The mayor mentioned that the alderman favored redheads. And blonds, brunettes, and midgets. But that's not a state secret. A story like this, Mr. Roopini, is just pebbles and twigs to us."

Sunny didn't know the term.

"What one Neanderthal man offered another to get a better pelt." Then Brooks Whetstone lowered his voice; Sunny had to cup a hand over his right ear to hear. Rula and Rita waved the light-green check from their table, and Sunny tried to use both elbows to point to himself; he must have looked like he was trying to take off.

"We're more interested in how a major corporation buys influence in a major American city."

Sunny turned around from Terry's bar again and emphasized a dramatic, weary sigh.

"No one bribed anyone to get Yello here," he said. "Sweep out all the opera tickets, celebrity chefs, autographed jerseys, and Jerry Springer, it was a business deal."

"Giving up tax revenues for ten years?" Brooks Whetstone asked. "Some business. Great deal."

"Tax revenues are projections," said Sunny. "Pie charts on a wall. Jobs are *real*. We traded flickering images for bread, butter, and salt. We got the headquarters of a company that will shape the world."

"And fund your political machine," said Brooks.

"Oh, please." Sunny fairly spat out the words. Rita, looking cool and cross, had brought over the check, which Sunny scarcely surveyed before fishing into his pocket and shoving a sheaf of twenties into the slipcase.

"You folks say *machine* the way the mayor said *antediluvian*," he told Brooks Whetstone. "Or the way some people say fascist, terrorist, and high cholesterol. Political machines went the way of steam engines, coughing, gasping, and conking out. You only see them in carnivals and museums now. Nobody listens to anybody. Everybody knows about everything. There is no *they* in politics anymore. *They* don't decide who becomes dogcatcher. Politicians take a poll before they go to the bathroom. *Number one or number two? You tell us, Chicago! Soap my hands or just rinse them?* Politicians don't get a dog until they figure out which breed polls better. Felix Kowalski counts all the *Frutas y Vehículo* signs across from his ward office on Archer and names his daughter Concepcion. I tell him, 'Felix, a few more Ethiopian families have moved in on Fifty-fifth. Get busy! You need a boy named Tesfaye!' If we have a machine here, Mr. Whetstone, I wish to hell someone would tell me where the plug is."

Terry held out the slipcase of Sunny's check, the edges of four twenties sticking out like the folds of a pocket square. Sunny waved it away, silently mouthing, *For her, for you.* He overheard Rula and Rita show Diego the autographed picture of some crime movie star. "*Amore.* That means love," Sunny was disconcerted to overhear Diego explain. "The Italians have a concept of love that's more cosmopolitan than our Anglo-Saxon views." Muriel and Virginie announced to Terry that, on the basis of their survey, Cub players looked more handsome in their photographs than White Sox, Chicago Bear players appeared bulbous and gross, and that Bulls were cuter than the Blackhawks.

"Hockey players have no teeth," he advised them. "Toothless Poles and Russians with more stitches in their chins than a pair of drapes. We had, what's his name, Vasily Stroganoff or whatever, in here last week. He ordered chicken vesuvio. We had to put the whole thing—thighs, breasts, peas, garlic, red pepper, and potatoes—through a blender for him. Looked like baby mash. I asked his wife, a hot young Czech, if I should bring over a few crayons, too."

"I always learn something from our conversations, alderman,"

Brooks Whetstone suddenly announced in Sunny's ear. "I hope we talk again."

Rula, Rita, Muriel, and Virginie chatted about Diego in the back seat of the black car as Sgt. McNulty saw them back home to the 48th, stopping once on Goethe to let Diego slip home. No sooner had Sunny unfolded his legs than his phone rumbled in his chest pocket and he had to take a call from Chief Martinez. He affected not to react to the fact that he overheard the girls whisper *scrumptious* and *lean* in proximity to Diego's name, but had to hold his hand up in the tumult of backseat giggles to hear the chief say heavily, "Nothing from Ponce and Said, sir. Maybe nothing at all. We have people picking through everything. We have to break now, but we'll start in on them again at four."

"Break?" asked Sunny. "Look, Matt, if this is some kind of union rule . . ."

"Our own, sir. Six hours of sleep for people in custody. If we get anything out of them, the last thing we want is—"

"Absolutely right, chief," said Sunny. "Put mints on their pillows if you have to."

"As a matter of fact, we ordered in for them," said Chief Martinez. "Thin crust from Marino's. A competitor, I know, but they ate heartily."

"You know some judges, Matt," said Sunny. "They'll only say, 'What, no cannolis?' "

Sunny was splayed on his bed when Rula came to find him. He had kicked one shoe from a foot, but the second refused to fall and gripped his toes like a window washer who had slipped on the platform. His trousers had been pulled nearly up to his knees in little corrugated rumples, and Sheldon had burrowed into a ridge of the blanket between his pinstriped thighs, blinking and dozing while Sunny played his thumb over the channel changer.

Rula sat down on the side of the bed to scratch Sheldon's gray head. His older daughter's eyes were glassy, like the surface of a dark lake.

"You've had a beer," remarked Sunny.

"Two, bloody hell. Isn't that alright?"

"Of course."

"Diego?" she demanded.

"He seems nice."

"Oh, great, bloody hell." She bit off her words. "That's a rice flour comment. Why not just call him an ass?"

"I liked him," Sunny insisted. "We didn't really have a chance. . . ."

"Yes. Always a phone call. Always something."

"Darling," he tried to say gently, "you know what's going on now."

"Now?"

Rula had pulled back her hair, so that when she wrenched her head suddenly around the black tail snapped in Sunny's face. He looked at her heavily and tried to reply lightly.

"I know. All of our lives. But I made dosas for you most days—until you started leaving early to avoid them. Or me."

"You noticed? Seriously? How? You were always everywhere else."

"We're in the service business," he said softly. "You have to serve uthappam at seven p.m., when most people have dinner. You have to have community meetings at eight, when most people are home from work. When you and your sister want to go to Northwestern or Columbia, they ask for money, not whether or not I was there every time you fell off your tricycles. I tried to be at the places I could."

"Only if you ran out of other places to be. Is that why they call it running for office? Running away?"

"Why would you ever—"

"I know I was a mistake. Mammaji told me. It slipped out. She was angry, she had a third glass of wine, you weren't around—as usual—and she tried to take it back. But—"

"You were a surprise," said Sunny. "That's different."

"Rita?" She practically spat her sister's name. "You wanted someone else to ignore?"

Sunny hesitated in reply, and then realized any hesitation would envenom any words he might try.

"We loved you so much, we wanted to be surprised again," he said. Rula shoved his words back, like burnt toast.

"You have to be around to see a surprise," she said. "You were closing the restaurant, sitting through a stupid bloody fucking ward meeting, making sure you were seen out with the snowplows, swapping lies with the mayor. . . ." She swished three quick circles with a hand, to suggest an infinity of insincerities. Then Rula turned away, showing Sunny her neck: the supple, tawny limb that was Elana's neck, too.

Sunny tried to touch her with just a thumb; she arched her back, as if his very touch were some kind of excruciating live wire. She finally let Sunny put two fingers of his hand lightly on her left shoulder, as if he were touching the skin of a cobra.

"Why would you have wanted me around more if you hate me so much?"

Rula stood up instantly. The bedsprings whimpered, Sheldon jerked awake, and red from the neon lights of the Riviera Theater rippled over the bedroom curtains.

"I don't hate you, Pappaji. I'm just bored by you. Like our mother was."

A century seemed to pass between them. Pages flipped and fell into history. Steamships pulled out and airplanes landed. Sheldon tucked his head into Sunny's knee. Sunny heard his shoe finally plop onto the floor. They both heard the squeak of a spigot and the rush of water: Rita brushing her teeth—or just running water to let them know she was listening, or trying to blot out the sound of a late-night phone call. Rula sat back on the bed, a bottom's length farther from Sunny than she had been before.

"She never told you?"

"Of course. She said that I bored her, that she couldn't stand me, that she didn't like my friends, that I watched too much football. We loved each other."

His daughter dawdled a toe under the bed, a few inches closer. Finally, Rula offered a few inches of her face to Sunny, her almond skin flushed with pink.

"Why did you bring more children into this world anyway?" she asked. "All the wars and lies."

"That's why," said Sunny. "A new chance."

"That's all? That's bloody it?"

"Nothing is harder to come by. You should know that," Sunny shot back without reserve. When he saw Rula's shoulders sink like a doll's being put back on a shelf, he knew that he had finally gained something back.

"I'm sorry."

"You bloody well should be," said Sunny. "There's lots and lots of other things in the world to blame me for."

Rula held her hand behind her back and opened it in front of Sunny. Long fingers, quivering slightly, three long lifelines slashed deep across her palm, a small purple bandage swathed over her thumb. Sunny rubbed it gently.

"Kitchen cut," she offered. "Mincing chilis."

"The unkindest cut," said Sunny. He laced his fingers lightly into hers and squeezed softly. He put the palm of his other hand onto Sheldon's head and rubbed it back and forth, slowly, until he could see the cat's eyes begin to blink and close. Rula sat forward, an elbow on her knee, as her voice got softer.

"Diego says it's all over the place that you're leaving the council."

"Probably."

"You could have told us."

"If I knew for sure myself. Right now, it's an idea I try out."

"Eldad says you could be secretary of state."

"Not the one with a plane, who goes to Geneva and Paris. The Illinois one goes to a fish fry every Friday night in Rantoul or Bloomington. I'm not so fond of fried fish. Or Bloomington."

"Congress?" Rula sat back and held the back of her hand to an eye, while Sunny squirmed and resettled himself against a twisted pillow, taking care to put Sheldon's head back against his knee.

"I'd like to get elected," he said. "I'm not sure I'd like the job. All the back and forth, like a ball bouncing around in a stairwell. All the votes going nowhere. Running again every two years—like never getting out of high school. I'm thinking—your mother and I used to talk about this—of getting some partners and financing while my name means something. Opening a classy place. There's an old bus garage on Clark, right off Devon. Something might open up on Lincoln."

"Bloody hell, we'd never see you," she said.

"Isn't that what you want?"

"We could help, you know," said Rula. "We've grown up ass deep in masala."

"Yes. Yes. It could even be fun," said Sunny. "But I don't want you to miss out on all the things you should be doing." He held up for a moment to offer a smile and waited for Rula to flash one back.

"Temple meetings and youth groups," she said.

"Book clubs and sewing circles, yes," Sunny added.

"You'd miss politics, Pappaji."

"Now and then. The St. Patrick's Day parade, for sure. I'd miss election nights."

"Not me," said Rula. She reached back for the elastic loop behind her head and pulled, shaking her hair across her shoulders.

Sunny recalled the last election night that he had taken his daughters along on his circuit of ward offices. They had yawned, squirmed, and traded tart observations over dreary buffets of pygmy carrots and limp bell pepper slices guarding puddles of desiccated hummus (in deference to the age and cholesterol of most precinct workers). City precincts reported first, with dramatic Democratic majorities. But then the returns from suburbs began to come in. Then, those from farther down the pie slice shape of Illinois. Totals changed. Margins tightened. Leads deflated. By ten p.m., the incumbent Democratic governor had been defeated, along with the Democratic attorney general, whose campaign had never recovered from his cosmopolitan explanation of his relationship with seventeen-year-old interns. "Anytime you have to say, 'This would never be a scandal in France,' " the mayor told Sunny, "you know you've got a problem in Peoria."

"There's no drama," Rula countered now from the bed. "All the polls tell people what they think and what's going to happen."

"Still everything is at stake," said Sunny. "There's something majestic about that. For a few hours, everything that self-important people hope is in the hands of a lot of people who fill coffee mugs. It may hurt me just to sit and watch. But if I stay much longer . . ." Sunny made a churning motion around his head. " . . . my brain will turn to rice flour."

Rula put down a hand against one of Sheldon's whiskers, then her head against Sunny's shoulder, and then her chin against his chest. She tried to rest against him the way she had when she was six. But the parts no longer fit. Their knees knocked against each other, her chin ground into his collarbone.

"Maybe I'm too big for this," she said. She giggled and burped a few dainty, beery bubbles into his shoulder.

The rippling red lights from the Riviera marquee had stopped rolling over the bedroom curtains. They could hear paper cups blow over the Lawrence Avenue El platform, scurrying and popping. Rula's hair smelled flowery. Sunny put his palm softly on Elana's slender birch neck. It filled his hand.

"Baby," he called out softly, so as not to wake her. "Baby."

21

SUNDAY MORNING

"We've got an oon-yun problem," Matina announced.

Sunny, in a gray suit and nursery blue tie, had just slipped down to his restaurant's kitchen where Sgt. Gallaher was already on-duty, standing with her backside grazing a stainless steel prep table and sipping from a coffee mug. Rula and Rita were still showering and fussing. The sergeant had drawn her hair tightly behind her head; it played up an almost perfect roundness in her face, the leanness of her neck.

"No onions Friday—the funeral, everybody take off, remember?"

"How many?" he asked, and Matina took one from her smock and held it up between them, as if they might want to memorize its appearance.

"Two-hunnert I'd say. Mebbe."

Between all the dosa and uthappam on the menu, Sunny could expect the kitchen to use about three hundred onions on a Sunday in late January. He took a cup of tea in his hands and sat down at the small round table in front of their grill.

"Tell Oscar and Wilmer to recommend the special rava masala dosa."

Sunny noticed a small, teasing smile flash across Sgt. Gallaher's face.

"We go through a lot of onions here," he explained. "Onion masala dosa, rava dosa, butter masala dosa—even the tomato and pea uthappam has chopped onions. But the special rava dosa has so many chilis, a slight reduction might go unnoticed. Does that violate a city ordinance?"

The sergeant held her chin for a moment as she pondered an official reply.

"Our orders are to protect you and your family, sir. Not count onions. Unless someone threatens you with one."

"You show a flair for politics," Sunny told her.

Sunny noticed how the flat, white edges of the sergeant's teeth tended to lightly bite her lip when she laughed; she licked her tongue over her teeth to wipe away any smudges of lipstick.

"Anyway, sir, it all smells delicious to me."

"Onions, chilis, and garlic—the trinity of south Indian food."

"Then we're all set for church, sir," said the sergeant, but Sunny held up his hand. Alderman Slavinskas was about to begin his press conference, and the three of them turned their heads up to the screen just above the long steel service table.

"Good morning, ladies and gentlemen," Linas began.

He spoke comfortably, firmly, and insistently, his glossy fingertips lightly gripping the top of a small lectern.

"I thank you for being here so early. I am sure we can conclude our business in plenty of time for you to make ten o' clock mass at Saint Maria Addolorata."

There was chuckling, quickly hushed, and a shuffling of feet from reporters in folding chairs. Linas waited for silence to return.

"I absolutely deny the charges made last night by a television channel whose call letters I will not dignify, and a group that has the impudence to call themselves the Good Government Association of Illinois," he said, and stood back to allow them to take in the tall man in police blues to his right.

"Many of you will recognize Commander Walter Green."

The commander nodded unsmilingly down at the reporters while Linas went on.

"As those of us who care about law and order and our men and women in uniform know, Commander Green is a man of towering integrity. I don't know as he would say the same thing about me," Linas added in the same, sharp tone, and the sheer, insolent shock of his remark caused reporters to gasp and laugh. "The commander is here to take any questions you may have that relate to the police in this matter.

"About ten days ago," said Linas, "I noticed that a new bar called the Oasis had opened in our ward on Western Avenue. I stopped in to introduce myself, and asked if, as their representative to city government, there was any way I could be helpful. This is usually code for, 'Can I leave some campaign brochures here?' "

Snickers and titters ran around the room.

"That woman—Ms. Belle—was quite personable. In fact she was so personable, I suspected at once that it was probably not entirely in response to my famous killer charm."

In his restaurant's kitchen, Sunny turned to see Sgt. Gallaher break into a smile even as she kept her eyes locked determinedly on the chained back door.

"She told me that my drink was on the house. I don't like people to do that. I also don't like to make gracious people feel like they've done something wrong. So I finished my drink—Oban, a West Highland single malt, I'm impressed that they had it; like they knew I was coming—and left a tip that more than compensated.

"Fifty dollars, to anticipate your question," Linas said, as the feet of several folding chairs squeaked as they dug into the mauve carpet. "My tax returns are public record. Every citizen of Chicago can find out what I'm worth. I can't leave the kind of cheap tip that you gentlemen and ladies do."

"My God, he has them going," Sunny told Matina and Sgt. Gallaher. Oscar and Wilmer arrived through the back door, stamped their boots, and looked up at the screen as laughter flared up again.

Linas contrived to look disappointed and grim as he went on.

"Ms. Belle informed me that the owners—whom she identified only as Jed and Julia—were worried because a city inspector had threatened to close their place until they could bring the tavern's ventilation and water pumping system into compliance with code," he said. "She said the owners needed to stay open to make a little money before they could afford such extensive repairs, which were estimated at fifteen thousand dollars.

"I told her that we had a soft drink cooler installed for our kids that costs twice that.

"She said that the owners would be grateful if I could intervene in their behalf. I replied—and notice, Channel Who and the Good Government Association didn't show you this—that city inspectors protect our citizens. Ms. Belle said—and I'll just bet that the Good Government Association won't show you the video of this—'But ahlder-man, ah heauh that heauh in Chi-town'—a big tip-off because honestly, do you know anyone in Chicago who says Chi-town? That's straight out of Dogpatch—'folks is accommodating. We'all would be sooo grateful. What's a po', honest businessman to do? I'm sure we could work out something. Just between you and me. I would be sooo grateful. Personal grateful, Mr. Ahlder-man.' "

Linas's impersonation had the reporters catching their breath and wiping their eyes. He tamped down their laughs with his hands, like some masterful old comic who has unexpectedly shown up at open mic night in a cellar club.

"I'm sorry," he said. "Every Australian actor does a better southern accent than she does. That woman—Ms. Belle—knew there was a camera on her. Maybe she wants a shot on the Grand Ole' Opry."

"He's utterly hilarious," Sgt. Gallaher offered from her perch against the tall steel table.

"Like my first husband," Matina volunteered, unimpressed.

"I'd pay a cover charge to see him," said Sgt. Gallaher. "Still, the charges, the video, the envelope . . ."

Linas settled the knot of his pink silk tie and went on soberly.

"I contacted Commander Green. I informed him that I had received what transparently seemed to be the offer of a bribe. The commander and I agreed that to protect the citizens of Chicago, and my own family, I should pretend to comply with their requests. Once the crime was on record, warrants could be issued. The conspiracy could be traced. Arrests could be made."

Walter Green held up a black wire, a beetle-black microphone smaller than the nail of a child's thumb, and a small, shiny disc.

"The alderman agreed to return to the Oasis wired last Thursday night," he said. "These recordings are being held as evidence."

Linas Slavinskas turned slightly to snap on a nearby monitor. Once again, there was the white circle of light over the white envelope and Alison Parker Belle's lingering red fingertips.

"What you see here isn't a public servant accepting a bribe," he said. "It's a public servant protecting the people of this city—at some risk, I don't mind saying—to document a criminal conspiracy."

Linas raised a white envelope right next to his face and paused. White lights shined and cameras snapped.

"I have the proof right here. That night this envelope and recordings were turned over to Commander Green and officers at the Deering District on south Lowe. In fact," added Linas, "I was with Commander Green when we each received calls that summoned us to City Hall. Where the mayor, God rest his soul, had just died."

A sharp inhalation seemed to suck up every breath in the conference room. Sunny recalled the studiously casual appraisal Linas had given in his office that night: *Walt Green is a real smoothie.* The commander spoke smoothly and sternly from his stepladder height. Reporters peered up from their chairs like kindergartners.

"Warrants will soon be issued," said Commander Green. "Trying to bribe a public official is a crime. I don't care if you call yourself the Good Government Association or the Girl Scouts of America."

"Whaddya want to bet?" Sunny wondered aloud to Matina and Sgt. Gallaher. "We're going to hear that little sentence every twenty minutes for the next forty-eight hours."

Linas took the sides of the podium into both of his hands. He rocked back on his heels before bringing his head forward for emphasis, his chin like the head of a chisel.

"And who *is* this group that has the impudence to call themselves the Good Government Association?" he asked. "People so self-righteous they think their bribes don't stink as much as anybody else's?

"Look at the list of their major contributors," he said. "Look at their addresses. Wilmette, Winnetka, and Lake Forest. How much do you think they care about Chicago? Do they live here? Send their kids to school here? They descend on Sears Tower, Michigan Avenue, and the Board of Trade by day and load up their attachés with money. At night they take it all home to their leafy suburbs and shake it over their hedges. Maybe they take their kids into the city once or twice a year to sit in a skybox at Wrigley Field and marvel at all the ethnic people with funny last names. 'Oh look, Dad,' says little Dunstin. 'I see a Negro! Just like on TV! Mexicans, too, just walking around, like normal people. And look at all those long, funny names!' "

Linas lowered his voice and elongated his vowels, in mimicry of a North Shore father.

"'Oh, thaaat's just Polish, son, don't worry,' " he said. "'Nooo need to bother yourself with thaaat language.' "

The reporters were soaked, hoarse, and giddy with laughter, as if they'd been munching cookies at an all-night dorm party.

"Look at some of the zip codes of their contributors," Linas went on. "10012. 10018. Know where they are? *New York City*."

Linas lavished scorn over each syllable, as if uttering the name of an old love rival.

"Walk down any street in New York" he demanded. "If you dare. Heaps of steaming garbage. Crack addicts hiding behind the bags. Now stroll down any street in Chicago. You tell me what city knows more about good government!"

He stood back from the podium, fastened the middle button on his jacket, and awarded the reporters a half bow.

"Ladies and gentlemen, I respectfully await your questions."

Sunny heard a chorus of small yelps from the folding chairs.

"Why did you visit the Oasis at all?" said one yelp that rose above the rest.

"To welcome a new business," said Linas. "I do the same for any hardware store, pet shop, or bakery."

"What did you mean when you said, 'Let me know personally if I can ever help you?' "

"What do you think? Extra trash runs during the holidays. Snow plowed on Western Avenue. Every citizen has a right to expect that from their city government."

"Do you always say that to redheads?"

Linas drew back, looking shocked, hurt, and maligned.

"And do you always have your mind in the gutter?"

With wounded dignity, he surveyed the worm basket of upraised reporter's hands, and called on a woman from the *Sun-Times*.

"Why did you accept the envelope?"

"To document a criminal act."

"Why not just say, 'No thanks?' " she followed. "Then walk away?"

Linas shook his head sorrowfully.

"All I knew about these people was that they were criminals. If you refuse to do business with criminals, they don't let you just walk away. I have a family to protect. I have a wife, three daughters, two dogs, a cat, a silver Porsche 911 Turbo, and Meridian 490 cruiser tied up in Jackson Harbor. I love them all very much."

A man from the *Tribune* stood up with a question for Walter Green.

"Why didn't you arrest them on the spot?"

The commander moved slightly in front of Linas and bent down to the podium microphone.

"Basic police work," he explained. "We knew the woman behind the bar had partners. We didn't want to arrest that woman—the redhead—and tip off her coconspirators until we had evidence on them, too."

"The GGA says the bartender is a law student from Duke."

Linas stepped back into the hot white light.

"Any junior college in Chicago would have given her a better course on the laws against entrapment than what she got there," he said.

"Why did you call her gorgeous?"

"I call all women gorgeous," said Linas, "including nuns and tough lesbian activists in leather motorcycle jackets. I'll bet I've even called some of *you folks* gorgeous," and once again he had to hold out his arms to rein in wild bursts of laughter as they flared from the reporter's seats.

"I've never heard any woman complain," Linas finally said in the quiet. "Or get the wrong idea."

"How much in the envelope?"

"I don't know," he said simply, then turned to Commander Green. The commander held a hand over his mouth and called across to Linas in a low voice that fell just shy of the microphone. Linas nodded, turned back to the room, and pointed at an ebony-haired reporter in the third row of seats.

"Jacqueline," he asked, "can you help us out here? *Gorgeous?*" he added to much laughter.

She was delighted. Jacqueline was a former Miami of Ohio homecoming queen and worked for the next station just up the dial from the one that had broken the Oasis story. A row of reporters let her by to step to the podium and take the white envelope from Commander Green's hand. She held it just in front of the microphone and ran a pink fingertip along the top. She turned the envelope over and the edges of green bills fell in a palm.

"One-hundreds," she announced, and began to count. At twenty-one, Linas called out, off-mic but loudly, "Benjamin Franklin? He wasn't even a president."

"Fifty one-hundred-dollar bills," Jacqueline announced.

"Five thousand dollars?" said Linas, striving to sound aggrieved, offended, and demeaned. *"That's not even enough for a decent pair of cufflinks!"*

Sunny picked up his phone and dialed one of Linas's mobile numbers. He guessed that the phone would vibrate in the bottom of a red silk pocket of his cashmere coat, or in the snug custom sleeve of his Gucci briefcase. When he heard the beep, Sunny said simply, "Linas? Sunny. Slam dunk."

Vera Barrow called before Sunny could snap his phone closed. Without introduction, her softy, husky voice announced, "Slam dunk, Sunny."

"He heard them coming. A flaming redhead pouring free drinks and making a proposition. They might as well have been wearing army boots."

"The son of a bitch was brilliant," said Vera. She so seldom used profanity, her epithets seemed like accolades.

"He was good," Sunny agreed. "He was great. Still, I don't think he won any new votes. Not tomorrow at least."

"I'm not so sure. It's the times, Sunny," said Vera. "People want someone who is smarter than the bad guys."

"Linas is smarter than the good guys, too," Sunny pointed out. "That's the problem," and Vera laughed.

"Not smarter than me, Sunny." Vera didn't bother to add, "or you, Sunny." They knew each other well enough—Vera knew herself well enough—that the vain, inconsequential compliments of the kind politicians usually paid were suspect.

"He sure is nervier," she said. "You get points for that in this game, too. I'll make my calls. My best to the pastor, Alderman Roopini."

22

The First Baptist Gospel Congregation on west Washington had polished dark wood walls, red velvet cushions, fraying and smooth along the edges, and a grand brass pipe organ with forty-eight tall pipes soaring from behind the keyboard like steely tulip bulbs. Radiator jets whistled and hissed steam. People clapped gloved hands and clasped coats across their shoulders. Frost glazed the windows, but people still fanned themselves with flimsy beige programs and raised the lower edges of stained glass window panels to admit winter air. The choir rocked and clapped; the congregation stamped and swayed. Miraculously, some children still snoozed, or blinked woozily on shoulders.

Sunny, Rula, and Rita were taken to seats in the sixth row by a smiling usher who kissed his daughters' hands and glanced a white-gloved hand off of Sunny's forearm.

"My man. Good to see you, Mr. Acting."

The pastor, in a pink and black robe that rippled like a flag as he rocked his arms, raised his hands above his head as if to ask for quiet; for a moment, the choir held back while the organ warbled and the pastor gave a steady shout into the microphone.

"There are those among you who are homeless, hurting, haunted," he announced. "They *neeeeed* a blessing!" and the pastor stepped back into a roar of raw voices, slick foreheads, and sliding feet.

"*I heard an old story,*" they sang, "*how a savior came from glory, how he gave his life, to help someone like me.*"

"Praise the Lord!" the pastor shouted out, above and beyond the microphone, and when the song died down he put his arms over the huge dark wood podium as if collapsing in God's embrace.

"Let everyone and everything that has breath," he said wearily, "praise the Lord in heaven while they have it. What are you going to use that breath for anyway?" he asked worshippers with new strength. "Cheering on Satan?"

"No sir!" they barked back.

"Arguing with your mother-in-law?"

"No sir!"

"Rapping, hip-hopping, and singing about hos, pigs, and bitches?"

"No, *sir*, Pastor Evans," parishioners declared even more emphatically.

"Shouting at your kids?"

"No sir!"

"Well, maybe a little," replied the pastor across a ripple of chuckles. "If they're playing with fire. Or playing around with drugs. But why use the breath that God gave you for those things that are small, silly, negative, depressing, discouraging, *dee*-praved, *unnn*-necessary, *immm*-material, unnn-wholesome, and generally negativity-producing no-count *nonnn*-sense, when you can p*rrr*aise God Almighty in His Heaven!"

Sunny got to his feet and brought his daughters up with him. They grabbed outstretched hands all around, setting off a clanking of bracelets and a rustling of heavy sleeves, and smiled over at Sgt. Gallaher, who stood to the side of their row, elbows folded and eyes playing over the mass of upraised hands and fists.

"Praise the Lord! Praise the Lord! Praise the Lord!"

People sat down hard, as if after an uphill trudge. Applause flickered and faded. It was soon hushed enough to hear a few sneezes, an isolated cough, and a couple of babies' cries.

"We have guests here, of course. We will ask them all to introduce themselves after the offering—make sure they'll stay." There was a quiet tinkling of laughter. "But there are also a few people who may want you to see they're here right now," the pastor resumed. "State Senator Melvin Simpkins," he announced. "County Board Commis-

sioner Nikki Sherman. And down there, with his beautiful daughters—
and lovely police guard—Alderman and Vice Mayor Sundaran Roopini, who has always been a good friend, and especially in these recent,
tragic days. Gentlemen and ladies, please!" bid the pastor, and Sunny
stood with an arm around each of his daughters. He could see Rula's
face redden. He could feel Rita stiffen against his arm. Sunny smiled
and sat down swiftly. When he looked toward the end of the row, he
could see Sgt. Gallaher flustered and blushing.

"D y'all see the police guard?" he asked. "Tall lady in blue. When
did *that* happen in the Chicago Police Department?" There were soft
snickers and calls of, "She's pretty, pastor."

But when the pastor could see Sgt. Gallaher's smile curdle, he called
out gently, "It is good to have you here. We'll pray that our Lord keeps
you safe. Thank you for serving the city of Chicago."

The pastor shuffled papers on the lectern; he did not want to proceed until all was in order.

"We have another guest here this morning," he announced. "I ask
you to receive him with courtesy. He has asked to worship with us
today. Of course I said yes. The House of God is open to all. But I know
you would also be disappointed if you didn't hear him speak, as well as
say amen. Some of you have probably seen him on the TV this morning. Better than Oprah, wasn't it? Oprah, who is such a dear friend."

Rula wrenched her mouth against Sunny's ear.

"You don't suppose—" she said.

"Of course not," he assured her.

"Ladies and gentlemen," the pastor began . . .

"Who else?" hissed Rita.

At first, there were more gasps than applause as the intonation of
Linas Slavinskas's name. But suddenly it was indisputably Linas strid-
ing with a full plume of steam across the stage: sandy hair swept back,
blunt lizard chin, and his sharp pink tongue licking, a deep blue blazer
set off by a white collar and high-pitched magenta tie. Hot white camera lights painted the podium as he arrived.

"Thank you, Pastor Alfred," Linas said soberly, and paused for
mothers to shush children and adults to mutter behind their hands.

"We've known each other a long time, pastor. And liked each other about half of it."

The pastor, sitting in a portentous wooden throne nearby that was engraved with scripture and cherubim, laughed and called out toward Linas.

"A little more than that my friend."

Linas bowed toward the pastor, and turned back to the congregation with a challenging eye.

"I—*loved*—the mayor," he said, rolling out each word. "I disagreed with him. I argued with him. We called each other names. I won't bore you with examples. Let's just say, that when it came to name calling, I always finished second."

Shy, tentative laughter swirled over the ranks of seats.

"The mayor was a man of his word," said Linas. "And a man of words, wasn't he?"

Voices rose around Sunny and his daughters.

"That's true, Mr. Slavinskas."

Linas nodded in thanks, and went on.

"We knew how to fight," he explained. "We knew how to jab each other. That's what old couples do, don't they?"

The floor of the church began to flower with pink, white, and yellow-brimmed hats, swaying with laughter and blunt, short shouts.

"That's right, that's right."

"When the mayor and I quarreled, we didn't need translators," said Linas, "We understood each other perfectly. The mayor said to me once—," and here, Linas risked his own gravelly impersonation— " 'Linas, at least you and your folks didn't fly out of here when my folks started spreading our wings. Cleveland, Dee-troit, Dee Cee, folks just up and left. The same folks who now pay dearly for their kids to go to schools with a carefully selected representative sample of Nee-groes, Hispanics, and Asiatics turned down the honor when diversity moved next door. Look at those cities now—block after block like empty ash-trays. *Least your folks stayed.*' "

Linas dropped his right hand against the podium, as if laying down a large rock.

"And we did," he said quietly. "Maybe not always next door. But across the street and down the block. Look, I know I've been called 'honky.' My grandparents were hunkies. If you worked in the stockyards or steel mills, you were a hunkie—hunched over for life. That's how the word began. You worked with your back, and your work could break your back. Dirty, smelly, bloody jobs, pouring white-hot steel in the mills, or getting soaked in blood when you hacked cattle. And for too long, a lot of black men couldn't work there. What miserable jobs to fight over. But hell—forgive me, pastor. No: hell is the right word. *Hell!* Those jobs were everything to us."

Cries and shouts moved over the room. Sunny felt his phone shudder in his pocket, and kept his eyes on the church's podium. Linas had removed a crisp linen square from his pocket and blotted it thoughtfully against his forehead.

"All those jobs have gone to Kansas and Nebraska now. God bless them—and good riddance. Those jobs were good enough for our fathers and grandfathers. But we have the largest financial market in the world here in Chicago. Our sons and daughters can have better jobs, with higher pay. They get to work indoors and wear suits. Our grandfathers worked in blood and sweat, but our children can wear cufflinks in air-conditioned offices and lift billions of dollars with just their fingers. Isn't that what life is all about?"

Rewarding Linas with laughs was one thing; applause was a greater gift entirely. But handclaps began to break out across the rows now as he went on, chopping out phrase by phrase with his right hand, and stepping back slightly from the rostrum to raise his voice.

"In your ward and mine, we rear our own children. Have you seen the nannies and the *aww-pears* wheeling around little apple-cheeked children in Lincoln Park? Or down Michigan Avenue, looking in the big store windows? But in our neighborhoods, we don't subcontract the most important job in life to hourly employees, God bless them, from El Salvador, Guatemala, and Haiti. Hourly employees that the folks along Astor, Bellevue, and east Lake Shore Drive pay *below* minimum wage, *off* the books, and *under* the table."

Rita leaned over to hold her fingers over Sunny's arm and whisper.

"Didn't the Slavinskases have that Danish girl who helped with the kids?"

"Larissa," he remembered. Colossal blue eyes, corn-yellow hair, and slender limbs in close-fitting jeans and sweaters.

"But Rosie was always at home," said Sunny. "I think Larissa was more help to the alderman."

"When we need help, we ask grandma," Linas continued. "We ask a neighbor. The older ones raise the younger ones. Sometimes, we need a day-care center. Thank God they have them in churches like this. As Pastor Alfred knows, over the years I've given a few small contributions—nothing grand, just enough to help out."

The pastor, legs crossed and smiling, waved and called out from his carved chair below a large embroidered gold cross.

"You have, my friend, you have."

Linas rested his hands on the podium and leaned back toward the choir.

"You know, Pastor, I was paying attention to the words," he said. "The singing is beautiful. But the words make it so, because they're the words of God."

Shouts of, "That's true, Mr. Slavinskas," sprouted around Sunny and his daughters.

" 'He sought me, and bought me, with his redeeming blood,' " Linas quoted. He narrowed his eyes in recollection; an expression Sunny had seen only when Linas had recalled the taste of some exceptional wine.

"Well your people and mine know what it's like to get blood on our hands. In the stockyards and hospital rooms. In the army. This week, there were people in my neighborhood—including our family—who shed tears right along with you. I thank you for letting me and my lovely wife"—Rosie rose a few inches from her seat, and raised a slender blond hand, waving trim pink nails—"join you for worship this morning. May our grief help us realize how many hopes and dreams we share for this city."

Linas ducked his head humbly as he stepped from the podium. He gently held the heel of his hand against the corner of an eye to blot a tear. The brims of huge yellow, pink, lavender, white, and cornflower blue hats swayed like petals in the rows of seats.

It wasn't until Linas had taken a couple of slow, grave steps down the winding stairs leading down to the floor that Sunny could catch his eye with one of his own and, in blinking back tears, flash an unmistakable wink across several rows of heads bent in prayer and reverence. The phone in Sunny's pocket jiggled over his heart. He nodded to Sgt. Gallaher, who led him through the aisle, and out into a small, dim alcove stacked with dog-eared children's Bible storybooks in which it did not seem impious to speak of politics.

"Shameless. Shameful. *Shameless*," she said.

"Lots of applause, Vera," Sunny told her. "But when it's over, just a bunch of red hands to show for it. Something else is going on."

After hearing only silence from the other end, Sunny went a sentence ahead.

"He's not running tomorrow."

When Vera replied, Sunny noticed just a trace of wobbliness.

"Surely that's what all of this has been about," she said.

"He must have counted and figured that he'd come up short," said Sunny. A shiny-headed deacon on patrol for straggling children heard Sunny's rushed, strangled voice and peered into the alcove; some soul must be hurting. Sgt. Gallaher waved the man away. "This way, Linas bows out in a blaze of glory," said Sunny. "And starts next year's campaign."

"That's diabolical," Vera said after a pause. "He told you he had to run because if I got in he'd have no chance next year. Or for ten years."

"I feel stupid, Vera." Sunny scolded himself. "Stupid, stupid, stupid."

"Not your mistake," Vera said crisply. "Every politician has to keep books for herself."

"He got us to start playing our hand, Vera. Put down our cards with Rod, Evelyn, Miles, Luis, Ivan. He knew all along that he couldn't beat you on the floor. But . . ." Sunny let his voice trail off, so that Vera could complete his thought.

"But he figures now that I'll come up short, too."

Sunny admired the way in which Vera did not resort to *we* when it came to bad fortune. He heard the organ rumbling and voices wailing before she spoke again. *Let Him in your heart today, Throwing every window open, O receive Him while you may.* By the time she spoke, Vera's sentences hissed down quickly, like short, hot fuses.

"I thought Linas was going to lead the crowd in 'Kumbaya.' I wonder how long Walter Green has been in his pants. Who do you figure he figures? Arty?"

"No," Sunny quickly replied.

"Daryl?"

"*Nooo.*"

"Rod?"

Sunny paused to run this new name through his mind; it swiftly returned, unmarked.

"I doubt it. The only chit he earns from that would be Rod's. Which is as valuable as old francs. No, it's something—someone—we're missing. Someone Linas can trust to get out of the way—or not be too hard to move out of the way—next year. In the meantime," said Sunny, "I have an idea. . . ."

Wooden doors sprang open. Organ blasts pealed. Voices roared. *Joshua prayed for to stop the sun. The sun did stop till the battle was won. Hallelujah!* Snowshoes squished over soft red carpet. Sunny looked for the two, bare dark heads of his daughters in the surge of violet, coral, and daffodil brims flapping out of the service and past his alcove.

23

It was the worst—by far the worst—time of the year.

Cold whistled in through battened windows, locked doors, and buttoned coats. Fountains froze. Sidewalks cracked. The lake turned gray. The holiday lights of December were packed away. The sun didn't show itself until most people were already on their way to work, and vanished before they began the trek back home. Whole days—whole weeks—went by, cloaked in slate, smoke, and silver.

Skyscrapers whipped up the wind, so that to turn some corners felt like walking into a wall with your face. Your skin was stung red; your mouth was pushed back against your teeth; tears blew back into your eyes. Sometimes, you could see people who had turned into the wind shove vainly with their arms, as if striking back at a mugger.

Snow offered spots of relief. The city was good at getting it off the major roads, so that the snow could sprinkle a kind of softness and light over the streets and sidewalks—until it was scorched brown by car exhaust, stomped gray by a million heels, and melted by sunlight until the downy shawl of snow became a fraying, graying fringe. Ice wrapped around branches and limbs, giving trees the silver gleam of candelabras, but they rattled like old bones with each blast.

In the early days of January, people knew the siege ahead and were determined to see it through. By February, they were grimly resigned; those who could afford it went to Florida or Puerto Rico for at least a few days' relief from the heavy coat weighing on their necks and the everyday trudge of heavy, soggy shoes. By March, everyone had had an explosion of exasperation: They'd dropped a coin or key and just couldn't bear to take off a glove to retrieve it; they'd stepped into a cold bathroom on a bleak morning, shivered and swore, "Shit. Enough. I'm tired. *Stop.*"

The city put on exhibits and festivals as diversions. Thoroughfares bristled with whimsical sculptures and thickets of lights. Many buildings strung gaily colored bulbs in trees and hedges; empty office floors glowed like casinos.

Gray was the color of the season, but not gloom. Many people went about their days and nights professing to be oblivious, or anyhow impervious, to the sting of the wind and wetness. A few brave or craven souls still ran along the beach. Bundled schoolchildren scampered, tumbled, and played ball in playgrounds and parks where the earth underfoot was as unrelenting as stone. Taverns bubbled late. People stamped their boots and clapped their arms to keep warm along the El train platforms, but still joked, gossiped, and made plans.

There were places on the planet that were colder and windier. But Copenhagen, Irkutsk, and those Himalayan towns that clung, like flowers, to the side of a grand gorge, did not have nearly so many millions of people heading off to work and school, restaurants, shops, churches, and movies, walking the dog, hauling groceries, or otherwise carrying on the semblance of warm and orderly lives.

Sometimes, the gray of the sky turned pearly. Sometimes, the gray lake rippled with slow-moving streaks of pale blue, slashes of deep blue, and ripples of foamy white light. Sometimes, spikes of light poked through clouds, like spectacular scythes. Sunny had been told, and came to believe it himself, that the ferocious weather seemed to breed a kind of pride: a loony but appealing conviction that people who could live and laugh at such temperatures possessed a special crazy toughness. They didn't break a sweat about small things. They savored a hot meal, hearty friends, a bracing drink, and belly laughs, with the abandon of people who thought they had earned the right.

24

After Sgt. Gallaher had brought Sunny and his daughters through the worshippers, guided them into their car, and tapped the thick security glass to signal the driver to pull out, Sunny noticed a message symbol winking on his phone and lifted it to his ear.

"Sunny? Arty," he heard. "A blessed Sabbath. You've got your two hundred dollars a ton. I'd like to bring it up first item tomorrow. Love to your girls."

"Alderman Agras sends his regards," he told them.

The officer pulled their black car over on Wabash, under the thunderclap of an El train trundling overhead, to let out Rula and Rita, who said they wanted to go to the Cultural Center.

"There's an exhibit of gilded silver cups and dishes decorated from the Sassanian Dynasty," Rula explained.

"Muriel? Virginie? Diego? Funny names for silver cups," said Sunny, and his daughters pushed down hard on Sunny's shoulders, laughing.

"Just remember," he told them. "The wedding reception at Jia's tonight."

When Sunny had settled back into his seat, Sgt. Gallaher turned to him with a slow smile.

"Back at church," she said. "That man wasn't the Alderman Slavin-skas that I know."

"It's among the ones I know," Sunny laughed. "All politicians say, 'We must not be bound by the nostrums of the past.' Linas isn't bound by nostrums he uttered five minutes ago. *Shameless.* But a professional has to admire his flexibility. Like a python."

Sunny clasped his hands together like a charmer playing a flute, then fluttered his fingers, like a snake rippling out of a basket. The gray of the day glazed over the gray tint of the windows.

"I should be outraged. But I enjoy the show. Most of us stop thinking. We take positions. Which *saves us* from thinking. Your supporters don't mind. They just hold you up against a list to see that what you say about gun control falls in line with what you say about abortion. What you say about capital punishment falls in line with what you say about gay marriage. Sometimes I think, my God, what possible link? But people see them, like the face of the Virgin Mary on a peanut butter cookie."

The sergeant parted her long black coat over a folded knee as the tires of the car thrummed with an iron whine over the Clark Street bridge.

"Gun control?" she began. "I say fine. Melt all the guns down into a big ball and shoot it toward Mars. Only cops and soldiers should have guns. Anyone says they need a gun to go hunting—use a bow and arrow. Or bare hands. Make sporting odds for an innocent deer. Abortion? I don't like it. I'm not sure I want to get rid of it, but I don't like it. There are lots better ways to stop from getting pregnant. Gay marriage? Why not? Everybody should get to live their own life. You don't like gay marriage—don't have one. Capital punishment? Anyone who takes a life ought to pay for it with theirs. Sorry, but I'm not sorry for them. Babies and deer are innocent. Killers aren't."

Sunny heard the tires bite into snowflakes, sand, gravel, and grains of blue road salt.

"You would drive the consultants wild," Sunny told Sgt. Gallaher, and he could see her jaw flush slightly as the heat in the car rose and she rolled a window down a quarter inch.

"Well that's how it all makes sense to me," she said.

Ingo's on west Irving Park had faded old paneled walls festooned with framed plates, soccer photos, Bavarian flags, and pictures of schnitzels, wursts, and bier. A yellowing old sign said, "Sauerkraut: German Natural Gas." The U.S. Attorney had taken a stool at the bar and held a blunt knife against the throat of a smoky brown thuringer.

"No last minute appeal?" Sunny called out from behind. Brooks Whetstone turned his head with a grim smile as the casing crackled and snapped.

"Denied," said the U.S. Attorney. "No mercy." The knife's edge clinked against the heavy ironstone plate. He placed a dollop of tawny brown mustard, flecked with speckles of horseradish, on top of the severed slice of sausage.

"I need some water with this," he said.

"That just spreads the fire around," Sunny told him. "Beer douses it."

Sunny nodded to the bartender—he was one of Adam Wojcik's best precinct captains—and he began to draw a soft brown liquid slowly into a heavy glass, until a thick white head, almost of the kind you'd see on a chocolate sundae, began to rise.

"Do I eat the topping with a spoon?" Brooks Whetstone asked.

"Slurp through the suds," Sunny advised him. "Have a napkin nearby. Or all the foam—you'll look rabid."

Sunny sipped from his own mug and could feel a spray of bubbles break near his nose. The dark beer had a tart, smooth taste, like unsweetened caramel.

"I am. Thank you for meeting with me," Brooks Whetstone said as he held a napkin in his palm over his chin. "And for suggesting this place. I don't get to see as much of the city as I'd like."

He slipped a slender brown envelope onto the bar and unwound the red thread from the top flap.

"I could use your interpretation skills, alderman. And as I've told you before, I know how to show my gratitude. The mayor—frankly, it surprised us, in this day and age—wrote lots of letters. By hand."

"A human touch in a depersonalized age," Sunny said after a pause.

"Why were some written by hand and some typed?"

"Don't you do the same?" asked Sunny. "Dictated letters, or something drafted by aides for official business. Handwritten notes for condolences, weddings, the birth of a child."

"So, the mayor would dictate something like this," the U.S. Attorney said as he slipped a letter from the envelope. It looked like a stiff ivory-brown sheet of the mayor's official stationery; Sunny could see the backside of the city emblem at the top. Brooks Whetstone read out half-sentences.

"'Dear Mr. Whetstone, congratulations on your appointment, blah-blah, I extend my warm personal welcome to Chicago and trust that you will come to cherish our city, blah-blah.'"

The froth on Sunny's beer subsided, and he took two long swallows while Brooks read.

"I don't know how to break it to you, Mr. Whetstone," he said. "But I doubt the mayor ever saw that. It's a form with your name inserted. I don't know how it is over at the federal building. We get just a little too busy to personalize a routine letter like that at City Hall."

Brooks Whetstone smiled slightly and licked a small streak of spicy mustard from the top of his knife. Sunny held himself back from saying, *I tell my daughters not to do that.*

"All these personal notes," he continued, tapping the envelope with the cleaned edge of his knife. "Why not phone calls? Email? Saves time and postage."

"A personal letter is *personal.*"

"More private, too, isn't it? One hand to another. Nobody reading or listening in. That's how terror cells communicate, isn't it? A man writes a note in a cave, passes it on, and six months and sixteen thousand miles later, a skyscraper goes down."

"Am I supposed to dignify that?" asked Sunny. "Not that you feds are any better at finding terrorists."

But Brooks Whetstone already fingered a new ivory brown sheet from the thicket in front of him.

"Here's one to Commissioner Rivera of Streets and San. Who was,

I might add, pleased to provide it. 'It is my pleasure,' blah-blah, 'to heartily recommend Justin Keenan, blah-blah, for a position with you. I have known Justin,' blah-blah-blah, 'for many years. Sincerely, etc.' "

"If a man knows the mayor, he's supposed to ask his second-grade teacher to write a letter?"

"As a matter of fact, he *wasn't* hired," Brooks Whetstone announced, a small light kindling his eyes. The U.S. attorney pulled another note from his brown envelope with a wizard's snap and began to read.

"'Dear Commissioner Rivera: It is my pleasure,' blah-blah, 'to heartily recommend Eric Rector, blah-blah, for a position in the Department of Streets and Sanitation. I have known Eric,' blah-blah-blah, 'for many years. 'Sincerely, etc., the Honorable. Blah-blah, Mayor.' "

Brooks Whetstone turned the letters around to face Sunny. Even in the bar's dim light, he could recognize parallel features: tall, looping first letters, trailing off into infinitesimal obscurity, each letter framing three lines of matching length. Each 'Sincerely,' looking similarly so.

"Almost word for word," Brooks explained as Sunny tried to exhibit interest and brought his nose closer. "What makes Commissioner Rivera hire one man and not the other?"

Sunny made a point of hesitating as he looked from line to line.

"Could it be—wild guess here," he said, "that he just made an honest personnel decision? Read the letters, but considered qualifications and experience?"

"To shovel shit for Streets and San?"

"Pushing a mower or a plow that's practically as powerful as a tank? You and I should know how to do something as useful."

Brooks admitted no reaction on his bland, blond face and withdrew another sheaf of paper, tapping the bottom edge against the bar.

"Some people were pleased to let us have a look at this one," he said, and read again quickly. "'Dear Barry'—this is to Barry Nygaard of Yello—'Blah-blah, Peter Mansfield, very exciting, Ninth Congressional District, I ask you to support him. Legal scholar, blah-blah.' Both Nygaard brothers gave the legal limit to the Mansfield campaign fund."

"I know," said Sunny. "I feel like a local coffee shop competing against the international chain."

"But their sister Karen gave a couple of thousand to you, alderman. A Yello executive named Gurkeerhat Singh gave you $2,000. You know him?"

"Maybe we shook hands on a subway platform. A name like that—must be a Punjabi. I'm Tamil. Do you know every member of the Montreal Canadians hockey club? Being white guys on the same continent and all."

Brooks Whetstone turned away from Sunny's taunt by wrenching a chunk of rye bread from a wedge that had been placed between them. Sunny could see two or three caraway seeds fall onto the bar. As Brooks spoke, Sunny blotted one of the seeds with his finger.

"So what could cause a stranger to give the legal limit to someone he doesn't know?"

"*Issues,*" said Sunny firmly. "Imagine—a smart guy like that actually paying attention. Maybe he likes my position on taxes, city services, or tax abatement on the fifty-two hundred block of Sheridan Road."

Brooks Whetstone daubed a crust of his bread in a smear of mustard and halted it just before his lips to tell Sunny, "Mr. Singh—and Karen Nygaard—and a few other names I'm sure we could find—gave contributions to you. This baffles me. You would think that all Yello executives must be passionately interested in doing favors for the founders of the company. Who have a strong interest in doing favors for the mayor."

Sunny widened his eyes and smiled, as if listening to a four-year-old count to twenty by missing every other number.

"Yello has the money to buy the moon," Sunny reminded him. "It gives money to hospitals, gospel choirs, one of the world's great symphonies, and the Polish Sports Hall of Fame. *Every* politician would oblige Yello. Even Greens and Wobblies."

Sunny had heard Sgt. Gallaher come up behind them during his last few words and turned his head just as she had stepped into place behind his shoulder.

"The chief," she said, just loud enough for Brooks Whetstone to hear. She held out a small black department phone. Sunny nodded at

Brooks Whetstone and took a couple of steps farther down the bar as he held the phone to his ear.

"Alderman Roopini, there may be a development," Chief Martinez said in a measured monotone. "The man we have been questioning at the Eighteenth. He now says he was in the vestibule where the stack of pizzas was waiting to be picked up by the mayor's security detail. He says a woman kept asking which one was the mayor's. She said she was a big fan. The man admits that she gave him three twenties to pop the top of the box. He says it was open just a second. But . . ."

Sunny kept his voice low, but turned toward the U.S. Attorney, who listened as he seemed to absently review the brown ranks of Goldwasser and Rumpleminze bottles behind the bar.

"Yes. Time enough."

"We're pulling receipts, flashing photos," said the chief, but then added, "You have to know this, sir: the suspect suffered cuts and contusions during interrogation."

Sunny could feel his neck redden and his ears boil. That was police parlance for "holding court on the street." A man that police had to chase down an alley who took a blind shot at them would predictably *suffer cuts and contusions in the process of being apprehended.* It was their way to ensure that any attempt to harm a police officer would receive swift reprisal before some myopic jurist could interfere.

"You were supposed to put mints on his pillow, Matt," Sunny curtly reminded him.

"The cuts and contusions were self-inflicted. *Sir,*" he replied equally.

"There's a special place in hell—not Dubai, Matt—for a department that breaks this case but gets it thrown out because they couldn't keep their hands in their pants."

"The suspect is at Weiss Memorial. We have a recording of everything. Our people are clear. I'll keep you informed, sir. On all counts."

Although the police chief clicked off with no further niceties, Sunny could feel the fever of Brooks Whetstone's vigilant interest from several seats away. He improvised a farewell into the phone.

"Thank you, chief. Please proceed as we discussed. *Official busi-*

ness," Sunny finally raised his voice in explanation to Brooks Whetstone, as he kept the phone at his side and nodded to Sgt. Gallaher to resume her stance.

"I appreciate your time," the U.S. Attorney said as Sunny inched back along the bar. He slowly drew out seven or eight sheets of ivory stationery with the blue and gold city seal, and fanned them across the bar.

"I don't think these letters indicate anything illegal, Mr. Roopini. By themselves. But I think they may help us crack a code."

He ran a thumb across the sheets of paper; lightly rubbing the raised lettering that said OFFICE OF THE MAYOR.

"We put them under a strong light. We've had cryptographers go over them, letter by letter. What if you string together every second consonant? Every third vowel? Is there some hidden message? What if the mayor was writing one letter in ink—the one we can read—but hiding a second one between the lines by writing with lemon juice?"

"Hold it over a candle," Sunny told him. "My daughters did that in the second grade. Sorry you missed it at Stanford."

Brooks Whetstone smiled cheerlessly.

"So all these notes from the mayor asking people to do something," he began. "Hire this man. Don't give money to that man. 'I would regard it as a personal favor.' They mean exactly what they say?"

"What else?"

"The mayor sent notes to you?"

"Every alderman. For the opening of a community center in Humboldt Park. A new library in West Englewood—"

Brooks waved off all further examples as uninteresting, like hearing about a choice of salad dressings at a diner.

"Personal ones," he stressed.

"Like when my wife died?" Sunny spoke softly, so the slap in his voice could be plain and flat. He watched Brooks Whetstone step back slightly and reach a hand over to press his fingers lightly on the coaster below Sunny's beer.

"No," he said softly. Then, "*No,*" more firmly. "I meant the ones asking you for something."

"What can an alderman do for a mayor?" asked Sunny. "He had my vote in his pocket. He had *me* in his pocket. There've been lots of people that wanted to run. Better, richer, smarter. Lawyers, professors, real community leaders. Younger and cuter, too." Sunny picked up his glass and took a small sip from the dregs. "But they all backed away because people said, 'He's close to the mayor. He gets things done.' The mayor had to write letters asking for my favors? How quaint. All he had to do was lift a finger."

Brooks Whetstone held the brown envelope out between them, so that the top flap came out just under Sunny's chin. Sunny even heard a scratch of stubble rub against the edge.

"All that devotion," said the U.S. Attorney quietly, "And he couldn't care less—it meant absolutely nothing—when it counted. Now you know what kind of man he really was."

But when Brooks Whetstone turned his gaze from the mirror to his glass on the bar with no further comment, Sunny began to laugh; he laughed so hard that he began to shudder and had to catch his breath, wipe his eyes, and clear laughter from his throat like a clutter of leaves.

"But you don't, do you?" he finally croaked. "You've just invested— what, a year? Two? And I'm sure enough money to pay for a good infielder. The oaths you had to give the Justice Department that all the court orders and special spending bills would be worth it because you were going to reel in a whole net of king salmon. And now, you're left just reading a bunch of letters, over and over, like some mooning teenager, trying to figure out why the mayor wrote *a* instead of *the*."

The white-capped glass was set down softly as Sunny reached into a pocket and pulled out three twenties to slip below his own empty glass on the bar.

"You were going to bring down a whole rotten temple of scoundrels. Now, you might be lucky just to snag a couple of sleazy building inspectors. It's what reporters do, too, Mr. Whetstone. You puff up fools like me to make it look like you're doing battle against dragons."

And then Sunny raised a hand in a crabbed, reptilian claw and opened his mouth, as if to bare fangs.

"Hahhh," he rasped softly.

Brooks Whetstone leaned forward deliberately and took the new glass steadily in his hand, tipping it slightly toward Sunny. The full white foam fell forward until half an inch flopped over and a driblet of beer trickled over Brook's unflinching knuckles. Brooks flexed the fingers with which he gripped the glass in turn, one, two, three, and four, as if counting down before speaking.

"I always find our conversation stimulating, alderman," he said.

In the ninth recorded hour of the interrogation of Carlos Ponce, aka Zambrano, Reyes, Rios, Contreras, Alomar, and Uribe, at the 18th District station on north Larrabee, a mommy and daddy team named Barry and Cindi had grown annoyed and exhausted. The subject twitched, scratched his pants, and pulled on his nose, as if tugging on a pin that could adjust the features on his face. He had gnawed his nails until the tips of his fingers dripped spit.

Worse, he had asked for a lawyer. A man had only to watch television to know that, and Carlos Ponce had traveled through courts and prisons the way some people drove up to Wisconsin every year to watch the leaves change colors.

Cindi and Barry had fended him off with reassurances. "We're just talking," Barry told him. "You help us, we can help you. A man with your background could use a little help," and they actually got him to say—interrogation camera purring and a milk-cheeked young state's attorney watching through the glass—"Okay, no lawyer now. I answer your questions, I get to go, no other trouble 'bout nothing."

Every hour, Carlos Ponce repeated that he had seen nothing—not nothing unusual, or nothing out-of-place, just *nothing*, he insisted, in stocky, heavy, stop-and-go sentences.

"You don' see. People, they don' see you. I'm just some guy 'gainst the wall. Some guy, picks up what they leave."

"Ever find anything?" asked Barry.

It was a question they brought back every hour or so, to see how faithful Ponce stayed to his replies. In the first hour, he had devoutly denied finding so much as a crumb among the litter and tumble of a vacated table. By the third, Ponce recalled that he occasionally skimmed a tip.

"Maybe once, twice a week, I see somethin' somebody don' miss, maybe. May-bee."

"Food?" asked Cindi, and Carlos Ponce waved the question away as too obvious.

"*Course*, that. People leave two, three slices. Nabieh and Tannous don' mind."

"I used to waitress," Cindi suddenly remembered in the fifth hour. "The Beef Baron's Barn just off Ninety-seventh. Some of the things they'd find! Teeth, dentures, engagement rings in the blue cheese dressing. She'd go off crying to the ladies room, he'd hurry back before the cab could come, put on a sad-dog face and ask, 'Say, I wonder if you found . . .' Funny thing, but if a couple was there to break it off, it usually happened during soup or salad. If the guy brought her there to pop the question, he couldn't get the nerve to ask until dessert. Nowadays, I wonder—maybe you know—with gay couples, how they figure who's going to ask whom? Some people left eyeglasses, keys, coins, rubbers, pictures, beepers. . . ."

She used her right hand to put the list in the air between them, emphasizing each word with her index finger.

"Anythin' I find, I turn over," he said flatly. "Can' use it any-noway. Keys? You don' know the apar'men. Glasses? I don' need. Wallets? Cards you can' use, only little bills, and pictures of people you don' know."

"Sounds like you thought about it," Barry observed.

"This all about a credit card?" asked Carlos Ponce.

In the seventh hour, Carlos Ponce repeated that he never followed the conversation of the people whose plates, cutlery, and castoff possessions he cleaned from the tables, because he couldn't hear it over the blare of the television over the bar, and he couldn't be less interested besides.

"Maybe if P'elope Cruz walks in, I lissn'," he said. Barry began to squirm with pique.

"Not if you were the only man left in the uni—" he began, but Cindi held him off with the palm of her hand.

"Well what if Penelope Cruz motioned you over and asked, 'Carlos, my dear, what are they talking about at table six?' " she proposed. "What would you say?" She was bargaining that in answering the hypothetical, he would have to resort to the specific.

"Table six that night?" said Ponce. "I thin' I change it three times. All guys I could'n understand."

"They weren't speaking English?" Cindi asked earnestly. "Spanish?"

"Computer shit," Carlos Ponce explained.

"Table three?"

"No' mine."

"Two?"

Carlos Ponce eyes widened.

"A couple. Eigh' to nine-thirty maybe. Fighting. 'Bout sumin' named Lola."

"Hola!" said Barry.

"I thin' her mother," said Ponce, and Barry sank back in his chair.

The officers departed to confer with their lieutenant and the young assistant state's attorney in the small anteroom on the other side of the glass.

"He's getting *too* vivid now," said Barry. "He's about to remember that they were plotting to rob the Royal Bank of Scotland."

"He's tired," said Cindi. "His defenses are down."

"Or he's tiring us out with *shit*," snapped Barry.

"Your analysis is noted," said the lieutenant coldly, and slapped a palm on the back of his neck to clear his mind and call the room to attention. Lt. Delbert Tompkins had been in the basement of the station, save for a dozen cigarette breaks, since shortly after nine a.m. Saturday morning. His mouth tasted of ash and rubber. His eyes burned as if he had to blink sharp gravel out of them.

They agreed that there was one play left, and returned to the cold, bright room. Cindi looked down at a sheaf of papers and made a mark with a pen, as if she had noted some small something that could be clarified with a comma or period.

"Table nine?" she asked, almost sweetly.

"Couple of girls," said Carlos Ponce. "Brown hair, long. Other short and dark. Just un'er the TV, I didn' hear much."

"Gay or straight?" asked Barry heavily, and Carlos Ponce turned to smile.

"Who know? I don' see them go down on each other," he said, and sat back with satisfaction at the way his joke had left his interrogators aghast.

"Of course," said Barry, in a bored monotone. "Or maybe that's what you have to say, because women never look at you."

"Girls fin' me," Ponce smirked. "Like birds fin' flowers."

"Like flies find turds," Barry suggested, and then stood up brusquely. He brought his arm down hard, as if drawing a steel door over the mirrored window.

"Turn that camera off. Turn that fucking camera off, do you hear? I am tired of hearing this *cock*sucking, mother*fucking, son*ofa*bitch* lie to us!" He stood in front of the window and swelled his chest as if to stop a bullet—or a cannonball. "Off, off, *off!*" Barry bellowed.

(In fact the camera that recorded interrogations could not be turned off once engaged. Police wanted to be able to attest to prosecutors and judges that they could not stop and start a recording; it authenticated a confession's integrity. But Barry and Cindi bet that Carlos Ponce's experience was not so extensive as to include this nugget of knowledge and would therefore assume that whatever followed was intended to escape the scrutiny of honest judges, conscientious defense attorneys, and the *Tribune*.)

Barry leered down at Carlos Ponce.

"My God," said Cindi, cringing. "You're not going to hurt him, are you?"

"Hurt him?" Barry demanded. He picked a lone pastel pink chair up by its poured plastic back and threw it into the cinder-block wall. It fell back, disconcertingly undented. "Hurt him? Hurt him?"

This time Barry picked up the pink chair by its thin tin wire legs and smashed the back hard against the cold concrete floor. The fluted pink shape of the seat stayed upturned, like a set of mocking lips. Barry wrenched the thin wire legs apart with his forearms. The tip of a leg fell off, unsheathing a sharp edge just below Barry's chin.

"I wouldn't *dirty my hands*!" he bellowed. "I would only *catch the clap* from choking him to death! I'm going to call in *fucking professionals*!" he said, and finally jerked the two rear legs of the chair into a sincere if inexact X. "His fucking legs will be sticking out of his throat! His throat will be sticking out of his ass!"

(*SC2000 Four-leg Y series plastic stack chair*, Barry thought to himself. *List price $64.95, and they take it out of my next paycheck if this doesn't bust something.* He had paid for a couple in the past.)

Cindi knew her turn, and crouched in front of Carlos Ponce on one knee. If he was reminded of a prayer card, so much the better.

"Please," she implored. "*Please.*"

The room's steel door flew open and clanked against the wall. A well-built man with a steely black beard wearing a black leather coat stepped into the room in lustrous, creaking black boots with tall, sharp heels that clopped off each step. He wore wire-rimmed sunglasses in the ruthless overhead light, kept his arms crossed across his chest, as if locking down some secret ingredient, and looked down at Carlos Ponce with scorching disdain.

"This is Colonel del Aguila," said Barry. "Of the Federal Security Directorate in Mexico City. You know them? The Seg-oorr-idad Fed-eee-ral?" Barry pronounced the Spanish title as if reading off the name of a small town on a map of Iceland.

Cindi turned her dark head down toward the floor. It approximated the silhouette of a biblical mother weeping though, at this point in their sketch, she usually had to bite back laughter.

Colonel del Aguila was actually Sergeant Leo del Aguila of the Mounted Police patrol on west Huron ("We Stay in the Saddle Longer" was the unit's motto—to be sure, unofficially so—and they sold T-shirts and refrigerator magnets with that inscription). His guest performances as a Mexican police colonel were booked several times a year at various north side station houses, as much for the authenticity of his glossy riding boots as his gruff beard and graying glower.

"She wan' to see, that's all!" Carlos Ponce shouted. "She said she just wan' to see! She gave me twenties! So I open' the top, an' she whistled! She look it over, maybe fi' seconds. I didn' see nothin' else! I didn' see!"

But before his last screech could die, Carlos Ponce threw himself on one of the upturned chair legs. After a pause and a splat, the sharp tip, soaking and dripping with what looked like bubbling, dark red wine, rose up like some nightmare blossom through the back of Carlos' neck, and a real scream—this time, not Cindi's—crashed and clanged against the foul brown walls.

The Krivas Museum of Lithuanian Civilization on south Pulaski had set out white-clothed tables in a large ground floor room, guarded by old suits of armor and unflinching male mannequins cradling crossbows. The wood-paneled walls were festooned with front pages from old Middle Europe newspapers, braying thick black headlines about Lithuania's occupations, humiliations, and massacres in bristling dark forests. The smells and sounds of bacon sputtering, onions frizzling, and butter burning grew in the room as staff brought out great, blistered blocks of kugelis, the Lithuanian dish of grated potatoes and beaten eggs. Men and women tucked paper napkins over their ties and necklaces.

Linas and Rosemary Slavinskas stood near the entrance; they each laced an arm around Sunny's shoulders.

"Lordship!"

"Mr. Acting Mayor," said Rosie, her lips brushing his ear. She wore a chestnut cashmere sweater over sensationally slim black pants, and a string of beautifully burnished old Lithuanian amber around her coltish neck. Sunny held on to Linas at his elbows and leaned into his ear.

"We haven't had a chance to chat since your 'I Have a Dream' speech this morning," he told him. "Very moving."

"I once was lost, lordship, but now am found," said Linas. "Was blind, but now I see—Sgt. Gallaher."

Rosemary stepped forward to extend her hand first, and Sgt. Gallaher reached back with her own. Ten long fingers clasped, and Rosemary Slavinskas's curvaceous coral fingertips entwined with Maureen Gallaher's blunt, clear sergeant's nails that were kept short by departmental regulation.

"Sergeant, I've heard a lot about you. I'm Rosie."

Sunny recalled that shaking hands was against operational procedure for a security officer. But Sunny supposed that all such rules were also subject to operational discretion.

"An honor."

"And all of our *children* want to meet you, too,"

Sunny realized once more why Rosemary Slavinskas still beguiled her husband. Linas swiftly opened another route of conversation.

"The sausage over there is naturally gray. Made by a guy over on Archer Avenue," he told them. "No artificial gray food coloring in the Twelfth Ward!"

Rosemary Slavinskas steered Sgt. Gallaher and Sunny through a thicket of seats toward a table in the front. Sunny found himself nodding at the headless suits of armor.

"The mayor came here for a dinner once," Sunny told Sgt. Gallaher as he walked behind her. "After they'd reached an agreement on a southwest side expressway. Alderman Slavinskas told him the suits of armor were re-creations of the great Lithuanian knights of fourteen-ten who defeated the Teutonic Empire. The mayor said, 'When I saw no heads, I assumed they were aldermen.' "

As he moved through clumps of folding seats and upraised faces, Sunny saw J. P. Mulroy from the 10th lift a wedge of kugelis into his ham slice of a face, Brock Lucchesi of the 13th tell his table the joke about why young Guiseppe always polished his Guccis before he went to dances, Collie Kerrigan of the 14th slip two twenties to a young waitress with braided blond hair and a tight-fitting red folk vest to bring their table a bottle of Asti Spumante, Tommy Mitrovic of the 21st hold somebody else's baby boy over his shoulders like a small, squiggling sack of fava beans, to feed the child the tip of his finger, and Jesus Flores Suarez of the 22nd tamp a layer of sour cream, like cake frosting, into place over the top of his kugelis.

"The girls can't make it?" asked Rosie.

"They're with friends," Sunny explained.

"Boys?" she guessed.

"One. Apparently they share him."

"Or they have a second they're not telling you about. And a third and fourth. The one you've met may just be to distract you from all the ones they don't want you to meet."

"Is every member of the Slavinskas family such a strategic thinker?" asked Sunny.

"It was months before I told my mother about Linas."

"Me too," said Sunny.

They swallowed their laughter as young Henry Krivas III, whose father started the auto dealership in the building that now housed their museum, got behind a lone microphone and tapped his knuckles.

"Test-test. Test-test. Can you—is this—can you—"

"Yes!" several voices called out from the back tables.

"We're so glad that everyone could join us on such a beautiful spring day," Henry Krivas said finally, as folding chairs tweeted and squealed as people squirmed around to see snow glazing over the large display windows.

A troupe of youngsters walked into the small, clear place just in front of the microphone: four girls and three boys, all in cinched red vests and tight green shorts. A recording of some small, brassy, cowbell band began to hiss from an audio player on a folding chair. The youngsters spun in place, reached down to the floor with their hands, and then pulled back their arms as if drawing back on a bow. "The flax harvest dance," Rosie whispered behind her hand to Sunny. The city boys piled imaginary sheaves of flax into the encircling, oval arms of girls balancing figment baskets on their hips. After several choruses of pulling and piling, they all raised their hands over their heads and began to slide them down to their knees, and then back up, as on a loom. The wheat-haired boy dancing, stacking, and weaving in the middle had to stand on his toes and reach up to match the others. The audience chuckled sweetly, but the boy's face smoldered like an electric coil.

Henry Krivas returned to the front and had just begun to explain the meaning of each layer of the Tree Cake set off to the side when two men backed into the room, spilling snow from their shoes and elbows and casting bright lights across the doorway.

Vera Barrow, a bright orange scarf drawn with artful carelessness across her throat, a loden coat draping her shoulders, stood in the center of the ivory cloud of light. She smiled shyly, like a child entering her parent's bedroom.

"The sign outside says 'All Welcome,' doesn't it?" she asked. Linas, his hands folded at his belt, stood just outside the circlet of light. Sunny heard Rosie's chair creak behind him, and then a soft scurry of steps.

"I tried to buy a ticket," Vera said in the sudden silence. "But my friend here said that he and Rosie wouldn't hear of it. Thank you for welcoming me. Thank you for welcoming our friends with the bright lights, too."

Handclapping broke out as Vera took Linas's elbow and Rosie Slavinskas's hand and began to walk through the audience. The backsides of television cameramen grazed upraised chins and knocked over butter plates. When they reached the front of the room, Linas leaned over to whisper something to Vera in her ear that was on the other side of the microphone and then raised his hands to call for quiet.

"I've asked Alderman Barrow to say a few words. I've certainly had my say today," and when Rosemary Slavinskas laughed, the room joined in; a few people clanged spoons against their saucers.

"So it's an honor to have the alderman say a few words to us," said Linas. "She's a great friend—a great speaker—and we'd be honored to hear from her, on this day on which we remember the late mayor and look forward to the future. Alderman Barrow," Linas said simply, and stepped back until he could feel a window ledge against his hip. Sunny could hear people unwrap cough drops, shake out small mints, and clear their throats to listen.

Vera had shaken her coat from her shoulders and handed it to Henry Krivas.

"I'll be brief," she began softly. "I know we'd all like to have some kugelis before the Bears game begins," and as the audience chuckled,

Vera turned up her brightest smile and slid her plain gold bangles back down her forearms, where they wouldn't clack.

(Sunny had never known Vera to express an interest in sports. Every time they had joined the mayor at a White Sox game, the mayor had made her fold her copy of the *Wall Street Journal* behind her scorecard, to look as if she were assiduously scouring pitching statistics. Sunny made admiring note of her punctiliousness.)

"I hope you will give me a few minutes to talk about why the mayor was so important to so many," she said. "I know he didn't get quite so many votes on this side of Western Avenue. But I know that my friend Alderman Slavinskas respected him, as he said so beautifully today."

The bone-dry electric light made Vera's copper face shine softly, and she pulled back her dark chiffon hair, as if drawing soft puffy ruffles around her face. Sunny heard voices all around him mutter, "Pretty. She's so *pretty*."

"This city has become so beautiful," said Vera. "Glittering, really. What a great and noble profile, all the tall buildings reaching skywards. Those grand, green parks. All the excitement.

"But sometimes," she went on in a sharper voice, "in some neighborhoods, you feel that the skyline belongs to some other city. Right next to the lake—and it might as well be across the ocean. In some of our neighborhoods, people turn to each other and ask, 'Do you know anyone who lives there? Do you ever go there?' You can take your kids down there for Christmas. See Santa, get some popcorn and a hot chocolate. Maybe a couple times in the summer, too, they can splash around in the park, and hear some music. But for a lot of people in this city, that stunning skyline might as well be Tokyo or Rome. The *moon*. It's as real as a postcard. A lot of people in this city have to live in crumbling buildings. They have to try to keep the kids out of parks that have been taken over by gangs. We've got some people in this city who complain that the city council banned foie gras. Do you know it?"

Sunny heard murmurs of familiarity move around the room.

"A French delicacy. I swear—of all the things. They stuff a goose with grain until his little liver bursts. Some delicacy."

The room rippled with laughter. Vera held out a hand, as if to call people back.

"Listen, we all eat some crazy things," she said. "You don't have to be in Chinatown or France. I've had kindzius,"—a pungent Lithuanian sausage—"and I like them. Well, once anyway. But I did ask myself, 'Why are you eating a pig's stomach?' "

Vera stepped back slightly from the microphone as laughter cascaded around her, and she deftly took the knot of her orange scarf and brought it over to the side of her neck.

"I had foie gras once. Visit France, and you have to try it. It's delicious. But I can live without it. You've got some people in this city who complain because they can't buy goose liver, and a lot of people who can't afford to buy bread and peanut butter. We can all be proud of the big, powerful, glamorous place this city has become. But we should also be embarrassed that we've got some people living in skyscrapers, and some others barely living in boxes."

Vera turned slightly, so that her profile seemed to be a kind of prow that cut ahead of her words.

"We've got some people," she began, "and I admire them, who get off a truck after hitchhiking here from Champerico. Or flying here from Guangzhou. Five years later, they're the foremen, and they've got two kids on the honor roll. Ten years later, they have their own company, and their kids are at Northwestern. I'm glad to have them. They make this city great. But we've also got people here whose families came up through slavery, bigotry, and poverty, and they haven't had a chance. They work hard. They struggle. But they haven't had a chance. Well to them—to us, if I may—our mayor stood tall in that skyline."

Sunny could see glistening in some eyes around him, and others who had to look down at the table to hide their eyes. Vera's voice grew so soft, Sunny heard snow pinging softly against the room's long gray windows.

"The mayor made us feel that all those shiny big skyscrapers turned around and bowed to us. He made us feel that his shoulders were big enough to protect us, too."

Vera stepped back and bowed her head slightly. Sunny heard people crinkling tissues and clearing coughs, and people pushing their chairs back slightly from the table, as if making room for another.

"Are there any questions?" Vera asked suddenly. Sunny looked for Linas, who was standing in grave respect over in a corner, and just as suddenly lifted his head in surprise. He had won points for withstanding questions from the press in the morning. But what could any reporter ask—about politics, his tax returns, some investigation or his personal life—for which Linas hadn't rehearsed an answer? It was risky to invite questions from the general public. They might ask a politician about space alien abductions, whether Lee Harvey Oswald acted alone, or if O. J. Simpson was really guilty. They could make a politician look foolish for not knowing the price of a gallon of milk, or that Ohio is a one-way street eastbound. A politician couldn't rely on the prospect of mutually assured embarrassment when taking questions from regular people. An ordinary citizen could humiliate a politician without consequence.

For several seconds, there was mumbling, whispering, and jangling, nervous laughter. Finally, a woman's voice called out, "Do you know Oprah?"

Sunny could imagine Vera, in another mood and circumstance, training a steely smile on the woman to demand, "Do you think that all black people live in one big shoe on the south side?"

Instead Vera smiled lightly and easily.

"A little. We've had lunch. She's as lovely in person as she is on TV."

"You ever get to go on one of those great Christmas shopping trips she takes her staff?" another voice asked. "New York, Milan . . ."

"No," said Vera. "But I can't imagine better shopping than what we have right here on State Street."

An elderly man, hunched as he stood, waved an old brown hat for recognition and Vera smiled down at him.

"I've got a question about—what are they?—TEZs. Have you ever heard them called Tax Exempt Zebras?"

Vera rewarded the room with a three-stop chuckle.

"Tax Enhancement Zones, and honestly, I've never heard that nickname," she said.

"If you see just one, you see a zebra," the man explained. "But put a bunch together, they're disguised. Half the empty lots they call TEZs belong to friends of the mayor, and friends of friends, and they just hide them in all the others." The man clopped his inverted hat over imaginary plots of land, one, two, three, as he spoke. "Some guy starts to build something, and it doesn't work out—or was never meant to work out. Soon it's empty again. Worse—an empty lot with bricks and boards, just catching snow, and a bunch of crack addicts sleeping below. You let a guy stop paying taxes on a property, and he has no incentive to develop it. My name is Vincas, by the way, and I can say this at my age: You're a great dame."

As laughs flickered through the seats and tables, Vera Barrow clasped her hands at her waist and pursed her lips thoughtfully.

"I've seen a few places like that, Mr. Vincas," she said slowly. "But I've also seen a TEZ over in Shirley Watson's ward, on the site of an old abandoned building on Sixty-third. Now there's a preschool, a wedding dress shop, and"—she paused to smile—"an off-track betting parlor."

"Two out of three," someone shouted, and Vera pointed out toward the sound with a graceful index finger.

"Brings in more foot traffic than the wedding shop," she laughed. "And over in Tommy Mitrovic's ward, there was an old abandoned garage on Seventy-ninth. We put through a bill to create a TEZ. Now some hospital has a walk-in health clinic on that spot, giving shots and lollipops to children, bandaging shins, and examining expectant mothers. It doesn't always work out. But you have to take a chance on neighborhoods."

"Should race count in hiring?" a woman's voice asked.

Vera expelled an audible breath into the microphone.

"Let me put it this way," she began. "No. *But*. Sometimes I wish we could do what they do in symphony orchestras—audition people behind a screen, so you never know. Here's the *but*. We can't put our society behind a screen. We have people from all over the world here. You should be able to see that in the police, fire, bus drivers, teachers, and sanitation crews. I simply don't believe that if you hire the best people, you won't get a pretty good sprinkling of all kinds. But sometimes you have to make an effort."

"Why have you never married?"

Mr. Vincas again. In the laughter and clatter of coffee cups getting topped and stirred, Sunny could hear new murmuration of *pretty* and *charming* move around the room.

"I was," said Vera. There was an abrupt, startled quiet, before she added, "A long time ago. A nice man. But we were young. I don't talk about him, usually. He's married, children, happy. Been married a couple of times, actually," she said, which seemed to unplug bottled nervous laughter in the room. "He and his family are entitled to privacy."

An auburn-haired woman in her mid-thirties got to her feet. She had dressed for the day: gray sweater over a black top, stretchy gray pants and black rubber boots that squished and squealed slightly against the floor as she moved her chair with her feet to be able to face Vera.

"Miss Barrow, you went to Harvard, right?" As Vera nodded, the woman went on. "And I'm sure—anyone can tell—that you earned it."

"My mother was a nurse's aide," said Vera. "She's the one who earned it. I didn't really know my father," she added.

"If you had a son or a daughter," the woman began, then checked herself, "well, I'm sure they'd be as smart as you. But you're a LaSalle Street lawyer. You travel in the best circles. You wear fancy French scarves," and as Vera clutched the orange knot at her neck and gave a comic grimace, the people at tables pushed back and laughed.

"I'm happy for *you*," her questioner continued. "But why should any child of yours—okay, I'm going to say it—just because of race, get into Yale, Notre Dame, or even a job in the county clerk's office, over some equally smart Lithuanian or Irish kid from Back of the Yards whose mother might be a nurse's aide now?"

The room stirred and then bristled. As the woman sat down, two diners next to her seemed to pull away, but one right behind her patted her on the back. Vera waited patiently before speaking softly.

"You know, ma'am, I'm on the Harvard Board of Overseers. We talk about some of these very things there. I'm not sure I have an answer that will satisfy you. And if that boy or girl was your son or daughter, well, he or she is going to have a big advantage in life anyway, because I can tell they have a parent who loves and cares about them. It's shocking to me—it's tragic—how many kids all around us, not just from poor families, have to grow up without that kind of love."

Vera paused a beat before proceeding.

"We're trying to make up, in just one or two generations, for crimes that took place a long time ago—"

"My family didn't come here until nineteen forty-seven!" a man shouted out.

"—a long time ago," Vera repeated. "And that injustice has put the dead weight of discrimination and poverty around the feet of millions of Americans ever since."

"My father worked a garbage route for Streets and San. My grandfather lost three fingers at South Works," the man's voice barked back.

Vera stayed blank-faced and silent as chairs scraped the floor and voices grated against each other to be heard. Instead, she fixed a kind, mild face on the woman in stretchy gray pants and spoke in a low, level voice as the woman wound the white drawstrings of her slacks around her fingers.

"Maybe in trying to make the world fairer now," said Vera, "we will occasionally disappoint a few people who don't deserve it. But if we don't do whatever we can to fix our society now, we may never get the chance. If your son or daughter never gets into Harvard—if they get passed over for a city job—I hope that's the worst thing that ever happens to them. Love them and support them. Love and support this great city. Plenty of opportunities will be there."

Vera stepped back from the microphone. The sound of an iron grind of plows nosing down Pulaski jounced the frames of the long gray windows. A bus spattered fat splats of snow against their gray glaze. Sunny realized that Vera's disquisition had sparked an uncommon reaction to a political speech: silence. After a pause, they heard Mr. Vincas speak up again.

"So why didn't *you* remarry?"

Gurgles of laughter crackled through the crowd. Vera waited until people had swallowed their snorts and straightened their coffee cups. Then she announced, as if revealing the answer to a fifty-thousand-dollar quiz question, "Alderman Slavinskas was taken."

The room erupted in laughs, claps, and shouts. Rosie Slavinskas stood up behind Sunny and cast her voice out above the din of smarting hands and rasping throats.

"Oh Vera dear," she said. "We can work *that* out!"

A half-hour later, as Sunny stood in the doorway, pumping Henry Krivas's right arm with thanks, he put his left hand out onto Linas Slavinskas's soft sleeve as the alderman showed Sgt. Gallaher a suit of armor nestling a crossbow.

"This guy worked security for Vytautas the Great," he told her. "But it would be a shame to keep some people on security details covered up like tin cans, Sergeant Gallaher. Positively antediluvian."

Sunny let his clasp of Henry fall away and brought his mouth low over Linas's shoulder.

"You were so eloquent this morning," he said. "I'm sure you agree with Vera's moving words on minority hiring."

"The words?" asked Linas, drawing back slightly. "Oh, absolutely. Great words. I just might have arranged them a little differently."

Sunny put a thumb on Linas's elbow, and brought him close.

"Any time you want to fill me in," he said. "You have the number I keep here."

Sunny thumped the lapel over his heart. Linas inclined his pomaded blondish head until it nearly touched Sunny's forehead. Sunny could smell coppery flashes of the best sandalwood and bay scents from his cheek.

"Let's just say that the tired old politics of the past cannot meet the challenges of the future," said Linas. "We cannot pour new wine into old wineskins. Lordship, you'll figure it out before I can tell you," he said.

Then Linas leaned over, his broad smile brushing against the outer edge of Sunny's ear.

"Viva la raza," Linas told him.

26

A rapid review of receipts from Quattro's at the 18th District didn't reveal new names; it would be too much to expect that the mystery woman who had asked Carlos Ponce to pop the top of the pizza box had paid by credit card. But they had pulled the surveillance tape of the automatic teller machine in the all-night drugstore nearby on Wabash—"God bless all night drugstores," Lt. Delbert Tompkins exclaimed. "Heaps of rubbers and lights as bright as floodlights!"—and saw bleary photos of a couple of dark-haired women who seemed to fit the basic description that Carlos Ponce had stingily croaked and gasped from his bed at Weiss Memorial during the third quarter of the Bears-Cowboys game.

During the first minutes of the fourth quarter, a mommy and daddy team named David and Nina knocked on the front door of a basement (name on the B1 bell: MEADOWS) in an endangered old railroad-style six-flat brick building on North Burling that was the address attached to the bank account of a Linda Marie Keely, who had withdrawn $200 in twenties at 21:08 CST on the Thursday night the mayor died. When David and Nina called their names and flashed brass in front of the peephole, they heard quick footsteps dashing away, a back door groan, and then a screen door bang. David plucked up the radio on his left hip to tell the two uniforms in the alley in back of the building to spear Linda Marie Keely by the shoulders before she could take a second step.

By the time David and Nina had scampered around to the German cars with broken aerials, parked between scuffed plastic garbage pails and puckered blue recycling bags, Linda Marie Keely was squirming, shivering, and swearing between the two uniforms, the longest strands of her brown hair spilling over trim soccer-player's shoulders and a green ribbed sweater.

"We just want to talk," said David, beaming geniality. "We need your help."

"Phone first, fuck-face," she spat back.

"You're not listed," David told her. "We checked."

"To avoid creeps like *you*," Linda Keely flung it back at him, causing Nina to chuckle over her remark all the way on the short ride over to the station on Larrabee.

"Creeps like *you*," she repeated every block or so.

A heavy black vinyl notebook sat on the table of an interrogation room. There were just six plastic-sleeve pages inside, each holding four black and white photos. Among the twenty-four photos there were three of Carlos Ponce. The balance was of curly-haired blond men, black men, burly Irish and Croatian men, and elderly, bald Asian men. "Can't we find a mug of a fucking Eskimo somewhere?" Lt. Tompkins had asked. But no other shot of a Mexican, Salvadoran, Guatemalan, Armenian, Indian, Lebanese, or Egyptian man, no one with the slightest tinge of a duskier complexion who could risk so much as a minute chance of bearing the slightest resemblance to Carlos Ponce.

"This is how we used to do it in the old days," said the lieutenant. "Before a bunch of lawyers had to hang over our shoulders, calling balls and strikes."

Katina Reed, the young lawyer from the state's attorney's office (who upheld her apple-cheeked aspect by actually being from Wadena, Minnesota, and fretting, "I don't *knooow* about that. . . .") had been anxious.

"We have to read the woman her rights," she insisted.

"That's only if you're going to try to get testimonial evidence," countered Lt. Tompkins, who, after twenty-six years of police work, had learned that lawyers could be held off, like demon spirits, by chanting a few of their own phrases back at them.

"She's just going to look at pictures. Might as well be reading *People*. If she says she doesn't recognize anyone, where's the testimony?"

"I don't *knooow* about that, Del. That's a little too cute."

"Ah, c'mon, Kat. *You're* too cute," the lieutenant joshed, and though Katina Reed had heard that particular blandishment several hundred times since she was in the fourth grade of the Deer Creek Middle School, she decided not to look too deeply into the blarney. She smiled and told Lt. Tompkins that if the purpose of the photo lineup was not to identify any of the men, but merely to see if Linda Marie Keely registered a reaction to Carlos Ponce—or pretended not to—his show could proceed.

"It's unexplored legal territory," Katina Reed told the officers, folding and wringing her hands. "I don't *knooow*."

"Okay, Kat," said Lt. Tompkins jovially. "You be Lewis, I'll be Clark."

As Linda Marie Keely flipped over the pages back and forth, shaking her head strongly, quickly, and doubtlessly, Lt. Tompkins received a call from the chief of the team that had taken a warrant into apartment B-1. He said there were traces of nicotine distillate on the lip of the drain in the shower. There were traces around the rim of the kitchen sink.

"Give us another fifteen minutes," said the sergeant in charge, "we'll find it in their plumbing."

He said that a team had found a litter of smashed glass in a trash bag a block in back of the apartment, and though the shards were trickier to test, they seemed tinged with an umber color.

"I'll bet it's not rum punch," the sergeant added.

The building's landlord, an elderly Serbian named Vinko, was found drinking crème de menthe while watching the Bears over in a tavern on north Cleveland. He said that the man from whom he received a rent check each month was a well-mannered young sandy-bearded gentleman named Meadows.

All of this was reported to Chief Martinez, who took the call as he stood in line for the men's room during the fourth quarter at Soldier Field.

(The police chief was recognized every minute or so. Fans shouted, "Hey, chief. Arrest our fucking lousy quarterback, why don't you?")

"I recognize that name," Chief Martinez whispered in a strangled shout above the tumult behind him. "Meadows. Claudia McCarthy's barista. *Toss that apartment.* Every thread in the rug, every loop in their towels. Bring in Claudia. Cuff the barista before he can draw off another latte. It'll take me half an hour to get out of here, Del. Do it *now.*"

Lt. Tompkins snapped the phone closed and walked heavily across the squad room. The Bears had just lost the ball at their own thirty-one. The defense stopped a Cowboy run into the right side of the line. Second and ten, but whistles blew before they could get off the snap. Cops groaned and slapped their desks. Announcers sounded amazed. Lt. Tompkins motioned for a sergeant to shut off the screen in the corner of the room, and as the din from the game died, Delbert Tompkins dropped into a chair that sat on the other side of the table from Linda Marie Keely.

"Do you have a lawyer?" he asked her softly.

"A lawyer?" she said. "Like you have a regular gyno or a dry cleaner?" She smiled in brown-eyed bemusement, as if he might want to share it, and twirled a strand of hair with a finger against her shoulder. "Gosh no."

"Get one," Lt. Tompkins commanded grimly, and as he rose from the seat, two uniforms moved behind Linda Marie Keely. She sat up suddenly, as if a drizzle of cold water had just slithered down her spine. One policeman laid a large hand on her head, and another opened a set of hinged model-100 nickel handcuffs with a metallic *clack!* and grabbed both of her slight twig wrists in one prodigious, pinching grip that made Linda Keely wince and squirm deep into her seat.

"If you cannot afford a lawyer," Lt. Tompkins informed her, "one will be provided for you." He nodded to the uniforms to proceed.

27

SUNDAY NIGHT

Sgt. McNulty stood alongside Sunny's black car, burps of tailpipe steam encircling his feet on the cold street and rising into wisps around his shoulders. The sergeant smiled and stood ready by the car door. Sgt. Gallaher turned to Sunny and blinked pearly snowflakes from her eyes. The patrol car that would take her and her crew back to the First District—Sunny was just beginning to learn the routine—was parked a few feet farther down.

"Tomorrow morning, sir," she said. "I'll escort you down to City Hall. During the session, I'll be nearby with half-a-dozen uniforms. But when they choose the new mayor, we'll move in to surround whoever that is."

Sunny could feel snow pile in his hair and melt slushily over his scalp. He felt a drip about to roll down, slightly left of the center of his forehead, and pushed it back with a knuckle.

"I understand," he said lightly. "One moment, I'm important enough to protect. Then, I'm an alderman again."

"I won't have a chance to say goodbye. And thank you."

Sgt. Gallaher stuck out her hand. Sunny took it carefully, squeezing only slightly, as he might nervously touch a small bird.

"I thank *you*," he replied automatically. "Serving the city is so vital. . . ." He let his voice fall off as he heard himself blather. Sunny drew back his fingers from their clasp of hands, but let his thumb still rest lightly on the top of Sgt. Gallaher's hand.

"I'm sad about the mayor of course," she said. "But getting around the city—talking about things—getting to know your daughters. Frankly, sir, it's been a blast."

They heard McNulty open the back door of Sunny's car. The officer at the wheel thrummed the engine, like an organ chorus, to keep it warm. Sgt. Gallaher leaned in closer to be heard.

"Your daughters," she began. "I've seen families—lose someone. Everybody tries to go through the motions. Eating, sleeping, working. But they have an open wound. They walk around dripping. Your daughters are aching. They're seething. They have to push back at something, but the world is a moving target. Except for you."

Sgt. Gallaher pushed a quartet of long fingers against Sunny's shoulder, then extracted her other hand from a pocket with a small white card.

"If I can ever help. I serve and protect."

Sgt. Gallaher tucked her simmering face into the high collar of her long black coat. Sunny heard her clicking steps quicken as she took long strides over the ice and sleet of south Pulaski on her way to the patrol car.

Sunny had just snapped on the small, hot, overhead light in the back of his car when Chief Martinez called from the 18th District.

"When Linda Marie Keely was being taken away," he announced, "she shouted in the squad room, 'It's the corn people against the rice people! And you fools don't know it!' "

"What possible—"

"We're asking commodity traders, agronomists," said the chief. "Who the hell knows? She said, 'We're becoming walking stalks of corn, can't you see?' "

"Is it some kind of racial stuff, Matt?" asked Sunny. "Are you a corn person, am I a rice person, and was the mayor—"

"An extra-cheese and sausage person, I'd say," said Chief Martinez. "I'll keep you informed."

Rula and Rita had called while he was on with Matt Martinez, and Sunny fumbled the phone open again just as soon as the tiny electric carillon pealed that he had a message.

"We've kind of got caught up," he heard Rula say. He made out something about dinner with Diego's family, a cousin from Brussels, the chance to hear about business school at or in Columbia (Sunny wasn't sure—her message gave no hint—if she meant the school or the country), and buses groaning and splattering gobs of snow. "Sorry to miss the reception, don't know Karen Wu, all anyone wants to hear is you anyway, Pappaji, see you at home."

"Sheldon loves you!" Rita called into the mouthpiece at the very end. Sunny held the phone to his ear for a few moments longer, until the electric wail began to grate against his ear.

Jia's sprawled over the second floor of an old warehouse on south Wentworth. Dim canisters spiked tines of lights down onto round tables wrapped with crinkly red cloths. As Sunny stepped into the restaurant, he saw people sign their names in sparkly gold ink on a red silk sheet stretched under a sign that said, "JERRY AND KAREN."

Mothers and grandmothers tucked drowsy babies over their shoulders. Little girls in flowery silk dresses held onto their fathers' hands, clasping small white boxes topped with gold bows against their chests. Little boys in snow jackets stood up straight and squirmed in their tight white collars while their fathers tried to knot their dark blue ties. As Sunny's eyes adjusted to the streaky dimness, he saw red lantern lights with yellow tassels jiggle like jellyfish each time the elevator doors rolled back and wind whooshed in.

Karen Wu was John's niece, the daughter of his brother, Paul, who had died six years earlier from the aneurysm John had always expected for himself. He saw Sunny and threw his arms over the acting mayor's shoulders, bringing his mouth next to Sunny's ear, as if murmuring the contents of some classified file.

"I ordered Chinese beer for the hoi polloi," John whispered above the din. "Brewed with formaldehyde. Let's get you something safe."

John waved, clapped his hands, and barked words that made the serving people in black uniforms step as if trying to run across a bed of glowing coals. A brown bottle of Corona, swaddled in a white napkin, was put in Sunny's hand. Sunny tucked it into his elbow as he shook hands with a line of Karen's bridesmaids in pale rose dresses: Carmen, Gabrielle, Lucy, Marilyn, and Rena.

"My buddy," John said with beery cheer. "The acting, interim, pooh-bah of Chicago."

But when the bridesmaids saw Sgt. McNulty, they cocked their thumbs, leveled their index fingers, and hid smiles behind their hands. A short-haired young man in a navy suit, whose shoulders looked like hard-packed sandbags under the stretchy fabric, walked over in well-shined shoes and stuck out his hand.

"My nephew-in-law," John Wu explained. "Sergeant Geraldo Cotto."

"I'm honored, sir," the young man said, and proffered a handshake that could open a Brazil nut.

"Honored," said Sunny, wincing slightly, and raising a hand over his eyes. "John tells me you're posted at Arlington."

"Yes sir. Third Army. The Old Guard," and when Sunny inclined his head with curiosity, Sgt. Cotto explained. "The unit that conducts funerals, sir. Can be twenty, twenty-five a week."

"Business sounds good," said Sunny. "That's terrible. Are we losing that many soldiers?"

"World War Two is dying out," Jerry Cotto explained. "Sometimes you help a frail old man into a folding chair, then realize, 'That's his *son.*' There's Philippine Army vets, and National Health Service doctors. More and more Korean vets. Vietnam ones just starting. And of course today," said Sgt. Cotto more softly, "every flight you hear come in over the Potomac, you wonder what's in the hold."

"It must get—depressing."

Jerry Cotto nodded. "The young mother with a swelling belly holding the hand of a child—that's hard. That's when you say, 'Why not me?' But lots of times, it's inspiring. You hear the citations, and shake your head—what people do sometimes. You fold the flag and give it to them gently. They hold it against their chest like a baby. It's a privilege."

Sunny turned his head as John Wu's niece came up and took Jerry Cotto's hand into both of hers. A song Sunny had heard a thousand times and couldn't identify as much as once chirruped like a trapped hamster through small tin speakers. Sunny looked after the couple as they stepped onto a small square of dance floor that had been unfolded like a game board. Karen Wu had to skip in her heels to put her slender schoolgirl fingers up to her husband's shoulders. Sunny turned to John Wu and said, "First time I ever liked this goddamn song." As the song faded, John Wu clapped his hands and called the guests around.

"Okay, okay, okay," he announced. "Put away the pot stickers for one damn minute."

Sunny saw young men in black suits with spiked hair, men of his age in gray suits and dull shirts, young women in shiny flower petal fabrics, and older women in red shawls and unbuckled snow boots. John put his thumbs under the belt line of his pants and rocked back and forth slightly.

"A few months ago, my niece said, 'Uncle John, I've met a fine young man. But he's not Chinese. In fact, he's Salvadoran. All he knows about China is chop suey. And I had to tell him that it's not Chinese.' "

There was laughter, and the ding of wine glasses against the rims of saucers. John doled out his words in half-sentence installments, salted by question marks.

"So I asked, 'Does he have a job?' She said yes. And I asked, 'Does he love you?' She got this gooey look and said, 'Yes.' I said, 'Well okay. Then he's my main man.' Can I meet this young Jerry? He was home on leave. He'd already given her a ring." Karen Wu, who had been standing behind John, reached around with an arm and fluttered her fingers in front of his tie. "Whooh. See? So I met him. I said, 'Jerry, you're in the army, right? You're going to move my niece around from

one dusty camp to another, like a couple of tramps, right? You're always going to have to squeeze your family into a compact car, and if
you ever get sent off to war—and if you're a soldier, that's where you
want to be, right?—she'll jump every time she hears the phone.' And
Jerry said, 'Sir—Mr. Wu—I love Karen and would never do anything
to harm her. And I love this country and will do anything to protect
her, too.' "

John Wu turned away, his face cracking.

"This is a good man," he said heavily. "His parents, Marydell and
Riccardo, got here like we did, didn't they? Like Paul and me, and a
dozen strangers sleeping in a basement on Cermak. I keep hearing
about all the opportunity in China. Good. It's about fucking time, isn't
it? China only gave me a kick in the ass, and I had to fight for that.
Maybe there is opportunity in China. But you have to shut your
mouth, right? Here, sometimes you got to scream to be heard. But you
get to scream, loud as you like. I think we have the best of both here—
Chinese people and American freedom. This city gets cold. But it's
great."

John's face shone and he turned to Sunny. His hands fluttered just
below his chest, and a jot of beer jumped up through the neck of his
bottle.

"A man here—my friend," said John Wu, "who has impressed us all
over the last few days. The acting, interim, whatever, of Chicago,
Sunny Roopini."

Sunny put the last eighth of his beer down on the table behind his
back. Applause broke out after his name, with more volume than what
he was used to.

"Thank you for that nice reception," he began. "Even though most
of you don't live in the Forty-eighth Ward, I'm sure we can accommo-
date you next election day."

He heard an encouraging chorus of chuckles and chortles play over
the room.

"You know, I come from a place where many marriages are still"—
and here Sunny trilled his rrr's with operatic flourish—"arrranged.
They use the latest computer software now. Ask some of the folks in

Bangalore that you talk to on the phone at night. There are Indian families in Chicago who do it today. I was back home a few years ago and said to my uncle Mohan, 'Arranged marriages! How primitive! How barbaric!' And Uncle Mohan said, 'So, you count on meeting just the right person if you walk into a bar? *That's* primitive—like expecting to see a message from the gods when you look into the clouds.' And then he asked, 'So, over there in the sophisticated west: what's the divorce rate?' I said, 'Oh, I don't know, I guess a little more than half.' And Uncle Mohan said, 'Sundaran, if you had a car that only worked half the time, you'd stop driving, wouldn't you?' "

Groans, gasps, and laughter rolled around the room. Women shook their drink glasses at men, and men shrugged at one another as Sunny continued.

"Uncle Mohan, by the way, has been married for fifty-some years. Unhappily, but enduringly.

"What these children—what this man and woman—have," he went on in a softer tone, "is a joy I see in discovering each other. The brave giddiness in suddenly realizing that two people who began on opposite sides of the world can come to this great, vast, churning place and find that in all of the important ways, they are from the same family tree," and here Sunny gently touched his chest with his closed hand, resting it slightly to the left side. In the dim light and red surroundings, his fist looked like a heart, and his thumb stood upright, like an artery.

"Some of us have been lucky enough to know that," said Sunny.

He opened his mouth for another word, but no sound followed. He looked over at John Wu, then felt breath come back into his lungs, and shook his head, as if he had just caught himself from tipping over.

"Your happiness makes us happy. Seeing you tonight makes us hopeful."

And then Sunny raised his closed hand just under his chin and opened his fingers like the petals of a flower.

"Our city has just had a great shock," he said. "But your love reminds us that the heart of this city still beats."

The applause broke around Sunny, and then began to build until it no longer crackled, clap by clap, but was practically seamless as people stamped their feet and thumped their palms against the cushioned tabletops. John Wu dropped his head against Sunny's shoulder. Jerry Cotto took his right hand, and Karen circled an arm around his neck to draw his head down and kiss Sunny on his chin; she had a small, rosebud mouth, and the brush of her lips reminded him of Rula's kisses when she was six. Strangers rushed to Sunny's side, tucked themselves under an arm, and signaled for friends standing a few feet away to snap. White flashes flared and faded in his eyes, making the guests look like Halloween skeletons smacking their hands.

Sgt. McNulty moved in, graciously but decisively, peeling a man from Sunny's shoulder as he asked, "Who is your spiritual auditor?"

Sunny put his own hands on McNulty's shoulders as the sergeant led him down a flight of broad concrete stairs. Sunny had to feel for each step with his toes. There was a small, quieter bar on the landing, and when he steered the sergeant into a clear space next to a window, he saw the U.S. Attorney for the Northern District of Illinois holding down the corner spot.

"That was a very moving testament to marriage," Brooks Whetstone told him. "Unfortunately, the women I know best are all serving time."

Sunny nodded for Sgt. McNulty to stand by a few feet down and walked to where the U.S. Attorney had a brown bottle and a glass waiting for him above an empty stool.

"A few good prospects must come up for parole," Sunny told him. "Pull the files and take your pick."

"I couldn't hear everything," Brooks Whetstone went on blandly. "But I could see everyone's eyes. You're a gifted politician, Mr. Roopini. I wonder why you've spent all this time in the minor leagues." His unruly sandy curls flounced over the back of his tweed collar like shirttails hanging out of a closed suitcase.

"I wonder if you've heard of a group called Madje," Brooks asked suddenly. "J as in jelly," he emphasized.

Sunny shook his head.

"Mothers Against Discrimination and for Justice and Equity," Brooks explained. "Their U.S. headquarters—a mail drop, really—is over on Madison. They give loans to poor women in Bangladesh to start handicraft businesses."

"Can my great-aunts in Mumbai get in on the action?"

Brooks Whetstone tipped his glass against Sunny's, and took another swallow.

"We've been turning up their records for a year. Chicago, Amsterdam, Dacca. Complicated, cryptic. But it looks like most of the dollars, pounds, and euros they take in wind up as takas in the hands of terrorist cells."

Brooks paused for Sunny to take a first sip before he went on. He heard his own swallow sound like a small ball going splat against a wall.

"The Carroll Family Trust is a major contributor."

Sunny took a moment to tap a small pile of coasters. Brooks Whetstone smiled coldly, as if his pale lips rose and fell at the end of a string.

"One point four million dollars over the last three years."

"You can't seriously think that Peter and Sharon meant to give money to terrorists."

"You can't seriously think that what they *meant* makes a difference," Brooks told him. He put a finger to his head. "*Dumb*," he pronounced, and pulled a phantom trigger. "Especially if you're running for office. A grand jury should get the case in a few weeks," he continued. "I look forward to giving them the chance to clear themselves."

" 'Questioned in connection with . . . ' " Sunny quoted from a future headline. "Put in the word terrorism. You play rough, Mr. Whetstone."

"I don't *play*," said Brooks Whetstone, with sudden hushed vehemence. "That's for dogs and children. I've got to stop people who would blow up Sears Tower for their god, and people—like your friends in City Hall—who would give away Lake Michigan for a few nickels. *I don't play*," he repeated.

The U.S. Attorney turned up his glass and let the last inch of beer down his throat before setting it down, a skein of small white bubbles sliding slowly as a spider down the sides of the glass.

"I'd say a seat in Congress can be yours. You'd get my vote, if I ever voted . . ."

Brooks Whetstone let his words run out and turned his glass on its side to roll it slowly back and forth between them.

"Just help me understand how the mayor did business. How he kept the gears oiled and the machine running."

"He ran the city well," Sunny suggested. "He gave the people bread and circuses."

"I'm glad the inmates are happy in the asylum," said Brooks curtly. "But you know what the other option is here. A subpoena. Getting 'questioned in connection with an investigation into City Hall corruption.' A lot of old friends—not real friends, mind you, but the kind who fill a politicians' holiday card list—might suddenly find your friendship inconvenient."

Brooks almost brought his voice to a hush under the laughter, the clack of chopsticks, and the clatter of dance music.

"We've both seen it. A politician's friends hear he's being squeezed, and suddenly, he *glows*." Brooks Whetstone made his fingers flutter under his chin, as if impersonating a starburst. "*Radioactivity*," he said. "Polonium. Kryptonite. No one wants to swing next to you on the playground."

Brooks Whetstone drew himself back about half a foot along the bar, then put his hand out toward Sunny's, along with a small, stiff white card.

"Let me know by the time you convene the council tomorrow. Just punch in this number. No need to say hello, leave a message, or press the pound sign. Just call. We'll know. We'll talk. We use a nice, woodsy place in southern Wisconsin for nice, long talks. Bring your daughters— skating, skiing, snowmobiling. I see all that stuff from the windows, at least. If I don't hear from you, we'll talk again. But that way, you really have to have a lawyer along. And then it's hard to have much fun."

Brooks Whetstone turned from the bar with a last pat of his hand along the edge. Sunny let his card and the ten digits stare back at him for a moment before picking it up and tucking it into his pocket, next to Sgt. Gallaher's and catching his thumb on a damp, wrapped, forgotten pot sticker.

Sunny sat in his car, lowered his muffler, and joggled his hands before removing his gloves and trying to unbutton his coat with numb fingers.

"You get awful cold in just a few steps," he told Sgt. McNulty.

"But that was quite a reception," the sergeant replied. "You may have trouble slipping back into obscurity." McNulty made no mention of his encounter with the U.S. Attorney.

"People were drinking," said Sunny. "They wanted to laugh and cry. People still don't get that *look* around me."

"Look?"

"Like they can't believe it's you," Sunny explained. "Like they thought you were somebody they knew, then they realized you're somebody everybody knows. Like they'll tell people later. With me, there's just a little nodding—like running into the kid who sat behind you in third grade."

"A couple of people wanted their picture taken with you," the sergeant pointed out, and Sunny smiled as he leaned his head back against the seat and lowered his eyes.

"Into the kitchen drawer tonight," he said. "Under matchsticks and takeout menus tomorrow."

The blasting dry heat in the car made him yawn. They had turned onto east Lake Shore Drive, and Sunny could feel light from bright white street lamps and glare from the piling snow seep under his lids. He heard his phone again, but not until the second set of trills. It was Eldad Delaney. Sunny marked the time in numerals on his screen: 10:06.

"There's something fairly sensational breaking," he told Sunny. "It's Arty."

A blog called Smoke-filled Room had run a story saying that Alderman Agras was engaged in "personal, intimate relationships" with two of the police guards on his security detail.

"Two at a time," Eldad stressed, sounding unexpectedly impressed. "I thought Arty's idea of a twosome was taramosalata and tzatziki."

(Arty had begged for a security detail, and the mayor had acceded. He hoped the gesture would flatter Arty during budget deliberations. It also enabled the mayor to astound Arty on Monday mornings, just before gaveling the council to order, when he would call from behind his hand, "And how was the Petrakas wedding over at Saint Athanasios?" even though the mayor complained that, "Keeping tabs on Arty is about as exciting as following a mud turtle.")

The web site said that as Alderman Agras's Budget and Government Operations committee set the annual police budget, any such relationship would violate the city's statutes against fraternization. Alderman Agras would be nominated for mayor the next day; the people had a right to know. The police officers, sniffling and sorrowful, had confirmed the reported details. Alderman Agras had declined comment.

"Arty, Arty, Arty," Sunny told Eldad. "Sofia has been having chemotherapy. One of his girls is a Moonie. His son got stopped with hashish in Japan. Arty, Arty, Arty," he repeated, and whispered the bare facts to Sgt. McNulty.

"Oh, God. I know who's on that detail," he said.

"Sgt. McNulty knows the women," Sunny told Eldad, but the sergeant was already waving his hands.

"Their names are Dix and Terrell. And, sir, they're not."

Sunny and Sgt. McNulty looked at each other across the backseat for a moment before Sgt. McNulty spoke.

"Mr. Roopini, there are things in anyone's medicine cabinet," he said. "Things in the kitchen. A car and a blanket in the garage."

He turned to lean down into the small window between the front and back seats. "I'll tell the uniforms in front of Alderman Agras's building on Burton to be ready for anything," said Sergeant McNulty. "And I'll see if I can get an ambulance—quietly—parked down the block."

Sunny did not often resort to the personal e-mail device that all aldermen had. Some seemed to grip it in their fists the way chain-smokers clenched packs of cigarettes. Sunny and Aidan Ruffino of the 38th had once been sent to a conference of legislators in Cuernevaca. Aidan had spent most of his time thumbing messages to his Irving Park car dealership with his left hand, and to his aldermanic office with his right.

"Hey, Aidan," Sunny told him. "Leave at least one hand free for chilaquiles. We're in sunny fucking Mexico."

Sunny preferred the phone. The mayor had caught him punching in a message once and pointed out, "Can't put that posh accent of yours in an email, Sunny."

But he considered the implications of a late-night call to the Agras household. It would put Sunny in the same intrusive company as reporters and cranks. Arty—Sofia, for that matter—would not be able to unburden themselves in front of each other, and would merely hold him off with reassuring brio. So Sunny fished the small, black slab from his topcoat pocket and pecked out a short message:

This will pass. Love to your family. What can I do? Sunny

His phone trembled and lit up with Vera's number—from her firm's office on south LaSalle—as he reached his own name. Sunny held her voice next to his left ear as she announced without preamble, "This is a tragedy. I regret that this unwonted intrusion of gossipmongers into a public official's private life has caused pain and embarrassment. My thoughts and prayers are with Alderman Agras and his family at this difficult time."

"Exactly right," said Sunny.

"I also think that I just promised to make Rod Abboud ambassador to the Vatican."

"Can the mayor of Chicago do that?"

"If Rod has such confidence, why disappoint? I also promised Wandy Rodriguez a TEZ for a lot on west Belmont. I promised Cassie Katsoulis to name a new vest-pocket park on Kedzie after Colonel Mordechai Frizis, the hero of the battle of . . ." Sunny could hear Vera shuffle papers, rustle coffee cups, and clink a pen against an ashtray.

"Kalama."

"Eight votes on the block, Vera," he told her. "We can get six—maybe even Arty's. As much as I despise taking advantage of tragedy."

"A person shouldn't be in politics if he doesn't know how to take advantage of tragedy, Sunny," she said crisply. As she spoke, Sunny saw a message flash in above the one he had just sent to Arty Agras.

Were fine. in bed. Mss's from vera linas ivan janet jane. facing chee-wowows in morning.

Can I come over? Sunny proposed.

In my pjs sunny, Arty Agras thumbed back. What would people say?

28

It was a stroke after eleven when Sunny turned the key and opened his door into a dark apartment. Rula and Rita were not home. Sheldon snoozed in a shadow of the pyramid of mail on the disordered dining table. Heat hissed in the front hallway. White light from the street and snow glowed against the drawn white shades in the windows.

Sunny snapped the switch in the hallway and Sheldon scowled and twitched, putting a gray paw with pink pads over his eyes. Sunny snapped the light off. He crept quietly into the kitchen, opened the refrigerator, and found a quarter bottle of South African white, capped with tin foil. "Didn't I teach them better?" he groused. He felt Sheldon circle his heels. He felt Sheldon's small, warm head butt his ankle. He found a carton of blueberry yogurt with the foil pulled back, took a smudged spoon from the sink, and held down a brittle gobbet for Sheldon. His small tongue lapped and scratched.

Sunny took Sheldon under one arm, the uncrowned bottle in the other, and turned down the hall. He passed his daughters' room: both beds were empty, unmade, and turbulent with mussed covers, outcast shoes, and rejected blue jeans. He stopped at the bathroom, lifted the lid with a toe, and put the bottle down on the ledge of the sink while he did his business. Sheldon whirred and tweeted softly while he watched Sunny's arc and nosed forward as Sunny rubbed his fingers under the spigot.

Sunny finally sat down heavily on his bed, his back against the wall.

Sheldon circled his lap and outstretched legs, before scrunching into a pillow while Sunny reached over into a plastic case and took out one white oblong pill for cholesterol and a small yellow aspirin for his circulation. He upended the bottle to swallow. He heard a couple of isolated guffaws, a man and a woman, ringing in the street. He heard the Lawrence Avenue bus groan as it pulled across Broadway. He heard the bones of the building under the floorboards creak in the cold and wind, and as he took a second swig of wine he saw a few lashes of Elana's nutbrown hair against the dark of the doorway, and then had to sit back and clutch his chest while his face blazed and his eyes burned when he realized that there were still sounds in the walls and floors that brought her back.

Sunny's phone trembled and danced in front of the blue numerals on the alarm clock next to the bed. It said 11:24. It was Linas.

"Arty. Arty, Arty, Arty," he announced. "*Moussaka a tois*. Poor bastard."

"I sent him a message."

"Me too."

"He told me was doing okay."

"Me too."

"The depressing truth, your lordship, is that there's almost no sex in political sex scandals," said Linas. "Nobody has the time. Nobody has the *oomph*. You see someone, you flirt, you send off sparks. She writes something on a napkin. But before the night is over you've got twenty business calls to return. You've got a stack of cards thick as a gin rummy deck in your pocket that's stiffer than a boner. And you've got to get to sleep because you've got to get up early. For a prayer breakfast.

"Bill Clinton: What was that all about?" asked Linas. "A couple of licks of the popsicle stick. I got better nookie than that in the seventh grade. *At a Catholic school*. Most powerful man in the world, and he can't get a full-court, bow to stern, stash the sausage, tickle her tonsils,

'Watch out, thar she blows!' screwing. Most of the time, he just talked dirty on the phone while bombing the wrong pharmaceutical plant in Sudan. Textbook frustration, I'd say. JFK? A collector, not a lover. Marilyn, Angie, Jayne, Judy—his back was so bad, he was so hopped up on uppers, downers, and diet pills, all he could do was lay back, blast off in his shorts, and fall asleep before they unhooked their Wonderbras. From Jack Profumo to Bill Clinton, it's all about phone calls, messages, secrets, and signals. *Not sex.* Even French politicians don't get laid as much as they'd like you to think. Their mistresses cook them *coq a vin* and let them fall asleep on the couch watching soccer. *Ooo-la-la, le head butt!* They conk out, wake up at three, and go home to their wives. You get so tired in politics, you dream about a good night's sleep, not a good night's screwing. Sex in politics? It's politics. It's about winning, not doing. Poor Arty—he probably just wanted someone to rub his neck."

"What an extraordinary confession, Linas."

Sunny had let his eyes droop to darken the room. Sheldon kneaded his elbow and bent his small, ashen head into Sunny's shoulder. If a wink could be heard over a phone, Sunny heard one now from Alderman Slavinskas.

"Exception proves the rule, lordship."

"What are you going to pull tomorrow?"

"I can't say," he answered after a pause. "Promised not to."

"I think I know," said Sunny. "I think I have the what, when, and where. But not the who or how. You sure that's what you have to do?"

"Gave my word, lordship."

Sunny understood: Linas's position was not subject to disclosure or revision. Giving your word was different from making a promise. A man could leave promises behind. Circumstances changed. Events intervened. A politician could promise, "I'll do everything I can to help," or, "I'll support you every way I can," and adults understood that the expression was like pledging, "I'll always love you," to a sixth-grade girlfriend. The phrase came with a time stamp.

But a man's word was hard currency. It meant "I'll vote for you tomorrow," "I'll hire you today," or "I'm with you if that happens." A pol who went back on his word had no credit and couldn't do business. He might as well sleep in a box on the street. Linas had been in politics for twenty-five years, and though he had lied, cheated, and connived in almost any given week, Sunny had never heard a complaint—Linas would hardly have lasted if he had—that he had broken his word.

"Hey, where are you calling from?" was all Sunny asked.

"My deck."

Linas lived on south Mozart, a street lined with neat miniature lawns in front of small, spotless, brick houses with screen doors in the back, barbeque grills in the driveways, and inflatable pools filling small backyards. But the alderman's home stood four floors tall on a corner plot. It held a two-story living room, a four-car garage with a wine cellar below (including a 1787 Château d'Yquem that had once rested on Al Capone's wine racks), huge, color-dribbling Leroy Neiman oil portraits of Michael Jordan, Muhammad Ali, and Abraham Lincoln, a cedar-clad cigar humidor the size of an ice cream truck, a basement swimming pool, and a dazzling roof deck from which the Slavinskas family and guests could behold the lights of the Loop blinking sixty blocks north.

"Must be cold out there," said Sunny.

"Got a Montecristo to keep me warm," said Linas. "And a radiator lamp designed by the guy who keeps the Bears toasty along the sidelines. Just me and the view out here. Quite something. Even late on a Sunday night." Linas paused to dispatch a pole of smoke into the frosty air. "The light shoots up from the streets and skyscrapers and seems to freeze in the clouds. It's the Magic Kingdom. It's Oz. It's Never-Never Land. Next time you're here, lordship, we'll ditch the others, come up here, and fire up a couple habanos."

"I'll look forward to that," said Sunny softly.

"Rosie knows a gal from the gym," Linas announced. "Acquisitions and mergers. Just divorced. Smart, pretty, funny. Natural blonde—they're in the locker room together. Unnatural bazooms—she's had them installed, like new kitchen cabinets. To say, 'Can you believe the bastard left *these* behind?' I've seen this gal on a NordicTrack, Sunny. You'll want to send flowers to her surgeon."

Sunny chuckled mildly and said, "I don't think I'm ready. I saw Elana tonight. Just a few minutes ago," he explained quietly. "A dark flash in the doorway. I thought . . ." It was as if Sunny's voice had been running on a track that just ran into a gravel road. Linas paused until he could hear Sunny clear his throat.

"She stopped in to say hello, lordship," he said. "That'll happen for a while. A man who loses his right arm still feels his hand and fingers twitch. He reaches out to touch something before he remembers that he can't. You never—you're never meant to, I guess—make a complete recovery. Just smile back, lordship. Blow her a kiss. Sleep happy."

A longer pause fell between them while Linas leaned back, Sunny closed his brimming eyes, and a Red Line train pulled away from the Lawrence Avenue platform, its steel wheels screeching with swarms of sparks.

"You know, I'm not from here," Linas said finally.

"Good God no," said Sunny. "I always thought you were found in the tall grass, like a Pottawatomie babe."

"Novelty, Ohio," he explained.

"Novelty?"

"No shit."

"Novelty?"

"Near Cleveland. Near nowhere. Came here when I was three."

"*Novelty, Ohio.*" Sunny pronounced the town as if it were a name on a topographical map of the moon. "Imagine if you'd stayed."

"Ouch," said Linas.

"Yeeow," said Sunny.

"Great fucking town you've got here, mister," said Linas. "Least-ways, to a small-town boy like me."

Sunny had been asleep for an hour before he felt Sheldon press his ear with his wet nose, as if he were trying to call an elevator. He let Sheldon lick the outside of his ear in a slow, deliberate circle, as if Sheldon were cleaning it for some inspection. Sunny opened his eyes halfway.

Sheldon's blue-rimmed eyes glimmered in the dark. His blunt gray paws grazed the midnight stubble on Sunny's chin. The blue numerals on the clock flipped to 1:04. He heard Rula and Rita giggle and hush at the other end of the hallway and decided to pretend that he was asleep. But his feet in his shoes suddenly felt as if they'd been filled with sand. His slacks wound around his legs like a snarled garden hose. Sunny sat up straight and tried to lean forward, but Sheldon pushed him back with his small pink nose. He smiled and put a palm against Sheldon's gray head.

"You know, Sheldon," he whispered. "The same letter could mean different things. You'd get a note from the mayor saying, 'Please hire this man,' but know you could ignore it. Or you could get the same note and know to help. Someone could get a note saying, 'I support this man, give him money,' and they'd know they could throw it away, or the same note—exact same words—and know that the mayor really wanted them to do it. You know the difference?"

Sunny drew his lips next to Sheldon's cheek and spoke just loudly enough to brush the small gray hairs standing in the white of the cats' ears.

"The ink, Sheldon," he whispered. "Black ink meant to do as he asked. Hire the guy, give him money. Blue-black ink, you knew you could ignore it, it was just for show. But the poor bastard in the note never knew the difference."

MONDAY MORNING

Sunny found his daughters by following the echoes downstairs into the kitchen. He turned the corner in time to be thrown back by a blast of guffaws. Sgt. Gallaher quickly unwound her tall, trousered legs, scraped back her chair, and stood, tucking the last gasp of a laugh into her chin.

"Am I the punch line?" asked Sunny.

Sunny thought the sergeant's face simmered again. Eldad stood and extended his hand.

"Good morning, alderman," he said, and inclined his head toward the sergeant. "She's a pistol."

"Yes. Bang-bang," said Sunny.

Rula and Rita stayed seated, while Matina poured out a cup of coffee for Sunny on the counter next to the grill.

"Diego says we should consider Columbia Business School," said Rita. She had put her long black hair back into braids that she had taken care to place across the front of her shoulders along the line of a pearly gray sweater that had belonged to her mother. "He says that with our backgrounds, we could do deals all over the subcontinent and Middle East. It's a fertile crescent of opportunity."

"That's why we were a little late last night," Rula added. She wore a high-necked burgundy sweater that Elana had worn to school meetings because she thought its slim form suggested youth, while the high collar reassured teachers of seriousness.

Sunny paused while Matina added a thimble of skim milk to his coffee, nodded thanks, and took a sip.

"With your fertile knowledge of Hindi and Punjabi," he told them, "you should be able to tell any cabdriver anywhere in the world, 'Starbucks, please, chop-chop.' "

Sgt. Gallaher broke into a soft smile while Rula floundered in her seat from side to side, and Rita flailed with her hands for Sunny's attention.

"India is the largest English-speaking country in the world, Pappaji," she said. "You've always told us."

"Well you might try studying a little English, too," he said, and then his voice softened.

"I'm sorry," he said. "Just a little tired and being an ass. You can be anything you want to be. Your mother and I always said that. Any homework I can pretend to understand? Or were you too busy doing deals?"

His daughters exchanged squishy, rueful looks that Sunny began to notice included Sgt. Gallaher.

"Not exactly," said Rita.

"No," said Rula. "We thought—Sgt. Gallaher suggested it actually—that we'd go into City Hall with you."

"To see your day as mayor," said Rita.

"I'll write the note," Sgt. Gallaher came in from the counter behind Sunny. "For school. A field trip, a civics lesson. 'Rula and Rita Roopini were absent so they could watch their father be mayor until noon.' "

Sunny frowned. He put his knuckles to his chin and scrunched his forehead before saying, "Three ballots, I'd guess. That should keep me on the throne until nearly one. Let's stay down for lunch in Greektown."

His daughters pushed back their chairs and sprang to their feet, snapping their fingers, chanting and cheering, "Opah! Opah!"

"We really want to go, Pappaji," said Rula, while Rita tossed her braids behind her shoulders—the gesture was distressingly flirtatious and startled Sunny—and said, "Since Sheldon can't."

Sunny decided to make dosas. "Tiene gusto?" he asked Wilmer, and "Tiene gusto?" he asked Matina. She was Greek, but they spoke kitchen Spanish together.

"Na*ddd*-ah," she trilled.

"Potatoes, onions, and chilis," Rita called out.

"Add cheese for me," said Rula, who then turned around to the counter. "But make one for Sgt. Gallaher!" she said. "Sgt. Gallaher should get the first."

The sergeant shook her large, dark head. A sable spray of hair fell against her neck like a fat feather.

"I'm on duty," she demurred. She'd worn a red and black scarf that day, knotted just below the neck with a small silver band, which her fingers seemed to run up and down, like changing messages on a signal flag.

"No dosas on duty?" said Sunny. "I'd never heard . . ." and as Sunny strode toward the scalding grill, Sgt. Gallaher pulled the ring down to just above her belt.

"Okay, sir. One."

"One done right is all you'll need," said Sunny.

Matina stepped up with a green apron she pulled around his white shirt and silver tie. The apron bore a flaking yellow seal of Local 81 of the United Food and Commercial Workers Union. Sunny held his hands, abracadabra style, over the small tubs of chopped ingredients that Wilmer and Nelson had prepared.

"Cheese, carrots, chilis, peanut butter, whatever," said Sgt. Gallaher. "Nothing special, no trouble."

Sunny ran a splash of water on his fingers and dribbled it onto the griddle. The water went whoosh then splat and quickly steamed into bubbles, which danced and disappeared.

"No trouble at all, sergeant," he announced over his shoulder above a new commotion of bubbles as he squirted a slick of corn oil over the hot silver surface.

"The key is touch and timing. I made my first dosa—oh mercy, in my father's place on Brick Lane, just before we came here. Young boys in the Amazon, I suppose, slay a jaguar."

Sunny dipped a tin ladle into the large white tub of rice and lentil batter, which had been churned and fermented overnight. He swirled a line of the batter onto the grill, holding it, his daughters noticed, just a little higher than usual for Sgt. Gallaher.

"When I was a teenager, we counted one Sunday," he said. "I think I made one hundred and two in an afternoon."

"A lot of hot work," Sgt. Gallaher called out above the escalating sizzle. Sunny smoothed the batter with the butt end of the ladle over and over, into an oval about the size of a football.

"You know the worst part of making so many dosas?" Sunny asked as he worked the ladle slowly up, down, and around. "Seeing so many bits and pieces come back, with the nice brown edges that I strived to get. You want to send them back out and say, 'You left the best stuff, don't you know?' Maybe it was my first lesson in politics. You can never tell what sticks with people. You can figure out how to bring peace to Jerusalem, but if you ever voted for a bus fare increase . . . Okay now, you can't lift the edges to check the browning," Sunny announced. "Or it will be lighter on that side. You stare into the batter and watch the bubbles. See? One, two. Now it's six, eight, then they begin to sprout all over. The smell should just be opening in your nose. You sprinkle the potatoes and onions over the inner two-thirds of the oval. The bubbles come quick now. You add the chilis last, so they don't get soggy. You hold off for a moment. You think, 'Got to flip it now,' but you hang back for the count of one . . . two!"

At the beat of three, Sunny slipped a slender spatula under the left side of the oval and turned it over, once, twice, then a third time before lifting a browned dosa, successfully crisped at the edges, onto a thick ivory plate. Sgt. Gallaher clapped her hands.

"Voila. As we say in Tamil," Sunny declared. Matina took the plate and plopped a dollop of pale raita alongside the dosa and pinched small

twigs of chopped cilantro over the top. Sunny had turned back to prepare the grill for more when Matina caught his arm and pointed to the
screen above the kitchen counter.

Arty Agras had just appeared. Sunny turned around. Wordlessly,
Wilmer moved over to the grill to make dosas for Sunny's daughters
while he watched Arty Agras wipe the back of his hand across his
mouth and give off a wobbly smile, like a man trying to hold his balance on a shaky ladder.

"God bless Arty," Sunny said, and then wondered, "Whatever will
he say?"

He recognized a scuffed white wall of Arty's 1st Ward office on Ashland Avenue.

"TV crews must have put him there," said Eldad.

Arty had been stood up against the wall. He wore a brown-bag-
colored suit and an orange tie and stood in front of a ragged row of
snapshots, citations, and declarations that listed as if they had been
hung just last night by a man who had come home drunk. Sunny
thought he could see a shot of Arty standing on his toes to pose alongside Jennifer Aniston. He recognized the only pictures he had ever seen
on a politician's wall of an office holder shaking hands with Spiro
Agnew and Michael Dukakis.

"Arty needs a good Eldad," Sunny said.

"Someone should at least drag a flag behind him," Eldad suggested.
"That flat wall—like a firing squad."

Arty licked his lips, darted his pale pink tongue over the back of his
hand, smiled shakily, and stopped for a moment to reach deep into a
pocket for a handkerchief, which he drew across his mouth and pressed
against his nose. Microphones bristled in front of his face.

"Good morning, ladies and gentlemen. I know it's a busy day. I'll do
my best to be subcinct."

Eldad groaned. But Sunny called up to the screen, "Take your time,

Arty," and onscreen Arty Agras paused and looked out with astonishment.

"Am I dead?" he asked. "It's the first time so many people have been interested in anything I say." The reporters stayed so silent, Sunny could hear someone's gum popping; someone's pen scratching paper.

"Well: it's true," Arty Agras announced in a slow, husky voice. "They got some details wrong. I'm sixty-three, not sixty-four. Get to be my age, you're in no rush.

"But me and those two boys? I guess that's true. What can I say? My family knows. My kids, my wonderful kids, my wonderful wife. We spent some time talking about it. They . . . they say they still love me," said Arty, his voice falling to a sigh. "They say we're still a family. I didn't want to drag them up here with me. They've been through . . . so much already. They didn't do anything. They have nothing to answer for. That's me. Only me.

"I don't know if I can explain this," he said. As he looked out, his blue eyes bubbled. "What are most of you folks—twenty-five, thirty? Are a couple of you forty? How many of you are married? I've been married thirty-five years. It's been good. Sofia—a lot of you know her—is a wonderful woman. Loving and kind. A wonderful mother. Tough, when she had to be. I . . . I can't live without her. I don't want to. But a marriage that long, I don't know if you're old enough to understand. You love each other. But love goes through seasons. Sometimes it's wonderful. Sometimes, it's not bad, it just gets a little cold to the touch. But you love each other and stay together because you know it's just a season. That's why you make a promise to each other. And to God."

Arty raised a quavering hand next to his face. His cupped palm was red and wrinkled, as if he had been pulling a rough rope through his fingers.

"You don't quit on each other just because you're going through a cold snap," he said, his voice rising slightly with defiance. "But sometimes, you get a little chilly. Ten years ago, it never would have happened. Ten weeks from now, maybe nothing. But something happened now.

"Am I gay? I don't know. I wouldn't mind. I wouldn't care. All I know is I hurt my family, and that makes me ashamed. But nobody forced anybody. I don't know why this is supposed to have anything to do with being mayor. I guess some people must feel that way or you wouldn't be here."

Arty seemed to shiver in the scalding light. His mouth snapped open for an instant, as if he were gulping a hook. Then his hands tightened along the silvery neck of the microphone stand, his lower lip came back into his chin, and he pulled back his shoulders, which threw his voice into the horde of gnat-black microphones.

"I'm going home to my family," he said. "There are a couple of hours before the session begins. I've got my job. If somebody wants to take this to a grand jury, I'll walk the plank, take a plea. But today, I still represent my ward. I'll do the job I'm sworn to do. If you have questions, I may have a lot of time later—soon. But right now, I just want to go home to my family," said Arty Agras.

Sunny could hear a chorus of chihuahuas bark and cry, "Arty? Alderman? Arty? Arty!" as Arty Agras ducked his head, thrust his hands in his coat pockets, and walked away. Just as quickly, the shouts were shushed.

"Not now," someone snapped, and then another voice added more softly, "Not now."

30

A field of yellow sawhorses blaring POLICE POLICE POLICE in black block letters had been planted along LaSalle just after the river bridge. Sunny was leaning forward in his dark city car to tell Rula and Rita they would have to get out and walk when a red face, blinking cold tears under a blue-checkered police cap, pressed his forehead against their glazed window and billowed a string of steamy words.

"Roopini! It's Roopini!" he called to officers behind him. Sunny heard the shouting through the glass, as another uniform thumped their roof and another smacked their trunk as Officer Mayer nosed the car through ranks of television trucks.

"Which one of us do you suppose they mean?" asked Rula.

Sgt. Gallaher, still smiling at that remark, led them onto the sidewalk just in front of City Hall through a row of uniformed officers. Reporters with bright, cold cherry faces flung questions over the sawhorses, hatching clouds of steam above their heads.

"Sunny, what will happen today?"

"The council will transact a little business," he called back, his feet slowing and crackling over blue grains of salt that had been spread over the snow. "Then elect a new mayor."

"The one you want?"

"The best one for the city."

"Did you see Alderman Agras's statement?"

Sunny shook his head, sorrowfully.

"And my heart goes out to him and his family. I think it's outrageous to drag people's private lives into headlines."

The reporters absorbed Sunny's reproach without any visible indignation.

"Does Alderman Barrow have Alderman Agras's supporters all locked up?" someone shouted.

"Locking up aldermen!" Sunny mused, as if someone had just suggested some small, surreptitious indulgence, like a glass of wine at lunch. They had reached the revolving brass doors, and as Sunny turned around to pitch back a last remark, uniforms inside began to push the door so that Rita and Rula could step in without delay. "Should we throw away the key?"

Laughter followed Sunny into the door. He turned to push the glass around and found that Sgt. Gallaher was already on the other side, turning it with her long, sturdy arm. Rula and Rita turned to greet him with a grin.

"*That* was exciting," said Rula.

"They were really listening to you, Pappaji," Rita added.

"Imagine," said Sunny.

His daughters took Eldad Delaney by his elbows and announced that they wanted to get coffee and muffins at a stand in the concourse below City Hall. They glanced kisses off Sunny's cheek and turned toward the escalator. When Sunny turned back, he saw that a couple of uniformed officers held an elevator car open for him. Four uniforms waited. He rode up to the second floor encircled by blue shoulders, dripping brims, creaking boots, crackling radios, and jingling keys.

"A lot of protection for a short-termer on a short ride up," Sunny said as the brass doors pulled open. Sunny's phalanx of uniforms laughed and shook. They took him through the entrance into the warren of aldermanic offices, and as they came around the corner into a hallway, Sunny noticed a striking woman with tawny hair standing in front of the plum-colored door that said SUNDARAN ROOPINI 48.

It was Dolores Carroll, in a brown alpaca coat that swept down spectacularly to the tops of her spiky black boots. She saw Sunny and his entourage at the end of the hallway, and looked to them with wide, beseeching brown eyes. Collie Kerrigan of the 14th had her trapped in a joke. His small eyes shone pink as he reached the punch line, his pate wrinkled like reptile skin, and gray flecks of ash and psoriasis sprinkled over his greenish-gray lapels. Sunny could hear Collie say, "So the judge says, 'Mr. O'Rourke, I've reviewed the case, and decided to give your wife seven hundred dollars a week.' And O'Rourke says, 'Quite fair, your honor. I may throw in a couple of bucks meself!' "

Collie turned his head to laugh, bringing up puffs of pipe smoke and coffee phlegm. Dolores Carroll brought her cheek besides Sunny's and smacked a kiss beside his ear.

"Alderman Kerrigan has been entertaining me," she said.

"A gal like this goes all over the world," said Collie, "and still hasn't heard these. Can you believe it, Sunny?" He reached over to bounce a fist against Sunny's elbow.

"See you on the floor, sport. Hotcha-hotcha, rock and roll, hasta lumbago. We're riding different mounts, bucko, but we'll come at the same time together in the end, right?"

"Beautifully put, Collie."

Collie patted Dolores Carroll's cheek so roughly, Sunny thought he could see the red imprint of three fingers along her jaw. Her smile hardened; it didn't crack.

"And you, darling, later at the Ritz," Collie told her. "While your hubby gallivants around Microfleasia or some place."

"Order room service and start without me, alderman," said Dolores Carroll, smiling hugely, sending him down the hall with a soft tap on his ear.

A uniform opened Sunny's door, and another felt the wall for the light switch. Sunny heard a low hum before he saw the small, drooping schoolroom flags lit up. Sgt. Gallaher strode ahead to open the door into the second room, and by the time Sunny turned the corner she had lowered the shades in front of his small conference table.

"A precaution," she explained, more to Dolores Carroll than Sunny.

"He's a very important man," said Dolores Carroll, and with a slight nod to Sunny the sergeant whisked almost silently back into the outer office with just three strides of her long legs.

"Well, at least for a couple more hours," said Sunny, and he and Do-lores Carroll broke into a laugh at the same time in front of the patch-work quilt of listing certificates. Her hair had been lightened slightly, but her eyes seemed more than ever to be glistening brown-black cin-ders that a man would want to touch, even as he knew they would burn.

Sunny muttered something about coffee. Dolores Carroll held up a tall paper cup, dangling the string of a tea bag.

"We haven't seen you," she began. "Since . . . I'm sorry Peter and I couldn't be there. We were at a conference in Dubrovnik."

"Your flowers were beautiful," said Sunny. "Your call. Your contri-bution."

Sunny couldn't exactly remember if it had been to an Israeli-Palestinian student orchestra in Jerusalem, or an Israeli-Palestinian summer camp in Maine. They had gotten a card, a coffee mug, and five blue-green wristbands emblazoned SHALOM SALAAM—so he said sim-ply, "What they're doing is so important." Dolores Carroll nodded.

"March fifteenth," she said after a pause. "We're having a party for Turkmenistan. The president there has suspended the Halk Maslahaty—the People's Council. The jails of Ashgabat are filled with dissidents, Christians, homosexuals, and reporters."

Sunny pursed his lips and smiled.

"That's an outrage," he told her. "The first three should be freed im-mediately."

"Come. Please," she said. "In fact, we'd like to put you down as a co-sponsor."

"What does it . . ."

"Your name would be the most important contribution," she said smoothly. "I saw your two lovely daughters downstairs. They must come, too. We had Wyclef Jean over the other night. Do you know his music? I'll bet they do. Lovely man. We're organizing a benefit for the Fanmi Lavalas party in Haiti."

She opened her coat by slipping a single tie at the center and sat down on the other side of Sunny's table.

"You've shown a great deal of poise over these last few days," she told him. "The city has been fortunate."

"Poise is the word that people seem to pass around," said Sunny. "Like saying that a schnauzer has dignity. Actually, it's been a treat. But Peter's commission will help reassure the city."

Dolores Carroll smiled—but the mild kind that people sometimes hid behind a hand.

"If I were investing in political stock, I'd buy some of yours," she said. Sunny shook his head.

"Would it surprise you to know I'm thinking of getting out of politics?"

"It would surprise me if a man as bright as you thinks he can," she told him. "People who sell shoes are in politics, Sunny. Surely you've learned at least that."

Sunny drummed three fingers over a yellow pad at his elbow.

"I need to provide for my family," he said. "Finally. I've been thinking about the restaurant business."

"We're interested in restaurants, too."

"I didn't mean the Guide Michelin," he replied. "There's an old bus garage near Clark and Devon. With a loan, a few investors who recognize my name now, I might be able to swing that."

Dolores Carroll drummed her own three sharp wine-red nails on the other side of Sunny's pad.

"I know a space," she said. "Ground floor of a rehabbed bank building in Lincoln Park. Clark right off of Eugenie. They're looking for something classy."

"Sounds pricey."

"You have to interest the developers into taking a position in it. It would give him—or her—an interest in seeing it succeed."

Sunny sat back from his edge of the table, but did not move his chair.

"Friends of yours?"

"Business partners," said Dolores Carroll imperturbably.

"That would make us partners."

"I've always thought that made sense."

"I didn't know you were interested in restaurants."

"I'm interested in partnerships," said Dolores, and when Sunny turned to look into the shade that had been drawn down over the boot crunching and traffic whistle hooting of LaSalle Street, she went on quietly.

"You keep a little cash in a political action fund," she said. "Vera appoints you to boards here and there. Crispus Foster won't go long without making trouble for himself."

As Sunny turned around, she splayed her fingers, as if putting quotation marks around pirouetting headlines.

"'Pretty Welfare Mom gets two a.m. Visits from County Board Pres.' 'Foster Drunk at Board Meeting.' Three years from now, the presidency of the county board is up, and the party will want a quality replacement. We could help. From there, it's secretary of state. Or governor. By then, Peter and I are in the senate. I know it would make some people cringe to hear it laid out so coolly," Dolores Carroll said almost sweetly, as if cooing over a sleeping kitten. "So—nakedly. But nobody gets anointed in this business, Sunny. You want to change things, you need clout. You roll up your sleeves. You get dirty hands. Clout isn't a chocolate they put on your pillow at night to bring you sweet dreams."

Sunny looked across the table. Dolores Carroll's eyes flared and did not blink.

"Outside the city limits, people think Roopini is some kind of corkscrew pasta," he said finally.

"That's not fair, Sunny," she told him. "This is Illinois. We have our little hatreds. But Illinois has elected Jews, blacks, Greeks, cranks, and crooks for quite a while. An Indian? No stretch at all. People know a family that runs the motel, an optometrist, a friend from school. I doubt you'd let your daughters make that kind of excuse."

Sunny was genuinely stopped. He started to reply, heard it a half-sentence ahead in his mind, and drew back.

"I'm sorry," he said finally. "I assumed something. I was wrong."

"Carroll is a name my grandfather saw on a street sign," she said.

"He asked, 'Who's that?' They said, 'A founding father.' He said, 'Well so am I.' The family name was Pekary. Romani from Hungary. Our son, who's at Cranbrook, wants to be called Kyle Pekary now." Dolores Carroll bit down on her thin, eggshell smile. "So no one will think he's taken advantage of all of his advantages."

Dolores stood up from her chair. They could hear other office doors around them creaking and groaning as aldermen arrived, coughing and sniffling, clicked on lights, shucked coats, and murmured, "Whaddya know?" The wall behind Sunny shuddered briefly as Salvatore del Raso of the 39th, who had taken the Brown Line in from Kimball Avenue, beat the toe of his boots against the baseboard of the wall they shared to shake off blue salt from the street. Dolores Carroll ran a finger just a fraction of an inch above the dream catcher Sunny had been given by the American Indian Center.

"Fantastic beadwork," she announced, as if it were under glass in a museum—or a gift shop that sold handicrafts made in village cooperatives in Chittagong. Then she turned around.

"Sunny, Congress never made sense for you. Roland"—it was the first time in years Sunny had heard anyone refer to the mayor by his first name—"wanted a way to let you raise money. He wanted us to pour more money into the party. He couldn't stand me, above my legs and ass. He thought Peter was a blessed fool. He loved you. So he figured out a scheme to milk us and make something nice happen for you—after your loss. He wanted you to have options, a future. The job itself? It never made sense. Aldermen don't become congressmen in this day and age. You've got to know something about butanol, Vanuatu, derived fuels, and proliferation. Not just potholes."

Sunny took a long time to reply. In fact, he liked Dolores Carroll. She could be generous and funny. He overlooked loutishness among aldermen the way you pardoned children for throwing a toy car at a playmate. Dolores Carroll was far more desirable and sophisticated company. Yet her expansive catalog of causes and certainties suddenly annoyed Sunny. He didn't understand how someone who had spent so much time in politics could feel so sure about everything.

"I wish more congressmen knew how to fill a pothole," Sunny finally told her. "It would give them something useful to do with their hands. You know," he continued, "I could win that seat. That's the hell of it. You get points for timing in this game, too. Forget what I don't know. *Timing* is on my side. Due to a terrible loss, as much as any"—he hesitated before realizing that she could not take issue with her own word—"*poise*. Three years from now, who knows how the table will be set? The music stops and you run for the open seat."

Dolores Carroll's eyes stayed steady and may have even grown a shade softer. She sat back and held a finger gently against her full coral lips as she spoke.

"We can spend five dollars for every one you'd have to raise, Sunny. More, if you force us. And when it's over, we'll owe no one, much less the friends that the mayor tried to shake down for you. A million dollars? Two? I'm sure we can both find better things to do with it."

"At the moment," said Sunny so softly he had to sit forward, "I don't think I can."

"I hope you'll let that moment pass," said Dolores Carroll gently. "And realize—"

But Sunny decided to interrupt her. He was an elected official and thought there had to be a limit to the admonition he could be expected to endure from someone who had risked only her money in politics. Sunny put his hands on a fifty-cent blue stick ballpoint, bitten on the far end, which said CHICAGO DEPARTMENT OF ANIMAL CARE AND CONTROL. He wrapped his hand around the lettering.

"I've had my name on a ballot six times," said Sunny. "In the end, you know, for all our bluster, we're not really in charge. A bunch of people with hands dirty from filling potholes and scrubbing toilets can snap their fingers, and—"

Sunny snapped his, flattened his hand, and blew across his palm.

"—make us go away."

About three-quarters of the way through Sunny's oration it occurred to him that Dolores Carroll had no doubt been both praised and decried by virtuosos. He couldn't keep his face stern. Dolores Carroll leaned across the table, close enough for Sunny to take in whiffs of amber, lavender, and snow drying on soft wool.

"I'm suggesting a way to win a real life, Sunny," she said softly. "Not just another election. Look at Roland—*the mayor*," she amended when she saw how invoking his mortal name again seemed to sting. "How many people have you heard say, 'Face down at his desk? That's what he would have wanted.' What nonsense. He was *trapped*. He couldn't stop running. Master of his domain? He didn't even own a hole in a log. He knew that the day he stopped being mayor, so did the free desserts. The 'Get Out of Jail Free' cards, too. He'd have nothing to give his friends, nothing to frighten his enemies, and nothing to trade for protection."

Dolores sat back, pushing her fingers delicately back from Sunny's pad. He could hear voices rising and bouncing in the hallway—Torey del Raso and Harry Walker, Emil Wagner and Patrick Tierney. Dolores Carroll flipped the sides of her coat back across her lap. They fell with a soft swish and a plush plop.

"We'd be good partners, Sunny," she said. "A golden age. Let's have dinner."

"Of course."

"I don't mean, 'sometime.' " Her dusky eyes seemed to narrow into hard, dark prongs. "Tomorrow."

Sunny nodded slowly. He could hear his daughters in the small office outside, crinkling bags and giggling.

Dolores Carroll stepped off with a sharp click of her black Tuscan boots, and Sgt. Gallaher raised a hand to hold off Rita and Rula so that Harry Walker III and Salvatore del Raso could step in to Sunny's office. Torey turned his large pale hands over and over, as if wringing a washcloth. Harry ran his fingers through the underbrush of his great white beard, as if calming a small animal.

"We're here on behalf of the Gay Caucus," said Harry.

"I didn't know—"

"I joined this morning," Torey explained. "Arty inspired me."

"Something amazing has been going on," Harry added. Sunny sat up straight. He could feel his jaw grind and tighten.

"I've been in conference," he said simply. Harry began to draw one of his toes back and forth in front of him.

"I told Vera that I'd vote for her," he said. "But I didn't promise. You can't promise in politics, Sunny. You know that. Shit transpires. Fate intervenes. I told Vera I'd vote for her, and I will. Just maybe not immediately."

Sunny felt static electricity prickle his scalp and singe the back of his neck. He had learned that half the time he had felt such palpable pangs of anxiety, nothing happened—and half the time that he felt nothing, the world caved in. He kept his response pointedly short, to be sure of his voice.

"You've decided . . ."

"Not decided, Sunny," Harry rushed on. "Something has *called* me. I know you're not a spiritual man. I respect that. This thing with Arty—"

"Outrageous," Sunny assured him. "Outrageous."

"Exactly, exactly. And Sunny, the outpouring of support—"

"The feeling that enough's enough," chimed in Torey del Raso, rubbing his hands in excitement now. "That it's time to show the prying bastards."

"Arty Agras will be an indispensable partner in Vera's administration," Sunny said smoothly, but Harry was already shaking his head and rolling his fingers across his woolly white Inuit vest.

"That's why we're here, Sunny," he said with rising excitement. "The phone calls—the messages—Sunny, Sunny. I reached Arty. I think he's trying to reach you."

Indeed, Sunny's phone quivered on the yellow pad on his small white table.

"A gay man, Sunny!" Harry flapped his arms and shined his face upward. "A proud, gay, humble, patriotic, man-loving family man!" Harry's icy blue eyes beamed. "A man who cherishes his wife, his children, his community, his church, and his boyfriends!" The Reverend Walker stretched his arms to embrace multitudes and thundered, "He could actually be mayor, Sunny! I can't turn my back on that! Out of the closet and onto the fifth floor!"

Sunny's phone danced over the yellow pad until it dropped onto the small white table and made a sound like a rattlesnake set loose in the room.

Just a few hours before, shortly after six in the morning, three black cruisers and a van with COMVAD! and a fleet red arrow painted across the side had pulled up in front of the old redbrick filling station that was now police headquarters for Highwood, Illinois, twenty-five miles north of the city.

(There was no such thing as Comvad. The department's chief of in-

vestigations had created the name to embellish a police van for surveillance operations with a name to suggest some new communications
company that would dig up the streets and appropriate parking spots.
The chief was delighted to read case reports that noted that passersby
would sometimes bang on the parked van and cry, "Assholes!")

The Highwood police chief, Roy Geraci, had sounded unimpressed
and snappish when Commander Green had awakened him shortly
after five. But he shook his head and whistled softly after reading
through the sheaf of papers presented by Commander Siobhan Kearney.

"Whooo," he said, handing it back. "Wow." And then, so that Kearney wouldn't think that he had spent his whole career in the crabgrass-
and-barbeque belt, answering complaints about boozy parties thrown
by teenagers when their parents were in Florida, Chief Geraci informed her, "I was in Milwaukee for seven years."

"Tough break," she said. "You know the building?"

Chief Geraci nodded. He had scarcely had time to splash his face
since being awakened and felt a lick of his dark hair spring up, like a coil
from a sofa, from the back of his head.

"Smack on Prairie Avenue. The middle unit of three studios above
the Talk of the Town salon. Look commander, I can get a tac unit over
from Highland Park. They can put a team on the roof, come in through
the window, and take him in bed."

Commander Kearney ran a freckled hand through the red bangs
above her brown glasses and shook her head forcefully.

"A tac team to take down one skinny barista? We'd be embarrassed.
Besides, we don't want any lights, cameras, and action. Besides . . ." She
thumped the City of Chicago patch of stars and bars on the left arm of
her uniform. Chief Geraci nodded.

"All yours then," he said.

Shortly after seven, the entire day watch of a dozen Highwood police officers surrounded the building at 225 Prairie. Charles and Deborah, Alex and Megan, Peter and Jessica, and Fred and Linda crouched in
the dim, still hallway. Charles knocked on the door, softly at first, like a
high school boy in a movie tapping on the window of a girlfriend at

midnight. His knocks grew sharper, louder. Deborah called out, "Mr. Meadows! Mr. Meadows! Chicago police! We'd like a word!" No response; nothing stirred. "Mr. Meadows!" called out Megan. Her eyebrows rose as they heard something—a drinking glass, a candy dish, a small window—break and scatter over a hard floor. Eight radios crackled on thick, creaking police belts.

"He's on the roof," Chief Geraci announced.

Clifford Meadows had heard the knocking, scrambled into his bathroom, stood on the rim of the washbasin, cracked the skylight—which, Siobhan Kearney complained later, had not been shown on any blueprints—pushed it out with bloody fingers, and clambered onto the roof. He got to his knees. He had thrown a blue plaid woolen shirt on over a white T-shirt. His blue jeans were already sodden. He had plunged his feet, without socks, into unlaced running shoes. He crawled forward. Pools of pink from the heels of his hand spread in the snow. Clifford Meadows got to his feet and shouted.

"Shit. *Shit.*"

Prairie Avenue wasn't Broadway: 225 Prairie was at least thirty feet away from the nearest lot, 240 Prairie, the Oakwood Elementary School. Clifford Meadows couldn't leap to another roof. He couldn't jump to the ground without going splat in front of a Highwood police officer with a cocked assault rifle. He came to the edge of the roof and cupped bloody dripping hands around his mouth.

"It's the corn people against the rice people!" he shouted. "You're drinking fish genes in your orange juice!"

Charles, Deborah, Alex, Megan, Peter, Jessica, Fred, and Linda surged in through Meadows's door and up the hole in the skylight like birds up a chimney. They stumbled, stopped, and kept going. Alex, Megan, Peter and Jessica had their Walthers drawn. Charles stayed down when he fell, flipped back on his ass, cocked the slide of his M-16 so that Meadows could hear it, and drew a bead on the back of his head.

"Down. Down!" Peter shouted.

Meadows flopped face first in the snow and slush. He turned his head to shout.

"It's cold! Fuck!"

The cops wore slick-soled shoes and had to clomp slowly. When they stood in a circle around Clifford Meadows, they trained the snouts of their guns on his head. He blubbered as he sank into the snow. Blood from his slashed hands and fingers seeped into the slush around him and made a pale pink silhouette. Meadows began to twitch. Megan put the cold nose of her revolver against the back of his left leg, wrenched off his shoes, and flung them over the side of the roof. They thudded into snow with a *pffft*. Meadows' toes were pink, and his heels white with old skin and flinty calluses.

"Fuck! It's cold!" he shouted.

"Freeze! Die! *Fuck*!" Peter screamed—the last so loudly that children in the play lot of the Oakwood School left their games and ran to the link fence across from the building.

Peter put the barrel of his Walter P99 against Meadows's neck, where he knew its fifteen ounces would feel as immense as a cannon. He pressed down until he could see a white outline of the barrel on Meadows' red skin.

"Want a new asshole?" asked Peter.

Alex put his right foot over the base of Meadows's spine and pressed down to pin him against the grimy roof like an old museum specimen in a display case. Meadows gasped, but didn't shout.

"Stay down," Peter told him. "Fuck you, food Nazi crackpot fuckball."

But it was Jessica who holstered her revolver and leaned down, shaking snowflakes from her curls as she bent over Meadows and slapped one half of a Peerless chain-link cuff around his right wrist, then wrenched his arm around his back to grab and cuff his left. She had been running and slipping and had to catch her breath. She planted her feet and lifted Clifford Meadows by the back of his blue plaid shirt until he was on his knees in the slush and snow. Alex and Peter stood back. Charles crawled forward. Fred and Linda stepped to the edge of the roof and slapped their forearms with their wrists three and four times to signal Commander Kearney and two Highwood cops with M-16s pointing pointlessly into the gray sky. Megan turned up the crackle of the radio on her hip and turned her head to speak. Jessica's eyes were bleary and red as she blinked out snow.

"Clifford Meadows," she told him. Her long neck quavered, and her voice was thick. "You are under arrest for the murder of the mayor of Chicago."

Sgt. Gallaher brought Sunny up to the mayor's office on five in a procession of blue uniforms. The silence was uncommon and arresting. He heard the feet of the officers squish softly into thick maroon carpet. The immaculate cream walls of the outer office blotted breaths and stomach grumbles. They turned into the mayor's office, and Sunny stopped. The walnut walls were smooth, brown, and bare. The Eakins, the Lautrecs, and the Hoppers had been taken down; the Art Institute didn't presume to anticipate the preferences of the new mayor who would move in within hours.

The mayor's massive old groaning slab of a beech bridge-tender's desk had been removed. Sunny thought that it must have been like pulling a boulder out of a front yard. Something old, oaken, and imposing had been trucked in. The glossy surface was golden and empty. There were no crystal or silver ashtrays holding gray gobs of ash, no slick drink glasses with crackling ice, no creased newspapers (items and quotations rounded in red, with exclamation points screaming and slashing arrows pointing to howls of SHIT! ASSHOLE! and ANTEDILU-VIAN!). No Fannie's sandwich wrappers, dribbling gravy over the most critical clauses of legislation, no cinnamon rolls shedding sugar glaze over official memoranda, and no serried ranks of silver and leather frames displaying the mayor smiling alongside the last two popes at Soldier Field; or the mayor, implausibly adorned in a skullcap, squeezing his eyes in solemn prayer at Jerusalem's Western Wall; the mayor spinning a basketball under the Chinatown gate; the mayor fixing a kiss on Aretha Franklin's outstretched arm (her coral nails extended, like dragons' tongues, from under the folds of a massive red fox robe) at the Praise Temple of Restoration on West Madison; the mayor making Jennifer Lopez laugh between takes on west Lawrence; and the mayor on Columbus Drive, taking the hand of flaxen-haired Gina Marie Heenan as she was anointed by Journeyman Plumbers Union Local 130 as Queen of the St. Patrick's Day Parade.

Sunny turned around on his heels and took in the blank walls, the bare desk, and the gray windows. The sound of chants from groups gathered in the surrounding streets outside reached up; their words fell away against the glass and snow.

"I'll be right outside, sir," Sgt. Gallaher said softly, and closed the door just as Sunny had to wipe his eyes and turn away to look at the snow freezing into frosty, wavy shapes over the LaSalle Street windows.

A dozen aldermen were shown in: Vera, Linas, and Arty, Rod Abboud of the 26th, Donny Stubbs of the 27th, and Daryl Lloyd of the 9th, John Wu, Evelyn Lee, Astrid Lindstrom of the 28th, Wandy Rodriguez of the 30th, Kiera Malek, and Jaco Rapoport Sefran. They circled the mammoth space that used to hold the mayor's desk, clasping hands, joshing about ties and shoes, cuffing shoulders, squeezing elbows, and exchanging insincerities before facing Sunny. Linas Slavinskas cleared his throat conspicuously.

"Ahhhem, Arty," he announced. "I would have guessed goats. Or whips and chains. But a couple of guys? *Chicago's finest?* Geez, Arty, how can I scandalize anybody now? I could slip the plátano to the Mother Superior of Our Lady of Vilna and people would just say, 'Yeah, but didn't you hear about Alderman Agras?' "

Laughs and shrieks smacked off the walnut walls. John Wu's stout, grave face cracked open as he bawled and guffawed. Vera slipped a lace hanky from her sleeve, daubed her eyes, then Evelyn Lee's. Wandy Rodriguez waited for the gush to ebb slightly then said, "I applaud your interest in Latin culture, Alderman Slavinskas," which sat off another round. Arty Agras turned slightly toward the others, and the laughter faded. His eyes were wet and full.

"I got a lot of calls and messages. They mean . . . more than I can say. Sofia says thanks, too."

Sunny waited for Arty to turn back and press the back of his hand to the corner of his eyes.

"One of you men or women will be the next mayor of Chicago," said Sunny. He paused while each alderman seemed to skip a breath.

Sunny's assessment flattered them. He thought he could see Vera, Linas, and even Arty button smiles—they knew that his utterance was preposterous. The city council would never elect Daryl Lloyd mayor. But Sunny hoped Daryl might feel so exalted about being called to the fifth floor, his resentment of Vera would be dampened for a ballot. Rod Abboud was only slightly more plausible: another Chicago fire would have to flash through the chamber and boil most aldermen for Rod to be elected. But Rod would have heard about any confidential get-together (Linas or Arty would have told him on the way up, saying, "Can you believe they didn't invite you, Marad?") Rod would begrudge Sunny for leaving him out and then vent his disgruntlement against Vera. So Sunny invited him.

Don, Kiera, Astrid, and Wandy had been called because they might have to take over the chair for Sunny, depending on whether he wanted a stern courtroom bailiff, a spry legal scholar, a warm-breasted mother, or an encouraging coach. Sunny wanted to reward them with a sensation of importance. So little in politics takes place behind the scenes anymore. The process was now so indomitably *open*. A man or woman could anonymously donate a new wing of the Art Institute, troll for kiddie porn, or finance a terror network. But give a hundred dollars to a campaign, and his name was on lists and blogs (when Sunny heard activists complain about power brokers in smoke-filled rooms ignoring the will of the people, Sunny recalled all the times he had spent sucking sugarless mints in no-smoking meeting rooms, cringing about polling data and focus groups). So when Sunny saw a chance to give a few friends a sensation of being behind the scenes, he took it.

Sunny had invited Evelyn because he still hoped she might come over to Vera if she needed a last vote. Jacobo was there because he sat near Sunny in the council, and he didn't want to kindle some long, slow resentment that would smolder in Jaco's gaze when they saw each other at the Japanese American Citizens League dinner, or the Freedom Seder at Temple Sholom.

And Sunny had asked John Wu so that he could tell his niece and her new husband that he had stood right there in that huge, walnut chamber, where Sunny told him that he could be the next mayor of Chicago.

"I have been on the phone with Chief Martinez," Sunny continued. "Two arrests have been made in connection with the death of the mayor."

The aldermen sucked in breath and stayed on their feet with insistent quiet.

"They will withhold an announcement until the chief is satisfied that all of the perpetrators they have identified are in custody," said Sunny.

Sunny took a few steps toward Vera and Evelyn as he spoke, then moved slowly toward Wandy and Kiera, keeping his hands in his trouser pockets, and his head pitched down so that he had to lift his eyes to meet those of the aldermen.

"I have also told the chief not to delay his announcement until we have elected a new mayor. The people of Chicago deserve to hear of these arrests as soon as they can be revealed. If this means that the cameras will have to cut away from our session when you, Linas, are in full oratorical flight—"

Snorts erupted from the aldermen, like a dozen pop bottles fizzing open. Sunny knew that it was not much of a joke; they were desperate to laugh.

"That's why they have instant replays, lordship," said Linas.

"Does anyone have another view?" asked Sunny softly. "We have a few minutes."

Daryl Lloyd and Rod Abboud seemed to fidget, Rod smoothing the dots in his tie, Daryl folding his unbandaged arm over his chest and the lemon and chocolate leopard spots of his dashiki.

"Nothing," Daryl said finally, and Sunny paused.

"Fine," Rod added.

"It may soon be your opportunity—your responsibility—to make a different choice," said Sunny. "I've learned over the last three days that you can see things differently from here," and as he spoke Sunny crossed over to the windows and looked out on the crowds that now lined LaSalle Street, clapping gloved hands. Their chants and songs sent wisps and clouds above their snow-capped heads and braying placards.

"You have to decide big things in a great hurry, without knowing everything. Then hope it looks right to people who can study it for thirty years."

Sunny stepped back from the windows and smiled at the aldermen.

"Okay, I want a good, clean election now. Nothing below the belt. Shake hands and come out *not* fighting."

As they filed out, Sunny put his hand lightly on Jacobo Sefran's elbow.

"Jack, the Reverend Jackson is stuck on a runway in New York," he explained. "Snow over the Alleghenies. Could you give the invocation this morning? It's last-second, but . . ."

Alderman Sefran drew back, grabbing Sunny's arm.

"Me sub for the greatest speaker in America? At the last second? Natalie Portman could be watching."

"I wouldn't ask, Jack, but—"

"I've got a couple of things that might do," he said, touching the back of his head to feel for his black woolen yarmulke. "I'll try."

Sunny felt his phone tremble in his pocket, and took it out in time to see the gray letters USATTY NODIST IL. 9:56 strut across the smoky screen. He waited until it ceased to shudder and then slid the phone back into his pocket.

Sgt. Gallaher held her hand up for a moment until six uniforms could file past Sunny onto the mayor's rostrum in the council chamber. He fell behind her long strides toward the high-backed burgundy chair and fastened the middle button on his coat before settling down as Lew Karp, his bald head bent in the clerk's chair just below, called out, "Corcoran, Eighteen! Volkov, Nineteen! Wa-tah-nah-bay, Twenty!" Lewie enjoyed curling Janet's name over his lips and tongue, like the title of an opera.

Christa Landgraf from the Corporation Counsel's office tipped her white glasses in greeting. Tina Butler, the sergeant-at-arms, caught Sunny's eye with a dip of her head, and walked up the three stairs to the mayor's chair. She held a gavel in her hand, clad in brass.

"He got this just last week," she explained. "He looked forward to using it."

Sunny ran the smooth, shiny wood of the handle over his fingers as he twisted it to see the engraving:

PRESENTED TO THE MAYOR BY THE

NATIONAL ASSOCIATION OF BLACK SCUBA DIVERS

CHICAGO CHAPTER

DIVE DEEP—DIVE LONG

Tina leaned over and brought her chin down until it was just above Sunny's shoulder.

"I think the mayor—well, you know," she said, taking care to turn away from Sgt. Gallaher. "He thought it was a little saucy."

"I imagine so."

Sgt. Butler held out the chapter's business card, and Sunny rolled back the drawer on the rostrum desk to take out a pad of paper.

"Ko-walski, Twenty-three!" Lewie's voice cracked out. "Booker, Twenty-four! Goo-tee-arrrez, Twenty-five!"

The pad had the city seal, printed in blue, with an American shield, a sheaf of wheat, a ship in full sail, a sleeping infant, and an Indian bearing a bow and arrow, arranged above the *Urbs in Horto* motto.

(Sunny remembered how the mayor had often suggested that the seal be changed to sheaves of cash in envelopes, a Polish sausage sailing in a poppy seed bun, an Indian embracing a slot machine, and the motto, *All You Can Eat*.)

Sunny took up a blue CITY OF CHICAGO pen and wrote:

Dear Scuba Divers:

The mayor looked forward to using your gavel. I regret that he could not. But I have used it to call the council to order on January 22 to elect his successor. Sergeant Butler returns it to you as a memento of a great man whom we all loved.

With best wishes,
Sundaran Roopini

And then he held his pen above the pad for just a moment before adding:

Acting Interim Mayor for 84 Hours

Lew Karp called out, "Roopini, Forty-eight!" and Sunny called back, "Present." Sgt. Gallaher stepped back as Sunny handed his note to the sergeant-at-arms, Lewie barked, "Berggren, Forty-nine!" Anders affirmed his presence from the back row, Lewie called out, "Sefrrran, Fifty!" with a slight Iberian trill, Jaco answered 'Present" softly from the stairs—he was already on his way to the rostrum—and Sunny sat back in the high-backed burgundy chair to receive the clerk's tally.

Sgt. Gallaher leaned over slightly above the back of the chair and pointed one of her lean fingers at the next-to-last row of the gallery: Rula and Rita sat on either side of Eldad. It had been years since they had come to a city council meeting. Sunny saw that his daughters no longer flashed the full, delighted, five-fingered hand-wag of a five- or six-year-old. They rolled their fingers subtly, from just under their chins; as their mother used to do.

"Fifty aldermen have answered present," Lew Karp reported.

Sunny nodded soberly, as if the result was at least a minor revelation. He brought the scuba diver's gavel down on the rostrum with a *crack!* that smacked louder than he had expected; the muttering and hubbub that ordinarily had to be gaveled down had already subsided.

"I thank the council for coming to order," he said. "We will now receive the invocation from the alderman of the Fiftieth Ward, Alderman Sefran, who of course is also the head of the Shaare Mizrah congregation."

"Devon between Francisco and Richmond," said Jaco, turning around to Sunny from the microphone just a few steps below the podium, then turned back. "For those of you who would like to join us some Saturday. *Ha-noteeyn tish-shuah, lam lakeem umem-shalah, lan-seekheem,*" he began in Hebrew, squinting, scrunching, and bending his knees to rock back and forth. "Let He who grants victory to kings and dominion to rulers, whose kingdom is for all ages, who released David, His servant, from the sword, who gave us a road through the sea and a path through mighty waters, may He bless the late mayor, and the new mayor we choose today."

Sunny kept his head down but opened an eye to try to catch Vera's. Vera lifted her eyebrows in surprised approval. But Jaco Sefran went on.

"And as our Christian friends say," he intoned, "may He bless even evildoers, and forgive them, Father, for they know not what they do, as that great Judeo-Christian Jew, Jesus, said from his cross of thorns."

And just as Sunny had inclined his head from prayerful repose and wondered if he should step in to begin the session, Jacobo's voice grew firmer.

"May God give us wisdom today," he said. "And if we don't choose the best or the brainiest candidate, please let us at least find a good man or woman who loves this city and will grow wise in the job."

He widened his eyes and looked out, as if expecting questions, and hearing none, went on.

"May God bless this city and all the peoples of the world who call it home. *V-kheyn y-hee ratzon, v-nomar ameyn.* So may it be His will. Let us now say amen."

"Amen!" aldermen called back, expelling fretful breaths. Sunny waited until aldermen had folded themselves back into their seats, and the cloaked groan of springs and hamster squeals of wheels below their chairs had quieted.

" 'And all the peoples of the world who call this city home,' " Sunny repeated. "Thank you, alderman."

He looked down at Vera Barrow. She wore a trim bronze suit with a muted sheen and thin violet pinstripes, clinched at the neck with a concealed clasp. She kept her arms relaxed but disciplined at her sides as she rose, taking Sunny into her glance with one eye, then the council with another.

"Mr. President, I move to suspend the reading of the minutes."

"Without objection, it is so ordered." He brought down the gavel softly.

"Before we proceed with the agenda, I ask the council's brief consideration of an item that lingers from last week," he began. "The council approved a new contract with Earth First that would pay the company three hundred forty dollars a ton for recycling services. The city has since been contacted by the officers of Earth First, who say that they have reviewed how new technologies may assist them in lowering their costs. They are confident that they can now provide the city with recycling services for two hundred dollars a ton, affording the city substantial savings."

Christa Landgraf lifted a small pile of papers in front of her face, like a slice of birthday cake.

"There should be copies on your desks of the new contract," said Sunny. "Do I hear a motion to approve?"

Arty Agras had gotten to his feet while Christa waggled the pages, and said, "So moved, Mr. President," then sat back down.

"Second?" asked Sunny. He looked to the right hand side of the second row for Wandy Rodriguez. But it was impossible to overlook Kiera Malek, rising from her seat in the center of the last row. She wore candy-cane striped leggings and a gray skirt below a puffed-up black blouse, and waved her arms as if trying to hail a low-flying plane.

"Mr. Prez-i-dent!" she called out. "Mr. Prezzz-eee-dent!"

Sunny turned his gaze from the right side of the chamber; he liked Kiera.

"Does the alderman wish to second the motion?"

He heard snorts from Linas Slavinskas and one or two others.

"I have a question," said Kiera, and Sunny nodded.

"Does the president know—does Alderman Agras know—what inspired the officers of Earth First to bring down their price?"

Sunny leaned forward earnestly.

"Alderman, I think they simply reflected on the best service they could give the city. Is the alderman opposed to saving the city millions of dollars?"

Kiera had walked to just in front of her desk and shook her bobbed brown hair.

"Indeed not," she said. "I just wonder if there is something missing here."

"I would invite the alderman to review the new contract language," said Sunny. "There is no one whose opinion I would respect more." He sat back, and ran the neck of the gavel through his fingers. "But at the moment, we have a motion on the floor. Is there a second?"

Sunny heard a chorus of voices, and saw Mitya Volkov of the 19th, Janet Watanabe, Tomislav Mitrovic, Jesus Flores Suarez, and Felix Kowalski of the 23rd cup their hands and call out in the row just below Kiera.

"Mr. President!" she tried to roar above them. "Earth First executives have been indicted for fraud in several jurisdictions. Austin, Texas, Madison, Wisconsin—

"Local yokel affiliates, Mr. President," Arty Agras shot back. "Just a bunch of fines."

Sunny struck the gavel against the podium and insisted, "Aldermen will please take their seats." He paused while Kiera begin to migrate back to the rear row.

"Trash is a dirty business, alderman," said Sunny. "Until we can find Benedictine monks who specialize in municipal waste recycling, our choice of service providers is limited. A motion and a second have been made. All those in favor of the new contract with Earth First, please signify by saying aye."

Ayes abounded. He could pick out Arty, Linas, Vera, Miles Sparrow of the 7th, his chin spiky after being shorn just that morning, and Cyril Murphy of the 40th.

"Opposed?"

Daryl Lloyd called out "Nay" for sure. There was a second; Sunny figured Rod Abboud, but couldn't tell. Kiera leaned over and exchanged words behind her hand with Sidney Wineman of the 42nd, but did not call out to oppose or affirm.

"Evidently a sufficient number," Sunny announced, and brought down the gavel. It smacked like the cracking of an iceberg.

"We turn now to our next item," he said quietly, and then drew a breath before going on.

"No one who serves even as acting interim mayor for just—"and here Sunny made a show of consulting his watch"—eighty-two hours can fail to be affected by the beauty and brilliance of our city. Next to being a father," and here, Sunny nodded up toward his daughters in the gallery, "serving this city over the past few days has been the greatest reward of my life."

He stopped to move onto the agenda, but heard John Wu call out, "You've done well, Mr. President."

Then Evelyn Lee and Wandy Rodriguez cried out, "Well done!" He heard Vera and Linas call out, "Alderman Roopini!" and applause began to roll through the seats and into the gallery. Sunny looked up and could even see strangers behind the glass of the gallery smack their hands. He looked for Rula and Rita. He didn't want to catch their eyes, but wanted to see their faces. They slumped in their seats, their butterscotch skin burning behind the hands that hid their eyes as strangers behind them clapped them on their backs and shoulders. Sunny halted and looked down until he could clearly look out at the council and speak without catching his voice.

"Thank you," he said in the silence, and then turned to Lewis Karp in the desk below him on the left.

"The clerk will call the roll."

Sunny had kept his head down during the applause. Even as he spoke his thanks, he let his eyes play over a crinkled sheet that Eldad had come around to place at his elbow. Each ward number was printed in black. Red, blue, or blue-black squiggles were beside each, sometimes with arrows, or question marks.

The estimate that Sunny had made out of his colleagues' solemn commitments, vague inclinations, and his own calculations, put Vera's base of support at nineteen. Sunny was more certain than ever that Linas would not go forward. Linas must have deduced, as had Sunny, that he would stall at eighteen. Rather than lose in the council, Linas had conjured a way—it was brazenly clear to Sunny now—to look triumphant, magnanimous, and cunning. He would run against Vera next year, and cast his vote today for Tommy Mitrovic or Astrid Lindstrom; or for maximum mischief, Dr. Daryl Lloyd.

Arty's nine votes had always been subject to change. Sunny doubted that even two aldermen thought that he should be mayor. But Arty was a powerful committee chairman and popular colleague. Aldermen whose wards would not accept a vote for Vera or Linas could curry favor with Arty by voting for him; a vote that could be borne without guilt by the confidence that Arty stood a better chance of being elected the Panchen Lama of Tibet than he did the mayor of Chicago.

The political effect of Arty's *scandale* had surprised Sunny. But he figured that even those who were tempted by sympathy or fealty to vote for him would pull back as it was clear that he couldn't win. Sunny had reminded Harry Walker III and Salvatore del Raso that there was more reward in voting for Vera, whose record on such issues was beyond their reproach, than for Arty. Aldermen might fight for principles. But giving their vote away for nothing in return violated a law of nature. It overturned the gravity that kept their planet spinning, feet planted, and blood flowing to their extremities. As each alderman began to grasp that his or her vote could bring Vera closer to being mayor, their votes were their last chance to earn her conspicuous gratitude.

Sunny folded the sheet of paper and kept it at his elbow. None of the red, blue, or blue-black squiggles, the arrows, slashes, or exclamations had surprised him. He saw Lew Karp hold a black marker over a yellow tablet that he had ruled with half-a-dozen columns. In the uncommon silence among fifty aldermen, he heard muffled chants, cheers, and slogans from the streets below. *"The people, united, shall never be defeated...."*

Linas Slavinskas sat back, tucked his intense lavender tie back under the center button of his shark-gray suit, and called, "Sing it, Lewie!" The sharp end of the pen trembled, like a gnat circling, and Lew Karp's voice roiled in the back of his throat as he declared in the still chamber, "Agras! One!"

33

Arty stood up from the very first seat in the front row to the very left of the chamber and bowed his head slightly in Sunny's direction.

"If I may say, Mr. President—"

"Briefly—"

"I am humbled by the spontaneous combustion of outpouring I have received."

He brought back his shoulders and lifted his head.

"Agras," he said with quiet defiance.

"Washington, Two!" barked Lewie Karp. Evelyn raised a long hand with a single finger extended to the sky, a lacy tan hankie in her fist. She ran half-a-dozen Higgledy-Piggledy storefront preschools on Madison and Harrison and usually had tissues trailing from her hands and wrists.

"Vera Barrow."

There was a burst of handclaps from the gallery seats just behind the council. Sunny thought they were a few smacks short of demanding to be gaveled down.

"Fisher, Three!"

"Vera, Vera, Vera," Dorothy sang out from her round, shy face.

"The clerk will record that vote for Barrow," Lew Karp said, with his head still bent low over his legal pad. "Jackson, Four!"

Wanda wore a pink wool suit with thin bone stripes and an ivory hat with a brim like swallow's wings.

"Barrow," she called from underneath.

"Barrow," Lew said. "Five!" and Vera stood up smartly to call back her own name.

"Brown, Six!"

"Vera Grant Barrow," Grace said, and there was a dash of friendly laughter and handclaps at the unfamiliarity of Vera's middle name.

"Sparrow, Seven!"

Miles let a moment pass before uncrossing a leg and standing up halfway to hail the clerk.

"I was jest wondering when you'd call on a man," he said, and anxious aldermen let out more laughs, as if they'd been punctured.

"I call them as they come, alderman," said Lewie.

"Well I'm surrounded by the queens here," said Miles to more laughter. "And I can't think of a better man to be mayor—man or woman—than Vera."

"The clerk records Alderman Sparrow's vote for Barrow," said Lew Karp. "Reginald, Eight!"

"Barrow," the attorney called.

"Lloyd, Nine!" and as Daryl stood up in his jungle-spotted tunic, Linas Slavinskas ducked below his desk. As aldermen and spectators noticed, laughter rolled around the chamber and up into the gallery. Daryl raised his hands for quiet. Then he found that he could clench and unclench his hands to show nothing was in them; which drew more laughs.

"I had a little chat with Sarge this morning," he said finally, gesturing toward Tina Butler in her dress blues. "She told me she didn't care if I had a sheriff's badge or a letter from the king of Norway, I'm not bringing a firearm onto this council floor ever again. Now that puts me in a persnickety position," said Daryl, who then stopped and put his hands in his pockets, as if to feel for the right word. "I deplore the police abusing authority. And I am scared to death of Sarge." There was another surge of applause as the sergeant-at-arms waved her white-topped cap.

"I respect her," Daryl added quietly. "And I respect this council."

Daryl was easily a sentence beyond the preface that Sunny usually abided during a roll call, but he chose not to insist that Daryl hurry to his vote.

"No problem, Sarge," he said.

"None here, alderman," said Sergeant Butler, and Sunny decided to insert himself only gently.

"We await the alderman's vote."

"Lloyd," said Daryl quietly, and sat back down. There was a flutter of muttering between Dorothy Fisher and Wanda Jackson, but Sunny stayed impassive in his seat; Daryl's vote for himself didn't upset Sunny's calculations.

"Lloyd votes Lloyd," Lew Karp repeated. "Mulroy, Ten!"

J. P. puffed out his buff pastry cheeks and rolled his knuckles over the surface of his desk.

"Pass," he said.

Lew Karp looked up in a puzzle. Voting was one of the few real tasks of an alderman. Lew Karp thought that J. P. had just waved it off, like chopped chives on a baked potato. Sunny leaned away from the small serpent's head of the microphone in front of him.

"The alderman will think it over," he told Lew.

Lewie lifted his mouth into a reluctant smile of resignation, and then rang out, "Sannndoval, Eleven!"

Fred hunched under his orange-plaid horse blanket sport coat, and his great mattress-stuffing eyebrows narrowed in contemplation.

"That sounds like a good idea," he said. "Pass."

Droplets of surprise began to scale Sunny's back, like spider legs. J. P. had wanted the Minnie Minoso Seniors Assisted Living center put up at Ninety-third and Harbor, rather than in Miles Sparrow's 7th, as the mayor chose. Fred Sandoval was touchy because his brother-in-law, a hoisting engineer, was suspended for ten days when inspectors saw him having a beer at the Cork and Kerry when he was signed in at the Sixty-eighth Street pumping station. ("Who are they hiring as inspectors these days, Sunny," Fred had exclaimed. "Puritans? Peeping Toms? People who never get thirsty?")

Neither man would have voted for Vera on a roll call. But Sunny suddenly wondered if the smallest gesture of inconsequential concern—an

insincere note, an unredeemable phrase of encouragement—might not
have made at least one of the aldermen less eager to sign on to whatever
scheme Linas Slavinskas now rose from his seat to reveal.

He was on his feet before Lew Karp could read off his name. His suit
shimmered as blindingly silver as the skin of a hammerhead. He wore
an opulently pink shirt and a lavender tie with as many thick folds of
silk as opera curtains.

"Slavinskas! Twelve!"

"Mr. President, I have heard from a few colleagues who have urged
me to offer myself for this high office," Linas began.

"Is the alderman casting a vote?" asked Sunny.

"May I have a moment to put my vote in context?"

"A sentence," Sunny replied with a smile. "Our context is that we
have fifty aldermen."

Linas smiled. He rocked on his heels and jammed his hands into his
coat pockets. He lifted his chin until the cords in his neck seemed as
taut as a cobra's. "While I welcome the esteem of my colleagues," said
Linas, "I have concluded that I can best serve the principles I hold dear
in these important times by supporting the candidacy of a colleague
who has served us ably and well and represents a new era in the history
of this city—"

"Sounds like a period, alderman," Sunny interrupted.

"Merely a pause for breath, Mr. President," replied Linas, who then
raised his voice above the babble of laughs that followed. "A comma!"
he pleaded.

"When the chair said a sentence, I meant Hemingway, not Dick-
ens," Sunny declared, which won small snorts of laughter from Kiera
Malek and Grace Brown, but not many more.

"I will therefore simply and gladly cast my vote, Mr. President,"
said Linas. "For the alderman of the Eleventh Ward, the home of great
Chicago mayors—Alllfredo Saaandovalll!"

There was a rush of gasps. Pads of paper plopped on the floor. Seat
springs groaned, and shoes smacked the carpet. Fred Sandoval stood up
from his desk. Gerry White and Astrid Lindstrom leaned over their
desks to pat his plaid shoulders. Linas grasped his hand, then his elbow,

and then raised both of their hands above their heads. Wandy Rodriguez in the row behind began to flap his own arms above.

"Mr. President!" he called. "I ask for a recess!"

Linas turned around from the gallery, lowered Fred's hand carefully, and turned his face up toward Sunny.

"Do we need a recess, Mr. President?" he asked. Linas was rollicking over the observable chaos, like the bad kid who set off a firecracker in a high school girls' room, just to see a lot of girls run out, adjusting their pantyhose.

"Why do we need a recess?" he repeated.

Sunny wavered. A recess would be a sign of confusion; even retreat. And now that he had gaveled the council to order, Sunny couldn't simply crawl down from the rostrum and reappear as Vera's full-time cheerleader. But he needed to give Vera the chance to reorganize and reload. He stood up from the high-backed chair and held his hand conspicuously over the microphone.

"Because I have to go," he announced, patting his belt for emphasis. He heard Collie Kerrigan crack a laugh at the end of the front row and saw Felix Kowalski in the middle tier put his elbow into Jesus Flores Suarez to repeat his remark. Linas Slavinskas threw his head back.

"When you got to, you got to," he conceded, and Sunny fumbled for the handle of the scuba diver's gavel to give a *thwack*! to the desk and declared, "Fifteen minutes," and walked off the stage. He looked for Rula and Rita's faces in the gallery, just before he had to turn the corner into the mayor's bathroom.

The tile was an eye-splitting yellow. The dual sinks were stainless steel that screeched in the bright light, the countertop was glassy, with small globs of purple suspended inside—"lost dinosaur sperm, looking for a mate," the mayor used to say. It was said that the mayor himself had overseen the renovation, authorizing a design scheme that would make prolonged conversation painful. Two uniforms stood outside. Sunny was washing his hands when Wandy Rodriguez sent word through the uniforms at the door that he'd like to see him. His hazelnut face was long and gloomy.

"Sunny, I'm sorry," he said. "I know I told you . . ."

"I understand, Wandy. Sometimes the wind changes."

Several bitter phrases flashed in Sunny's mind. But he would take no pleasure sticking pins into Wandy Rodriguez; he still hoped for his vote on the next ballot.

Sunny also knew that if his own 48th had run a little farther west and a little farther south—if his ward had a few more Salvadorans and Mexicans, and a few less Gujaratis and Hanzus—he might have had to make the same choice as Wandy.

Sunny stepped back into the hallway just as Linas strode by, shoulders gliding with the nimbleness of a panther springing from the bushes.

"Refreshed, lordship?"

Sunny reached around one of the blue uniforms to take hold of Linas's arm.

"Positively effervescent," he told him. "Fred Sandoval! He's a half-bright career bachelor who can't cut the tusks of hair in his nose without professional help. He runs a half-crooked insurance agency on Halsted that finances every factory and tavern fire in Bridgeport."

Linas had smiled through Sunny's entire denunciation.

"That what you tell him when you need his vote?"

"I think I promised him a stoplight," said Sunny. "Not to make him pope."

Linas turned his face upward, looking like the choirboy who had caught Father Dan with Mary Catherine Flannery, and who was now free to take ten from the collection plate.

"Oh ye of little faith!" he grinned.

"What you figure he'll get?" asked Sunny. "Seven, nine?"

"A dozen and counting."

"And what happens when he believes that little speech of yours and runs next year—against *you*?"

"That's Hay-*zooses* problem," he said, rolling out the first name of the alderman of the 22nd Ward with a Mexican soap opera accent, to distinguish him from the Nazarene.

"Besides—I count on the chihuahuas and the U.S. Attorney to head that off."

"This is dangerous, Linas," Sunny said sternly. "Dangerous and stupid. You're setting off clan warfare. Fred's people against Jesus' people against Vera's and Daryl's."

"Grown men and women, lordship," said Linas.

"*Aldermen*," Sunny reminded him.

Linas laughed with a broad, strapping smile that looked like it would be unscratched by a head-on collision. He squeezed Sunny's shoulder and patted his cheek.

"I love you, lordship," he said. "I swear I do," and after Linas had turned the corner Sgt. Gallaher approached Sunny quietly from behind. He nodded for her to step ahead, but first she averted her eyes toward Alderman Slavinskas in the hallway.

"If you don't mind me saying, sir—that's a little snide."

"Saying he loved me?" Sunny laughed. "It was the only thing he really meant."

As soon as Sunny gaveled the council back into order, J. P. Mulroy stood up and waved his five stubby salami fingers for recognition.

"Mr. President, am I recorded on this vote?"

Sunny looked over solemnly at the clerk.

"The alderman is recorded as having passed," and when Sunny heard both Linas Slavinskas and John Wu wheeze with laughter, he rushed ahead to amend, "That is, he is recorded as deferring his vote. I'm glad to confirm that the alderman is demonstrably alive before us."

"And I would like to cast my vote for Sandoval."

Sunny pulled back to have a word with Christa Landgraf, who raised her curvaceous glasses onto her brows.

"You pass, you have to wait until everyone else has voted. Am I right?" he asked.

"Except he's asked if he's *recorded* on the vote," she whispered.

"Meaning?"

"That he's had expert advice," she said, cocking her head toward Linas Slavinskas. "It lets him cast his vote right now. If you let him," she added. "It's the chair's rule."

"He can appeal the rule of the chair," Sunny pointed out.

"Alderman Slavinskas won't push it," said Christa, turning her small chin toward the wall. "Even he won't get twenty-six aldermen to say that they didn't hear J. P. Mulroy pass." Sunny held his hand over the rostrum microphone.

"I'm going to permit it," he said after a moment. "I don't like it. But Fred is next, and it's better for everyone to let Fred vote for himself straight off. Any alderman deserves that, no tricks." He nodded to Lew Karp.

"Mulroy, Ten, Sandoval," Lew repeated, and Fred himself raised a hand from his seat.

"Mr. President? Am I recorded on—"

"Does the alderman wish to change how he is recorded?" asked Sunny. He cringed to hear himself sound snappish and could see Alfredo lower his arm.

"Please. Yes. Sandoval," he called softly.

"Sandoval, Eleven, Sandoval," said Lew, who cocked a look above his glasses at Fred to add, "My apologies for previously incorrectly recording what everyone here heard."

There were hoots and claps. Sunny drew back his gavel, but they ceased in time for Lew Karp to resume the roll.

"Lucchesi, Thirteen!"

Brock had been clicking one of his ballpoints back and forth against his chin. He drew it back, leaving a tiny, red depression, and rolled the pen into his hand before calling out, "Agras."

"Kerrigan, Fourteen!"

"Sandoval!"

Lew Karp lifted his eyes into the second row of the chamber, on the left-hand side.

"Wu, Fifteen!" he called, and John, who had been stalwartly for Linas, answered in a measured, muffled voice, "Alfredo Sandoval."

"Watson, Sixteen!"

"Vera Barrow," said Shirley, who leaned over to pat John's arm.

Evelyn Lee struggled to stand on her slim legs as Lew Karp called her name. Her ankles often swelled on cold mornings, from thirty years of putting her short arms around heavy garments enrobed in plastic and stuffed with wire hangers and carrying them onto a truck. Kevin Corcoran of the 18th leaned over, but Evelyn put a hand heavily on her desk and waved him back with a nod. She wore a gray suit with oatmeal-colored speckles, and an orange kerchief tied at her neck. She took off her blue glasses to pick out Fred Sandoval on the other side of the chamber.

"Ah, Fred," she said. "I love you, Alfredo. But you're not a real candidate. We've had enough fun and games today. We've paid off favors and flattered a few friends. It's time to choose a real mayor—the best possible person for mayor."

"Vote. *Vote*," shouted Sidney Wineman from the row behind. "This is a roll call, Mr. President, not Open Mic Night at a comedy club."

The laughter began in the knot around Sidney, Ivan Becker, Kiera Malek, Felix Kowalski, and Sanford Booker, and by the time it reached Evelyn Lee, she joined in. Sunny gave one soft tap of his gavel, but said nothing.

"I thank the alderman. Was that Sidney?" she asked. "Sixteen years here, and I've learned to cherish the few truly funny remarks. Mr. Clerk," Evelyn said finally, "please record my vote for Vera Barrow."

Sunny saw Vera swivel quickly around. Screeches and claps burst from some of the visitor's seats on the council floor. The gallery behind the glass buzzed. He saw Linas push back in his chair, but otherwise hold himself pointedly still. Aldermen in the last row, from Emil Wagner, to Cyril Murphy, and then to Jacobo Sefran, turned their heads to huddle behind their hands. Alfredo Sandoval leaned over; Linas heard him out, smiled, shook his head, and patted his arm with dramatic reassurance. Sunny looked down at his list and saw that the next dozen or so votes would bat back and forth between Vera, Arty, and at least six more for Alfredo Sandoval. Sunny decided to send the aldermen out of the chamber while Evelyn Lee's switch was the last broad stroke in their minds.

"It's twelve-twenty something," he observed, and brought down the scuba diver's gavel. "We will recess for lunch until two."

Sgt. Gallaher leaned down toward Sunny as he sat in the small, windowless conference room behind the rostrum and delivered grave news.

"We have a lockdown," she told him solemnly. "By order of Chief Martinez. All access into the building is blocked until the end of the session. The crowds outside are just too large," she said. "He would have phoned except—"

"Yes, I've been busy," said Sunny. "This means—"

"That's what I've been getting to, sir," she said, letting a smile skip over her lips. "No food deliveries."

"Fascism," said Sunny. "Bloody *fascism*," he repeated vehemently. "Who says it can't happen here?"

"Wherever the Lord closes a door She opens a window," said Sgt. Gallaher. "The First District has snapped into action."

Rula produced a white plastic sack with Fannie's green script crawling across the outside. It crinkled as she hefted it onto the conference table. She parted the top and a contrail of spice and smoke rose into the center of the room.

"Limited menu, of course, sir. I think we just got two lean brisket, two pastramis, and one turkey pastrami."

"The vegetarian option," said Sunny. "Anyone mind if I take that?" Eldad spread out a broadsheet from that morning's *Tribune*, and Rita shook out the sandwiches.

"No potato salad or cole slaw," said Sgt. Gallaher over the commotion of Rula, Rita, Eldad, and Sunny passing, crinkling, unwrapping, checking, rewrapping, and passing sandwiches in white paper swaddling around the table. "Or sour dills or knishes. But the officers were able to put their hands on these."

The sergeant shook a bag of potato chips in her slender fingers.

"Come hither," said Sunny, and then felt embarrassment rise in his face.

"With crab seasoning, for some reason," she added, and Sunny threw his pin-dot tie over his shoulder and tucked a napkin over his shirt.

"In my dwindling minutes of power," he said sonorously, "I would like to give all officers involved keys to the city for this humanitarian mission.

Rula and Rita hatched back the rye hinges of their pastrami sandwiches, delicately picking the thin strings of red meat up from the wrapper and lowering them into their mouths.

"How did they bring them in?" asked Rula.

"The ledge of the men's room on the second floor, right outside the council chamber," said Sgt. Gallaher. "A couple of patrolmen, a couple of reporters, and Alderman Mitrovic are leaning out, and hauling up bags of sandwiches on ropes." She leaned back on the edge of a chair back and laughed.

"That must make a sight for the cameras," said Sunny, as he worked over the turkey pastrami on whole wheat. The sergeant smiled.

"I'm sure it's exactly what they do in the House of Lords," she said.

"The Baroness Warwick of Undercliffe always has the turkey pastrami," said Sunny, and when Rita looked with palpable bafflement from Sgt. Gallaher to her father, he added, "Something my Mummyji said the other morning."

"Evelyn Lee sure came through," Eldad rushed in to observe. "That puts us at nine, one more than we'd estimated. Alderman Slavinskas found me and said, 'Looks like I'm not the only one with surprises around here,' and then he said, 'Eldad, just remember, for every action, there's an equal and opposite reaction.' "

"Newton's Third Law," said Rula.

"My first," said Sunny.

Sgt. Gallaher felt a twinge, reached into her jacket, and suddenly waggled a mobile phone at Sunny. He sat up as she held out the screen so that he could see the identity of the caller, then asked his daughters, Eldad, and the sergeant, "Give me a moment?" They left the curls of pastrami, crusts of bread, and smears of mustard among the crumbles on the table and moved into the hallway.

"And get the door, please," asked Sunny as he pressed a button to answer the call.

"Some show over there," said the U.S. Attorney. "Reminds me of the ones where they lock up a porn queen, an old child star, a nuclear scientist, and a piccolo player to see who survives."

"Very similar, yes," said Sunny.

"You never call. You never write," said Brooks Whetstone. "No puffs of smoke."

Sunny had gotten to his feet. A 1933 map of the city's wards, a photo of Lincoln Tower, and a framed program cover of the first Ferris wheel from the Colombian Exposition clacked like a chorus line of katydids against the walls as a couple of Pink Line trains pulled south away from the Washington Street platform.

Sunny sat on an edge of the conference table and ran his fingers absently over the smooth grain.

"I fingered the slip of paper you gave me," Sunny said. "But I never smoothed it out to read the number. You know why? You're shrewd, Mr. Whetstone. You knew that the way to get me into your game was to make me feel guilty—and I do. Sometimes I wake up screaming and crying. I haven't spent enough time with my daughters. Now, they're just about gone. I've bought posh ties and worn them once. Now, I can't find them. Stupid, wasteful. I took it for granted that people I loved would always be around. Now, she's not. I wasted so much time—so much care, so many feelings—on silly, senseless, useless things. I was always going to make things right later on. Now I'm out of time. But I doubt that giving you seduction tips on a lot of old friends will help me," he said. "I helped some people who needed jobs and made sure they did them well. I figured out ways to fix and do some things. I'll live with that."

There was a long silence on the phone, which Sunny felt distinctly as a silence between two men. They could hear each other breathe; they could each hear the scratch of the other man's afternoon beard on the mouth of the receiver. When Brooks Whetstone finally replied, he seemed to let his voice out slowly.

"You've been through a lot, Alderman Roopini. For all you've given to politics, you have an embarrassingly small amount to show in return. End your career in the council, go on to something else, and you won't find anything nailed to your door from me. It's a gift, really. And as you can guess, I'm the kind of man who usually says, 'Christmas? *Bah humbug.*' Can we have an understanding?"

Sunny could hear the howl from a train as it turned into the Lake Street curve a few blocks away. He heard police whistles peal in the streets outside and, before he could answer—before he could even take a breath to answer—a soft rap of knuckles against the conference room door. Sgt. Gallaher called from the other side.

"The council will please come to order," Sunny began. It was two twenty-two. Aldermen were uncommonly quiet in their seats; he plucked up the gavel, but then put it down. Lewis Karp discovered a speck of pastrami clinging to his glasses and rubbed it against his black knit tie. Christa Landgraf had brought a cup of tea up to her desk on the rostrum, the string of the bag looped through the handle, and she patted her throat as she cleared it and smiled at Sunny.

"Watered, fed, and ready," she said.

"When we recessed, the council was conducting a roll call vote," said Sunny. "Am I correct, Mr. Clerk, that we recessed after Alderman Lee cast her vote?"

"Correct sir," said Lewie. "For Alderman Barrow."

"That's not necessary," Daryl Lloyd shot back from the first row.

"Thank you, Mr. Clerk. I think a great many others are keeping tally as we go along," he said, and cast a smile out toward the cameras on stilts in the press section. "Would you resume the roll call?"

"Corcoran, Eighteen!" cried Lewie.

Kevin had his fingers tilted like a steeple under his chin.

"Sandoval," he said.

"Volkov, Nineteen!"

Mit rubbed his thumbs in the corners of his smoky grey eyes.

"Barrr-ow," he called.

"Wah-tah-nah-bay, Twenty!" Lew announced, as if proclaiming a destination for an international flight, and Janet tossed back her curly head to reply before Lew had warbled the third syllable.

"Barrow!" she emphasized.

"Mitrovic, Twenty-one!"

"Agras," Tommy said quietly.

"Sss-wah-*rez*, Twenty-two!"

Jesus, whose desk was in the smack center of the chamber, cupped his small sand shovel of a beard against the palm of his hand. His eyes narrowed and seemed to darken into searing brown blisters.

"Sss-" Lew Karp began again, but Jesus raised his head and cut him off with a single sideways nod.

"I'm ready to vote, Mr. President," he said. "Alfredo Sandoval."

Christa Landgraf slid her pad under Sunny's gaze. Linas slid his chair back, as if to make room for plaudits, but kept a blank face. Vera found Sunny with her eyes, and raised her chin slightly. Sunny tapped Christa Landgraf's pad with a pen and spoke slowly into the hushed chamber.

"I am informed that the chief of police will make an announcement in just a few moments. I am sure it is of interest to aldermen and to those watching. It has become a long afternoon, in any case, and it is the feeling of the chair that a recess would be welcome. Without objection," he said, pausing only briefly, "it is so ordered," and Sunny brought his hand down softly on the rostrum, as if tapping the head of a child.

At 4:04 p.m., Chief Martinez announced that Linda Marie Keely and Clifford Meadows had been arrested and charged with the murder of the mayor of Chicago.

Sgt. Gallaher and a phalanx of uniforms took Sunny into a service elevator and ascended to the twelfth floor, on the top of City Hall. The sergeant had to duck slightly as the doors opened into a gray and green jungle of overhead pipes and the crash and roar of boilers and elevator cables. They turned down a hallway Sunny had never seen. The sergeant threw her shoulder into an iron door that groaned open, like the top of a horror movie casket. Snow flurries surged in like fireflies. Sgt. Gallaher brushed them back with an arm, as the door opened onto the roof garden on top of City Hall.

Vera Barrow stood under a heat lamp of the kind that warmed waiting passengers at elevated train stops. She smiled, dropped a cigarette from the tips of her pink fingers into the snow, and stamped on it lightly with the toe of her high-heeled boots. Sunny heard the slightest hiss.

"I thought Matt did well," she said.

Sunny nodded and took Vera's hand. He kissed her cheek. They sat on a painted green bench that had, to all appearances, probably also been appropriated from the stores of the transit authority.

(A previous mayor had ordered the roof garden installed, to absorb rainfall, reflect heat, and confirm the city's environmental policies. Sunny had only seen the roof garden when the late mayor had invited him up in warm weather to smoke cigars. He remembered that under the crust and tumble of the current snow, there were 150 or so species of wild onions, in salute to the city's Pottawatomie name, butterfly weeds, buffalo grasses, and blue aster. In spring and summer, field sparrows, juncos, and peregrine falcons came to call.

When the late mayor had first been shown around, he asked a young man from the city's Environment Department how much money the garden saved each year in energy costs. The young man proudly and promptly replied, "About four thousand dollars."

The mayor grunted.

"And how much does it cost to maintain this little rain forest?" he asked. "You know, water, plant food, landscapers, horticulturalists, and whatever you call the highly paid professionals who clean up peregrine shit. Which I'm sure is recycled and made into exquisite jewelry for the City Hall gift shop."

The young man opened his mouth before he realized that he was stumped.

The mayor grunted again and walked on, stopping to flick an ash onto the bright yellow inflorescence of a blue aster. The young man hurried to catch up with his stride.

"I think the point is less to save money," he said, "than it is to *show* people how to save money."

"By *not* saving money?" The mayor strolled on, shaking his head. "Interesting approach."

"I know, sir, four thousand dollars doesn't sound like much against all the billions you deal with. But—"

"No sir," the mayor replied, dismissing the young man's apologia with a cutlass slash of his cigar. "A man can buy himself a couple of aldermen for that.")

Vera shook a monogrammed leather cigarette case from her sleeve and held the cigarette out between her fingers.

"I'm not going to make it, Sunny. Am I?"

Sunny took her hand and held it against his cheek to shake his head.

"When Jesus voted for Fred, we fell back," he said softly. "We had him down for Arty. Just as a place to park. I figured that by the time it got to him, you'd be three votes up. He'd calculate that he could get the TEZ on Twenty-sixth, and that would help him next year, even over in Sanford, Collie, and Linas's wards. But we didn't count on Fred. Jesus must have made some calls, taken some soundings. . . ."

Sunny's voice faltered.

"We can get you to twenty-one. Twenty-two with my vote. But . . ."

Then Sunny's voice gave out.

"Next round?"

"You might get a couple back from Fred," Sunny said softly. "But lose a couple to Daryl. Back to twenty-one. Do that twice and . . ."

Vera gently let go of Sunny's hand and put the cigarette to her lips. Flashes from her gold lighter made small sparks twinkle and disappear in her face.

"Folks start throwing over their shoes looking for lifeboats," she said to finish his sentence. "The time has come for me to tell you something," Vera continued. "Maybe I should have told you a year ago. I think I've got a few minutes to tell you now."

The sky above them was blackening. Wisps of heat from nearby rooftops and building grates froze into small bluish clouds that floated against the lights glaring from frosted glass windows in the buildings looming above them. Sunny heard screeches and a rumble of wheels from the elevated platform along Wabash. Wordlessly, he reached over for her cigarette case, and Vera tapped it against her alligator watchband until two filter tops poked out.

"I had a client named James Masterson," Vera Barrow began.

34

MONDAY NIGHT

"As a kid, James got caught up in South Side Insane Popes," Vera continued. She had taken a puff from her cigarette and passed it over to Sunny so that he might start up his own without fumbling for the lighter.

"He was in prison before he had to shave every day," she said. "By the time I heard of him, he was at Menard, and coming up for parole—again. He was *not* innocent. He was the lookout for a team that beat down some El Rukn in an alley near a school. So they could deal. This girl with three kids looped with chains and diamonds and everything black and gold got in to see someone at the firm. Flash around a few—more than a few—hundreds, and the drawbridges on LaSalle street snap off salutes. The girl said that James was a changed man. If he didn't get out, he'd be crushed. I guessed her money convinced us. Nobody asked, 'Did you win the lottery? Invest in Microsoft at just the right time?' "

She shook her head and expelled a cloud of smoke and frost.

"Our car service brought me down to Menard. 'When I heard the call was for you, Ms. Barrow,' the driver said, 'I thought we'd be going to Bloomingdales.' Two hours later, we were at the prison. The gates clanked. I had to clamp a tissue over my mouth and nose, daubed with Jean Patou. People piss and cum on every corner in that place, like it's the only way they have to chip away at it. But finally there was James in a conference room, beaming, like some kind of buff carnation. Shaved head like some wise walrus. Beautiful manners. 'Please. Thank you. Pardon.' He smelled—I'm not sure how he managed it in there—like tangerines.

"Sunny, I got to *know* James," she said with a shiver. "*Respect* him. He'd cleaned up. He'd read. He was trying to make peace inside between the Almighty Vice Lords, the Gangster Disciples, and the Popes. He'd been jumped, thrashed, and cut plenty—gave a little of it back, too—until those wild kids with electric eyes began to get what he was. The warden called him Mahatma. Third or fourth time I saw him, I noticed that he always had bandages around his wrist. I worried. Carefully, I asked how they got there. He said they covered his tattoos—the IP with the bloody sword piercing down. From then on, I started looking when they brought me through any common areas. Every fourth or fifth prisoner had bandages over their wrists. I thought, 'That's James. That's his power.' Sunny, what kind of man gets thrown into a hellhole and figures out a way to make it better? Have you known anyone in politics who'd done something that bold? That worthwhile?"

Sunny shook his head and shrugged his shoulders; the cold sharpened and leached into his bones.

"So I made a good argument," said Vera. "The warden was eloquent. James got parole. Moved in with his sister and began to work in our mailroom. Eighteen months, sterling record. People would leave packages with him—Macy's, Tiffany, Bloomies, never a problem. People would leave *their children* with him for the afternoon. One of our partners offered to put him through school. But James was already forty.

"I agreed to help get him a job on the outside. A man that noble shouldn't have to spend his adult life fetching coffee and steering a cart."

Vera shook her head as if just the right words might come out on top.

"But you know, Sunny, companies don't jump to hire someone like that. It's much easier to buy a table for a dinner for an ex-offender rehabilitation group. You get a tax deduction and rosemary garlic chicken.

"So I asked for *his* help," said Vera. "The mayor's," she added, unnecessarily. "There were maintenance openings in Chicago Park District field houses. James was good with his hands."

Sunny thought that he could see Vera's face flush slightly, even in the cold.

"It wasn't commodities trading. But a solid job. The mayor wrote Lucy Julian," said Vera. Sunny knew the name; she was in charge of Facilities Management for the South Region. "James was hired."

"Good Christ," said Sunny. "And James was the one. . . ."

"Yes," said Vera quietly. "Last November. Arrested for running drugs out of an equipment shed in the Douglas Nature Sanctuary."

"Old habits die hard?" he asked softly.

"Old friends don't let go."

"He needed the money?" asked Sunny. "The friends?"

"He needed to be free of me."

Vera clinched her collar against her throat as a tendril of wind slipped under the hot glare of the heat lamp.

"Sunny, there's something I left out," she said, looking over the edge of the Hall toward a bank building on Clark Street. "James and I. We were involved."

Sunny paused and smiled gently.

"Once or twice?"

"A week," she smiled back. "I told you once, Sunny. Everyone has a personal life. Whether they know it or not."

Sunny clasped his arms over his chest. He stretched his legs, and rocked back and forth on his heels for warmth as Vera went on.

"Always my place," she explained. "Of course—I'm sorry if that sounds smug. I had the cab downstairs to take him away at six because, after all, I had to go to the gym. I had a breakfast meeting. He began to feel humiliated. We never went out. Never a movie, never a restaurant. I was always getting bean and tofu pancakes delivered, because prison food fouls your guts. Sunny, what could I do? I was at the right hand of the mayor. I go to China, climb the Great Wall, and there are always a few tourists who wave, 'Hey, Alderman Barrow! We're from Glencoe!' I represent the Archdiocese of Chicago. I'm on the Harvard Board of Overseers. I couldn't bring a man covering up gang tats on his forearms into the University Club. I'm sorry if that sounds cold. If we took the Olympic committee to the Lyric Opera, I had to tell him he could stay home and watch TV in bed—like some kind of four-year-old."

The wind had begun to blow icy white grains from the top of the encrusted piles on the roof. The snow made Sunny rub the back of his hand over his eyes.

"You didn't ask me if I loved him," said Vera, and Sunny just shook his head. "I've been thinking how I'd answer when you did."

"That's a question for teenagers, Vera," he told her. "People who think love can make everything right."

"People will do things out of loneliness they wouldn't for love," said Vera, and Sunny drew his toe into a small pile of snow.

"Yes," he said simply. Vera's eyes seemed to scrunch against the snow, too.

"The mayor wrote the letter, Vera," Sunny pointed out. "It's on his hands. His cold, dead hands."

By the time she turned to Sunny, real tears simmered in her eyes; she held them back like gobs of spit.

"He wrote the letter, Sunny. It said, 'My good friend, Alderman Barrow, highly recommends Mr. James Masterson. I have misgivings.'"

"Black ink?" Sunny asked softly.

"Of course. Granted me my favor, and gave me away."

"*Bastard.*"

"No need for a blood test for that, is there Sunny?"

He blew burps of steam through his hands.

"The mayor could put your foot in a bear trap and make you think it was a glass slipper," he told Vera. "I just didn't think he'd do it to you. To *us.*"

Vera laced an arm through Sunny's and put her chin against his shoulder.

"Roland wanted to be mayor forever, Sunny. He didn't want anyone else to be mayor, ever. Not me, not Linas, not some Kennedy or Jesse Jackson IX. He thought he'd just be buried in that big leather chair and they'd never roll in another. The more times I got mentioned as his successor, the more he worried that I wouldn't wait around. He made sure to bury a land mine for me."

For the first time in their talk, Vera sat back on the bench and smiled without hurt and strain. She even opened the top of her coat at the collar.

"James took a plea," she went on. "We got a junior partner to handle it. I said I was too busy with council work. Everybody thought it was because I felt let down by him. It was a little more complicated, wasn't it? James is back in Menard. Happy, too, in a way, that he never was out here. In there, he has image. Authority. He counts. Out here, he's an ex-con—a middle-aged man pushing a cart down the hall. In there, he's the Mahatma."

She put a hand on his knee, squeezing lightly, as if touching a child's hand. She brought her polished bronze profile close to his mouth and chin.

"I'm radioactive, Sunny," she told him. "You can't see it yet. But . . ."

She shook her hands under her chin and flashed out her fingers, as if sending off sparks. "Weeks, months from now, it'll come out," she said. "It's not the story, but the headline, right? *Alderman Uses Clout to Put Drug Dealer in Park' 'Wise Old Mayor Issued Warning' 'Ex-Con Dealt Drugs from Alderman's Love Nest.'* "

Vera splayed her nails like a thousand sharp rays pinging through the night.

"You don't think some people won't be happy?" she asked. "Uppity colored girl brought low. . . ."

Sunny took Vera's hand, placed it softly under his chin, and gravely kissed her palm. True tears began to roll. Vera shuddered and squeezed her ribs to recover her breath. She began to turn around, left and right, flailing for a handbag, and realized that she hadn't brought it, only her cigarettes and lighter. Sunny drew the white linen from his lapel pocket, and Vera pressed it, folds and all, against her eyes and nose.

"What do I do now? Right now."

"Nothing," Sunny said after a small pause. "Make them play the game all the way through. See if something occurs. You've got votes in your pocket, and the sale is on. There's always the unexpected."

"Collins sent me a message Thursday night," she said. "Seems years ago, doesn't it? Within minutes, I'd guess. Something like, 'Dear Vera: We've lost our best friend. My heart feels so inky black.' "

"Oh good Christ," said Sunny. "That was supposed to be some sort of clever code?"

"I imagine," she said. "That rock will get turned over, too."

They both sat back on the bench. Fat flakes zipped over their heads, floated toward the hot light, then dropped wetly onto their hair and hands.

"I got to go with Arty over Fred," said Vera. "He's a clown and a fool but there's something there, somewhere."

She held a closed fist against her chest, but Sunny waved it off with the last glowing inch of his cigarette.

"Well no need to go diving into the earth's molten core just yet," he told her. "Let me try a few names first."

He saw Sgt. Gallaher wave from the groaning iron door, and Eldad Delaney trying to clop around the snowy clumps of bins and planters.

"Vera. Vera *dear*. Is there anything else I should know?"

She smiled and then buried it in her palms, raised her eyes to Sunny but put her fingers across her face, like slats in a fence.

"Linas and me," she said. "A three-day weekend in Aspen at a conference on 'restoring and rehabilitating urban ecosystems.' Never left the hotel room. Croque monsieur sandwiches, strawberries, and sparkling wine."

"A shame," said Sunny. "Aspen is lovely. I've seen postcards."

Vera shook her head.

"Altitude makes you do crazy things."

"Things you regret?" he asked, and Vera took her fingers down, one by one, before answering.

"Things you decide not to do again," she said softly.

From below, they could hear police whistles cheep and twitter as they turned back rush-hour traffic on LaSalle.

"Vera," said Sunny suddenly, "I thought we could do things right this time. I loved the mayor. Even—even now. But I thought this was our chance to do things right. Not always winking and scheming, begging and money grubbing, jiving and conniving. I thought we could do it right."

Eldad steadied himself on his smooth heels as he pulled up within a respectful distance of Sunny and Vera. He stayed silent, but Vera smiled back, and replied to Sunny in a low, hoarse voice.

"Sunny, maybe we just waited too long."

35

Sunny slipped into the big burgundy chair on the rostrum shortly after six-thirty. Aldermen began to drift back, mopping their mouths with the backs of their hands and resettling their belts, from pools of gossip. Sgt. McNulty came up behind Sunny and placed a hand gently on his shoulder.

"Second shift, sir," said the sergeant. "We didn't plan for quite so many curtain calls."

"Neither did I. Sgt. Gallaher is off duty?" he asked, perhaps a little too anxiously.

"Yes, but," said the sergeant, and when Sunny looked up he thought McNulty looked a little too blank-faced to be sincere.

"Sgt. Butler cadged a seat for her with your daughters," he explained. "She said the show was so good, she wanted to come back on her own time."

Sunny looked out into the gallery and picked out Rula and Rita among the bright-colored drooping snow parkas and sagging mufflers. He feigned surprise at the sight of Sgt. Gallaher, smiling alongside Rula.

"Sgt. Mo said that she went over the drill, sir."

"Yes. We pick a new mayor, and you drop me like an empty candy wrapper."

Sgt. McNulty rocked back on his size twelve brogues and stuck out his hand.

"If I don't get a proper chance to say goodbye. You ever need a parking ticket fixed, sir, I'm at the First District."

Sunny took McNulty's hand warmly and rose from his seat to the height of the sergeant's shoulders.

"And if you ever want the biryani of your life. . . ."

Lewis Karp tugged noisily on the coiled serpentine neck of his microphone. All but a few aldermen seemed to be in their chairs. Sunny nodded, pulled his own chair into the rostrum, and began in a soft voice, holding the scuba diver's gavel in his hands.

"The council will come to order," he began. "Again," he added, and soft chuckles wound around the chamber.

"I understand several aldermen have received complaints from citizens who do not appreciate having their favorite shows preempted by this prolonged session. And I am also told that television stations have received even more calls saying, 'These are the best afterschool cartoons we've ever seen.' " Sunny said in the rising clamor of handclaps and laughter.

"So we will endeavor to continue this important session with spirit, but also with a seriousness to reassure the city."

From a corner of his eye, Sunny saw Eldad approach and put a small, ivory scrap pad on the corner of the rostrum. Sunny rolled back slightly from the desk on his gilt wheels.

"Mr. Clerk, please resume the roll call," he said, and Lew Karp looked down into the center of the chamber.

"Kowalski, Twenty-three!"

"Artemus Agras," Felix called from his seat.

"Booker, Twenty-four!"

Sanford decided to stand, in his light gray suit with a blue stripe, and turn back to the gallery as he revved up an arm.

"Vera Barrow!"

The cheers rose and fell before Sunny could try to quiet them.

"Goo-tee-airrrez, Twenty-five!" trilled Lew Karp, and Alonzo shot up angrily from his seat, flailing his arms so fiercely that his red tie jumped.

"Question! Question Mr. President!" he cried.

"Questions are not usually entertained during a vote unless they are procedural," Sunny explained in an amiable tone. "But I don't want to stand on procedure."

"My question is germane, your honor," said the alderman. Alderman Guttierez had absorbed the phraseology of courtroom procedure from appearing as a witness in robbery cases of his own currency exchanges. "Why does the clerk announce every Spanish name like he's shouting '*Goooaalll!*' at the World Cup?"

Hoots flew up from the aldermen's seats as Alonzo tried to shout above the laughter.

"I don't hear him go, 'Ko-va*lll*-ski!' I don't hear him go, 'Kat-s*ooo*-lis!' "

"He sure has fun with my name," shouted Janet Watanabe, and Lew Karp steamed and burned above his tight white collar.

"Mr. President. Mr. President," he stammered, but Sunny was not about to let Lewie return fire. He held him back with a flat, friendly hand.

"I know the clerk. I think we all know that he enjoys every syllable of the immense variety of this city. I am glad to say that a roll call here is as diverse as the United Nations. I enjoy when Mr. Karp calls out, '*Rrrr-ooo-peee*-knee!' It makes me feel like I'm onstage at La Scala. But I will ask the clerk to tone down some of his artistic impulses."

Lew Karp began to clear his throat, but Sunny leaned forward into the microphone, and looked directly at Alonzo Guttierrez.

"And I will ask aldermen to keep a sense of humor and an open heart. Mr. Clerk," he said, gliding his chair back smoothly.

"You say my name just fine, Lewie!" John Wu barked from the second row, and Lew Karp let roars of "Wu! Wu!" subside before he went on.

"Guttierez, Twenty-five," he said softly, and Alonzo, who now simmered and slumped in his seat, called out even more softly, "Sandoval."

"Abboud, Twenty-six!"

Rod polished a gold pencil against his gray vest and called out,

"Agras," as blandly as if he had been asked to choose between mundane condiments.

"Stubbs, Twenty-seven!"

Donald's smooth copper head gleamed above everyone else's.

"Barrow!"

"Llll-ind-strom," trilled Lewie, and caught himself just as quickly, and so articulated "Twen-tee-ayt," as if an electronic chip had uttered it.

Astrid hunched forward on her elbows and drew a deep breath. "Sandoval," she said quietly.

"White, Twenty-nine!"

"Barrow."

"Rodriguez, Thirty," said Lew Karp in a studious, unaccented monotone.

"San-do-*vahl*," Wandy called back, then smiled and shrugged when Linas Slavinskas and Brock Lucchesi turned around from their desks in the front row.

"Zamora, Thirty-one!"

"Agras," said Luis, and there was a small stirring in the seats around him at the end of the row.

"I love you, Fred," he called down to the front row. "But Arty's got the *corazón* today." Sunny surmised that Luis had also calculated that Arty, even unelected, would be more likely to deliver the appointments Luis desired in the Department of Constructions and Permits than Alfredo Sandoval could in defeat. The roll call moved into the third row.

"Wagner, Thirty-two!"

"Excuse me, Mr. President. Mr. Clerk," said Emil. His doughboy cheeks burst cherry red with something he couldn't contain. "That's *Vahg*-ner."

Sunny let the laughter roll over the chamber. Linas Slavinskas chortled so hard that Brock Lucchesi had to pat his back, as if to bring up an egg roll. Eldad discreetly slid another message pad over to Sunny, who pointedly stayed with his smile even as his eyes played over the few words that Eldad had sketched on the pad. Alonzo Gutierrez looked up from the seat between Sandy Booker and Rod Abboud and announced, "All right, I'm an asshole." When this set off new whorls of reaction, Sunny leaned forward and began to rap the gavel gently.

"I'm sure the clerk will so note. Does the alderman of the Thirty-second Ward wish to give us his vote?"

"Sandoval," said Emil.

"Tierney, Thirty-three!" said Lew.

"Sandoval."

"Gregory, Thirty-four!"

Regina removed her black reading glasses and raised them over a shoulder.

"Barrow!"

"Viola, Thirty-five!"

Carlo, wearing one of his signature slouching black sweaters, rolled his thumbs over the Sanskrit green granite mandala around his neck.

"Eternity, unity, and Sandoval," announced Carlo.

After Keith Horn of the 36th and Vernetta Hyne Griffin of the 37th cast votes for Vera, Sunny caught Wandy's eye in the second row and beckoned him to preside. Sunny slipped back into a conference room. Aidan Ruffino of the 38th voted for Fred Sandoval. Torey del Raso stood when Lew Karp called out his name and hailed back, "Arr-tee! Arr-tee!" Cyril Murphy of the 40th voted for Fred. Ivan Becker of the 41st pretended to nap, jolted awake, rang his head from side to side like a cowbell, and said, "Barrow! Uh, Barrow!" Sidney Wineman was resting his head between his thumb and forefinger when he heard his name, then pulled on his wire-rim glasses to answer, "Barrow, absolutely," as if making a diagnoses. Kiera Malek said, "Me, too," which Lewie Karp did not stop to make her clarify. Sunny had returned to the rostrum to hear Lew ring out, "Walker, Forty-four!" when Wandy crept back and whispered to Sunny, "Keith needs a few minutes to recharge."

"So do we all," said Sunny, then pulled back to the desk.

"I think all aldermen could use a recess to refresh and restore before
we complete this roll call," he announced. "Our labors may stretch on."
He brought down the gavel hard to say, "Without objection, the council will return at seven *p.m.*," he added and set off scattered laughter.

Sunny motioned for the uniforms to hold back so that he could step
down and walk to the last row, where Keith Horn had piloted his chair
into an aisle.

Keith had a law office on west Belmont. He specialized in settling
estates and handling drunk driving pleas. He called his chair, powered
by a four-ampere charger, "my Learjet." When he was sixteen, Keith
had fallen during the first steps of a hundred-yard dash at a high school
track meet at Winnemac Park; other runners cursed and kicked gravel
into his eyes as they stepped over him. He was diagnosed with multi-
ple sclerosis. Keith's muscles were now as lean under his slacks as the
legs of a nine-year-old. He wore the same black shoes each day—and
why not?—that dangled, unscuffed, just above two flat footrests. For
the past few years, Keith's optic nerves had been popping and going
dark, like old lightbulbs in a dimming hallway.

"Keith, can we make you more comfortable somewhere?"

"I'm fine, Sunny," he said. "Sarge lets me lie down on a cot. You
know what you can do? Send down a couple of hot chicks."

"Sorry, Keith, the building's locked down. We can't even get hot
soup."

Keith pulled back slightly on the stick that steered his chair until it
locked with an electric belch.

"How's she doing?" he asked more softly. Sunny leaned down to
answer (which he usually refrained from doing with Keith—it made it
seem as if he was stooping to speak to a child).

"You know Vera," he told him. "Class. Pluck. Stiff upper lip."

"She'll get a better go at it next year."

Sunny kept his same, still expression, and answered only, "We can
hope."

Keith's red-rimmed eyes sizzled in his dark brown face.

"You got another plan?"

"Just to think of something else."

"Too late to think, Sunny," Keith told him, and began to push his chair forward over the sloping carpet. "You know politics. You have to do all your thinking before the votes are counted. Afterward, all you can do is live with your mistakes. Thanks for our annual conversation, Sunny," Keith called back sharply over the whizz of his small motor. "You don't have to worry about me again until next year."

Sunny had Arty Agras, Vera Barrow, Daryl Lloyd, Linas Slavinskas, and Alfredo Sandoval shown into the conference room. They left a chair at the head of the table for Sunny, and it was an unusual sensation to see heads swivel as he entered with Sgt. McNulty and two uniforms, and to realize that the meeting began as he sat down. Stuart Cohn and Christa Landgraf followed.

Linas had a white-lidded cup of coffee before him. Sunny asked, "Are you going to drink all of that?" Linas popped the top to spill some into a drinking glass for Sunny and pushed it across the table.

"Clearly, we seem stuck," Sunny began. "We are blessed with several outstanding candidates. But unless my calculations are wrong, none of you have enough votes to be elected mayor on this ballot. Or the next."

All heads seemed to swivel before fastening on Vera Barrow. Her delicate smile stayed sturdily unflustered; her sienna hair sprang back over her ears, unmussed. Her voice, when she finally broke the room's silence, was clear and strong.

"Yes, Mr. President," she said. "That's certainly true for me."

Arty Agras grumbled agreement. Daryl Lloyd shifted in his seat, but said nothing. Fred Sandoval nodded once, down and up.

"I think the time has come to explore a few other names. We have a real election coming up in a little over a year. But the city needs leader-

ship until then, too. The people in this room represent such an invigo-
rating range of ideas." Linas Slavinskas appreciated Sunny's phrase,
and fought down a smile. "If you can agree on a candidate to occupy the
office for the next year, his or her name can be proposed before this ballot ends. He or she might be approved by acclamation. The city will
have united leadership at a challenging time. And be grateful to you all,
I'm sure."

The aldermen sat back in their office chairs.

"Grace Brown," Sunny suggested without elaboration, and pushed
back from the table, as if he had just overturned a water pitcher. Linas
pressed both hands against his chin, and Vera pushed the tip of a gold
pen over her front teeth. Arty Agras flicked a dot on his tie, before
Daryl Lloyd offered the first reaction.

"She's a stalking horse for Vera."

"I'd suggest a stalking horse for you, Daryl," said Sunny. "If you
could win even one other person's vote."

The aldermen erupted in snickers and ooohs. Arty Agras finally
reached across the table for Daryl's unbandaged hand.

"Grace, I love Grace, but he makes a good point," said Arty. "She'd
be extremely suggestible to suggestion."

"At least Grace doesn't sit on my lap," snapped Vera, looking at
Linas and Fred Sandoval, side by side. "Singing 'Bye-bye Blackbird'
when I pull the string."

Sunny folded his arms over his chest and shook his head. "Grace is
smart and honest," he declared, but knew that he was beginning to
scold; aldermen turned away with showy indifference.

"Alright," he announced. "Astrid Lindstrom."

The aldermen turned to look at Daryl Lloyd. He let the fingers poking from his sling drum a line over his forearm.

"I love Astrid," he said. "But . . ."

"But?" Sunny asked sharply.

"I *love* Astrid," Daryl repeated with audibly escalated sincerity.
"Love her, love her, *love her*. More than once, she's picked me off the
floor. Ways you don't even know," he said, and had to break his gaze

away from the table. "But we've got millions of people in this city who would consider that a setback. The council would let a couple of assassins—young white assassins, you see their pictures all over TV now—take away something that we worked for."

"Is that how you feel?" Sunny asked, staying stern.

"Of course not. I love Astrid. But others . . ."

"Yes. It's always the *others*, isn't it?" Sunny shook his head with dramatic despair. "Twelve years on the council, and that's the worst you have on Astrid?"

"Don't tell me color doesn't count, Sunny," said Daryl Lloyd. "In this city? It comes in with the wind. You can't brag all the time on all this diversity and not expect people to keep score."

"Well I'd support her," Vera declared, crossing her legs with a silken rustle and raising herself notably above Daryl. "Smart, tough, good."

"So would I," said Linas, but Fred Sandoval was already moving a large hand over to Linas's shoulder.

"You don't have votes to give away, Linas," he reminded him.

"She just voted for you," Sunny pointed out.

"I love Astrid, too, Sunny," Fred implored Sunny. His brown eyes looked like swollen acorns under his heavy black glasses. "And I don't go for any of that other stuff. But we've gone too far down a different road to turn back. People expect the kind of change they can see now. Something different."

Sunny rose and began to walk around his seat. When he had settled his hands on the back of his chair, Linas Slavinskas actually raised his hand for recognition.

"No offense to my friend here," he said, nodding toward Arty Agras. "But we've got a guy sleeping with two guy police guards who's considered middle of the road, and a mother of seven kids is too controversial. Only in America."

The aldermen had all pushed back from the table to throw back their heads with guffaws when Sunny pulled up his chair and threw them another name.

"Steven Price," he proposed.

Steve Price was the founder of Muriél Aeronautics. He was a self-made man, round-shouldered and steely-jawed even into his sixties, who had earned a Bronze Star in Vietnam and millions in his helicopter business. His name was often bruited between elections as a candidate that either party wanted to recruit for governor. He had grown up in a fatherless household in Detroit's Sojourner Truth housing projects and excelled at West Point. Every few years, Steve piloted one of his own copters to some new airspeed record. Every February, his calendar brimmed with school assemblies during African-American history month. Every May, six engineering students from poor families graduated from the Illinois Institute of Technology because (as they had no idea) Steve Price had paid their tuition.

But Steven Price had never run for governor. He was too fond of gun control for Republicans and disdained teachers' unions too much for Democrats. Once, as he contemplated running as an independent, the *Tribune* ran a feature on Steve Price's daredevil high-altitude balloon expeditions. An accompanying photo showed Steve in his silvery flight pajamas, next to the lissome young co-pilot to whom he was not married. The caption said, "Cabin temperatures can sink to 40 degrees," and the mayor, along with hundreds of thousands of other readers, murmered aloud, "Betcha Steve stays warm."

Steve Price forswore politics thereafter. He figured out that each party had flattered him only to pick freely of his fathomless pockets and deduced that spending thirty million dollars of his own money to win a $200,000 a year job was a preposterous business model.

The aldermen quieted at his name. Vera looked across the table to Linas Slavinskas.

"Brooks Whetstone had something."

"The usual," said Linas. "Gifts to people purchasing for the Pentagon, the RAF, and Israel. A few low-down indictments, nothing tied to Steve."

"I'll bet they were wined and dined pretty fancy to buy helicopters," said Arty Agras, swabbing a hand against his chin.

"If he's mayor, our police can't buy his helicopters," said Fred Sandoval, and Sunny turned tartly toward the alderman.

"When did you read an ethics regulation, Fred? If we have to, we'll buy them from North Korea," he added.

"Poland," said Linas Slavinskas.

"Of course Steve Price is a Republican," said Daryl Lloyd, with the same studied nonchalance Sunny's daughters displayed to tell him that a famous film star was absolutely, positively (everyone knew it; how had Sunny never heard of it?) gay.

"Who knows? He gave a lot of money to the mayor," Vera pointed out. "It's the only way you get a seat in the game."

"Then he's perfect," Linas concluded. "Smart. Unindicted. And if he fucks up, he's a Republican."

"Sunny, he doesn't want it," Arty Agras said suddenly. Sunny paused before he replied.

"I've had a word with him, Arty. Mr. Price says he understands these are special circumstances. He would be willing to serve until the election next year. After that, he intends to run the foundation that bears his name. Near his place in West Palm Beach."

But Arty Agras shook his head so widely that his shoulders twisted and his tie slipped out.

"He doesn't want *it*, Sunny," he persisted. "Steve Price might like putting hiring and firing. Or going to mayor's conferences, though a guy like that has probably already been to Sun Valley and San Juan. He'd probably like showing the queen of England around Wrigley Field. But he doesn't want *it*, Sunny. Anyone who's mayor, even for just a year, has to be able to spend Thursday night at the South Austin Community Council listening to every goddamn gripe about slow bus service on Roosevelt Road and hearing the parking regulations on Cicero compared to the Nuremberg Laws. He can come back here to the Hall and make fun of the blue-haired lady who got up in the middle of something important to say that the purple martin swallow should be the civic bird. But he also has to love it a little, am I right? The city deserves that. At least that."

The pause that followed was so long, Sunny began to count to himself. Aldermen looked across the table, looked down, looked back. By the time he reached six, Sunny said, "Artemus, you brim with wisdom today."

The aldermen began to stand, brush their hands over wrinkles, shake out their legs, and stretch their backs.

"I might have another thought," Sunny said before they could begin to step away from their chairs. The overhead lights buzzed and made the aldermen blink their eyes as they turned.

37

Arty, who was ordinarily fastidious to the point of fussy, had tiny green glops of exhaustion in the corners of his eyes that he tried to catch with an index finger. Vera's richly painted eyebrows had begun to flake, faintly. Daryl Lloyd's forehead shone. Linas Slavinskas had bitten three of the nails on his left hand, and Linas usually wore clear polish. Sunny sat down, smiled, and lifted his phone in his hand.

"I've also been speaking to Taber John Palmer," he began.

Dr. Palmer was the recently retired chancellor of the University of Illinois campus in Chicago (and with distinction, though several reports had raised questions about spending he had authorized to recruit promising athletes in west Africa). His name summoned an image of an elderly, sunny-faced man with a soft crown of silver hair, courtly manner, and kindly uncle eyes.

"A distinguished educator," Sunny continued. "The author of acclaimed biographies of Fredrick Douglass, Leroy Paige, and Duke Ellington. Winner of the Bancroft Prize for American History."

Sunny looked at a paper he had taken from his coat and paused to find something that he had circled on. "He has served on and chaired presidential commissions on poverty, race relations, and preschool education. He has more honorary degrees than Alderman Slavinskas here has cufflinks." The aldermen sat back and barked. "He also serves on almost as many corporate boards." Sunny read off the names, like items on a takeout menu. "All-State Insurance, Bally Total Fitness, Northern Trust, Quaker Oats, the *Tribune.* Yello."

"Free checking, free breakfast, free Internet, and a gym pass," said Linas. "I've met him. He's a hoot. He's clever. But I don't know. . . ."

"You want this Taliban John Palmer to chair a commission, Sunny?" asked Arty Agras.

"Alderman Roopini wants him to chair *us,* Arty," Linas Slavinskas said, looking across the table. "With a chair and whip. The other names were just tin cans. Sunny gave us a little target practice. He's suggesting that we make the professor mayor."

Arty's jaw slumped. He looked over at Vera, then Fred Sandoval, then back at Sunny.

"He's written good books, I'm sure," he told Sunny directly. "But he has no experience."

"So he has fresh ideas."

"Would you choose a brain surgeon who didn't have any experience?" asked Linas. "Just a lot of fresh ideas?"

"Maybe to operate on you, Linas," Vera offered.

"Politics isn't brain surgery," answered Sunny. "We're living proof. Someone who can choose good people to do a few worthwhile things— I'd settle for that."

"He doesn't know *politics,*" Daryl Lloyd said more sharply.

"A university president?" Sunny raised his eyebrows in return, as if challenging something his daughters had passed on from a smart-aleck friend. "I'll bet he plays politics at least as well as someone who's never run for office north of the Orange Line."

The other aldermen groaned and clapped at Sunny's gibe, so tellingly tailored to Daryl's ward. But before they could catch their breaths, Stuart Cohn had made a thrumming sound in the back of his throat until the aldermen had turned around to face him. Sunny had made sure that Cohn and Christa Landgraf sat against the wall. They had been summoned there to counsel elected officials, not share their deliberations.

"This is all very creative," he said with his courtroom raptor's countenance. "But I've just checked statutes. The law states that the council has to elect an alderman mayor. No civilians. So someone in the council would have to resign. Let's say you can get someone to do that tomorrow. Even tonight. Then Mr. Roopini here could appoint Dr. Palmer to take that seat, and he could receive votes for mayor. But the law also clearly states that the new mayor has to be chosen at the first business session following the resignation or expiry of the old mayor. That's this session. The meeting we're in now. Your interesting idea, Mr. Roopini, may be a few hours too late."

"We're recessed," Vera Barrow pointed out. "Can't we just stay in recess and come back in a few days? It's a legalism, but—"

"You mean leave without ending the meeting? Get out before we choose a mayor? We'd be laughingstocks," said Fred Sandoval.

"We're not?" asked Vera.

"I'd have to gavel that down," said Sunny quietly, after a pause. "As Stuart says, the law is clear. And it's right. We're elected to disagree, raise our voices, threaten, trade, but finally *do something*. Politics isn't supposed to be just putting a live wire up the public's ass and turning their stomach rumbles into policies. Some things—this thing right now—we're supposed to do on our own. We can't just duck and wait to hear voices from a burning bush. We have to decide."

The buzz of the lights suddenly made Sunny slap the back of his neck. He could feel his shirt chafe and sting like a grimy bandage. His feet itched. His hands tingled. He wanted to open a hole in the back of his head. Steam and brine, he guessed, would trickle out. After a pause, he looked down the table to Stuart Cohn and Christa Landgraf.

"Let me ask our learned counsels." Sunny paused to take a breath. "What if I resigned as alderman of the Forty-eighth Ward right now? And then, as acting interim mayor, I appointed Dr. Palmer alderman in my place?"

Christa Landgraf began to run a thumb over the spine of an ordinance book, but Stuart Cohn offered an answer instantly.

"You can't resign as alderman and be acting interim mayor."

"What if I did it in the same second?" asked Sunny, lifting one of the white printed sheets in front of him. "Not page one, then page two, but two sides of the same paper at the same instant?"

Sunny flipped the page, back and forth, back and forth, as if performing a card trick. Cohn stared into the wall behind Sunny, as if trying to count the rustles and swishes.

"That's a chicken or egg question," he said. "Which comes first, the resignation or the appointment? As presiding officer, your interpretation would prevail. As long as it were upheld by the council."

"*Yes*," said Christa Landgraf. "But, no." She had thrown back a page and pressed the stub of a short pencil into a boldfaced line. "You couldn't appoint Dr. Palmer alderman until he's registered in that ward. I'd guess he's registered in the Second or Forty-second. Not the Forty-eighth."

"This time of year," said Arty Agras, "he's probably teaching in-amorata, or whatever you call it, in Orlando or Cuernevaca." Arty pronounced the name of the Mexican town as if it were a country Irish dish.

"That just shows he's smart," said Vera. Sunny pressed his fingers together in a steeple below his chin.

"This is Chicago," he said. "The dead can vote. Surely we can figure out a way to register a man who's still alive."

Stuart Cohn had turned his forehead down into his palms and rubbed his temples with the heels of his hands. Then he stopped. Stuart never took off his glasses in public—he felt it would be as perturbing and revealing as removing a toupee—but now he raised his glasses from his nose, pinched himself between the eyes, and resettled his spectacles.

"The clerk could call you to cast your vote," he began. "You could pass, you could vote for Alderman Barrow, you could vote for Mickey Mouse."

"There's an idea," said Linas, but Vera Barrow held out a hand to hold off another jest.

"The specific vote doesn't matter," said Stuart Cohn. "But once you cast it, it has to be counted at the end of this ballot. So you could write out your resignation from the council, and present it to yourself as acting interim mayor. You could accept it. You could tell yourself what an honor it has been to serve with yourself. But you would remain acting interim mayor until the roll call we're in now is over and the results have been declared. So on the same sheet of paper, Acting Interim Mayor Roopini could appoint Dr. Taber John Palmer to succeed Alderman Roopini as alderman of the Forty-eighth Ward. Then one of the fifty aldermen could rise, ask if they are recorded on this vote, and cast their vote for Dr. Palmer. The stampede of popular support would be free to proceed."

Cohn looked over to Christa Landgraf, who had folded her glasses into her palm; as if she couldn't bear to watch.

"The registration problem is real," he conceded directly to her, then looked down the table toward Sunny. "So you should establish an address for Dr. Palmer in the Forty-eighth right now. A spare bedroom, somebody's sofa. Wait—a motel room. You can book it and get a printed confirmation back by email. An alderman must be a registered voter of his ward, and you can't be a registered voter unless you've lived in the precinct for thirty days. But if the council elects him mayor, it would take thirty days for a challenge to reach the courts. I can practically guarantee such a delay," he said softly. "By the time any case was heard, Dr. Palmer would have been freely elected mayor by a duly constituted City Council. And I can't see any court overturning an open democratic election that millions of people have followed, vote by vote. Especially if it leads to Taber Palmer."

Cohn sat back and tossed his gold pen into the open pages of the city code. The aldermen sat back, waiting in unspoken consent for a first reaction.

"My God, Stuart," Vera Barrow said finally. "That's breathtaking."

Arty Agras put his head against the smooth oak table, turned his head to the side, then sat back up to speak.

"My God yes. No offense to you, Vera. Or Linas. Or you either, Miss Landgraf. But Jewish lawyers . . ." Arty shook his head with reverence, the way some people paid homage to Cuban cigars, continental cuisine, or Nazi storm troopers.

Linas shifted in his seat, impressed but unconvinced.

"When you want to head back into private practice, Stu, give me a call. But that may be too much of a trick shot, even for me."

"Taber John Palmer is a man of quality," Sunny said in a subdued tone just above a whisper; for the first time, it conveyed a note of pleading. "The city deserves a little of that now. I've spoken with him a little. He says he is eager to serve the city he says gave him a chance when Itta Bena, Mississippi, didn't. It's getting ugly out there on the floor, all laughs aside. All the back and forth over Lewie Karp's incredible performing tongue came too close to breaking out into clan warfare. I don't want to give tired people more opportunity to say things we'll all regret tomorrow—and hurt this city."

"Silly, scattered, late night arguments, your lordship," said Linas.

"Like most homicides," said Sunny. They heard the satiny swoosh of Vera Barrow stretching her legs again.

"I like it," she said. "Extraordinary developments call for an extraordinary solution. And he's retired—not likely to run next year. We all get extra time to sharpen our knives. Or class up our acts."

Sunny held a hand over Alfredo Sandoval's elbow and clutched it just lightly. Fred ran his tongue over his lips and finally let out a sigh. Sunny could see Fred's chest constrict under his plaid coat.

"I can live with it," he said.

"What does the professor teach?" asked Daryl Lloyd.

"History. Political science," said Sunny, and the aldermen could hear Daryl run the back of a hand back and forth over the bristles on his cheeks that had grown back over twelve hours.

"Maybe he'll find out that politics isn't as easy as it looks in the books," he said.

"Hear, hear," Arty chimed.

All the aldermen looked away from Linas so that Sunny, at the end of the table, was the only set of fretful, imploring eyes.

"You have your votes," Linas told him flatly.

"I *want* your opinion, Linas," said Sunny. "Anyway. Regardless. No one's voted yet."

Linas uncrossed and stretched his own long legs and sat forward. There was a debonair creak of leather from the heels of his slim Italian boots. He found a tissue from his breast pocket, pressed it to his forehead, and spent a moment looking for something in the folds.

"People always look for someone above the battle," Linas finally told them. "No mud on their shoes, blood on their hands. The Immaculate Contender. Well, I think the battle teaches you something. Every single scar."

He sat back and moved the heel of his hand slowly across his chin, until it sounded like the edge of a steel door scraping a sidewalk.

"Will he help my daughters with their homework?" he asked.

Eldad Delaney had entered softly through the door behind Sunny. As the aldermen broke into a last round of worn-out laughter, and he whispered something. Sunny looked down the table at Christa Landgraf.

"Let's put the pieces in place," he said. "Mr. Delaney will call Dr. Palmer. Let's book him a room at the Argyle House." It was a bed and breakfast in the Forty-eighth that won four stars in many gay travel guides. "They have fresh poppy seed muffins in the morning. And I'll enjoy watching you and Professor Palmer do best by this city over the next year.

"Chief Martinez is outside," he added. "Under the circumstances, I suggest that he speak to us all."

38

Matt Martinez had not changed from the blue leather service jacket he had worn to preside at the booking of Clifford Meadows in a holding cell on south State Street twelve hours earlier. The creak of his jacket's blue sleeves in the cold had irritated him for at least the last four hours. The chief felt gray, as if his skin had grown a top layer of scales. Sunny surrendered his own chair, and the police chief sat down heavily.

"God's Good Earth Warriors," he began. "They are—I don't know. Activists. Concerned citizens. Militants. Terrorists. Shits. *Shits,*" he finally pronounced.

"They say they wanted to dramatize the dangers of unknown substances creeping into food supplies. So they slipped a toxic substance into the mayor's food supply. The mayor? He was just unlucky enough to be a target of opportunity. If Meadows had met a monk with the Dalai Lama, or Oprah's hairstylist, there might have been a different victim. Claudia McCarthy stopped in for coffee every morning when she got off the Brown Line. Men notice her, right? Meadows worked behind the counter, and he noticed her. Noticed that she used soymilk. Found out—maybe he overheard—that she worked for the mayor. His mind began to work. I mean, if you're going to penetrate the mayor's inner circle, what better way than Claudia?"

Matt Martinez finally took off his checker-brimmed hat and laid it in his lap. He quickly ran his fingers through his hair to lift it from his scalp.

"Between all the frothing and sprinkling, Claudia told Meadows about the mayor's routines. His habits. His appetites. She didn't realize it, of course. She was just making conversation. Maybe trying to impress Meadows a little with her job. Meadows probably didn't have to ask very much. After a while, Claudia realized that they never went to his place. He said it was being renovated. He said he had roommates. He said he had dirty dishes. He never answered his phone. He said it was his brother, and they didn't get along. Which seems to be true, by the way. After a while, Claudia figured out that she was being used. She just thought it was in the traditional manner. Six weeks ago, she stopped seeing him. By then, Meadows had gotten all he wanted. All the information that was necessary to plant the poison and kill the mayor to make . . ." Chief Martinez fairly spat the last words, "their point."

Arty Agras was the first alderman to speak. His words were slow, and tinged with incomprehension, as if he were trying to read words in a book in a dream.

"So, Matt. The people who killed the mayor. They—they're—orgasmic food nuts?"

Linas Slavinskas caught Sunny's eye. They both fought down grins. Chief Martinez ignored, or didn't catch, Arty's phrasing.

"What did you expect, alderman? Mafiosi? Hit teams from the KGB? Nuts do the job just fine."

Vera Barrow had reached over to see some of the sheets from police reports.

"They're protesting transgenic life forms," she reported with a rare tone of wonder.

"What the hell," said Daryl Lloyd. "Martians?"

"Scientists putting fish genes in tomatoes," the chief explained. "Genes from a flounder being put in tomatoes to keep them from freezing. Rat genes being put into cattle so that cows reproduce like rats."

"What the hell?" said Fred Sandoval. "Here? Not on Mars? Not even California? I never heard . . ."

"Now you will," said Sunny. "For a couple of days. These people are against it."

Arty stood up from the table. He began to take short, stumbling, teetering steps, like a clubbed boxer trying to stagger to the ropes.

"Christ, I think I am, too. Fish crap in tomatoes!" said Arty. "What the hell, what the hell. But Sunny, what did the mayor have to do with that? How could anyone possibly think that something like this helps whatever the hell they're for or against? Killing a good man . . ." Soft, fat tears began to bubble in Arty's eyes. "A man who looked his enemies in the face." Yes, thought Sunny. Only his friends had to worry. "It's indecent. It's stupid. It's barbaric."

Sunny let silence take over the room. They heard a lone cry from a late-night elevated train, the click of a door nearby and low, muttering voices of police shifts coming and going as clock hands began sweeping up toward midnight. Sunny rose and put his arms around Arty and guided him into a seat.

"That's what they count on, my friend," he said gently. "That's what they *believe* in. Nothing gets attention like a shot, a blast, a satchel going off in the subway. People don't have to know what you stand for, just what you're willing to do. Are you willing to rig bombs in a school? Drop a rocket on a hospital? Strap a bomb to your guts on the bus? Fly head first into a city? That's what makes a mark. That's how thugs make smart people cower. Blow up babies, behead bystanders, send old ladies crawling, and little girls screaming and crying like sirens—that's when crowns change heads, talking heads blather, and armies march. How does something as drab as politics compete? And the way we behave—why should anyone think that politics could even change a man's socks? So people try to capture history with a single shot, a draught of poison, or stealing planes in the sky. Politics? Ridiculous. You might as well throw pebbles under a train. How tiresome. How compromising. How square."

Sunny settled Arty into a seat, and Vera Barrow took his hands.

Arty began to shudder, like a small boy with blue lips, wet beside a swimming pool. Linas Slavinskas rose and put his hands on Arty's shoulders. Sunny turned around to the chief of police.

"Thank you, Matt. *Chief*. Let's take a moment, aldermen," he said. "I have a couple of short notes to write. Then let's finish the roll call."

They could hear Lewie Karp in the hallway outside. He drummed the top of a tin popcorn can with his knuckles and called out, "Does anyone here want to play this game?"

39

The conference room door sprang open with a bang of the door against a chair. Rula and Rita burst in, eyes brimming, noses running, wiping their fingers over their eyes and onto the bottoms of their sweaters. Eldad had told them . . . something.

"Oh, Pappaji, are you sure? Are you sure?" said Rula.

"You'll be bored, you'll be angry," Rita sniffled. "You'll blame us. You'll just sit around with Sheldon, scratching."

"She never wanted this, you know," said Rula. A thick tuft of her sable hair had fallen over an eye. When Rula clamped a hand over the tears in her other eye, she couldn't see what was in front of her; her legs began to crumple. Sunny took her into his arms. She was so convincingly independent that Sunny had to remind himself that their older daughter felt responsible for everything—bird flu, Great Lakes pollution, the valuation of the yuan—and registered hurt like a thermometer.

"Mammaji would say stay," Rula burbled and rasped. "She loved you. She was proud of you. She used to say, 'It's a dirty job but someone has to do it? My husband does.'"

"I'll count on you to keep life interesting," said Sunny.

"Bloody hell," snapped Rita through a slick of tears. Then she laughed. "Not that, too."

Eldad stepped back into the room and tentatively approached their giggling embrace. His face was full, red, and beginning to break.

"It's terrible, alderman," he said. "A terrible, irrecoverable, magnificent loss."

"You gush to my face now, Eldad," Sunny told him. "But the next alderman you work for, you'll tell how I pick my teeth with my fingernails and sneak a nap after lunch. How I don't always digest asparagus."

Sunny's daughters parted partway from their embrace, so their father could face Eldad.

"You're opening a new restaurant?" Eldad asked. "All my life, I've heard that I'm supercilious enough to be a great headwaiter."

"You have all the tools," Sunny agreed. "But you've got important work to do. Aldermen to paper train. Maybe you can help the new mayor. I can write you a letter of recommendation now, you know, once I'm a civilian. Just come by our place for dinner now and then."

Eldad held on to Sunny and Sunny squeezed back, gripping his shoulders and patting his back. Each man tried to croak, "Thank you, thank you," through his clotted throat. They clasped each other so tightly that Sunny's daughters stepped around them and pretended to look at the maps and photos on the wall. Their father had become so ridiculous to them: scratching, drinking, curling up with their cat, and falling asleep in front of old cops-and-robbers, next to a bottle on the nightstand. But they had to heed, even as they couldn't quite decipher, the devotion of an outsider. It gave a glimpse of a part of their father that their mother must have once seen. It was like finding a forgotten family photograph lost in the back of an old book and thinking, "My father? Are you sure?"

Sunny wrote his notes and reached the rostrum a little after nine. Word had passed around the chamber. He could see chihuahuas chatter in the press seats and look toward him more than usual; he even caught one pointing to Rula and Rita. He caught a glimpse of a monitor, and saw that television trucks had turned stadium lights on Taber John Palmer's home on west Sixteenth Street (which was indeed in the 2nd

Ward). An excited voice announced that the professor had flashed a quick wave from a second-story window, then drew his curtains. Another agreed that his books were judged to be extremely distinguished by those who had read them.

"The council will please come to order," Sunny announced. "Welcome to the late show."

The laughter was much larger than such a meager line deserved; even reporters laughed. Sunny knew that he was being flattered.

He looked down into the second row, to the first desk in that cluster of five seats, and nodded at Donald Stubbs. "The chair will ask the alderman of the Twenty-seventh Ward to preside." Sunny came down to the floor from the right side of the rostrum, landing just as Don reached the four-step stairs. Don took Sunny's right hand into his own and then threw his left arm around Sunny's shoulders.

"My man," said Don Stubbs.

Sunny had to tilt his chin to look into Don's face; it made his neck twinge as if he were trying to see the top of a tall building from the street.

"I'd like to go out in my seat," he told Don.

Sunny walked past Collie Kerrigan of the 14th, who reached out for his hand, and Luis Zamora of the 31st, who patted the small of his back. He turned left past Jacobo Sefran and Anders Berggren, finally pulling out the back of the blue leather chair and sitting down beside Anders and Cassie Katsoulis.

"Missed you," said Anders. Jaco blew him a kiss from two seats away and laughed. Cassie leaned over and smacked her lips loudly against his cheek. "Love you madly," she said. Wandy, Astrid, and Gerry White turned around in their seats from their desks and extended their hands to Sunny. Astrid let her hand linger on Sunny's for a moment and squeezed. They heard Lew Karp call out, "Wojcik, Forty-five!"and Adam, just three seats down, call back, "Art Agras." Sunny's note on the single sheet of paper rested under Lewie's elbow. He had had to clutch his right wrist to steady and strengthen his hand as he wrote his name. Should the note wind up in a plastic sleeve in a library some day, he wanted whoever tried to decipher it to be able to make out at least his name.

Sunny was so absorbed that he didn't hear Lew call Jane Siegel's name. But Jane's snap-crackling whip of a voice brushed his ears when she called back, "Barrow!" Sunny ran his hands over the stubby leather arms of his blue chair. He had known aldermen who had bought their chairs when they left the council (in fact old Stefano Tripoli of the 11th, who objected on principle to paying for what a man could have for free, had been caught trying to roll his chair into the trunk of a cab on Clark Street). You'd see their old aldermanic chairs appear thereafter in a basement or alcove, tagged with a brass plaque, like a hunting trophy for the desk-bound. Sunny didn't think he'd do that. His chair would only be in the way among the tubs of onions, cloves, moong dal, cumin, and cardamom seeds.

"Katsoulis, Forty-seven!"

"Agras," she said, and patted Sunny's arm. Lew Karp seemed to pause, then rang out, "*Rrrooo-peee-kneee*, Forty-eight!"

There were ripples of laughter; no objections. Sunny decided to stay in his seat, but swiveled slightly to his right to be able to catch the look of his daughters. Rula and Rita beamed back, eyes brimming. He turned his seat back toward the rostrum and announced, "Very proudly, for Vera Barrow." Several handclaps burst out in the gallery. Don Stubbs let them be.

"Berggren, Forty-nine!" called Lew. Anders pulled up to his desk to say, "Agras," and Sunny sat up and steadied himself against the desk for the last vote and what would follow. Don Stubbs had turned to Lew Karp. His hand folded over the small microphone reminded Sunny of a bear enwrapping a berry. He could hear his note brush Lew's microphone as he lifted it up. Donald took off his hand and turned back to his microphone as he looked down at Sunny.

"The alderman of the Forty-eighth Ward," he said, "should preside for this last vote."

The clock behind the rostrum gave off a tin *pop!* as it snapped down to nine-fifteen as Sunny walked back to the stairs in the chamber's sudden, consummate silence. He heard the sole of his shoes scuff against the hard brown carpet of each of the four stairs. Don Stubbs was there to take his hand and swing the back of the mayor's burgundy chair around so that the deep red seat faced Sunny.

"Go out in the big chair," Donald told him.

Sunny sat down and drew himself up to the rostrum with a smile. He nodded down at Lew Karp to proceed.

"Sefran, Fifty!" called Lew. Sunny could see Jaco begin to rise, but before he could answer, Evelyn Lee had climbed to her feet and waved a yellow legal pad of paper for recognition.

"Mis-ter President!" she called. "Mis-ter President!" Shirley Watson of the 16th, sitting to her left, put her arms against Evelyn's hip to steady her as she waved; so she waved harder. Sunny was puzzled but not displeased; it was another minute to hold the smooth gavel in his hand, to call out names, and thread a way through problems with immediate and practical answers.

"Does the alderman have a procedural question?" he asked.

"Yes. Am I recorded on this vote?"

"Oh," Sunny heard himself say. Now that Vera had fallen short in this ballot, Evelyn might want to record a vote for Fred Sandoval before the count was closed. The change would do Vera no harm on the ballot; it might do Evelyn some good in her ward. You had to let someone who gave you a vote when it really counted make the best arrangement for herself when it no longer did. Sunny nodded gravely to Lew Karp.

"The alderman is recorded as voting for Vera Barrow," he replied.

Evelyn had handed the pad to Shirley Watson. She wrung her knotted hands.

"Well I would like to change the way you have recorded my vote," she announced.

"To what, alderman?"

"Sundaran Roopini," said Evelyn. There was a quick handclap from someone in the gallery, swiftly hushed. Sunny was perplexed, but leaned forward with a smile.

"The chair thanks the alderman," he said. "But my service here has been honor enough. Maybe a tie for the holidays; I have always ad-

mired the alderman's taste. But the chair is not a candidate for mayor."
Sunny tugged up his tie again and sat back from the rostrum.

Evelyn Lee stayed on her feet.

"The alderman is not offering a tribute. I am casting a vote. I think
the ringmaster ought to know the animals by name," she said, and
when the aldermen surrounding Evelyn began to laugh and clap, including Dorothy Fisher of the 3rd and Wanda Jackson of the 4th in
front of her, and Regina Gregory of the 34th at her desk behind, Sunny
decided to amiably move on.

"The chair thanks the alderman. And now, Mr. Clerk—"

"Mr. President! Mr. President!" It was Wandy Rodriguez on the
other side of the chamber. "Mr. President, am I recorded on this vote?"
Sunny could not look past Wandy; he had carried too much for him. He
lifted his left hand to hold back Lew Karp's reading of the final totals
for a moment and answered, "I remember that one myself. You are
recorded as voting for Alderman Sandoval."

"However," said Wandy. "I would like to change the way I am
recorded."

"It is the alderman's right," said Sunny, uncertainty making his
voice quaver, as if he had tried to hold a long note.

"Put me down for Roopini, too," said Wandy.

"Rodriguez, Thirty!" Lew Karp repeated at full cry. "Votes for
Roopini."

Then John Wu was on his feet, from the first desk in the second
row, waving a water glass for recognition. Two seats down, Kevin
Corcoran stood up, and in the row behind them, Emil Wagner, who
flapped his arms and called out, as if trying to catch the attention of a
search plane. Sandy Booker rose in the center of the second row, barking, "Mr. President! Mr. President!" as if trying to keep a spaniel
from running into the street. Sunny could see Astrid Lindstrom and
Gerry White stand, just in front of his empty desk. He looked out
over all the bobbling, bawling heads, for Rula and Rita, and finally
saw them; Sgt. Gallaher, too, standing just behind. His daughter's
eyes bubbled. Rula, then Rita, raised their hands alongside their faces,
and when they were sure they had caught Sunny's gaze they nodded

their heads and shook the tears from their faces. They nodded up and down.

"Perhaps," Sunny began to speak from the rostrum. "Under the circumstances . . ." He looked down to Vera Barrow: fifth desk, first row on the left. Her face was amazed and amused. She put her hands together, as if to clap, then kept them folded at her chest, and simply bowed her head to Sunny.

"Perhaps," he went on in sudden quiet, "I should remove myself from the rostrum. If the alderman of the Twenty-seventh Ward would please return . . ."

He came down the stairs in a daze, four steps after another, and not feeling a toe against the ground. The sergeant-at-arms cocked her head at someone from the City Clerk's office to give up his seat, a folding chair just below the rostrum. The young man *moved*, legs, arms, like a marionette being shaken and snapped. Sunny heard Don Stubbs's voice boom above him.

"Doesn't anyone here know how they voted?"

Jaco Sefran's trained voice carried above the others. "Mr. President," he implored. "I didn't get to vote! The clerk called my name and before I could answer, this tsunami started."

"Let me assuage your grievance," said Don. "Mr. Clerk?"

"Sefran, Fifty!" Lew Karp repeated.

"Sunny Roopini!" Sunny heard Jaco call back. Don Stubbs called on Sanford Booker, who changed his vote for Vera Barrow to Sunny, and then on Astrid Lindstrom, who changed her vote to Sunny from Alfredo Sandoval. Sunny felt a rising sensation in his lungs and had to bend over at his waist to breathe. He saw the boat-heavy, black, thick-soled shoes of about eight men and women in plain blue or gray suits begin to form a circle around him. The radios at their belts squawked; they replied and turned them down. When he could sit back up, he saw the backs of half a dozen uniforms. Sgt. McNulty drew by his side, and leaned down.

"Breaking up is hard to do, sir," he said. "I'm back."

Sunny looked up to smile, but McNulty's eyes scoured the crowd standing and waving behind the glass of the second-floor gallery.

Sunny could peer between two stout elbows. Vera Barrow had waved for recognition, and as soon as Donald Stubbs had said, "The alderman of the Fifth Ward," the chamber was hushed. Sunny heard only small static squalls from police radios, the click of ballpoint pens, the mousy squeal of chair wheels being pushed back from desks. Vera began with a breath.

"Mr. President," she said and paused, then raised her chin. "I move that Sundaran Roopini be made the choice of this council for mayor by acclamation."

"Second! Second, Mr. President!" Sunny could see Arty Agras, Dorothy Fisher, and John Reginald in the first row.

"Roopini! Roopini!" John Wu began a chant in the second row. Emil Wagner and Shirley Watson picked it up. Janet Watanabe of the 20th and Mitya Volkov of the 19th began to clap along as they sang out each syllable. "Roo-pee-knee! Roo-pee-knee!" Along the rear row of the chamber, Keira Malek and Harry Walker III began their own cheer. "Sun-knee! Sun-knee!"

Somewhere in the clamor and commotion Don Stubbs called the question. The room was swept with a welter of Ayes. He called for Nays. Sunny was sure that several aldermen would have cast ballots against—Daryl Lloyd; Felix Kowalski; maybe Keith Horn and Cyril Murphy—but they did not feel emboldened to shout back at a mob of hurrahs. He heard none. Don brought the gavel down. Sunny felt hands at his back and elbows push and steer him through the blue and gray suits and onto the rostrum. Don Stubbs placed the gavel in Sunny's hand. The chamber turned quiet, as if a plug had been pulled. The clock above the rostrum sizzled with a small buzz as it swept down to the half-hour.

"Good lord," said Sunny, "I hope we'll be able to explain this in the morning."

Sunny used the gentle babble of laughter that followed to turn his eyes down to the rostrum and think before he raised his head. He raised it just slightly.

"I came to this city as a child," he began. "Our children were born here. My wife is buried here. We miss her—painfully. But in Hinduism, we like to think that her soul has been released. We are pretty sure, though, that her soul chooses to stay within the city limits. . . ."

He heard Linas Slavinskas laugh, then Brock Lucchesi and Collie Kerrigan.

"Long before I ever got the hang of Christmas, Hanukkah, or even Super Bowl parties, I learned about St. Patrick's Day," he said. "It was always among the first things we were told about the city. People said that the lake is east, the Cubs are north, and the Sox are south. The Loop is the circle of elevated train tracks. Well, an oval, really. And we were told 'They dye the river green on St. Patrick's Day.' We thought, 'Ah, this is our holiday.'

"You see," Sunny continued, "there is a Hindu holiday called Holi. It's usually in March. For a few days, we can paint ourselves in bright colors and say to hell with all the formalities and restrictions of caste, gender, and age. People dance, they drink, they question gods—whatever they're not supposed to be able to do. And so it seemed to us that this was St. Patrick's Day here. All the babies in green snugglies and jammies, the grown men and women wearing green bowler hats and top hats. All the green sprouting in lapels and wound around necks."

He wound a hand near his shoulder in illustration.

"So there was this St. Patrick's Day, about ten years ago," he said. "At noon I marched in the parade with my ward. The Great Forty-eight. We were miles behind the Slotkowski Polish Sausage float, the Journeyman Plumbers Union float, and the float from the Pipe Fitters Union. All the brass bands from St. Patrick, Sacred Heart, St. Benedict, Cardinal Bernardin, Francis Xavier, and Our Lady of Perpetual Help. All the city workers, from Parks and Rec, and Streets and San, holding brooms and shovels over their shoulders like parade rifles.

"I remember the weather that day—so improbable for March. You could take off your topcoat. The parade ended in the late afternoon. I decided to walk north, toward home. I crossed the bridge over the green river. I looked west and saw the El running alongside. I looked east and saw the blue-gray lake, and the sun setting off these streamers of light in all the skyscraper windows. I walked down Michigan. I turned onto Rush, and then State. People spilled into the streets, talking and laughing. People in the park tossed footballs, and danced with their dogs.

"I sat in the window of this coffee bar. I'm trying to remember—perhaps it wasn't really coffee that I had. Sitting there, I saw a second parade of faces and slogans. 'Irish Girls Know Italians Do It Better'—that was my favorite. Perhaps Alderman Ruffino would agree."

From his seat in the left side of the third row, Aidan Ruffino called out, "My mother sure did!" Sunny acknowledged him with a smile, and went on.

"You know, on St. Patrick's Day, you often read the button or the scarf, then see the face. So you'll see a sweater saying, 'South Side Irish,' look up and see an Asian woman, or an African-American man wearing it. And I believe they mean it—Irish as a word for having a little bit of boisterous fun in your heart.

"So as I was sitting there, two young women passed the window. Early twenties, clad in green, laughing loudly and dancing as they walked. It took me a moment to see that they were Indian. I'd take them to be from farther north than our family, maybe Gujarat or Madhya Pradesh. No matter. We saw each and smiled. As if to say, 'Fancy seeing you here, such a long ways away.' It wasn't until we nodded that I noticed their foreheads. Right at the center."

Sunny held his index finger to the center of his forehead and pressed gently and perceptibly before bringing his finger back and going on.

"Where some women might put a bindi, or a reddish dot of reverence on her forehead, or even a caste mark, they each had a green shamrock. There is no caste here. No reverence. Just—Chicago."

He turned his head down for a moment, kept his hands folded on the rostrum, then brought his mouth subtly closer to the microphone as he brought his voice down.

"I know this place can be cold—very cold," said Sunny. "Brutal, and uncaring. I know it can be hard, unsparing, and loveless. I know—my daughters and I know—how in a single, unpredictable instant—"

Sunny drew his hand across his chest; as if to suggest the weeping drip of a wounded heart.

"But we also have so many amazing lives to fulfill. This city takes in people from all over the world. It leaves its mark on us all."

Sunny stopped. He raised his head, and opened his mouth, but only breath came out, and he halted. He looked out into the chamber. He saw Linas Slavinskas stand, then Jesus Flores Suarez and Tommy Mitrovic, then Vernetta Hynes Griffin and Astrid Lindstrom, Jane Siegel and Adam Wojcik.

"Chicago!" Linas cried. Then Fred Sandoval sprang up with the same cry, and Vernetta, Astrid, and Regina Gregory in the back row. Cries of "Chicago! Chicago!" rang the chamber.

Sunny looked down toward Vera Barrow; he still couldn't speak. He raised the gavel in his hand, feeling like a child wielding a toy hammer.

"Mr. President," said Vera imperturbably into her microphone. The cries and chants died down.

"I believe our business is concluded," she said in the quiet. "We have worked the night shift and done an honest job. I can hear birds twittering, and smell bacon frying. Mr. President, I move to adjourn."

"Second! Second!" called out a chorus of voices; cries from the gallery chimed in. Sunny could feel his own voice surge back into his throat, even though he could only say, "Without objection—" and bring down the gavel.

"Keep it, sir," said Sgt. Butler when Sunny handed the gavel back to her. "It should be your souvenir."

"They gave it to him," he told her. "It should go back."

"You'll get plenty more," she said.

Sunny looked around for his daughters. The floor of the council seethed with bleary, blathering aldermen staggering between their desks to talk. Most of them turned their faces to try to find Sunny.

Daryl Lloyd raised his strong arm in salute, and when he caught a look from Sgt. McNulty, flexed his palm open and shut to say, "See? Nothing there." Collie Kerrigan shouted something about a contract to remove solid waste from an abandoned site on south Kildare. "Six-hundred cubic tons of *pooh*, Sunny!" he shouted. "Stuck in committee!" Sunny tried to lean down from the rostrum to say something, but he was deferentially and forcefully nudged along at his elbows by Sgt. McNulty, who muttered behind his ear, "The scrum is getting a little thick, sir."

He saw Rula. Then Rita. And then Sgt. Gallaher, her long hands curled like pink talons over a shoulder of each. She steered the girls through the droves toward Sunny, in tiny, faltering steps. He waved. He kissed his fingers and blew it their way. His daughters laughed, and Sgt. Gallaher's blue eyes brimmed when they caught Sunny's. They drew close and as the girls left the harbor of her long arms, her arms wound up around Sunny. He turned his head to put a kiss on her cheek, thought better of it, thought again, and then the two of them found each other's lips, as quickly and imprecisely as children trying it for the first time. They tried again.

Tina Butler had climbed through to crowd to Sunny's side, and fell in step. As they nosed along she called up to him, "There's about a thousand chihuahuas right outside the chamber, sir. You want to talk to them?"

"Might as well give them a chance to get their teeth into my ankle, Sarge."

"Okay, I'll break a path," she said, but before she stepped ahead, she tightened her fingers along Sunny's arm.

"Oh God I miss him," she said suddenly. "Such a rotten, gutless thing they did to him, may they rot in Hell. But I'm happy about you, sir. Maybe my crazy bastards here finally got something right."

"We'll try to give them a good show, Sarge."

They stopped at the swinging doors that opened onto the large, walnut room just outside the chambers. Vera Barrow had managed to scrape her way to Sunny's side and took an arm. Linas Slavinskas had been bumped so hard, his sandy pompadour was bucked from its perch and hung down over an eye, peek-a-boo style. He took Sunny's other arm and patted his hand, "Pallie," he said. Art Agras and Alfredo Sandoval had scrambled through the uniforms, and clambered to stand right behind Sunny. They raised and wriggled their heads above his shoulders, looking for the blink and glitter of camera lenses. Sanford Booker, Gerry White, Vernetta Hynes Griffin, and Carlo Viola pressed themselves against the locked arms of uniformed officers, who tried to hold back the throngs. "Sunny!" they pleaded and waved. "Sunny!"

"Hey, Arty," said Linas. "A ménage. Your kind of scene."

The aldermen threw their heads back and laughed. Tina Butler asked, "Ready?" Sunny nodded and took a breath. The big doors rocked open. A swarm of cameras began to chatter, whine, and pop. Blackheaded microphones darted and hovered. Streetlights scattered snowy midnight fireflies in the windows along LaSalle Street. Skyscraper lights winked back. In the dark blocks beyond, all-night trains groaned around turns and fire sirens warbled and shrieked.

Bright lights gushed. Cameras fizzled and hissed. Linas Slavinskas churned his right hand in the air and called out, "Ladies and gentlemen, the mayor of Chicago!" as about a thousand chihuahuas yelped and shouted, "Mr. Mayor! Mr. Mayor! Mr. Mayor!"

Under the smoke, dust all over his mouth, laughing with
    white teeth,
Under the terrible burden of destiny laughing as a young
    man laughs,
Laughing even as an ignorant fighter laughs who has
    never lost a battle,
Bragging and laughing that under his wrist is the pulse,
    and under his ribs the heart of the people,
    Laughing!

                                    CARL SANDBURG

ACKNOWLEDGMENTS

I am indebted to many people for their advice and kindness:

Michael Bauer; David Bradley; Peter Breslow; Judge Anne Burke of the Illinois Supreme Court, Alderman Edward Burke, and their son, Travis; Nishant Dahiya (wearing a Bears hat and eating Garrett's Chicago Mix in Daley Plaza on the day of the Super Bowl); Frank Delaney; Amy Dickinson; Karen Bass Ehler and Rusty Ehler; Monica Eng of the *Chicago Tribune* (who may have the best assignment in American journalism—covering ethnic restaurants in Chicago); Mary Glendinning at NPR News; Will Grozier; State Senator Roy Herron of Tennessee; Wen Huang; Anshul Kaul; Stephanie Leese of the Talbott Hotel; Jordan Matyas; Jim and Laurie Nayder; Robert N. Nicholson; Dr. David Reines at Virginia Commonwealth University; Carolyn Reed at Rush-Presbyterian Hospital; Jim Rogers; Fanchon and Manny Silberstein; David Spadafora and the staff of Chicago's Newberry Library (there is no better place in which to work on a book, and I do not overlook the isle of Capri); and the peerless Ed Victor.

Kee Malesky reads and improves every line that I write for publication. Well, not this one.

The present alderman of the real 48th Ward is Mary Ann Smith. The alderman and her assistant, Greg Harris, have been helpful, candid, and hospitable. Alderman Smith has convinced our family that if we could relocate to Bali, Monaco, or the 48th Ward, the 48th would be the obvious choice. I hope I do no damage to her career by saying that any citizen in the world would be lucky to be represented by her.

Martin Oberman, the former alderman of the 43rd Ward, was a technical advisor on his former forum, and gave me the benefit of his counsel and friendship. At this writing, he is not a candidate for public office. The only way in which it seems to me that Chicago could be more marvelous would be for Marty Oberman to be returned to public life.

My friends Rick Bayless of Chicago and Gordon Hamersley of Boston shared insights on their life's work of running a restaurant. Shalimar's Restaurant on London's Brick Lane, and Swetal Patel and the staff of Mysore Woodlands on Devon Avenue in Chicago taught me the unique features of an Indian kitchen—and how to make dosas.

I don't know of a more enjoyable way to spend a snowy Sunday than to be uplifted in the morning by services at the First Baptist Congregational Church and nourished in the afternoon at the Kugelis Festival at the Balzekas Museum of Lithuanian Culture. We thank the Reverend George W. Davis and his congregation, and our old family friend, Stanley Balzekas III, for making us welcome.

Lynn Cutler honors the profession of politics. No doubt whatever insights I have about political life began when I saw her, many years ago, stand among the carcasses of a meat packing plant in Waterloo and talk about aid to Africa. Over the years, Lynn has become a mover and shaker. But her great gift is for friendship.

The Sergeant at Arms of the Chicago City Council is Tina Butler. I have chanced to make her a character in this book because my imagination is simply too poor to envision anyone else in the job. The city's much-maligned aldermen are lucky to have her as their protector.

All mistakes are mine alone.

I am grateful to Dan Menaker and Jennifer Hershey at Random House for their confidence and to Stephanie Higgs for her surgical skills. I owe thanks to David and Jean Halberstam for David's encouragement and powerful example. And to my late cousin, Paula, for the love of laughter and animals that she has given in trust to those who loved her.

Novelists learn to look for unexpected moments in which lives turn. For me, it came when I arrived at a friend's house in Brooklyn, hit my head on the cab door, and met Caroline Richard. My head wound healed. But I have never stopped swooning over Caroline. My wife is a Frenchwoman who loves Chicago even in—especially in—winter.

I write this just as we welcome a new daughter, Paulina, into our lives. Her arrival only amplifies the joy we have known with our first daughter, Elise. We have spent enough time in Chicago so that Elise

(perhaps with her father's connivance) exclaims, "Go Sox!" and "Go Bears!" and seems to treasure those things that Chicago offers in such abundance: warm friends, hearty meals, and sturdy laughs. Elise and Lina have veins of Asia, America, and Europe running through them. But wherever we land in the world, we like to think that they have the hearts and souls of Chicagoans.

SCOTT SIMON
SHANGHAI, CHINA

ABOUT THE AUTHOR

Scott Simon is the host of NPR's *Weekend Edition with Scott Simon*. He has reported stories from all fifty states and every continent, covered ten wars, from El Salvador to Iraq, and has won every major award in broadcasting. He is the author of *Home and Away*, a memoir, *Jackie Robinson and the Integration of Baseball*, and the novel, *Pretty Birds*. He lives with his wife, Caroline, and their daughters, Elise and Lina.

www.scottsimonbooks.com